The Emerald Ta...

The Emerald Tablet

JENNY JOBBINS

PHARAOH PRESS

LIVERPOOL BOOKS ONLINE

liverpoolbooksonline.com

The Emerald Tablet

ISBN 1 901442 15 2

First Published in 2003 by Liverpool Books Online

liverpoolbooksonline.com

www.emeraldtablet.co.uk

Design and Typesetting by
John Saunders Design & Production, Southmoor OX13 5HU
Printed in Great Britain by Antony Rowe Ltd.

Or let my lamp at midnight hour
Be seen in some high lonely tower
Where I may oft out-watch the Bear
With thrice-great Hermes, or unsphere
The spirit of Plato, to unfold
What worlds or what vast regions hold
The immortal mind, that hath forsook
Her mansions in this fleshy nook:
And of those demons that are found
In fire, air, flood, or under ground,
Whose power hath a true consent
With planet, or with element.

JOHN MILTON – *Il Penseroso*

"In the city of Wardabaha, situated behind the citadel of al-Suri, you will see palms, vines and springs. Penetrate into the wadi and pursue your way up it; you will find another wadi running westwards between the two mountains. From this last wadi starts a road which will lead you to the city of Zerzura, of which you will find the door closed; this city is white like a pigeon, and on the door of it is carved a bird. Take with your hand the key in the beak of the bird, then open the door of the city. Enter, and there you will find great riches, also the king and queen sleeping in their castle. Do not approach them, but take the treasure."

From the Book of Hidden Pearls
RALPH A. BAGNOLD – *Libyan Sands: Travel in a Dead World*

The events of late 1020 and early 1021 ....

Contents

For Martin and Guy

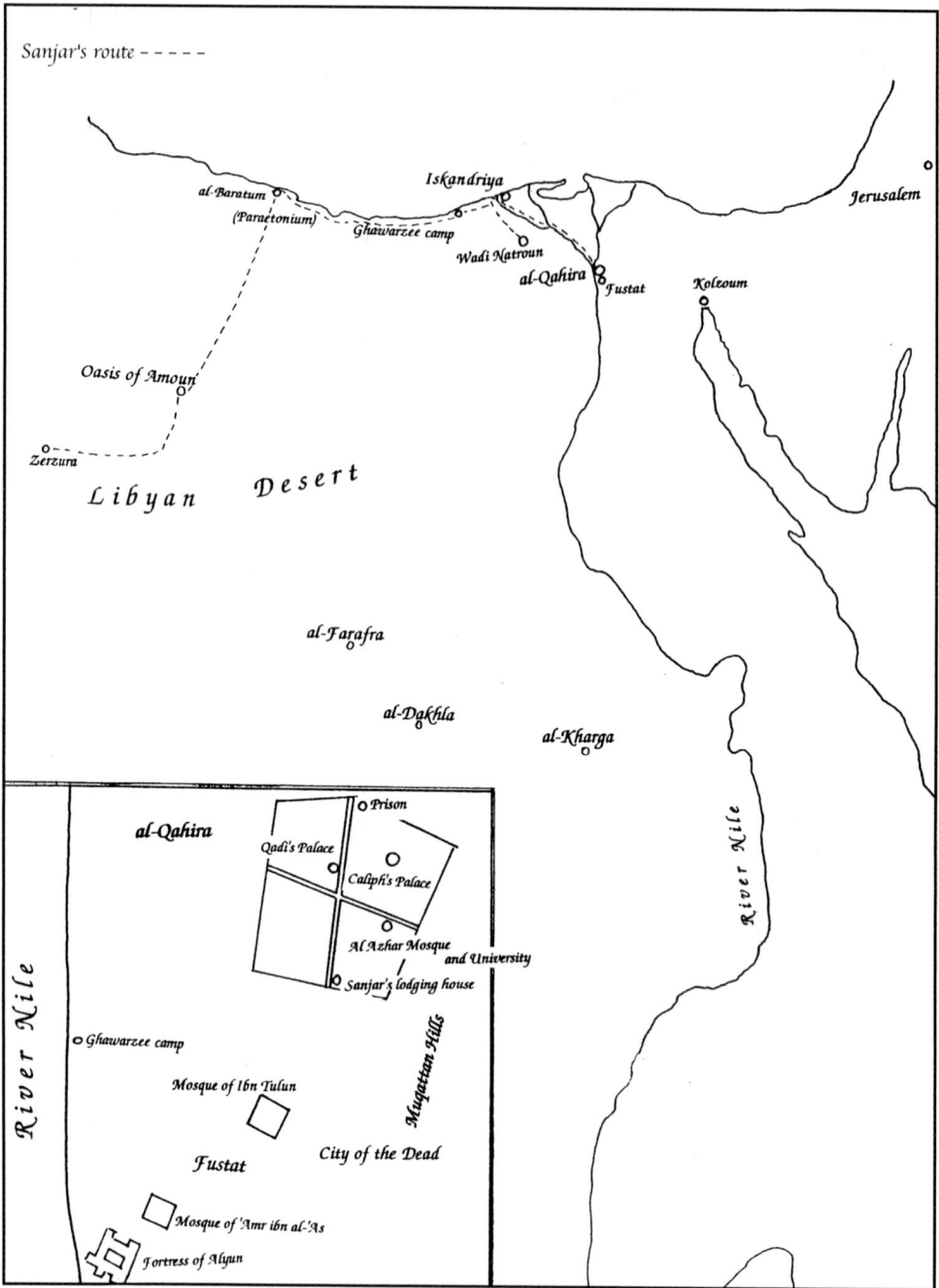

al-Baratum
(Paraetonium)

Iskandriya

Jerusalem

Ghawarzee camp

Wadi Natroun

al-Qahira
Fustat

Kolzoum

Oasis of Amoun

Zerzura

Libyan   Desert

al-Farafra

al-Dakhla

al-Kharga

River Nile

al-Qahira

Prison

Qadi's Palace

Caliph's Palace

Al Azhar Mosque
and University

Sanjar's lodging house

River Nile

Ghawarzee camp

Muqattan Hills

Mosque of Ibn Tulun

City of the Dead

Fustat

Mosque of 'Amr ibn al-'As

Fortress of Alyun

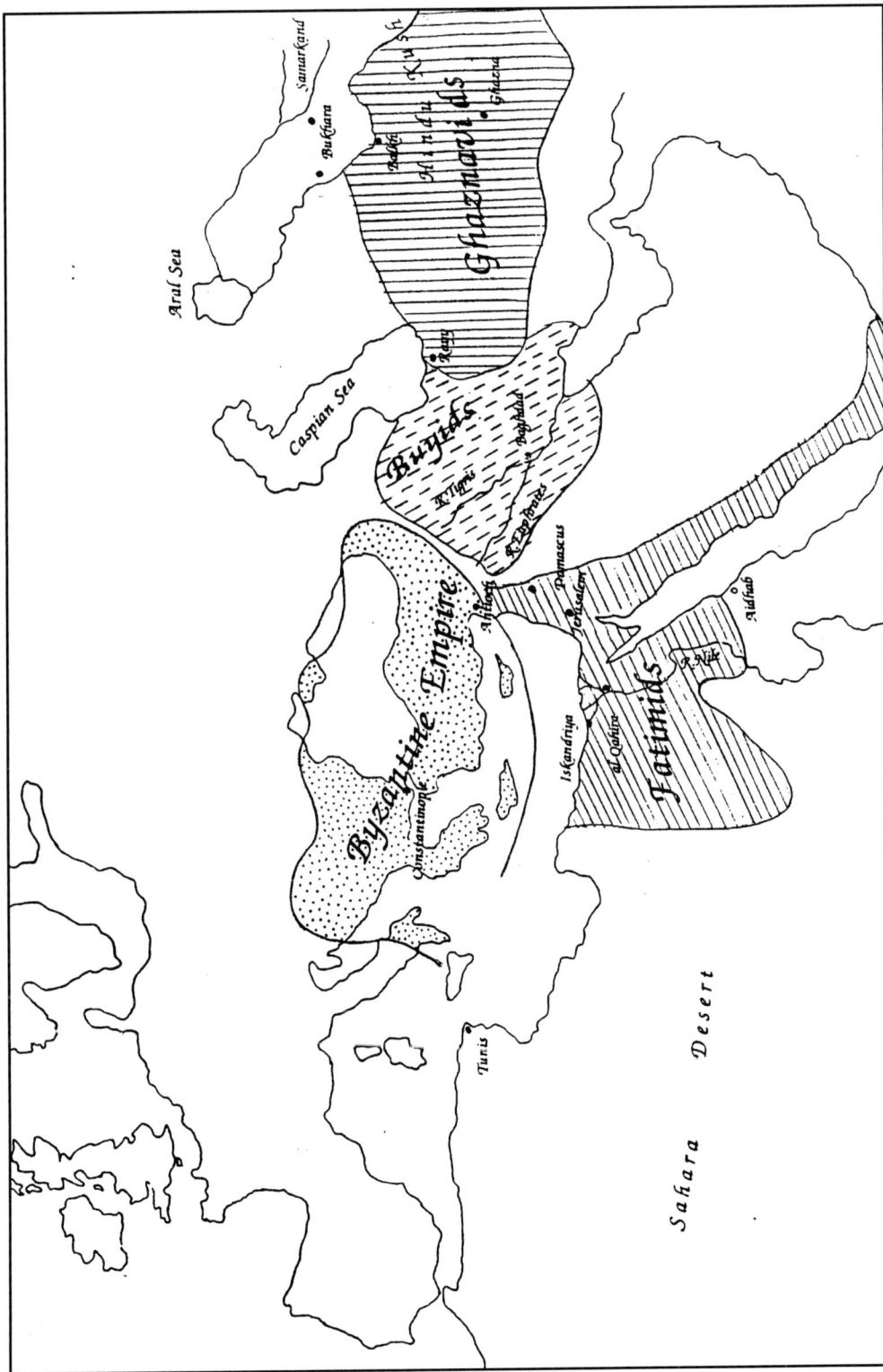

Samarkand

Bukhara

R. Khash

Balkh

Ghazna

Ghaznavids

Aral Sea

Caspian Sea

Rayy

Buyids

Baghdad

R. Tigris

R. Euphrates

Byzantine Empire

Constantinople

Antioch

Damascus

Jerusalem

Iskandriya

al-Qahira

R. Nile

Aidhab

Fatimids

Tunis

Sahara Desert

1 · A Trade, a Trust, and a Gilded Cage

THE FULL MOON hung over the city of a thousand minarets, throwing her prying beams along streets and round corners, through corridors and courtyards, and through latticed screens into sleeping rooms where few citizens were sleeping. The moonbeams traced through the wooden screen a web of diaphanous lace over the couch of Bahiga as she lay, arms flung wide, on silken sheets, black hair tumbled about her pillow and her white skin glowing in the pearly light. Below and around her the city rubbed its eyes and tried to keep awake. The minarets, guided by the moon, stood sentinel; silent, unresponsive witnesses to the bustle in the lamp-lit streets, to muted footfalls in dark corners; here a cat, there a ragged figure flattening itself in the shadows. Donkeys thrashed in their stalls. Nightjars called on the river-bank. But no dogs barked.

The gates of al-Qahira, unlike those of other cities, were by decree not locked or bolted against the night. Without the walls merchants approached with their pack animals, showed their manifests to the guards, and waited until ushered in. Soldiers rode to and fro, many of them messengers from far-flung garrisons. Yet while the officers of the court and the merchants and traders went about their business, some parts of the city and the quarters around it were still: the homes of those who were at peace, and the homes of those who wished to be left in peace. The morbid marble tombs of the City of the Dead, and further down the river the ancient, massive, profane monuments of the vanquished people, not to be spoken of, not to be seen.

Within the walls of al-Qahira people seldom rested. At daybreak, without changing their clothes, without the solace of darkness, they tumbled down with a blanket to keep out the desert chill or else thrashed in the summer heat; thus they tossed, dozed, woke, and tossed again. At dusk they rose and obeyed the call to prayer, leaving their wives to enjoy the doubtful pleasure of lying alone through the night.

They were awake, too, in Fustat, the merchants' city outside the walls of al-Qahira, where in the night coolness man and beast scampered amidst the fetid odours of the narrow, unpaved streets leading to the port. There lamps were lit among the merchants' stalls and exchanges, where goods and produce were bartered and ships loaded and unloaded. In the night hours fortunes were made and lost, bringing riches or despair, while overhead hung shadows, the shadow of bankruptcy, of arrest, of fear and of death: death to the rat from the stalking cat; to the snake from the strike of the mongoose; to the fevered child in its crib; and death to the night walkers removed from the safety of the crowd, robbed of a purse or a coat and left to die alone on hostile ground.

Al-Qahira, where the ruler scorned the day, and rode by night. Here, for one, Bahiga slept, in her moon-laced room, her breast gently rising and falling, her soft damask coverlet draped rose-red over her slender body. On a mat before the door her nurse snored, stirred, turned and dreamed of sibling soldiers homeward bound on the sea.

* * *

On the road that ran alongside the river where waving date palms, silhouetted in the moonlight against an indigo sky, striped the path with long shadows, a tall figure walked. Skin paled by the moon to a shade of milky topaz was drawn over fine, handsome bones. The nose was long and angular, the cheekbones high, the chin smooth. A long moustache was blazoned across the upper lip. The eyes were black and fearless as the night, but the lips were full and sensitive. A lock of black hair spilled from beneath a black helm, which was smooth and polished but for a ring of silver studs. Beneath a long grey surcoat of wool woven with silk, worn in those parts as protection from both wind and sun, the soldier wore a silver-studded light mail shift, while on the feet that strode with such purpose along the moon-stippled path were soft boots with silver spurs. Sanjar Mouseback, servant of the Sultan of Ghazna and of God, a ghazi, veteran of wars against evil and the infidel, was afraid of nothing.

Or almost nothing.

Fear on the battlefield in defence of God and Honour, fear of ghosts and demons, this he did not know. But fear of a ragged old man? If the sensation of Fear perpetually eluded him, could he not have found Respect?

Caution, however, was another matter. Sanjar Mouseback encountered Caution at every corner, at every unexpected meeting. But caution towards a senile vagrant? His left hand caressed the knob of air where the silver scabbard of his sword should have been, and his right, weaponless, flexed in readiness of another meeting, another wager in this accursed country where every old man was a magician.

His black eyes flashed in anger as it crossed his mind that the Caliphs might have done well to wipe out these heathens when they swept into the country during the Holy Wars, instead of permitting them to live and practise their sorcery and devil-worship and to wallow in their obsession with graven images and tricks.

Sanjar Mouseback had visited the city of Fustat several times in the month since he had arrived in al-Qahira, and on these visits he had learnt only three things about it: it stank, it was noisy, and it was full of very odd things indeed. The smell and the noise did not concern him unduly, for in these it was not much worse than any other large city, and, though one complained, there could be no reason why it should not be so, given the reluctance of its citizens to refrain from throwing their waste and filth from the windows into the streets, and the lack of rain to wash it all away, and given the cries of hawkers and the level of shouting resulting from so much congestion in the streets. But the oddness was different. It was largely that there were several layers of citizens forming different castes, and that many of these castes stretched way, way back to times before recollection, so that the city, although it was founded by the harbingers of Islam, the true religion, was in fact only an ornament in an old, old country. Not even the newest ornament, for that was the city a mile or so north at al-Qahira, where Sanjar, who lived on a pension from his distant master, was quartered.

Sanjar Mouseback was well travelled and had grown to know and respect his Arab allies and their ways. If al-Qahira and Fustat were different from cities in his homeland, the country outside them mystified him even more, for it did not belong to the Arabs at all. Though it was ruled by the Fatimid Caliphs, and by the Ikhshidids and Tulunids before them, it was no more a part of the Caliphate than were the depths of the ocean off its shores. Sanjar had travelled the breadth of Asia from the heart of India to the foothills of the Himalayas, and across the wild deserts of Persia and Arabia, but he had been to no place as alien as this. He had been born far to the East, near Balkh, in the foothills of the Hindu Kush, where his Samanid ancestors had ruled for generations. At this moment he would have given all his possessions to be home with his tribe in the place he had not seen for so long.

The silent noises of the night lurked behind every bush and whispered in every clump of reeds along the riverbank. The moon outlined the rutted tracks of carts, horses, camels and footprints, but Sanjar's eyes were on the shadows on either side, and his footsteps, falling softly in the dust, found the path with an expert tread. The long grey cloak swung and now and again the buckles on his mail shift jangled.

As Sanjar walked he became aware of low voices and laughter. Approaching the sound carefully, he turned a bend round a clump of date palms and saw the light of a campfire beside a few pitched tents. He hid in the shadows barely a few yards away. Half a dozen people sat around the fire in jovial conversation, a common enough scene when travellers stopped to

3

make camp for the night. But this group was unusual, and he observed them closely. The men, in bright robes and turbans, bearded and wild eyed, were animated in their raucous laughter. But two figures sat among them coy and kittenish, like women. Their white gowns were resplendent with gaudy strips and sashes of jewelled satin, and satin bands gleamed in their hair which curled over their foreheads above the melting, kohl-lined eyes. Lascivious lips curled under a faint black shadow. No woman would have sat, unveiled, around a campfire in such company. He had chanced upon a group of travelling entertainers.

Sanjar had few qualms about making his presence known. He had little to fear from these Ghawarzee, for he carried little (except for his fine physique) to lead them to prey upon him. Perhaps the silver embellishments on his helm and what remained of his armour might tempt them, but they would have to fight hard, and the laws of hospitality precluded murder before dawn. He was confident that he could keep them entertained with tales of his exploits and wanderings while he rested.

And so, with his hands slightly raised to indicate that he was unarmed, he stepped out of the shadows and hailed the group.

"Greetings in the name of God."

"And his grace to you," several voices murmured in reply.

Sanjar noted from his manner the leader of the band: a lean, wiry man in middle age with small, piercing eyes.

"Will you not sit a while?" he asked, indicating a space the others were making for him, "with our fair ladies?"

The dancers giggled. Sanjar had seen performances of other Ghawarzee, and their tone did not surprise him. They were dancers and musicians, jugglers and conjurers, outcasts from society who journeyed from village to town and from wedding to festival where they played for a fee. The dancers who were now inviting him to share their corner of the fire reminded him of similar groups, their distant cousins, perhaps, who had visited his tribal village a lifetime ago.

Sanjar seated himself between the dancers and the men, the musicians and conjurers, while the leader, with his cool eyes, faced him over the fire. He was plainly an object of curiosity: a horseman on foot, a soldier without a sword. They guessed there to be a tale behind this, and waited for him to tell it. One of the men brought small glasses of sweet black tea, and while he sipped Sanjar recounted his story.

"I had just left the mosque after the noon prayer, when I met an old beggar on the road near the walls of the fortress of Alyun," he began, "behind which lie the churches and synagogues of the unbelievers. Before the wall was a stone with strange carvings upon it, and the old man wagered he could decipher them. Now I told him he could give the carvings any

4

meaning he chose, for I should be none the wiser, and I countered him by swearing I could cleave the stone with my sword. Now my sword, Moonflinger, is a Holy Sword, fashioned in Yemen as was Zulfikar, the Sword of the Prophet at whose side it once fought, and it is very precious to me."

Sanjar, aware that his audience was spellbound, sipped his tea. "I assured him that the stone was a simple matter for Moonflinger, which could slice through sandstone as easily as through butter," he went on. "How was I to foresee what the magician would do to me, for he turned the sword into a stick of kindling in my hand, and the scabbard at my side to a filthy rag! As for poor Moonleap, my mare, whom I have drawn into more perils than I wish to admit, never did I put her in such a spot as this, for he turned her, hair by gleaming white hair, to marble, her black and silver saddle no more than a carved piece on her back. And, as I raised my hand to strike the old man, I felt the flesh drain and tingle as it began to turn grey." Then Sanjar described how, turning from an examination of his petrifying limb to the magician, he had found there was no sign of the old man, and he was alone in this strange place with the marble statue of Moonleap and a broken stick. Tearing off the rag that hung from his side and flinging it angrily down, he had begun to trudge back to al-Qahira where he lodged.

There were murmurs of sympathy, but the Ghawarzee could scarcely contain a certain glee at this wiseacre: anyone who had half an eye open in these lands, they felt, would have shown some circumspection before accepting a wager from a stranger.

After a while the dancers had heard enough of Sanjar's complaints, and began to banter him with ill-disguised innuendoes. Being familiar with their tactics from his earliest youth he countered their suggestions with good-humour, and the group soon fell to talking of other journeys and other lands: one of them had visited Sanjar's homeland and spoke of it with affection, remembering, perhaps, some long-abandoned lover. Before long one of them began to strum the tambura, and the two dancers stood up and began to dance. One with castanets in hand, the other with a tambourine, they cavorted to the drum and tambura, spinning now to a slow, now to a frenzied rhythm. The firelight caught the sequins on their garments, and the sashes tied around their hips emphasised their lascivious movements; effeminate and sensual, they had adopted the postures of those city women they never saw. Men everywhere feasted their eyes on such a vision of sensuality, for women had once danced, long ago, but now it was only rarely that they did so for the eyes of the world.

At last the dancers resumed their places beside the fire, and still they teased until, abandoning all hope of fulfilling their desire, they asked if Sanjar's interest might lie elsewhere, and that one of the real ladies of the

5

group, lying now asleep in her tent, might better accommodate his pleasure. At this Sanjar felt the contours of his money-purse, to which at least one of them had doubtless already let his prying fingers slip, to test its weight; he felt it to be sadly depleted: the cost of his lodgings, not forgetting some carousing in the city, had left him a poor man. He would be lucky if he had the price of a new horse. He was about to decline the offer with a pretence of regret when all hell burst loose.

* * *

The Ghawarzee camp on the riverbank lay half way between the Roman fortress of Alyun and the new city, al-Qahira, the princely city within whose walls, among the gardens, marble halls and lofty dwellings the Caliph al-Hakim bi-Amr Allah lived. Beside Alyun was the merchants' city where most of the people also lived: Fustat, founded by the Arab conquerors as they entrenched the fortress held by the Roman Byzantines, and its river port, where traders met and merchants landed their loads of cotton and grain, porphyry, ivory and spices.

Near where Fustat bordered the river lived a physician, Boutros, a Christian, as many physicians were, being skilled in the arts of herbal medicine and healing. He considered himself, in most respects, successful in life; ill health and disease, rife in this unhealthy city, made him prosper. He was well satisfied with his position and thus given, on occasion, to pomposity; though his self-esteem was tempered by the disappointment that his wife (Christians, like geese, married once, and for life) had borne him no sons, nor even daughters. Yet he was not bitter, nor cruel as a man or master. His servants were all Copts, members of the Egyptian Church, like he, and all shared the burden of conquest by another race. Though many Copts had embraced the new faith after its tempestuous arrival nearly four centuries earlier, others clung to their Christian beliefs. But those who stayed Christian lost many rights in the land that had once been theirs. So they shared a brotherhood of sorts: Christians did not keep slaves, and those who worked for them were not restricted by the tyranny of absolute bondage.

Boutros the Physician had taken into his household a small boy named Tadros. Abandoned by his poverty-stricken family to the privileged elevation of a hayloft in the physician's stable, the boy knew no great love or kindness but, having been encouraged to say his prayers, was not sufficiently deprived of compassion to lose his natural friendliness and intelligence.

While he was growing up Tadros helped with the mule and donkeys in his master's stable, and now they were under his charge. He rose before dusk to feed them and clean the stalls, then mounted the small white

6

donkey on which he ran his errands and set off to the fields south of the city to negotiate a new source of fodder, for his master had quarrelled with the old farmer who formerly supplied him. With this business over he started back to the city, but he was tired, and he began to think that what he would like most in the world was a jug of cool sherbet, so when he came to a roadside khan along the way, he stopped. He put the donkey under a shelter behind the building and entered the khan, barely glancing at the ill-assorted men who thronged the poorly lit room. A fat, surly man gave him the sherbet in exchange for a piastre, and Tadros perched on the edge of a wooden bench with it, relishing its cool sweetness, and trying to ignore a stranger sitting beside him who seemed to want to draw him into conversation. The man was young, and was dressed in the garb of the southern region; he spoke in a friendly enough way, but Tadros did not like his prying questions as he inquired about his business. He remembered that his master had often cautioned him about talking to strangers, and gave away no more than the time of day.

All of a sudden a group of farmers stormed into the tavern and seized upon a band of traders laughing over their drinks in a corner, loudly accusing them of shortchanging in the market place. The farmers demanded recompense, but the traders threw over their table and rose, protesting with foreign accents and dramatic gestures. Within a moment fists, jugs and baskets began to fly and Tadros, cursing the day, made for the door. Just when it seemed everyone but he had joined in the brawl someone seized his arm and dragged him into the mell. He received a punch on the arm and staggered back, only to be pushed forward once more. Suddenly his eyes focused on an object to provoke terror: a huge, black-bearded fellow bearing down on him furiously, his fist drawn back to deliver a blow which fell, not on Tadros, but on one behind who was in the act of bringing down a stone jar on the boy's skull. The jar crashed to the floor, smattering shards and contents with a resonance that was swallowed in the surrounding din.

All at once the doors of the khan swung open, admitting several soldiers of the city guard. Tadros knew how they worked: those brawlers who were lucky would be arrested.

"Come!" cried the huge fellow, and dived for the rear door. Blindly Tadros followed. There was a great crush, but at last he found himself thrust into the open. The large man was nowhere in sight, and of this Tadros was glad for he knew not to trust strangers. He determined to flee back to Fustat along a small road away from the highway, but he could not see the donkey amongst the crowd in the courtyard. While he looked a shadow fell in the moonlight, and the big man stood at his shoulder.

"No time for that," he advised.

Nor could he argue, for the man took his arm and forced him at a half-run to match his stride. Tadros was afraid as well as perplexed. What did the man want with him? From his appearance and dress there could be little doubt what he was – a donkey boy from a not-so-grand household.

"My master's donkey!" he stammered in protest.

"Never mind that now," said the big man. "Let's go before we get mixed up in this mess. An arrest wouldn't do either of us any good, me a foreigner and you a poor Copt in possession of a fine white donkey. Neither of us wants to be hauled before the Qadi for fighting in a street brawl. That's against the law."

Wondering how the big fellow knew so much about the donkey, Tadros twisted round to see his face, and recognised him as one of the men accused by the farmers when the fighting started. His fear increased, What did the oversized foreigner want with him? He made another attempt to break free, but the vice-like grip merely tightened. Tadros quickly decided that guile might be his only aid, and relaxed his pull. At this, the larger man steadied his pace.

He took Tadros to a quiet country road where fields of young wheat bordered by reed-fringed canals stretched in an orderly fashion, and a water pump creaked as a blindfolded ox pulled the beam round and round. There, resting in the shelter of a date palm grove, was a group of men. The big man spoke to them quickly in words strange to Tadros, and pulled him forward.

"Here, boy! This is Cviit, my master. Bow!" and he pushed Tadros down

This man was as strange as his name. He was hooked and bent from his fingers to his nose; his clothes were tied haphazardly round the bundle of his body and his turban appeared to be balanced rather than worn on his crown. His eyes darted to and fro and almost behind him, missing nothing. The big man, glancing and gesturing towards Tadros, spoke briefly to the older one in a foreign tongue.

"Boy, we need you," Cviit crooned. "We shall pay you well for your endeavours but, if you fail, we shall punish you severely." His eyes darted round his head at his companions, who grunted in assent. "We are new in this country, and we need someone to show us round the city."

Tadros did not believe this at all. "I should be honoured to serve you, lord," he replied politely. "But I already have a good master. I beg leave to return to him, and to recover the donkey which I left at the khan."

"Now, there's a pity," whined Cviit, "for should we choose to free you, then you would be forced to return to your master without the donkey. For Hrouv here took the precaution of removing it from its stall almost as soon as you left it. He took a look at you, you see, and saw you could be just the man we were looking for." He waved a small purse in front of his ugly nose. "Here is your donkey money, boy. Come and get it!" He made a croaking attempt at laughter, which the others joined in. "How will you repay your master now? Better stay with us and earn it as your fee, for then you will have the wherewithal to return to your master, pay him back, and start afresh."

Tadros heaved a great sigh, for he knew his life had changed for ever. His master, in spite of his avarice, was an honest man, and like many honest men he would not tolerate dishonesty in others. He would never allow Tadros the groom to return to his household, but would turn him away without a piastre or a name.

For the rest of the day he sat apart from the traders, refusing ale and crusts and even the mutton they roasted on a spit, and which he guessed was stolen. Sadly he contemplated all he had lost. By nightfall his heart was as thoroughly chilled as was his body from the night air, and without even a cloak around him he lay down to sleep on the cold ground.

The moon was high and bright when his captors roughly woke him and forced him to help them break camp. He could not understand their speech, but guessed that truly trade was bad, or else these were not traders but itinerant thieves who had crossed the sea and come to the river, and now planned to try their luck in the city. With a heavy heart he trudged behind them, planning his escape.

* * *

The Ghawarzee were travellers who lived by wit and guile; they were not fighting men, attuned to those slight changes in the elements that threaten danger. As they tried to charm their handsome visitor their minds were far from vigilant to the terrors of the night. When a huge figure with a black beard and flashing eyes leapt ferociously out of the tamarisk bushes, scimitar flailing, the Ghawarzee still sat numbed with surprise.

Only Sanjar, weaponless, reacted. With one move he seized a blazing fire-brand from the hearth and rushed at the attacker. The man screamed as the flames seared his face and set alight his robes and turban, and while he threw himself to the ground and rolled in agony as he tried to extinguish the flames Sanjar picked up his scimitar and ran him through.

Sanjar held the scimitar aloft. It was then that the other bandits burst from the bushes where they had silently gathered to launch their assault. Around and again Sanjar thrust his blade as the swordsmen struck to silence him. He had floored three more of the thieves when an unlucky blow from a swinging scimitar shattered Sanjar's blade, leaving the splinters gleaming.

Almost at once he felt and heard a sword flying through the air towards him. He caught the hilt, marvelling at such precision of movement, and the fifth attacker was upon him. He caught his balance to ward off the other's blows, parrying a thrust that caught his arm before he could retaliate with a

9

cut to his opponent's neck. The man fell, eyes bulging in surprise at his own half-severed head, and his body shuddered and lay still.

Sanjar, still beside the fire, paused, but a strange, muted whine caused him to turn. He found himself facing a bent, evil-looking man who was encircling him with insinuating, cat-like movements, his darting eyes glinting red in the firelight. Cviit lunged at Sanjar, but the soldier looked with pitiable scorn upon the man. Though he might be evil incarnate he was no physical match, and Sanjar considered it beneath him to strike such a person.

As the soldier hesitated, Cviit backed, turned, and ran for the cover of the tamarisks where he had planned his ambush. There was a crackle of dry twigs as he fled into the night.

Sanjar looked around at the chaos he had wrought. Six bodies lay scattered in the sand, and the air was filled with the stench of burnt fabric and flesh. The Ghawarzee had gone, deserting even the screaming women in the tents.

Out of the shadows crept a dark-skinned boy who flung himself at Sanjar's feet. "Spare me, master," he begged, clutching hold of the soldier's boots. "I was not one of them; they took me and held me captive. Spare my life, and I will serve you, for I have lost my master and have no place to go. Have pity on me, great lord!"

Sanjar studied the boy. He had not run away like the Ghawarzee, and neither spoke nor dressed like the bandits. Indeed he surmised it was he who had thrown the sword, and thus saved the day. Yet best be cautious: the boy might be turncoat, or a spy.

"Get off your knees, youth," he replied, "for perhaps we can assist each other."

Gladly, Tadros attached himself to his third master of the day. He covered the hero's hands with kisses, forgetting for a moment that he was embracing one of the heathens, a usurper, a soldier who upheld the Muslim faith, a faith for which he had probably fought. Confused, he sat back on his heels and considered his new situation.

The Ghawarzee crept back sheepishly to the fire. They dragged the corpses to the river and threw them in so the swift current could carry them through and beyond the city before daybreak. They raked over the bloodstains in the sand, then extinguished the fire and prepared to break camp, for they wished to be far away before their escaped assailant returned with the city guard and whatever tale he cared to tell.

While they worked Sanjar lay on a straw mat, his slumber undisturbed by the activity around him, and Tadros sat cross-legged at his feet. Though he was now free there was no point in returning to his master. It would take him years to save enough from his meagre wage to repay the physician for the donkey. Alone, he might face arrest for its theft: with a protector he could face the world.

Later the Ghawarzee woke Sanjar. As he rubbed his eyes and tried to clear a bad taste from his mouth, the taste of fire, carnage, and unrefreshing sleep, they cautioned him that they were about to leave for the northern towns. He refused their offer of recompense for saving them from the bandits; he merely insisted he had repaid them for their kindness in allowing him to share their fire.

While they finished loading their camels Sanjar debated whether to take his new disciple into his confidence. The boy still sat there, tailor-fashion. Something about him struck Sanjar as being different. His dark skin betrayed him as a native Egyptian, the Arab being so much lighter, the Turk fairer still. But it was something about the boy's dress that disturbed him, and Sanjar suddenly realised what it was. The bareheaded boy with his simple gown was a Christian, an infidel.

Nervously Sanjar backed away, putting an arm's length between himself and the boy seated at the other end of the mat.

It was the boy who spoke.

"My name is Tadros," he said. "I am a Copt, and a Christian. If I must serve you then serve you I must, though I don't know if I ought to, or if it is right that I do."

Sanjar thought this over.

"I am Sanjar Mouseback, and I am a veteran of the army of the Ghaznavids whose empire is far away to the East. I have fought the Infidel, in the Punjab and elsewhere. I hold that loyalty may be owned or given, but not bought. As a Christian, therefore, you may be my slave or my friend, but as a servant I cannot trust you." He paused, and looked the boy over with his dark eyes. "I think I may take you to be a friend – and as friends, let's walk together to the city."

"Then, friend, I will serve you as a friend and companion, which is truly what I wish, although you can see I have no other choice. So let's be on our way."

The Ghawarzee, with many salaams, set off northwards along the river. The two odd companions struck out northeast for al-Qahira, but Tadros warned that he dare not enter the city since his master had friends everywhere, and might discover him. It puzzled the young Copt why the warrior had no horse or weapon with him, but he concluded he had met with some accident and decided it would be inappropriate to ask questions.

They had been walking for about half an hour and dawn was almost breaking when the tall walls and minarets of the city, straddled below the rocky edge of the high desert plateau, came into view. On their right sprawled the huge cemetery, the City of the Dead, and Tadros begged Sanjar to pause.

"I daren't go any further," he explained. "Let me hide there, among the tombs. I shall wait for you until tomorrow, but if you don't return I shall know my destiny does not lie at your side."

"I don't want to leave you, undefended, among the ghosts and demons of the departed," Sanjar said. "Take this, the sword that binds me to you. It may not save you from the dead, but it might at least afford you some protection against the living."

Tadros took the scimitar, and pulled from his gown a wooden cross which he wore on a thong around his neck. "I wear a cross, and I can recite words of prayer," he said. "But I'll take the sword: there may be other spirits that haunt me tonight."

Sanjar shuddered at the sight of the boy's protective talisman, his crucifix. His thoughts, though, were on his own predicament. He needed to get back to al-Qahira, and he needed a horse. Leaving Tadros among the tombs he followed the road to the city wall and the Bab Mitwalli, the gate closest to his quarters.

Throngs of people were pressing through the gate, which would be locked at dawn: messengers, merchants with goods and peasants with donkeys and carts laden with vegetables or fodder, all bound for the palaces within; pilgrims, servant women with pots or packages upon their heads; and even a caravan, a string of camels up from the Red Sea with a cargo of rich merchandise brought from Africa or Arabia, or from as far away as India or China. At the gate customs officials checked the goods and manifests of everyone who tried to enter, turning away with a beating those who had no business there.

But it was the southern gate itself, with its ghastly demonstration of the city's mood, which held the gaze of all who approached it. Try as he might to avert his or her eyes from the ghoulish parade and its message, everyone who neared the gate was overcome by the impelling force to look, and to shudder, and to murmur soundlessly: "Bisma'allah, there but for the grace of God go I!" For the dome of the gate was adorned with the drooling, decaying heads of the city's offenders and renegades, thieves and murderers. The bodies of all who met their end in public execution were tossed over the walls to the scavengers below, but their heads festooned the pinnacles of the gate until the whitened skulls, picked clean by ravens, were knocked down to make way for others.

Sanjar Mouseback glanced unmoved at the morning's crop of cheerless faces. He was inured to the horrors of the battlefield where no prisoners were taken, and the death of a handful of villains, not his people and probably highly deserving of such a fate, meant little to him. Carried by the throng he plunged through the gateway into the cobbled street. He was suddenly aware of how tired he was, and how much in need of food and sleep.

As he neared the house he heard a sound that had become familiar over the past weeks, and his heart quickened; it was the cry of runners bidding the public to make way. The people in the crowded street parted, struggling to clear a path so as not to be beaten aside, upsetting carts and trays of fruit and bread, forcing pack animals to make space. Flattening himself against a buttress, but oblivious to knocks and jostles, Sanjar held his breath.

Around the corner trotted the runner, and on his heels two black-skinned Nubians ran, shoulders bowed, bearing a gilded sedan chair. The red velvet curtains were, as always, tightly drawn. But, as always, as the sedan passed Sanjar was certain that the velvet twitched. Through the cruel curtain Sanjar beheld his vision. The procession passed in a flash, but Sanjar held his post while he regained his breath, moving only when an impatient onion seller pushed him on.

Sanjar had never seen his love, had not been given even the merest glimpse of her face or form as she passed hidden in her gilded cage. But he knew she was slender, because of the lightness of foot of her bearers as they ran; and he knew she was beautiful, because of the gleam of fearless devotion in their eyes.

2 · Sanjar fails to find a Horse, while Tadros meets a Cat

SANJAR PASSED most of the day and much of the next night searching for a horse to replace Moonleap. He saw many, all with owners eager to make a deal: greys, duns, roans and bays, some white as snow, some black as ebony and some with a sheen of gold; most fit, some ailing. He was hustled from dealer to dealer by contractors eager to be in at a sale, but he found not one that suited him and returned on foot to his lodging in the alley near the south gate.

Thanks to an introduction through an envoy of the Sultan of Ghazna, Sanjar was quartered in a large house arranged round a quiet courtyard filled with fruit trees and vines and hidden from the street behind massive cedar doors. The doorkeeper usually sat on a stone bench outside the gate, where he was often joined by his cronies. But that night the door stood ajar and a small crowd had gathered in the courtyard garden. In their midst sat a black-skinned woman in a black robe. She was a geomancer: before her in the dust lay a handful of shells.

The crowd stirred at Sanjar's arrival. Although he was now well known in the neighbourhood, admiration for his physique and bearing had not abated. The doorkeeper jested with the woman to tell the soldier's fortune, and after some ribaldry she consented and threw the shells, examining the pattern in which they fell.

"Search no more for a horse, sir," she said, and the doorkeeper translated the words from the Nubian tongue in which she spoke. "A youth will find a horse for you, a youth with," and here she chuckled, "brown eyes, and wavy black hair," and she chuckled again, with which the crowd joined in, "every-one has brown eyes and black hair."

"Except Suleyman!" called the crowd, referring to the old gardener, who underneath his turban was quite bald.

"Who is the youth?" demanded Sanjar.

Through the doorkeeper, the woman replied in some surprise, "Why, he is known to you: don't deny you know him! His skin is dark, and he wears, round his neck – "

"Yes, I know him."

Of course, Tadros was a groom and would find him a horse. Sanjar decided to take a rest, and then return to the City of the Dead.

Still studying the shells, the geomancer hesitated to speak.

"What does she see?" Sanjar asked the doorkeeper.

"Wait, now she speaks. Many trials lie before you. You will venture far into the desert: she sees a garden in the desert and roses blooming. She sees an army, thousands strong, turning in circles among the dunes." The woman became very disturbed, and began to wail and roll her eyes. "She says, leave the Christian boy! Do not approach the Christian boy! Do not touch the stone! I think," the doorkeeper added. But the woman cried out loudly and shuddered, then, painfully it seemed, brought herself out of her trance and muttered something as though in agony. "She says she can see into your soul," he said.

The crowd was spellbound. To relieve the tension, someone called, "Are there no damsels in her vision?"

After a few moments the woman recovered her composure. "A damsel?" asked the doorkeeper, translating her words. "A graceful damsel with slender hands, beautiful as the day. She wears a gold bangle from the old times, set with turquoise and lapis lazuli." The geomancer, exhausted, was abruptly silent. The doorkeeper pressed her, but she muttered, "It is all. It is enough."

Sanjar tried to slip a coin into her hand but she would not take it, so he asked the doorkeeper to use it for her. He went through to his rooms. After a rest, he would find Tadros.

*　*　*

Seeing but unseen Bahiga sat on a tapestried cushion at the laced wooden screen that masked the window of her chamber, watching the people in the street. She paid almost no attention to her nurse who, embroidery in hand, chatted about life downstairs. Bahiga received gossip from the nurse, who heard it in the kitchen; usually she listened, but this night it bored her. She stared out of the window, musing as she examined the crowd of small traders, rich merchants, mullahs and soldiers, uninterested in the events of the house and the activities of her father being so faithfully related, but too lazy and too indulgent to tell the nurse to hold her tongue.

Behind her on a silver tray gleamed all manner of delicacies: peaches, grapes and apricots, white rice flavoured with nuts and spices, small roasted birds, creams and custards, sweet almonds and sugared delights. The food was untouched. Bahiga and her nurse behaved as though it were not there.

*　*　*

As the day drew to a close Tadros searched for a corner in which to spend the night. He did not stray far from the place where the warrior had left him, for he did not doubt he would return. He was lucky enough to find a way to appease his hunger: at noon a family arrived at one of the tombs and, unwrapping loaves of bread, meat, cakes and fruit, had cheerfully shared a feast with the soul of their loved one. It was the anniversary of the death: at any rate, the family communed with the spirit as though it was there and, when they went, left its share of the food on a baked clay plate. Crossing himself vehemently Tadros waited until their voices had died away, then took the plate – a brave act, for the spirit might be angered, and it was a Muslim ghost at that. But with his stomach rolling Tadros had little time for the supernatural.

He fell to examining, even admiring, the elaborate shrines which covered some of the vaults, built so enduringly to house forever the spirits of the dead. Did they have no heaven to go to, he wondered? Or did they dwell in a heaven of sorts, returning to earth to visit their relatives at will? Or perhaps, as the monks said, they were condemned to eternal hellfire and damnation, and all this tomb building was in vain, an innocent masquerade. The ground was littered with broken plates and scraps of food, offered, as was his mid-day meal, to the dead, but swiftly scattered by marauding animals.

Suppose, as some said, the ghosts of the heathen dead stayed close to their earthly remains, watching over the place where their bones rested? What also of the murdered, the executed, and the innocents? What if only Christians were privileged to leave this sad world to live in the heavenly skies, while the ghosts, the afarit of others remained to haunt indefinitely the vicinity of the tomb?

Tadros, of course, believed in afarit. Everyone did. People were especially afraid of the afarit of those who had died a violent death, for they never succeeded in leaving the place where they met their fate, but stayed to avenge themselves for their tragedy on all who passed by. And there were other demons, worse than afarit... for although the priests said there were none but angels and Satan himself, the monks knew otherwise ...

The day grew chill: still Tadros turned this way and that. Now he started at every shadow, and once a cat caused his heart to leap so far that it was some time before it quieted. But it was only looking for mice. The muezzin gave the final call to prayer. As the flaming evening sky hit the summit of the plateau a cold fear settled on his heart.

With his sword drawn, Tadros settled into a sun-whitened corner and waited for the night. Again hunger gnawed at his stomach, and he longed for his straw mattress over the stable and the sweet smell of the donkeys. He murmured their names over and over until he could feel their warm breath and soft lips in his hands, hear their hooves scraping the stable floor, the champing of fodder, the snicker of greeting. Inevitably, though, his thoughts turned to the white donkey and what lay in store for him now.

He could return now and throw himself at his master's feet, and tell the story of his capture. The physician would be in a good mood, having, at this hour, dismissed his patients, and dined. But without a witness Tadros knew he had no story to tell. He had little choice but to stay where he was until the soldier came back for him.

The lights of Fustat flickered in the distance. Tadros had spent his life amongst the milling crowds of the city and the constant proximity of people and animals. He knew how it felt to be alone in a crowd, but to be quite alone and quite outside was new, and he was filled with terror and dread.

While reflecting on his misery, with which he had met more in the past two days than ever before, he heard footsteps and saw a light bobbing in and out of sight as it wound through the necropolis. His first urge was to run, but then he thought perhaps he should flatten himself in the shadows and evade discovery. By the time it was clear that the light was moving in his direction he was rooted to the spot in terror. Though he tried to move – for surely they were coming for him – he could not. The two, Satan and his assistant, had come to take him for his sins of deception and cowardice, and the theft of the food. Had he been in a mood for reflection he would have considered himself a fool for thinking to hide in this place.

Terror closed his eyes and ears: he waited mutely for the ghostly hand to fall on his shoulder. Then he remembered to pray, and as he prayed he thought of the crucifix he wore around his neck. He took it in both hands, and the familiar smooth contours gave comfort to his heart. He opened his eyes as the light closed in and the steps drew near, and he heard a voice say, "Why, O my friend, about here lies the new cadaver that was brought in today."

So they had come for the corpse, thought Tadros, his mind fleeing to the still body on a palm-strewn bier he had seen carried into the cemetery just before dusk, to await burial in the morning. They had come for the corpse, and might leave him.

"It was Hussein the tailor, and a poor soul," said the other. "Not much meat on his bones."

Tadros froze. So they were ghouls, the wretched demons the Arabs told of, who ate the flesh of the dead.

"No trouble from marauding dogs tonight," answered the first, "for they are gathering in the hills to wait for the moon. Ah!" Something clattered to the ground. The figures stopped.

Tadros held his breath.

"My keys."

The companions lowered the torch as they stooped to search the ground, and by its light Tadros saw not devils or ghouls but men in cloaks and ragged turbans. Finding the keys, they straightened up.

"Aiee!" one cried in pain, "My back, O Abdu!"

His relief at seeing the night watchmen was so great that Tadros wanted to cry out in greeting, but he held his tongue. He risked a beating at best, and at worst he might be treated as a grave robber and have his head nailed to the city gate. The men passed on, and he murmured a prayer of thanks for his delivery.

He dozed. When he awoke the moon was high, and green eyes glinted. He started in fright. But it was only a tabby cat, sitting on he wall before him and regarding him intently.

"Hello, puss," he said.

"Hello," said the cat.

Tadros rubbed his eyes. There was a grey cat, licking its paws. He decided he must have dreamed the last few moments, or allowed his imagination too much rein in the night.

"Pussy," called Tadros. He would have liked to stroke the cat, wished he had saved a tidbit to tempt it over to him. His bones ached and he shifted position uncomfortably.

The cat jumped to another wall, and yawned. In this new position it looked lighter in colour, and he could see it was a large cat.

"I'm glad to see you," said Tadros to the cat. "I suppose you come here to catch rats. I'm here because I'm hiding from my master."

The cat stretched and seemed, perhaps in a trick of perspective, to be bigger still.

"Not many people spend the night in a cemetery talking to cats," said Tadros.

The cat's eyes caught the moonlight and turned a vivid red. Tadros was disturbed. The cat jumped off the wall and began to prowl to and fro. It was quite the largest cat he had ever seen.

"Son of a lion," said Tadros.

The cat sat down and regarded him, fixing him with its emerald eyes. As Tadros watched, it grew as large as a desert dog, then as a ram. It fidgeted as though irritated by its weight.

Tadros could not see through the cat. Its face, the tabby pattern on its coat, were solid as was plain to see, but...

And he understood.

Though the moon was bright, the cat cast no shadow.

It was now as big as a calf. Still it regarded him. Holding its gaze, Tadros gripped the scimitar, which felt heavy and unwieldy in his unskilled hands.

The cat did not move. Tadros called on fear to drive the blade.

The cat screamed. The scimitar sliced through its body, but through air, through a scorching blast of heat. With the merest flicker of green flame from the spot where its eyes had shone so brilliantly, the cat was gone.

The moon vanished behind a cloud.

And in the darkness they came for him, bestial red-eyed demons riding torrid creatures from the depths of the underworld, dull-eyed skulls dripping rotten flesh, winged devils that flayed the air about him. With hideous uncouth sounds they dealt blow upon blow to his body, blows unfelt save in his heart because he was praying for all he was worth; and he held up the little cross to the beasts, and would not veer from his prayer even when the lovely face of a woman gazed kindly at him, which he knew to be false when she stretched out her graceful hands to touch him but could not reach him, held back as she was by the crucifix. Tadros chanted until there came the sweetest sound he had ever heard, the call to the dawn prayer. Exhausted and ravaged by horrors he had never imagined, he fainted into sleep.

* * *

Sanjar woke in dismay. It was well past noon, and he had to find the Coptic boy and a horse. Hurriedly he dressed and left the house. Recognising people in the street, he called a greeting to a bread seller here, a doorman there, and dropped a coin into the hand of a blind beggar who often stationed himself near the Bab Mitwalli. As he passed the gate he glanced up, and grimaced when he saw the face of the wiry man who had escaped from the attack at the camp of the Ghawarzee: he looked down at Sanjar with a look of surprise that he could run no more.

Near the place where he had left Tadros a burial was taking place. A body wrapped in a white cloth and strewn with the palm fronds that would ensure eternal life was being lowered into the grave, while a group of mourners stood about: all men, so it was a man that had died. Sanjar found Tadros curled up behind a wall, fast asleep, tightly clutching his crucifix. Sanjar smiled to himself. He had probably spent a frightened night here alone in the cemetery, as well as almost two hungry days. Sanjar shook him, and he awoke with a cry. The boy had passed a shocked, near sleepless vigil, and wished to stay sleeping. But his good nature got the better of him, and gratefully he ate the bread and white cheese Sanjar had brought him and listened to Sanjar's tale of how he had lost his horse and needed to find a new one.

Tadros finished eating and wiped his hands on his shirt. He began to laugh quietly,

"It's no laughing matter," said Sanjar shortly.

Secretly Tadros relished the idea of such a warrior being hoodwinked into

19

losing his horse by an old man, but at the same time, as a true groom, he was alarmed for the horse. It was two days since it had been petrified. Where was it now?

"It's an old trick, an illusion," he explained, realising that as a foreigner Sanjar might not be familiar with the old magic. "Such masters make you see things you believe to be true, but when you cannot see them, or when you refuse to believe them, they disappear. I think they have to make special preparations, and summon devils, and then I think they write something on a paper which you have to touch. Do you remember touching a paper?"

"Not that I can think of."

"I don't know exactly how they do it. Real miracles can only be worked by the grace of God. That means no preparations and no papers. Raising the dead and healing the sick are miracles, but amusing the people by turning things into stone is a magic trick."

"But once, when I was in the market in Damascus, I saw a man pluck a chicken and put it in the oven to roast, but when he took it out it was sitting in the pan, alive and clucking and completely feathered. I saw that truly."

"It was a trick, a magic trick," insisted Tadros. "God did not bless tricks with the name of miracles."

This is a very pious boy, thought Sanjar, for these very words had been used by the Imam who had taught him the Qur'an as a small boy.

"How can I get Moonleap back?" he asked.

But Tadros was still thinking about the trick. "If, as I think, your magician used a paper, then we must find him and ask him to remove the spell, or we might get it removed by someone else. That is, if we can find someone who knows how he did it. And if we can find your horse. Of course the spell might have worn off. Let's hope he didn't plan to steal her, and sell her."

"I fear that might have been his purpose."

It was dark when they reached the stone-walled enclave of Alyun, the city the Romans built and to which the invading Arabs laid siege from their encampment at Fustat. The enclave was inhabited by a hotchpotch of people, mainly Christians and Jews, and the streets, some so narrow that a laden donkey could pass through only with great difficulty, ran between buildings of stone plundered from ancient temples and carved with strange symbols. There were monasteries and convents, churches, schools and synagogues, and houses for rich and poor. The massive, iron-studded wooden gates at their entrances were seldom closed, for the city was guarded by its ties with the Holy Book.

"This place is blessed," said Tadros, "for so many wonderful things happened here." He pointed to a stone church on one corner. "This church of St Sergius is built on the place where the Holy Family sheltered on their flight from Herod. Now it is the church of the Pope, who is the patriarch of the Egyptian Church. And here under the new synagogue is the very spot where Moses was found in the bulrushes."

Letting Tadros ramble on with his religious anecdotes, Sanjar retraced his steps to the place where he had left the sad replica of Moonleap. "St Barbara," said Tadros reverently, crossing himself, and disappeared inside a small church.

"I wish you would help," Sanjar complained when the boy reemerged a few minutes later.

"I am helping. I thought if your horse was turned into stone outside the church of St Barbara, then she must have seen what was going on, so I went to ask for her help."

"And what is she going to do?"

"We must be patient."

The stuccoed walls of the church were washed white, and its doors stood open. But there was no sign of the old man he had found seated near the church door: no passers-by, not even a dog. And no sign of Moonleap.

The silence was broken by a small boy with tousled hair and a torn striped shirt tugging urgently at Sanjar's sleeve.

"Boss, boss, you want sword, very good sword?"

Angrily, Sanjar tried to scrape the boy off his arm, but Tadros said, "Show it to us."

The boy dragged them to a small house. He ran inside and emerged holding in his outstretched hands a gleaming sword which glowed white, ultramarine, and many splendid colours. Its blade was of finely wrought steel, and its hub of steel and silver edged with gold, a design of moon and stars. Tadros shuddered when he saw it, for he knew it as a sword of Islam, a sword that had pierced many hearts. But Sanjar trembled with delight, for it was Moonflinger, his Holy Sword.

But as he stretched out his hand to take it, the boy snatched the sword away.

"How much?" he demanded, not in the least intimidated by such a powerful ghazi.

Sanjar towered over the little boy. It was absurd that this small fellow was brave enough to try to *sell* Sanjar the sword.

He said reasonably, "The sword is mine."

"No," snarled the child. "Mine. How much?"

Sanjar laughed. "I would take it, and use it to slice you in two, you little heathen, for stealing it."

"How much? I give you good price," he said in pigeon Arabic.

Sanjar's eyes flashed at the child's impudence, but Tadros intervened. "The lord will give you a good price if you can tell him where to find his horse," he said.

The boy looked frightened.

"And the scabbard," prompted Sanjar.

"And the scabbard. A good price."

The boy hesitated. "The head man called the city guard," he said finally.

"When?"

"Yesterday."

"Where can we find the head man?"

"Give me money."

"Give me the scabbard."

"Scabbard no have. Head man have scabbard."

Sanjar opened his purse and extracted a small silver coin. The boy's eyes widened for an instant as he grabbed it, but prudently he masked his joy.

"This not enough. Give me more," he complained, but his wail trickled away as he watched Sanjar's face.

"Now take us to the head man," Sanjar said.

The headman was small and plump, a Copt, appointed not in Alyun but by the council of al-Qahira. He spoke fluent Arabic, in spite of the wooden cross he wore to identify his faith, He received the pair in the courtyard of his house and invited them to sit on a bench strewn with rugs, while he squatted with a sallow-faced assistant on either side. Politely he asked their business, and in reply to their question admitted he had seen the wandering horse and had called the city guard.

"Indeed, it was a fine horse," he said, his mouth twisting into a smile. Clearly the headman had fought hard with himself before surrendering Moonleap.

"May I know where she was taken, and by whom?" enquired Sanjar, equalling the other's conventional courtesies.

"A Captain Guhar, of the guards at al-Qahira, came for her," replied the headman. "He was much taken with the horse. As for your scabbard, I have it here, and will return it for a small fee to cover the cost of the trouble you have caused." As an afterthought, he added, "As you may know, though a foreigner, it is not customary in our country for any other than a soldier to ride a horse. Donkeys and mules are more suitable for everyone else, by the Caliph al-Hakim's decree."

Sanjar rose. He was aware of the power of the headman in the community, and equally aware that this power rarely extended beyond it.

"If my horse was taken into custody merely until she could be returned to her rightful owner, then no money would have changed hands."

"No money changed hands," agreed the headman, bowing.

"He was lying," Tadros said as they again trudged along the cobbled street.

"Perhaps it was more a return of favours."

As if to confirm this, one of the headman's assistants rode up behind them on a scrawny bay mule, giving a perfunctory greeting as they squeezed into a doorway to let him pass. Further on he kicked the mule into a run and headed off towards al-Qahira.

The two walked back through Fustat and the wheat and vegetable fields lying between the cities, passing on the road an assortment of merchants, soldiers and peasants, a gypsy band with a dancing bear, and a north-bound caravan of twenty camels laden fragrantly with sacks of spices and frankincense. As they neared the gates and the garrison at al-Qahira they were not surprised to meet a reception committee, and Sanjar was glad to feel the weight and strength of Moonflinger in its silver scabbard at his side.

Yet the party barring their way looked as though it would make scant allowance for the protocol of a fair fight. Facing them was a giant Syrian, at least seven feet tall and broad with it, flanked by two Circassians from Masovia, each only a foot shorter, yet dwarfed by the Syrian. Sanjar and Tadros tried to work round them and carry on towards the walls, but the trio moved to block them. All the passers-by seemed oblivious to them, but in fact they were completely aware and wary, gazing fixedly in any direction but at the guards.

Sanjar asked the reason for this show of hostility.

"No one enters al-Qahira without a permit," warned one of the Circassians.

"I have a permit."

"You heard."

"How can I enter?"

"The city is not for the likes of you," said the Syrian enigmatically.

"Time to go," said Tadros.

Sanjar drew Moonflinger, but the guards leapt at him. He had no chance to fight before the world blackened the cobblestones leapt up to greet him.

*   *   *

They had no way of knowing how long they had been in the cell. The only light to filter through was cast by a flickering torch outside the door, which allowed them to make out that they were in a small room with bare stone walls, a filthy straw mat, and a jug of fetid water presumably placed there for ablutions. A foul-smelling sluice ran across the floor. At regular intervals a guard marched along the passage, and sometimes they heard muffled cries.

Sanjar recovered consciousness in this cell: Tadros ripped strips of his own shirt to stop the profuse bleeding of his head wound. He was half-delirious with weakness from the heavy blow.

At last they heard the feet of several guards outside, and soldiers opened the door with massive keys. They clamped iron fetters on their wrists, and ushered them out and up a narrow, winding staircase to the street, where the harsh sunlight blinded their weakened eyes. When they became accustomed to the glare they glanced back and saw they had been imprisoned in the dungeons of the tower of the Bab al-Futuh. Citizens thronged the streets as thickly as they did where Sanjar lived at the Bab Mitwalli on the opposite side of the city, intent on their own pursuits and barely glancing at the unfortunate prisoners being marched to the garrison of the guards and into the presence of the notorious Captain Guhar.

The captain kept them waiting. When at last they were summoned before him, he glanced at them contemptuously. Sanjar's anger reverberated around the room as he spoke.

"You are Captain Guhar?"

The captain did not bother to reply to such an insolent question.

"You should know that I am that I am Sanjar, known as Mouseback, veteran warrior of the Sultan of Ghazna, and have fought many wars for the glory of the Faith."

"Your master, your former master, is not the ruler here," rejoined the captain. "You are a stranger to us, but known already as a thief, a murderer, and a liar, and you are my prisoner. You claim property that is not yours to claim, You have no deeds, and no rights."

"I claim no more than my own," replied Sanjar, white with fury.

Suddenly the door was flung open and two figures burst into the room. Resplendent in scarlet and gold tunics and turbans of royal blue, these were Circassians of the Caliph's guard.

"We have a warrant for the arrest of Sanjar Mouseback," said one, "to appear before the Qadi." He slapped down a scroll before Captain Guhar.

And now it was the Captain's turn to be consumed with rage, for the warrant included a subpoena for the warrior's property, and for the Captain's appearance before the Qadi.

His pride injured by the indignity of the subpoena, but with no cause to doubt the successful outcome of his plea, Captain Guhar left at once and rode to the Qadi's palace, leaving Sanjar and Tadros to be marched through the streets under guard. It was here that Tadros was seen and recognised by an acquaintance of his master's; Boutros the Physician, on learning of the arrest of his groom, crossed himself and decided that discretion (accompanied by a small donation to the Church) was the better part of valour. A few days later he relented and made some enquiries regarding the fate of the boy, but by then Tadros was nowhere to be found.

It was as they neared the palace of the Qadi that Sanjar heard the runner's cry, and around a corner appeared the familiar red and gold sedan. The guards stopped while the sedan ran by. But did a curtain not flicker as it passed? Did he not feel the searing glance of those unseen eyes?

The Qadi, it was said, lived in more magnificence even than the Caliph, whose tastes were simple, even humble. It was whispered that under a Caliph who, in spite of his personal asceticism and bouts of generosity, was a dangerous madman, only a clever, scheming and ruthless man could have survived as Qadi. His palace was set in the hub of the city and was several storeys high, each wing backing onto a courtyard set with rare trees. Guards led the prisoners through the silver-studded gates and under a portal supported by granite columns to the judicial offices and the Great Hall of Judgment, which served less as a democratic court of justice than as a place for the apportioning of the Qadi's personal whim. Sunlight poured into the hall through windows set under a ceiling twenty cubits high. Marble columns graced its contours, while the floor was inlaid with marble pieces set in geometric designs. Scarlet-and-blue-liveried Circassians stood in position, and at the far end of hall, surrounded by officials, the Qadi sat on a dais in his crimson robes.

To the hushed silence of the court, a notary read out the case against Sanjar.

"It seems clear to me," said the Qadi smoothly when he had finished, "that such a fine horse and so unique a weapon can be the property only of the Caliph al-Hakim himself, and that if it is not so, then indeed it should be so. For if you, follower of a foreign ruler who is, how shall I put it, in no position of influence here, won these things as the spoils of war, then it is only right that they should go, along with other goods confiscated in this way, to our ruler. You did well, Captain Guhar, to bring this to our attention. You may return to your command convinced of our gratitude. You," he returned to address Sanjar in his treacly voice, "must present yourself to the Caliph al-Hakim in order for him to establish your loyalties."

Captain Guhar, his soreness over losing the horse giving way to relief over the commendation of his enterprise, left hastily.

"That man," said the Qadi confidentially to Sanjar when he had gone, "too frequently exceeds his duties."

"My lord, I request permission to speak," Sanjar said, bowing. "My goods were not granted me as a share of the spoils of war, nor as rewards for my conduct. My mare, who is brave and valiant, was bred by my father, a Samanid lord whose stable is renowned throughout Turkestan. My sword passed into my hands through the grace of the Imam of al-Aqsa in the Holy City of Jerusalem, where it had been kept since the days of the Hajira. These are rightfully mine, and remain so, and I beg justice from your Excellency in the restoration of my possessions."

"Hmm," said the Qadi, stroking his beard. "That was well put, but the

Caliph al-Hakim has expressed an interest in your situation, and this will be for him to decide. You are commanded at his court, and you will appear there forthwith. You are dismissed."

Sanjar, followed by Tadros, was escorted from the hall. As they left the Qadi was wearing a frown, and their last impression of him was of a man much troubled by the burden of his duties.

Sanjar was marched away with four guards: Tadros, as his servant, was left behind, and after waiting for half an hour for someone to tell him what to do, strolled unobtrusively through the palace gates into the street. From there he made his way to the Bab Mitwalli district where Sanjar lived.

It was not a great distance to the Caliph's palace, but to the prisoner, who had had no pause or refreshment that day, the march in the hot, dry sun seemed interminable. The road was quieter than in other parts of the city, for the common throng was kept well away from the neighbourhood of the Caliph. They joined a troop of soldiers as well as several carts laden with provisions and a small flock of sheep, all making their way to the palace gates. The cobblestones echoed with the thunder of trundling cartwheels.

The street opened into a square lined by the high walls and towers of the palace gardens. In the guardroom at the gate, beside a mango tree that waved in the breeze, soldiers clattered tric-trac pieces on a wooden board, and an officer emerged without haste or enthusiasm to scrutinise the prisoner before allowing him to be ushered in.

The Circassian guards flung open the gates, and so unexpected was the sight that met his eyes that Sanjar halted. Before him was a serene and beautiful garden lit with a thousand lamps, its scents and colours vying with the singing of birds to command attention. Winding between the almond and lemon trees, acacias and royal palms, roses, cypresses and small tamarisks, were beautiful ceramic floors, the tiles themselves resplendent in shades of blue, turquoise, green and gold. Pools of clear water glistened, caressed by playing fountains. Marble seats lined the paths, so one could rest to savour the garden. In gilded cages, coloured birds wept and sang.

The Caliph stood alone in a corner of the garden, eating a peach. The guards withdrew, leaving the Caliph's bodyguards, all with their tongues prudently removed, in their positions at the garden wall.

The Caliph offered Sanjar a peach.

Sanjar, embarrassed, declined.

"Oh come on," said the Caliph. "Home grown."

"I can see that God has blessed your garden most graciously," said Sanjar, falling to his knees. He was conscious of his filthy and dishevelled appearance, his bloodstained head and clothes, and his weakness from privation and thirst. But the Caliph himself was plainly garbed. Had Sanjar not known better he might have mistaken him for one of the ordinary citizens of al-Qahira or Fustat, for he was wearing worn robes much like those cast off by a travelling merchant. He was younger than Sanjar had expected, in his mid-thirties or thereabouts. The cheeks behind the long and straggling moustache were hollow, as of a man under-nourished, and the eyes flashed now demoniac, now benevolent. Small wonder those who frequented the court went in terror of this man.

"If you don't mind my saying so," suggested the Caliph, "you don't look much like a hero."

"I have been in prison, your Excellency."

"Ah, yes, the Bab al-Futuh. Well, perhaps you could do with a rest. But not on your knees, I can't abide obsequiousness. Or titles, so drop the 'Excellency'." He regarded Sanjar suspiciously. "Are you sure you're a hero?"

"There have been moments." Sanjar swallowed the compulsion to add the word 'Lord'.

"Yes."

The Caliph paced to and fro with his half-eaten peach. Not normally a man at a loss for words, he was finding it difficult to broach the subject nearest to his heart.

"You have attracted some attention. you know," he said finally. "And you are in trouble, quite definitely in trouble. However! We have a need for someone of your sort. I take it that, loyal as you have proved to your master, the Sultan of Ghazna, you pledge loyalty also to his allies?"

"His allies have only to command."

"Very well, then. As I say, you are in a precarious position. We only have to say the word ... But why am I threatening you? We are allies, and we must be friends! If you are amenable to my plan, you will find freedom the least of your rewards, for I can promise you riches beyond your wildest dreams. Have you heard," he demanded abruptly, "of the Emerald Tablet?"

Sanjar shook his head slowly. "No, I have never heard of it."

"Hmm. The Emerald Tablet of Hermes Trismegistus, as the Greeks called him. The thrice-blessed, or, as some say, the five-times-blessed. I want it."

"If this Hermes has an emerald you desire, then acquiring it for you will be my quest."

The Caliph tossed away the peach stone. "So you know nothing of the Emerald Tablet. Well, what could I expect? Unfortunately it's not so easy as simply stealing a precious stone. First, you have to find it. And second, you have to know how to take it."

"Can we not find this Hermes?"

"No."

Sanjar was bewildered. "Then I shall search for him."

"No, you miss the point. There is no Hermes, if there ever was. It's the Emerald Tablet I want you to look for."

"What is this tablet?"

"Ah! You are beginning to ask the right questions. The Emerald Tablet was found more than thirteen hundred years ago, on the other side of the Nile, in the Great Pyramid of Giza. Who found it? I can tell you that too. It was found by the Pharaoh Iskander – Alexander the Great, you might have heard of him – after he overthrew the Persians and came to conquer Egypt. He found it, and he wrote it all down."

"What did he do with it?"

"Not much of a classical scholar, are you? We don't know what he did with it. Perhaps he left it where it was! But it's not there now, I've looked. Somehow, though, I don't think he left it in the Pyramid. He had a destiny, and it was the Emerald Tablet that showed him his destiny. The Emerald Tablet was the most perfect artifact ever produced. Iskander found the whole of magic engraved on a single stone.

"What it would mean to possess that stone! To learn the secrets of the stars! To find a way to the most secret, the most inaccessible knowledge, hidden from man since the dawn of time!"

The Caliph's words fell among the trees and on to the ears of his mute bodyguards, for Sanjar had stopped his ears to such profanity and was waiting to be dismissed.

3 · The Master of Time

SANJAR WAS IN a room decorated with rich silk carpets and delicately carved closets, lit with sunrays filtered through a latticed window. It was a hariim room, full of feminine touches and pleasantries, embroidery and flowers and the scent of frankincense mingled with jasmine and rose. He wondered whose room it was. He had no way of knowing: he had arrived here with a basket over his head.

In the midst of this finery he was sadly conscious of his physical state: wounded, unwashed, unshaven, still in torn and filthy clothes, and with a gnawing pain in his stomach. As he took stock of his surroundings he noticed a dish of honey cakes set before the window, and after a few moments of battling with himself he picked one up. As he did the door opened.

"Don't touch it!"

Sanjar dropped the cake.

"Devil's food," Bahiga explained, sweeping across the room to move the dish out of his reach.

Sanjar wiped his fingers on his gown. Then, remembering himself, he fell on his knees. The young woman before him was the loveliest thing he had ever seen: had he tried to conjure such a face in his dreams, he could never have captured such beauty. Her features were small and fine, her eyes lustrous and intelligent, her mouth perfect in its sweetness. Her ebony hair was drawn back under a scarf of red chiffon, and was prevented from straying by a single strand of pearls.

Confused by his own indiscretion of gazing on her face, Sanjar ashamedly bowed his head.

"There is no need to kneel, soldier," she said in tones that were more of a command than a statement. "It is I who should apologise for your abduction. But, as you have doubtless guessed, you ought not to be here, and this puts me doubly at fault. It were better that this place and my identity were not revealed to you. Please get up," she repeated.

As he rose Sanjar noticed that another figure had entered the room behind her mistress: a maid or nurse, plump in middle age and soberly dressed. She hovered near the door; Sanjar guessed that if she made a move the guards who had leapt on him as he left the palace and carried him here would be upon him in a moment.

Bahiga regarded him less sternly. She took notice of his dress, of his wounds which were livid and in need of attention. It was when she sent the maid for medicine that she allowed a more personal interest to affect her glance, and when he turned to look at her she felt, to her shame, a blush rising to her cheeks that she could not control, and as being caught unawares and without mastery over her feelings was anathema to Bahiga she was further plunged into confusion. Sanjar, on the other hand, was encouraged by the blush, which he took not as a lapse in character but as a sign that she reciprocated his interest. So, with just a little hesitation, he smiled and she, pleased, smiled in return. When the nurse returned and Bahiga leaned over him to wash his wounds with warm, scented water and apply a sweet-smelling salve, she was acutely aware of his closeness. Sanjar, too, breathed in the soothing balm mingled with the scent of her perfume and felt, rather than calmed, alarmed by the passion her nearness awakened in him. He was still more perturbed when he caught sight of her gold bracelet, which was set with turquoise and lapis lazuli.

"Won't you tell me your name?" he asked, knowing that if he knew only this, he would be able to retain a little of her.

"My name is Bahiga," she replied softly.

"And mine – "

"Yes, I know, Sanjar known as Mouseback, a Samanid, a ghazi – or should I say a soldier of fortune – lately in the service of Sultan Mahmud of Ghazna, who has designs on carrying the Muslim faith into India. When you have eaten, Sanjar Mouseback, I shall tell you why I brought you here."

The nurse led Sanjar into another room, where fresh robes were laid out on a couch. By the time he had changed and returned dishes of yogurt, scented rice and meat stewed with apricots were laid out for him. He ate gratefully and silently, and as he sipped sweet coffee and cut open a pomegranate, he prepared himself for enlightenment.

"The Caliph al-Hakim has instructed you to seek and find the Emerald Tablet of Hermes Trismegistus," Bahiga began. "I am going to beg you to pretend you never heard his request, to leave al-Qahira and this country and never return, to erase everything he told you of it from your mind, never to think of it, never to look for it, never to find it.

"I don't think I need to tell you why it is I ask this of you. Al-Hakim has now been Caliph for more than twenty years without doing anything for his country or his people, apart from building a mosque or a fountain here and there. He has grown more and more eccentric, and is now quite mad. He hates Jews. He hates Christians – he put to death even his uncles, Bishops of the Church. He hates his sister, the Sitt al-Mulk. He hates all women. We

30

are not allowed into the streets and are obliged to stay at home, for he has forbidden cobblers to make shoes for us. He hates dogs. There are no dogs any more. He hates landowners, or anyone who could challenge his power. Even the common people suffer: they are forced to sleep by day and work at night, and he rides round on a donkey to inspect them. We all live in fear of him, yet we are all, still, in his grasp.

"But there is worse. Four years ago, he announced that he was divine. First he proclaimed himself the Messiah, which was a mixed blessing for the Christians and the Jews, because once he thought he was their spiritual leader he stopped persecuting them. But at the same time he angered the Muslims, who were expecting a more suitable Messiah. And it didn't stop there. He began to see himself as the god-king of the Egyptians, the divine Pharaoh, following in the footsteps of Cheops, of Ramses, of Iskander. He will not rest until he is omnipotent! Imagine what might happen if this madman got his hands on the Emerald Tablet! You can imagine it, can't you?"

Sanjar, being a soldier rather than a philosopher, had not thought of the consequence should he successfully fulfil the mission he had tacitly consented to undertake. He could concede that Bahiga might have a point, but he still understood very little about the Tablet, and he began to formulate a few questions in his mind that would not display his almost total ignorance. Before he could phrase his first question, however (and he tried to dismiss the thought that the riches he had been promised might be vanishing into dreams), Bahiga's room began to behave very strangely indeed. First a strong wind swept through it, unbalancing the brass tray which held the remains of his meal and swirling Bahiga's crimson scarves tightly round her shoulders, while a puff of smoke suddenly appeared in a corner. Then there was a great deal of shouting, and Sanjar felt himself propelled through the room by a powerful force, tumbled down the stairs in a cloud of dust so thick it choked him and forced him to close his eyes, and thrown into the covered back of a very dirty cart, from which, when he opened his eyes, the last thing he glimpsed through a hole in the boards as it clattered down the street was half a dozen liveried guards violating the crowds and overthrowing merchant carts. He had little doubt they searched for him.

The cart emerged from the crowded streets and turned as though heading for the river, so Sanjar decided to jump out without attracting the attention of the driver. He might have succeeded had he not chosen to climb out just as the cart became entangled with a mule ridden by a very irate Copt carrying a medicine bag who, seeing Sanjar emerging from under the cover, decided to vent his anger on one who, so richly if not tidily dressed, must have been in charge of the cart. Sanjar jumped, and the curses of the driver and the doctor echoed after him.

Weariness overtook him as he walked back to his quarters. Finding the door open, but nobody about, he climbed up to his rooms on the third floor and collapsed on the couch. Thoughts of Bahiga ran through his mind. Who was she, and why did she live like this, in a house with untouchable food and magic winds? With her image in his mind, he fell into a deep sleep.

* * *

Sanjar woke when it was dark to find a lamp lit in his room, while a jug of cool water and a pile of fresh linen lay at his side and fragrant incense burned over a pot of hot coals. Tadros sat at the foot of his bed, clean and shaven, in a new white gown.

Tadros brought him coffee spiced with cardamom.

"All right, you've made your point," Sanjar said. "When I've had a hot bath we shall discuss your wages."

"I don't need a wage, sir. I want to serve you because you are a great and a brave man." And well respected by the Caliph, who sent for you, he might have added.

"Where is my horse?"

"Downstairs in the stable, sir, well fed and resting."

Sanjar sipped the coffee.

"You can start by telling me what you know of the Emerald Tablet."

Tadros scowled and, arms round his knees, curled up into a ball.

"I don't know about things like this," he said sulkily.

"And you don't want to know, eh?"

"It's not for you or me."

"A legend?"

"A heathen legend. It's not good to talk of these things."

"What is it?" Sanjar gestured with impatience, wondering if the boy knew anything at all.

"I don't know."

Sanjar slammed down his cup. "Can't you say anything?" he shouted.

Tadros, terrified at Sanjar's unexpected anger, showed the whites of his eyes.

"It's not true, master, master! It doesn't exist!"

"Then why I am offered a large fortune to find it? And who is this Hermes, who owns it? Don't worry boy, I just need your help."

Tadros, relieved, offered a compromise.

"I'll find out," he said.

Memories of Bahiga flooded into Sanjar's mind, unfamiliar emotions that troubled and excited and unsettled him.

"There is a lady named Bahiga," said Sanjar. "Who is she?"

"I'll find out," Tadros promised.

*   *   *

Although he pretended to have been to great lengths, Tadros didn't have to look hard to find out anything. Information came to him in the form of the saqui, the thin, bent water carrier, named Hanafi, whose position gave him the privilege of entering the outer chambers of the hariim, otherwise forbidden to all but the father, husband and sons of the house. One morning the saqui told Tadros that Bahiga would soon pay a visit to Sanjar, but that she requested Sanjar not to leave his house until after she had come.

Sanjar was overjoyed, and accepted his imprisonment with elation. But by the third day he had become restive. He scarcely took his eyes from the window overlooking the Bab Mitwalli, and did so only to glance compulsively at the door. He had Tadros search the street for a sign of her, but there was none. He forgot the gilded sedan chair and the delight he had taken in its unknown occupant. He thought only of the lovely woman who had tended his wounds and enveloped him in her perfume and her beauty.

His meals were brought by Tadros, who reported that, as usual, there were no women in the streets, not even – as one occasionally glimpsed – a heavily-veiled figure hurrying by for fear of betrayal. Tadros was making efforts to find a sage who could explain the mystery of the Emerald Tablet. But he was a Copt, he complained to Sanjar, and no one trusted him. What he really meant was that he was afraid to become enmeshed in a web of disbelief.

When Bahiga came she was dressed as a boy. Her visit was so fleeting that it was over almost as soon as it began, and afterwards Sanjar had difficulty in recalling whether it had occurred, or whether her appearance was a manifestation of his dreams.

She arrived as night fell, accompanied by a eunuch who was also simply dressed. Bahiga herself wore white, with her blacks locks swathed in a white turban. Her eyes shone with the pleasure of the escapade: devoid of antimony she looked like a pretty boy, and Sanjar wondered fleetingly whether other women disguised themselves and moved about the city in this way.

They seated themselves on a carpet in the dimly-lit room, leaning on cushions, with one knee raised and the other tucked beneath. Tadros set a water pipe between them and withdrew to sit with the eunuch in a corner. His sullenness over the magical quest dissolved as soon as he beheld Bahiga, half woman, half youth. Though she was young and slight, a force emanated from her that commanded awe. It was not merely the aura that one of high birth wielded as a natural right; it was the aura of one skilled in the mysteries of good and evil, one who possessed the power of an enchantress.

Sanjar passed her the mouthpiece of the water pipe, and she returned it, each tasting the salty nectar of the other's lips. His eyes met hers, and for an instant he seemed to drown in the black, limpid pools. As he gazed he knew she was willing him to deny his quest.

"You want to learn about the Emerald Tablet," she said, replying to his unspoken words. "But first you must know the one who wrote it. We must go back in time to the dawn of Egypt's days. Not of your days, for your ancestors were wandering the Hindu Kush, and understood only the rocks beneath their feet and the icy chill of the mountains, nor of my father's, for his were Thracians who knew no more than the wind in their wild hair as they galloped over the steppes. But the days of the Egyptian, like my mother, and your friend here," she waved a languid hand towards Tadros, "stretch back through ancient days to the dawn of wisdom, for this is an old, old land." She paused to draw on the pipe, and the bubble echoed around the small room. In spite of the bustle from the street outside, now waking at the end of the Caliph's daytime curfew, there was no sound but the voice of Bahiga.

"While your ancestors roamed the cold hills contending with primitive spirits and led by shamans, and mine, or my father's, followed the herds of the horned Moon-goddess, the Egyptians wrested with the greatest of all mysteries, the mystery of life. They mastered it. And once they knew the secret of life, so they gained mastery over death. Their knowledge was of the highest level. Yet it was not for all: the secrets were for only a few, those initiated into the supreme priesthood, the disciples of Thoth.

"You can see the image of Thoth carved on the tomb and temple walls of Memphis and Thebes, though his image is safely blanketed from philistine iconoclasts by layers of drifting sand. His god-figure, quill in hand, records the sacred mysteries and the passing of time. He knows why we are here and where we will go. He knows the sun and the moon, he reads the stars; oceans and winds are at his command. He knows how to heal the sick and raise the dead, how we may travel and leave our bodies behind, how we may be at one with our knowledge of the Universe. He teaches."

Sanjar felt himself overwhelmed by a feeling of tranquillity, almost of euphoria. He felt an uplifting of spirit as she spoke, and then her words became disembodied. They drifted round him in the air, but they were not attached to Bahiga because he could no longer see her. He looked down at his hands, and found they were invisible too. But this did not induce a sense of fear or panic, rather one of peace, as though he were relieved to find his body was no longer necessary. He and Bahiga seemed to be flying, yet there was no sensation of it; instead they were ethereal in motion, suspended in air, and he found he was no longer listening to her words but feeling them.

She told him to look down, and as he did so he found himself forgetting himself and who or where he was, and accepting this unusual pose as one natural and quite in the order of things, much as he accepted his dreams as reality while he dreamed them. It occurred to him that perhaps he was dreaming, for the sensations he was feeling were very close to those of dreams. Again Bahiga urged him to look down, and doing so he was startled by the sharpness of his vision as he gazed on scenes which seemed to belong to another world. Below him was a river, and on either side brown, half-naked men tilled and tended neat, square fields yielding an abundance of produce. The waving date palms, the brown-spotted oxen yoked to the plough and the mud brick houses grouped on the river banks looked familiar, yet Sanjar could not place these scenes. Bahiga pointed his thoughts in another direction, and suddenly they were in the inner halls of a splendid temple. On the walls and columns were carved mysterious scenes of gods and kings, overlaid in rich and glorious colours: brilliant yellows and reds, blues and greens; and around them were strange marks and figures of birds. Before them was a huge statue of a god of shining gold, and before him an altar lit with flickering candles. Sanjar was so overawed by the vision that he forgot such idols were forbidden and profane: to him it was a thing of magnificence and beauty. The god stood erect and proud, but the face looking down on its worshippers was benevolent and kind, as though happy to bestow on them the wealth of the land they tilled, the warmth of the sun which brought life to them and their crops, and the abundant waters of the Nile which nurtured them. "O river! No one knows where you are from, you flow from your secret caverns to bring your gift to your people, O blessed one! And you descend as rain to water the lands of foreign people, so all can share your goodness! With your father the sun and your sister the moon you share the love and gratitude of your people! You who gives life to every living thing, we bow like reeds before your glory, O abundant one!"

Approaching the statue was a line of priests robed in white, with leopard-skin cloaks thrown over their shoulders and golden bands in their hair. Each carried a tray of offerings for the god: bread, cakes, and fruit, jugs of wine, or censers from which drifted the heady aroma of frankincense. As they came forward they chanted. "Hail to thee, Ra, thou who risest, and shinest, and art king of all the gods! Father of beginnings, thou who created the earth, and made the sky and the ocean, and brought the river to nourish us! Lord of heaven, thou who sails across the sky, prepare to slay Apep, the serpent of darkness, and wake to a new day!" Placing the trays on the altar before the god, they prostrated themselves while he satisfied himself. When he had consumed the spirit of the food, the priests carried out the trays, while the last one extinguished the candles and swept away the footprints they had left in the dust with a soft palm-frond brush.

Sanjar had not known, could not have known any of these things. How, then, did they enter his mind? He realised that he was no longer conscious of Bahiga putting messages into his head, as she had previously fed him with words. Now he seemed to be absorbing her knowledge, but without the process of thought. And though the language of the priests was like none other he had heard, he knew what they were saying.

So elating was the scene in the temple that he would have stayed to watch the sleeping god, but Bahiga led him on. He saw the vast, square foundations of the Great Pyramid, and again would have lingered out of curiosity to see how the construction of this wonder was undertaken, but the bustling desert, which was crawling with men as though they had disturbed a giant ants' nest on the riverbank, was swiftly enveloped in a mist which ebbed and flowed and finally cleared to show a large room, its whitewashed walls covered with strange designs. Dozens of baboons ran about the room, playing havoc with hundreds upon hundreds of papyrus pages lying scattered on the floor, and on a golden throne before a golden table sat an old man, his grey locks tumbling about his shoulders, and wearing a long amethyst gown embroidered with gold. In his thin hand he held a long quill pen which moved over the papyrus sheets at such a rate that page after page was swiftly completed and tumbled one after the other to the ground. A small boy with a long handled besom tried to sweep the pages into a corner, but as fast as he swept the floor filled up again. Sanjar heard Bahiga's word-thoughts reverberating silently through his mind.

"I can talk again here," she was saying, "he is too passionately engrossed in what he is doing to hear us. This is Hermes Trismegistus, or Thoth, the Master of Time. Thoth is the scientist of the gods. He has chronicled the cycles of the sun to chart the equinoxes and number the days and the years, the cycles of the moon that govern the fertility of all creatures as well as the tides, and he has mapped the stars and has told us when Sirius will rise, so we may understand the cycles of the Nile and know the seed time, the harvest time, and the flood time. He has invented the art of writing, so men may keep accounts, and write laws and edicts and chronicle events, and write down hymns, prayers and poems so the words remain sacred and are not debased or forgotten. He knows the art of healing the sick with the use of prayers and herbs, and he has taught people how to perform surgery, and how to lift the spirit out of the body of the patient while they do so, so that he feels no pain. He can raise the dead. He knows the other side of the moon and the stars. There is nothing he does not know, and that he has not taught those who sought to learn."

Though Sanjar fought to keep it, the vision began to fade and the white mist enshrouded him once more. When it cleared they sat again on the carpet on the floor. Dazed, he shook his head and breathed deeply, but the air was not the fresh, clean air of his journey but the stuffy, damp, smoke-filled air of his small room.

"And they knew how to learn." Bahiga pulled at the pipe. "But they learnt too much. Their power grew too great, and their knowledge was abased... Within a few generations it was almost gone. They crowned Thoth with an ibis head, and kept him in check by pretending he was a bird.

"When the power of his mysteries was at its peak, hundreds of years before they began to draw him as a bird, Thoth wished to write down his secrets. He let it be known that he sought a tablet that was beautiful enough to bear his sacred words, and strong enough to carry them for eternity. At length, someone brought him a piece of emerald, and on its flat and incandescent surface he engraved all he knew, all of magic written on a single stone. 'What is below is that which is above, and what is above is that which is below,' he wrote on the Tablet. He wrote the number of the stars and the nature of the wind, he wrote of light, and fire, and of the Creation. He wrote that the elements, born of the sun and the moon, are nurtured by the Earth.

"The high priests studied and practised what they had learnt from Thoth. But hand in hand with the knowledge of good they acquired a knowledge of evil, for one cannot learn one without the other. They were taught to know evil and to recognise it in order to combat it, but in the course of time they became curious, and wished to learn how they might benefit from using the darker side of their knowledge. They began to use their knowledge for evil as well as good. At first they were restrained, but, egged on by their Pharaohs, they began to use the tainted wisdom to gain power over enemies, or gain riches or privileges for themselves, or to conjure images and mirages that amused and overawed the people. Over time, they allowed the forces of the sacred magic to work greater and greater evil. They began to use it to predict the future, to work magic over spirits, over each other, and even over Pharaoh. Finally, they resorted to the lowest form of magic: they sold it. The highest knowledge became the deepest evil. It became one with the mundane. Folk-magic and god-magic, it was one and the same. The high priests of the Mysteries of Osiris became magicians, practising debased rights and selling amulets and charms.

"Who was Thoth? Thoth came from another world, before the Flood. He came with the Divine Family, Osiris, Isis, Horus, Nephthys, and Set; they were to govern men, and he to teach them. Thoth was the god of the Moon, as Ra was god of the Sun. As Ra became Amoun, so Thoth became Hermes.

"Many centuries after Thoth engraved the Emerald Tablet the High Priests, fearing the misuse of its power, laid it in the Great Pyramid so it would rest hidden and secure. There it lay for two thousand years until Iskander the Great entered the pyramid and found it. Iskander changed when he saw the Tablet: he became inspired, like a man with a great destiny to fulfil. He left at once to consult the oracle of Amoun in the desert far to the west, and on his way he founded the city of Iskandriya. But he never saw the finished city, for he went off at once to fight the Persians, and when he died Ptolemy became ruler of Egypt as Iskander had decreed. Influenced by Iskander, Ptolemy and his descendants embraced the knowledge of Thoth, whom they called Hermes Trismegistus, Hermes the thrice-great as he possessed the three parts of the philosophy of the world. And Hermes lived among them, but though some priests and scholars tried to hold fast to his instructions the depth to which his sacred magic had fallen distressed and perplexed him, and he did not show his face.

"He appeared, instead, to others, in different guises and at different times. Each body he used grew old, very old, but it did not die. It ascended to heaven, leaving another in which his spirit could live on. Thoth was Elijah and Elisha, he was the Hermes Trismegistus of the Iskandriyans, and he lives among us still. He still does not die, but he changes bodies. His physical parts ascend, but he clings to the world in his attempt to guide us. He is known as the Qutb."

"And may we see him?"

"Every day. But we do not know him, for he is known only to himself. But only he may give you permission to search for the Tablet. Not the Caliph, nor I. For the Tablet was and is his, fashioned by him at the height of the wisdom of the priesthood before they began the fall from grace, to be passed down in perpetuity for the use of mankind, but then withdrawn and hidden in a most sacred place, until Iskander disturbed it."

"But if I am to ask his permission I must first find him, and where may I do that?"

"Well, that should not be too difficult, for he is said to be a neighbour of yours. Although he moves around, of course." Bahiga smiled. "Unlike al-Hakim, he does not need a donkey to travel."

Sanjar's eyes narrowed, for he felt the young woman's strong will drawing him into combat. Moreover, he did not care much for ancient mumbo-jumbo, brought up as he was, desert spirits or no, to respect the word of God.

"And if I don't find him?"

"If he wishes, he will find you. If he does not, it is a sign you must not go."

Sanjar's eyes sparkled. "But if I find the sacred Tablet and bring it to al-Hakim, and win my reward, I can remove you from the house in which you are so ill at ease, and take you away with me anywhere we wish to go, and we shall have everything money can buy."

Bahiga's eyes flashed in anger. "You betray me with your seductive words," she countered. "I had thought more highly of you, even though you are only a soldier. Now I know what you are: a mercenary, one who would sell not only his own soul to the highest bidder, but the souls of the ones he loves. I prefer my house to yours: better the devil you know!"

Having so deeply offended her, and not knowing whether she was a high priestess or an angel, for she appeared at times as one, at times the other, Sanjar wrung his hands. He really did not know how to address the fair sex. Indeed, apart from his mother, his sisters, and his father's wives, almost the only women he had addressed were those he had encountered in his carousing when, in spite of his religion, he had frequently been in his cups.

"I am a very bad Muslim," he offered feebly.

"God will be the judge," was her formal reply.

"He might as well strike me dead."

"I know in my heart He has other plans."

"I have offended you and I want to die."

"That's very dramatic," said Bahiga, drawing herself up. "But then soldiery is a dramatic profession. Most men are conscripted, and do not offer their bodies to the service of a warlord. That is prostitution. Most people prefer to die in their beds." She stood up.

"If you pursue your venture without sanction, Sanjar Mouseback, I shall fight you. I do not use a sword, but my weaponry is formidable. I do not have a horse but I can move faster than the wind. If you find the Tablet you will lead others to it as well. You will lead me to seek to destroy it, and the others will seek to destroy you."

The boy in white had been replaced by a much taller, strikingly handsome being, august and asexual, whose crushing words were supported by a sardonic glare. But the startling effect was only momentary. She, or he, turned, and followed by the eunuch slipped through the curtained doorway and out into the busy night street.

4 · Like Daughter, Like Father

TRYING TO SILENCE his heart, the Qadi waited fretfully to be summoned to the kiosk where the Caliph was holding his evening audiences. He judged that al-Hakim was in a capricious mood. Some plaintiffs emerged relieved, cocky or even smiling; others were shaken, and a few had been dragged out screaming by Circassian guards.

At last it was all over. Those plaintiffs who still waited but had not succeeded in gaining an audience were shooed away without ceremony. Sitting for a few moments in peace, the Qadi lectured his heart on the folly of palpitating.

The summons came. The Caliph sat on a pile of cushions, looking smug.

"Were you satisfied with the warrior?" asked the Qadi, careful to keep his smile friendly rather than obsequious.

"I am not satisfied yet, but I may be," the Caliph replied affably. Secretly he thought the soldier had a very good chance of leading him to the Emerald Tablet, but he wasn't going to give the Qadi, whose protégé Sanjar was, any cause for complacency.

"Have his possessions been returned?" al-Hakim asked.

The Qadi nodded. "We sent back his horse, his weapons, and his servant, a little Copt who sprang from nowhere."

"We should keep an eye on him."

"I thought as much. I have in my pay the saqui who carries water to my house. He brings information, and I have made sure he will visit the soldier while he stays in the city."

Al-Hakim scowled. He was always disturbed at the thought of the Qadi, and others, getting too clever. The Qadi's heart pounded faster.

"Nothing passes your eyes or your ears," he said reassuringly.

The Caliph decided the Qadi's idea of employing the saqui as spy had been a good one.

"Of course," continued the Qadi, "one cannot expect the soldier to be completely trustworthy. Once – "

The Caliph flared. "Then why choose him?"

"We have no cause to fear him yet," explained the Qadi as calmly as he could. "But once he lays his hands on the Tablet... "

The Caliph nodded, understanding spreading over his thin face. "He must be closely followed and watched."

"If I may venture."

"What?"

"If you care to leave it in my hands."

"You mean," al-Hakim leaned a little closer and glanced furtively around, rolling his eyes and wriggling his outstretched fingers. "You mean...?"

"Precisely."

Nodding, the Caliph sank back into the pillows. A lesser man might sometimes have remembered to be a little afraid of the Qadi.

* * *

The Qadi left the palace in low spirits. It was all very well to be in the Caliph's good books, but it meant one always had to be achieving something, and the Qadi, by inclination a lazy man, found constant levels of activity tiresome. Moreover, they raised his blood pressure. He had tried to prevent the Caliph from getting too interested in the Emerald Tablet, had tried to insist it was well known to have vanished without any hope of recovery; now he cursed himself for mentioning it in the first place. How did he know his amusing little anecdote would be taken so seriously? He had an uncomfortable feeling that it would lead to his undoing.

He knew, too, that someone was fighting him.

Ah, Bahiga! His thoughts strayed. Bahiga, who would not give him her love; Bahiga, who nurtured the mysteries her mother would not betray to him, who understood more than he of the realms of darkness and the theatre of light, but would not lead him there. Who had closed those doors to him as she had closed her heart.

This brought his mind back to the Emerald Tablet.

Which was open to him, as well as to al-Hakim.

Hurrying home, he locked himself in his chamber and fell easily into a trance.

* * *

Sanjar turned his head so as not to see the old man wince with pain. His questioning had reached something of a stalemate: the saqui's fear of Bahiga's magic was too great for him to betray her for money. But Sanjar was too fastidious to resort easily to physical torture. Tadros suggested breaking him down by interrogation and intimidation, and, displaying a ghoulish side to his nature, was attempting to show the old man what it would be like to have his toenails pulled out.

41

The saqui decided to keep his toenails and give away one of Bahiga's secrets.

"She is not," he began, doubly disloyal, "a very dutiful daughter. She refuses to obey her father, who gave her life… the shame… "

Sanjar leaned over him, eyes flashing. "It is not your place to insult her! You, little more than a beggar! Curse you!"

Hanafi began to whimper. He wanted sympathy. He had hoped to rouse a manly passion against lack of humility in the gentler sex, and against the woman who had subjected him to this torture; but he had misjudged his man, and the moment.

"But her father is not a good man," he added.

The breath of relief in the room was audible.

"Go on."

The saqui shook his head, feigning sorrow. "She prefers not to acknowledge him. She lives under his roof with her serving maid and guards more loyal to her than to him, who spy on his militia. He is a Turk: her mother was Egyptian, and, it is said, she died of a broken heart on his account." The saqui paused; Sanjar waited expectantly.

"Like her and like her mother, her father is a magician. His magic is very strong. But his magic is black. He is cursed."

"Cursed?"

"He uses a jinni."

Sanjar turned to Tadros, perplexed.

"Very bad," explained Tadros. "People who bring jinn under their influence are disobeying the laws of God."

"Aye, aye!" agreed the saqui.

"Jinn are waiting to be summoned, but they must be ignored. It is forbidden, like seeing into the future, which is one of the things jinn do."

"Aye!" nodded the saqui vigorously.

"It all sounds against the laws of God to me, every bit of it, jinn or no. What does this jinni do?" asked Sanjar more conspiratorially, leaning towards the old man.

"It provides for him. If he reaches in his pockets, he finds gold. It spreads his table with fine things to eat." Here the saqui drooled. "Through this jinni he tries to win Bahiga, but she refuses the things the jinni brings her. She prefers her food cooked in the usual way."

Sanjar remembered the honey cakes.

"She scorns his gifts of silk and jewels, wearing only the things that were her mother's. And she is disobedient, too, risking her father's displeasure. She goes about in broad daylight, flouting the law. She is clever with magic too. She can command spirits and humans to do whatever she wants, and animals as well. Her father is afraid of her." The saqui renewed his whimpering. "Have pity on me, lord. Everyone is afraid of her."

42

"WHO IS SHE?"

The saqui took a great gulp.

"She is the Qadi's daughter, may God forgive me and the Prophets protect me."

*   *   *

The Qadi emerged from his transcendental excursion with a slowed pulse, and much refreshed. Muttering to the jinni he had dragged back with him from his trance to his chamber, he performed the customary routine. First he lit the censer packed with frankincense and charcoal, and lightly wafted the fragrance into the corners of the room and over the walls, windows and doorways. Then he changed his clothes, putting on first a white linen robe, then a cloak of gold silk, and round his waist a black sash. He took his almond wood wand and held it high, then placed it reverently on the wooden altar that stood at one end of the room.

He hesitated. He preferred the jinni, which was capricious and mischievous, to be well out of the way. In a severe voice he commanded it to leave his presence, but to wait nearby for his call. There was a slight, chill breeze, and the invisible jinni faded away.

His breast rounded with courage, the Qadi stood before the altar and performed his preliminary rituals, bowing to the south and to the west, to the north and to the east, murmuring incantations and calling on the names of the Guardians.

It was now time to consult the grimoires. Heavy, dusty, and worn with age, the leather-bound volumes with their thumbed vellum pages were heavy or light to hold, depending on the motive of the one who held them. Today as he lifted them they seemed to float through the air. Resting them on the ancient wooden lectern carved with griffins and simorgs' tails, the Qadi leafed through the pages inscribed with diagrams and characters in many scripts, reading aloud to himself but skimming over the passages he did not understand (for in magic, it was dangerous to surmise, or to practise in an unfamiliar tongue) he searched for knowledge of how to control Sanjar Mouseback's quest, and of what spirits he should call to his aid. The Tablet itself, once it fell into his hands, would provide the ultimate in knowledge and power. All of magic engraved on a single stone.

Daylight faded: the Qadi lit his lamp and then a candle, letting a stream of molten wax flow over the edge of the lectern and drip to cluster on a griffin's beak. Without pausing to rest or eat, he read on into the night.

*   *   *

"You are used to carrying heavy loads. I'll give you a choice: camel or donkey?"

The saqui, as prostrate as his bent back would allow, groaned.

"Well, I did warn you."

The saqui had avoided the Qadi's house for a few days, sending a friend there to take water in his place. This morning, however, the friend had not appeared, and the saqui was forced to bring it himself.

"Why don't you stand up?" Bahiga suggested. "It will be a last opportunity for you to stand on two legs."

With a pitiable effort the saqui tried to haul himself to his feet. She watched him half saddened, half amused.

"No use expecting justice from the Qadi," she advised, answering, to his astonishment, his unspoken thoughts. "He's been locked up with his books for the past three days." A thought crossed her mind, but she lost it, and let it go. One of the saqui's, perhaps.

She began to intone the spell that transformed men into beasts, or specifically asses, beginning with the invocation of the Evil Princes in whose department she was entering.

"Oshpuroth, Osmoleus," she called.

At the dreadful sound of these names the saqui froze and involuntarily held his breath. A draught of wind scurried round the room. With her arms raised, Bahiga stood poised.

Actually she was wondering what to do next. Although it was well within her powers to invoke the Evil Princes and to turn the saqui into an ass (though briefly, and more in fascination than in substance, so that though to himself and others he might appear to be a donkey he would remain, in reality, still the poor old water carrier) she had no intention of doing so. To begin with, to execute this dangerous spell she should have undertaken several days of preparation and fasting, and prepared her room with candles and frankincense, and used her almond wood wand. She should have prepared a paper and drawn on it the correct symbols of the charm itself, which the victim should see and touch. The spell could only take effect in the presence of the spirits she was now summoning by name, but she did not expect them to show themselves unless she made herself and her chamber ready to receive them.

All these things and more she would have done to punish the saqui for his disloyalty and to compensate for the irritation of having to find another messenger. She did not, however, wish to invoke the Evil Princes for such a trivial revenge. She did not fear the Princes, but she did not wish to make them feel wanted.

Bahiga, arms raised, apparently lost in the transcendence of her spell, scrabbled in her mind for a face-saving solution. She failed to hear the steps

44

on the stairs. It was her nurse who jumped up and tried to block the door.

Bahiga dropped her arms as she heard the voice of one of her father's servants summoning her loudly, and immediately, to his apartments. With a display of irritation that the saqui failed to interpret as relief she gestured to the old man to make himself scarce.

The Qadi held in his arms an ancient grimoire from which spilled and fluttered pages and papers inscribed with magic charms. His room smelled fustily of candle wax and incense, and he looked dishevelled and tired, still dressed in his white and golden robes.

"Father!" reproached Bahiga. "You look as though you haven't slept for days!"

The Qadi who, while pursuing his research, had stumbled on evidence that proved him right, and Bahiga wrong, in a dispute they were having over the exact Hebrew spelling of the name of one of the four fallen angels, was the first to notice a spiritual presence in the room. And when he asked, "Who is here, daughter?" she (and others) noticed the unsteady voice and the hint of alarm, the voice of one who fears the spirits because he, as well as they, is aware of his own weakness. The voice of one who succumbs to temptation, and fears the tempters.

"Who is here?"

Bahiga looked round and saw them, Oshpuroth and Osmoleus, phantoms very faintly visible in outline, with a hint of black robes and grey faces.

"How did I do that?" she asked herself.

"Go away," she said.

"I am ready to swear my oath of allegiance," said Osmoleus.

"I too," agreed Oshpuroth.

"There seems to have been a mistake," said Bahiga, "no one has summoned you."

"Too bad, we don't often get called up for this one."

"I accept your oath; now return whence you came until I call you again to perform my bidding." Bahiga was careful to use the correct formula to dismiss the Princes, although they were probably only too glad to go. Daylight hurt their eyes.

"I shall await your bidding," echoed Osmoleus.

"Wait!" said Oshpuroth. "Who summoned us? It was not you; I thought it was him!" and the Prince raised a ghostly finger which pointed unequivocally at the Qadi. The black sleeve shimmered back to his side. Bahiga looked sharply at her father, who shrank back involuntarily.

"But it was her voice!" cried Osmoleus.

"No, no, I am quite sure," insisted Oshpuroth. "He is, after all, correctly robed."

"And in a state of fast."

45

"Oh, father! Did you forget to eat again? How could you have been so careless!"

"Yes, it was he who called us, and he to whom we owe our allegiance."

"You know the rules, father! Three days of fasting, and leaving your wand on the altar! I bet you left the candles burning, too."

"But wait! It was she who called our names!"

"It seems to be a kind of," the Qadi drew a painful breath through his palpitating heart, "joint venture." In spite of his fear he managed to smile to himself at the irony of having joined his estranged daughter in this act of summoning two of the most powerful of the Princes.

Bahiga turned her contemptuous gaze from her father to the Princes.

"To which of us do you make your oath?" she asked sternly.

"Why, to you both, Your Highness," replied Osmoleus, and his brother nodded his ghostly head.

"So will you reappear to us as one, or to each of us?"

For a while the Princes communed, though motionless and in silence. Finally Oshpuroth spoke.

"You, together, called us together. That is how we must reappear to you; though each of you may make the preparations to summon us alone."

"But only after we have appeared to you both to honour our present command," added Osmoleus.

"Then go now whence you came, until you hear our joint voices. Go back to the dark places where you live, and may God keep you and the harm you do many leagues apart."

The Princes waited.

The Qadi swallowed. "Look here now, go back to your place."

Without another word they faded away.

The Qadi was embarrassed, sensing that his daughter suspected she had caught him convening with evil spirits. Bahiga glared at him unpityingly. She ignored the plea that came to her mind from his: Be one with me, for you are what I am.

The name in the book, the name of the fallen angel you wished to show me, the name of the-one-I-will-not-mention. There was a miscopying, it is incorrect, she sent back.

Her father turned on his heels, a tired and defeated man.

* * *

The saqui waited until Bahiga's steps had faded away, then he shouldered his water skin and slipped out of her apartment and down the stairs. He hid in the kitchens for a while, judging his moment to make a break for the street gate.

46

On his way down the stairs the saqui came across several scraps of paper that had fallen out of the Qadi's grimoires while he was looking excitedly for Bahiga, but with his mind more directed towards flight, and unable both to negotiate the stairs with the water skin and collect the papers, he let them lie. But once outside in the empty courtyard his curiosity got the better of him, and he reached to pluck a paper that had fluttered out of an upper window and caught on a mulberry tree. The saqui, of course, could not read, but he studied the drawings on the paper, which were of small squares like a checker-board, each containing a character. He tried to make out its purpose, scratching his ears, which itched in an odd way, and which felt uncomfortably long. He screwed up the paper and tried to put it in his pocket, but his pocket had disappeared.

Panic stricken, the saqui cantered off down the street.

* * *

Sanjar Mouseback decided that, for Bahiga's sake, he would look for the holy man she spoke of, but that if the search proved difficult he would abandon it and, sanctioned or not, begin to look for the Emerald Tablet. He had agreed to the quest, and to keep to his agreement was a point of honour.

On the evening of the day after Bahiga's visit he set out to walk the short distance to the University, where he judged such a holy man might be found. Tadros, as a Christian, refused to accompany him to this, the greatest seat of Islamic learning.

As he reached the Bab Mitwalli at the end of his street and turned, still inside the city, towards the University, he noticed that the blind beggar who usually stationed himself next to the gate had moved from his usual position and was now seated just ahead of him. Sanjar, as usual, threw him a coin.

He made fruitless enquiries at the University. Nobody had heard of a man who had lived for five thousand years. Indeed, he was obliged to leave quickly when unpleasant allegations of heresy were raised. The next night he tried several of the mosques, but this time asked more discreetly for a man of God. Almost everyone he spoke to had heard of the Qutb, but no one knew who or where he was.

Not knowing where else to look, and inclining to the opinion that Bahiga had made the whole thing up and was at this moment mocking him from her chamber, he decided to call an end to the search for the Qutb and begin to look for the Tablet. Bahiga had warned him of the consequences, but now, as he walked home, he tried to decide whether the story of the god who still lived among man was a practical joke, and if not whether she would forgive him for failing to find him.

He was suddenly forced to flatten himself against a wall as runners approached and the red and gold sedan, which he had not seen or thought of for days, flashed past. The runners splashed through a puddle and spattered him with filthy waste water. "Who IS that?" he growled at a passing liquorice drink seller.

The man looked at him with surprise. "What's this, brother?" he asked. "You must be a stranger here, if you don't know who that is."

"That's why I'm asking."

"Everyone knows who that is."

"Look, man. I'm filthy from the splashes, and bruised from the crush. Tell me who it is, and I'll make sure that next time the sedan tries to pass the runners act more civilly."

"You'll be lucky."

"Lucky? Is this person so special?"

"I'll say. That is the Qadi's daughter, Bahiga the Jewel, the woman they say no man may win, for she knows the secret of her destiny."

Bahiga, who saw him every time she passed in her sedan; Bahiga, for whom love bloomed in these crowded, plangent streets. Sanjar gazed after her, once again in love with the woman in the gilded sedan chair.

*   *   *

The beggar was in his usual place. Sanjar threw a coin, but it missed his lap and clattered in the street. The beggar gently poked the cobblestones with his scrawny fingers, and Sanjar recovered it and put it in his hand.

"May the blessings of God fall upon you and your family."

"Don't you have a different blessing for once, old man?"

"What blessing do you want, soldier? I cannot offer you miracles. You must always follow your own heart, and your heart will know what is best and what is right. You search for guidance, but you may not know it when you it is offered you."

"But if I cannot find the one who might aid me?"

"Then go alone, and he will find you."

Sanjar gazed in admiration at the beggar, wise in his poverty and blindness.

"How can I be sure?"

"You must have faith. Have faith, and he will find and guide you, and you will know what to do when your quest is over and you hold the Tablet in your hands."

Sanjar, shocked, straightened up and stared at the old man. Was this another fortune teller, one who could read the future or his mind? Yet his words were just. Sanjar reached in his pocket for another coin, thanked the old man, and strode off in the direction of his lodging.

48

As soon as he left a gust of wind whirled down the street. The beggar rose and, unnoticed by the milling crowds intent on their own pursuits and on saving their goods which were blowing about (for dawn was breaking, and they must finish the business of the night) he was caught in the whirlwind, and slowly ascended to the heavens.

At any rate, he was never seen there again.

As the ragged figure floated aloft to meet the clouds, a small drama was enacted in the street below. A poor man seeking work, so weak and exhausted by poverty and hunger that he had no energy to look where he was going, was blown over by the wind and collided with a pomegranate seller trundling his wares in a handcart, and fell headlong. As his nose came to rest on the side of the road he noticed a glimmer of silver, and his eyes focused on the coins scattered by the beggar on his ascent. He picked them up, rejoicing. Shame had prevented his returning home, for he had no money with which to feed his children; he had therefore abandoned his family to the charity of neighbours. Now he could bring them food, and they would welcome him. "Thanks be to God!" he said over and over. On his way home, however, and before he had exchanged any of the money, he happened to see for sale a bolt of fine cloth costing just the sum he had found. It occurred to him that if he purchased it and took it home for his wife to sew into garments they could make a profit on the cloth, and with it buy more cloth, as well as food. All this they did, and he and his family prospered as tailors for several generations, while not forgetting to help their neighbours and endow generous gifts for the poor.

As for the fruit seller, he wasted his time in retrieving his spilled pomegranates, for one, which he happened to eat, was tainted by filth from the street, and only a week later he died of plague; his wife died also. They had, as yet, no offspring, but the son she was destined to bear would have become a fanatical leader of unspeakable cruelty, and the world was better off without him. Which all goes to show that even that which is written may be changed by one on his way to higher things.

*　*　*

"The question is, what did Iskander do with the Tablet when he found it?"

Tadros and Sanjar repeated this question to each other several times a day, sometimes musingly, sometimes intently. Sometimes the words fell like a thunderclap when there was a silence between them.

They reasoned that the Tablet had almost certainly been handed to the High Priests. The capital had soon moved to the new city of Iskandriya, and surely it was there that the priests would have taken it. If so, there might remain a legend, a trace of a memory.

They set out at dawn, as the eastern ridge of hills glowed pink and the shimmering river waited for the day's traffic (for the night rule was ignored here following several accidents). A fresh breeze blew towards them from the northeast as they journeyed down river towards the sea. They would pass rich, green farmland for the first part of the way, then the river would divide into several branches and filter through the banks of silt that formed the rich black land of the Delta. Eventually the silt would form a marshy swamp negotiable only with difficulty, the reedy haunt of hippopotamus, crocodile, pelican and flamingo. To avoid the swamp Sanjar and Tadros followed the banks of the thin, reed-choked branch of the river that led to Iskandriya. Tadros rode a fine bay mule he named, with some irreverence, Hermes. Hermes was strong and willing, and did his best not to lag behind Moonleap.

* * *

On the third day Tadros noticed that Sanjar was travelling wary eyed and tight-lipped. Such a ride was arduous, and at noon they stopped to rest under a clump of date palms. Their garments were moist with perspiration and coated with a layer of dust, and it was pleasant to rest in the shade on the riverbank while the horse and the mule grazed. But Sanjar allowed them less than an hour. "If only there weren't so many people," he grumbled as they mounted and moved on.

Tadros looked about. He could see two women cutting clover for fodder, one at each end of a large field. Some distance away a man led a blindfolded ox round and round a water wheel, which creaked and groaned as it turned. The scene was, to Tadros, quite bare: he could not grasp the concept of 'so many people' when all he had seen for miles were isolated peasants. After the crowds of Fustat and al-Qahira, this was 'no people'.

"People notice us," Sanjar said. He was scanning the landscape keenly. He might have been looking for a landmark, or for a place with no people at all.

"Ride on the grass," he ordered suddenly.

Tadros moved the mule off the dirt track and on to the grass bank, carefully treading behind Sanjar. Before long they came to a wide fig grove where Sanjar halted and looked around. He motioned to Tadros, and they struck off through the fig trees. The road was soon out of sight.

Sanjar found some thick bushes growing before a carpet of rich grass, and there he tethered the animals. "They'll be too occupied here to make a noise," he said quietly. "Now, we are going back to the road, because the nearer we get, the better we can see."

They crept back to the riverside track and waited out of sight, concealed behind a clump of reeds. They heard their trackers before they saw them: a creak of a saddle and then voices, loud and free.

"They are still walking on the grass."

"Aye, if they are still ahead."

"The peasant back there said there was no other road in this direction."

They passed on. "Caliph's men," said Sanjar. He had seen the four faces clearly, and would remember them. Their black surcoats were trimmed with gold, and their long lances gleamed: an uncomfortable weapon to carry on a long journey.

"Why are they following? Are they checking on us?"

"I hope that is all."

"Shall we go on now?"

"No, let the horses eat for a while."

"They might come back."

"They might not." Sanjar unrolled his pouch of bread and dates.

"If they do?"

"They are supposed to be following us. What would they say if they turned round? That they lost us? No, they'll wait for us to catch up. And we are in no hurry." Lying back on the soft turf, Sanjar chewed dates while Tadros slept and Moonleap and Hermes grazed, flicking away the flies with their tails.

*　*　*

They only person who knew that the frightened grey donkey with pleading eyes was really her father was the saqui's seven-year-old daughter, but no one believed her, even though it hung near the family's mud-brick hovel in such a pathetic way that they gave it scraps of food. It even allowed them to ride on its back, but balked when they tried it with a bit, first angrily flailing its hooves and then looking for all the world as if it were going to cry. Being short of money since the breadwinner had failed to come home, the family decided to sell it. "Never mind, father," said the daughter, but that night she opened the door of the shed where they had locked it, and it slipped away into the shadows.

It had to find Bahiga. She would laugh, of course, but it would shame her into removing the spell. Had the saqui's belief in his metamorphosis diminished by one iota the spell would have begun to melt of its own accord, but he did not know this, and it would probably not have helped if he did, because his belief in Bahiga's powers was absolute.

But how could he reach Bahiga? He hardly dared go back to al-Qahira, where stray animals were rounded up. He wandered down to the river. There it was quiet and no one bothered him, and there was plenty to eat.

The Qadi's attempt to follow Sanjar to Iskandriya was thwarted by the Caliph who, having dispatched a small but competent group of soldier-spies, was confident of his ability to control the project in its early stages. In vain the Qadi begged to keep the mercenary in his sight, but his own role in the search was so dispensable that he dared not infringe the borders of diplomacy. He therefore agreed to stay at al-Qahira, while secretly he fumed, he fretted, and his blood pressure rose, both from fear of his master's unpredictability and the nagging dread that Sanjar Mouseback might scoop the prize. At last, watched with thinly veiled contempt by his daughter Bahiga, the Qadi resorted to gazing into his crystal ball, using a small boy he kept at hand as a medium.

Bahiga, closeted shoeless in her room with her nurse, laughed at his impatience.

"Your father is a sick man," scolded the nurse.

"Sick with greed."

The intense heat of summer had abated, giving way to lazy days when the weather was pleasant, yet it was still comfortable to do nothing. Of late, the preoccupied Qadi had forgotten to procure the mysterious delicacies with which he tried to tempt his daughter, and a calm had descended over the two women as though, forgotten, they would be left in peace. It was, they knew, a temporary respite.

Meanwhile the Qadi turned over his judicial duties to a deputy and, unless he was called to the palace, he retired to his apartment to gaze at his crystal ball and study his tomes. His collection of ancient books was great, and priceless. It was rumoured that he possessed papyrus scrolls from the ancient Library of Iskandriya, and many of the older volumes were so dry they crumbled to dust as they were touched. The Qadi was not a stupid man, but the classical education he gained in his youth, and his later study of the law, had been fragmentary. His method of research was greedy rather than scientific, and as he had also no great gift for languages, and since many of his books, especially those of a sacerdotal nature, were in Greek, Coptic, Latin or Hebrew, he lacked the patience for thorough investigation. His wife had taught him how to decipher some of the older scripts, but it had been so long ago and he did not know now whether she had taught him correctly, or had deliberately misled him so he could never read the signs...

He drew his attention back to the Latin volume lying open on the table in front of him. "I am Isis, Queen of every land," he read, "she who was taught by Thoth; and whatever laws I have ordained no one can revoke. I am the daughter of Geb, Lord of the Earth; I am the wife and sister of Lord Osiris and she who mourbed when he was murdered by his brother Set; I am the one who first found fruit for men; I am the mother of Lord Horus; I am she who rises in the constellation of Sirius; the city of Bubastis was built for me. Be joyful, O land of Egypt that nourished me."

The Qadi closed the book and drew his palm over his brow. The image of Isis had conjured the memory of his wife more deeply than ever. Whatever laws Isis ordained no one was able to put aside. He saw his wife in the white robes of a high priestess, wearing the serpent crown, the golden belt of the goddess clasped round her waist. She held above her head a small bowl in which burned a clear white flame, and the scent of heaven filled the air as she chanted. He should not have been allowed to see. She never forgave him because she allowed him to see.

With a deep sigh he turned to rummage through the books, knowing them by their size or cover rather than by title. He was trying to refresh his memory, searching for knowledge of Hermes Trismegistus. He picked up a loosely-bound codex of vellum pages written in Greek. "Hermes," he read, "scribe of the gods and keeper of the sacred records, brother of Isis, lord of astrology, medicine, and the sacred arts, he who spoke the sacred words that brought forth the universe at its creation. Hermes, he whom the ancients called Thoth, the ibis-headed scribe who knew all."

The ibis-headed scribe who knew all. At some time, somewhere, he had written down his knowledge. The Qadi cursed. A hundred times a day he cursed himself for having told the Caliph this story. He wished he had never heard of the Emerald Tablet. He picked up another book.

"*Campaigns of Iskander*," he said aloud. He turned over the first page. Someone must have been with Iskander when he found the Tablet. Somewhere, at some time, it was recorded.

* * *

Sanjar and Tadros caught up with the Caliph's guard in a small town which happened to be holding its weekly market. The guards were sauntering from stall to stall, picking over goods and produce and helping themselves to fruit and sweets. They learnt that no one in the town had seen the pair they were following, but left without realising not only that their quarry was on their heels, but that the ones they followed were shadowing them.

Soon Sanjar and Tadros arrived at a shallow lake where herons patrolled the banks and marsh birds called. Once they disturbed a hippopotamus, which dashed through the mud and hit the water with a heavy splash to join a small herd wallowing in the shallows. Laden camels sauntered down the paths, and they passed a caravan of some four dozen camels on their way from Tunis carrying ornamental metalware and woven blankets, which would be exchanged for pepper and spices in Aleppo or Damascus. They caught up with a pathetic band of Negro slaves stumbling on foot, their ebony skin bearing an ashen glaze of exhaustion and despair. On seeing this, Tadros crossed himself, but Sanjar gazed sternly ahead until they were about to pass the band and, by chance, one of the Arab drivers turned round to thrash a slave who was lagging behind. Sanjar drew Moonflinger and bore down on the torturer, who fell on his knees with loud protestations. But Sanjar knew this relieved only himself, for once his back was turned the beatings would be renewed with added vigour.

"Why can't we fight, and free them?" begged Tadros, fearing that his hero might not be so high minded as he would have liked him to be.

"And do what with them? Take them home? And how should we feed and shelter them on the way? They have crossed the desert once. Where would they find the strength to return?"

"Could they not find freedom on this side of the desert?"

"To the Arabs, they will only be slaves."

Tadros shook his head. There were many things he did not understand, not least the impassivity expressed by Sanjar. But Sanjar was lost in his own thoughts. The Prophet taught that one might keep slaves, but only if one treated them well. The poor souls dragged up from Africa were treated anything but that.

The landscape changed again. The brackish marsh lakes gave way to solid ground, and fields of wheat and barley, olive groves, vineyards and orchards stretched away on either side. On the fourth day they climbed a mound and beheld the sea, and before it the crumbling ruins of the ancient city of Iskandriya. The green land, as though exhausted by its attempt to reach the shore, fell short of the city whose ruins lay in arid wasteland. On a headland out to sea stood the tall, wide tower of the lighthouse, the Pharos, once one of the Seven Wonders of the World. The city to which it had guided fleets and emperors lay decaying at its feet, most of the marble columns of its halls and temples fallen and broken, its walls half-buried under mounds of rubble and sand. Had they stood here half a millennium before they would have seen gleaming white palaces and marble-paved streets lining the shore, but these had long fallen into the waves. Gone too were the long cedar vessels which had once lain in the harbour, and in their place was a ragged fleet of fishing vessels and three or four Cordoban merchant ships.

But Tadros had never before seen the sea, and had imagined no waters greater than the Nile in flood. He saw that Sanjar, who was wondering aloud where to begin his enquiries into the story of Iskander, did not appreciate the depth of his experience, so he confined his excited comments to the mule. The mule pricked his ears, shook his bit, and also contemplated the view. Sanjar woke from his reverie.

"Let's see what kind of a welcome we receive," he said. "I fancy we may be unpopular, not for our own sake, but for what we may bring with us."

"You mean the guards?"

"Indeed. But we shall see."

They rode down with a lingering look at Iskandriya, which glowed in the warm afternoon sun. The street leading through the outskirts of the city was straight and wide but badly pitted, sometimes displaying gaping holes. On either side were mounds of crumbled buildings and rubble, or gardens now wasted and dry. The stream of donkey carts, camels and men on foot thickened as they neared the walls the Arabs had built within the old metropolis a hundred years before. Here a crowd of travellers had gathered, all anxious to enter before nightfall, while the soldiers and customs officers manning the gates were equally eager to keep them out. It seemed travellers could enter providing they had the correct papers, but only if they also offered a bribe and a show of obeisance. There was a great deal of pushing and shouting as they tried to force the attention of the guards, and loud arguments as the zealous customs men relieved them of a sum of money or a portion of their goods in excise. Some, forbidden entry, retreated and clustered along the walls. It was obvious from the appearance of their camps that some of them had been there for days or weeks.

Sanjar's papers included a passport from the Caliph that stated the bearer was on a military intent, specifically that he was instructed to measure the sea walls and assess whether they needed to be reconstructed. The reasoning behind this bogus mission quite escaped Sanjar, who did not see why he needed to measure the walls or even go near the harbour, or why being on a mission for al-Hakim was not protection in itself. He knew better, though, than to question the working of the Caliph's mind. The passport satisfied the guards and he and Tadros found themselves on the other side of the huge double gate, amidst a crowd of Greeks, Persians, Arabs, Jews, Copts, Turks, Venetians, Cordobans and Nubians; it was a city of markets trading in goods from slaves to spices, where fortunes were made and lost.

Behind the walls the ruins sprang to life, and from the rubble rose whitewashed churches, limestone mosques and houses several storeys high, all built with stones from the dismantled Greek and Roman city. West of the harbour stretched a shanty town of low adobe houses, and on its far borders lay the black goat hair tents of a Berber encampment.

Four liveried guardsmen with poised lances posed on horseback on the sea wall. Sanjar and Tadros rode to the beach, where Moonleap trod the waves and dashed her mane in the wind.

* * *

"So they have arrived in Iskandriya?"

The Qadi nodded.

"What else?"

"Only the two of them riding on the beach. Your escort was also there."

The Caliph wished his escort were able to report back at such speed as the Qadi could by looking into his inkblots.

"Your method intrigues me. Bring the small boy tomorrow, and show me how you do it."

"I must say I find it more reliable than other methods." The Qadi suspected that Bahiga had an influence over his crystal ball, which was refusing to work.

They were in an upper room of the palace, where the Caliph often rested in the afternoon. Now, though, he was pacing the floor, his hands clasped behind his back. The Qadi hovered near him, anxious to catch every word.

"Do you know what they will find there?"

The Qadi took a deep breath, and spoke with an effort. "Alas, it is not for us to know the future."

"But some do, geomancers and soothsayers and so on. I've heard of kings wanting to know of an auspicious day to do battle, or of who will betray them. The servants say my sister uses a magician every day. Why don't you do the same for me? Who knows what the Sitt al-Mulk is plotting?"

"Holy men can see things, such as the time of their death. But I am not holy. I should have to use a jinni, and jinn often lie, out of ignorance or mischief. It's a risky business, being a prophet. I prefer to stay out of it."

The Caliph paused. "But you can see things happening miles away, out of sight."

"I have that gift."

"Very intriguing. But when I find the Emerald Tablet, I shall have that gift too."

"When you have the Emerald Tablet you will not need this gift, for you will know everything."

"Every power will be in my hands."

"Quite so."

He began to pace again. "Could I make my Caliphate last for ever?"

"Without a doubt."

"And conquer the Byzantine Empire?"

"The whole world will be yours."

What goes without saying, thought the Qadi, is that unless the Tablet is found soon my head will roll.

"You say you cannot see into the future. But that may apply only to mundane affairs."

"Indeed. For you, I see a brilliant future stretching ahead."

"Even divine."

"Divine, assuredly so."

The Caliph looked at him benignly. "You may go back to your magic. And don't forget, tomorrow, the inkblots."

Unless the Tablet is found, or someone gets rid of this madman, thought the Qadi as he took his leave. Already al-Hakim had forgotten him. He had turned to the window and was staring over the garden, where the lemon trees held their green fruit. But his mind was far away, seated on a jewelled throne in Constantinople.

5 · Rhoorogh

SANJAR GLANCED round at the merchants and officials sitting on divans around the public room of the khan. The air was heavy with scented smoke and rumbled with low chatter and the clatter of ivory pieces on tric-trac boards. "Who recommended this place?" he asked Tadros as they shared a water pipe.

Instinctively Tadros ran a hand over his lips as though to shield his answer from lip readers. "It was the warden of your officers' quarters at al-Qahira. He says he often stays here."

"Well there's something funny about it."

"I thought he was a friend of yours."

"He is. But there's still something funny about it."

"What exactly? It looks like any other inn to me."

"I don't know. If I knew I'd tell you. Something odd, that's all"

"When are we going to start looking?"

"Just as soon as I've finished this pipe."

An hour later they were walking through the ruins of the city that had seen such splendour in the days of the Greeks and Romans, making their way towards a tall column that rose in the distance like a slender tower. Granite columns, limestone blocks, and broken marble statues were spilled over the ground, half buried in dust and sand.

"If Iskander left anything behind, it will be buried under all this."

They looked helplessly at the ruins. Sanjar had never taken much interest in history. As a boy he had learnt the Qur'an, but the tales it told left many gaps in his knowledge. The aeons before the Prophet's triumphal entry into Medina four hundred years earlier belonged to the infidels. Now he gazed at what was once a colonnaded street paved with clear white marble, and he tried to imagine the ghosts which thronged it when it was new and its columns were tall and shining, He had to admit it must have been beautiful. And it seemed to him curious that the Greeks built in stone and marble for the living, while the Pharaohs used these materials only for the dead. They walked some way in silence, away from the sea, marvelling at the extent of the ruins.

"What about the famous Library?" Tadros asked suddenly, as he stopped to pick up a fragment of marble which appeared to represent a delicately-carved cockle shell.

The mysterious shell reminded Sanjar that they still had to look for information, however overawed they were by the past. "Where would you start to look?" he asked.

"In the church, always."

"The church? Al-Hakim, Christian hater, wants us to find something in a church?"

"His mother was a Christian. Her brother, Arsenius, was an Archdeacon."

"You mean the one he put to death? The Caliph hates women and Archdeacons."

"The Caliphs hates Jews, Sunnis, and dogs. What's left?"

"So much hatred."

"I still think the church."

They had come to a dusty, noisy quarter clustered beside a large mound. The hill was littered with stones and fallen statues, and now they could take a clear look at the tower that had led them there. It stood on the summit, a huge, red granite column mounted on a massive square base. At its top, set clearly before the deep blue sky, was a mounted horseman astride a prancing stallion. For how many centuries had the figure ridden over the fallen city, what had it witnessed, what could it tell? The Horseman's Pillar, the people called it. But who was he, and who had put him there? The remains of a town lay at its feet, the broken columns of its temples strewn on the hillside, while three or four whitewashed churches had been built among the ruins. They by-passed the modern quarter, with its dark-skinned, ragged people, its hovels and its pungent smells.

"The church, then. A church," Sanjar said. "Let's try the nearest."

"Right!" Leaping over a fallen pillar Tadros headed for a small church with the shadow of a fresco on the outer wall (the Caliph had once ordered all the saints to be painted over). He did not know quite what to ask for, but he hoped the priest, if he found him, would not let him down.

Slowly Sanjar turned to follow him. And as he turned, he caught a movement somewhere behind his left eye. He froze, and ran his eyes over the ruins around him. Sanjar looked up at the horseman, and his eye fell from its peak to the base of the column. There was the faintest shadow of movement, and, with infinite slowness, something began to creep from behind the solid granite block.

First he saw what appeared to be gnarled tree trunk wearing an enormous, loose fitting boot which stepped gingerly round, hugging the stone base. Then a great, knobby hand appeared, then a wrist, and a thick, sinewy arm inched its way round the block. Finally, a huge, ugly, leonine head emerged, with tangled, grizzled hair and beard, thick, curling lips, a flat nose, and large black eyes with an expression that was at once hostile and saturnine. The eyes fell before long on Sanjar, who stood atop a pile of stones with Moonflinger in his hand. For a moment the creature was quite still, then it let out a great roar and dragged the rest of its body into the open. It paused for a moment as though steadying its focus, then lurched towards Sanjar with a cry of rage. shaking the ground with its great strides. Aloft in its hand it swung a massive, knotted club. Sanjar glanced round for a higher point and found it a leap away on top of a wall overhanging the arch of a doorway. Here he was shoulder-high to the monster and could jump on its neck if need be. He sheathed his sword. Craning its neck upwards, the creature dashed against the wall, which shuddered at its weight. The wall made a great effort to hold itself together; as it fought to remain standing some mortar crumbled, and bricks began to fall. Sanjar sprang just as the giant jumped out of the way of the falling masonry. The wall crashed to the ground, sending clouds of dust billowing into the air.

Astride the wide shoulders, he rode the monster with a grip on its wild hair, but it shook him off as easily as it might have shaken off an insect. Sanjar sprang again, but the creature brushed him off. He knew he could not defeat it by strength, and he drew Moonflinger.

The Holy sword, poised in Sanjar's hand, began to hum. At first it vibrated softly, but then the sound grew steadier, then narrowed until it rang in a tone as pure and as clear as the ring of a glass bell. Sanjar felt his hand lighten on the hilt. He no longer held Moonflinger, Moonflinger held him. The blade turned, catching the sun, and as it flashed the creature, whose gaze until now had not left Sanjar, flinched and drew its arm over its eyes. Moonflinger caught the creature's scent. It twitched. Its note rang a tone higher, and then it sang.

The creature was mesmerised. It half lowered its club, and stood transfixed. It might have been thinking what it should do next, it might have been stunned by Moonflinger's song. The sword sang wordlessly of courage and victory, and as it sang it led its master to its goal.

Moonflinger closed in on the creature until it was just a few feet away, and then it swirled in a broad flourish. The creature's eyes followed the blade, and then Moonflinger abruptly stopped singing. It lunged, but it was merely a feint to throw the target off-balance. The creature raised its club to deflect a second strike, but it lunged too late and missed a third feint by the sword, and a fourth, It jumped back, but it lacked the agility to dance neatly out of Moonflinger's way, so the sword led it quite a dance. It crashed from foot to foot, shattering fallen bricks and sending rocks rolling down the slopes of the rubble. All at once it drew itself up and poised. It heaved its chest, and angrily shook its mane, and then it roared. The roar rolled like thunder over the stones of the fallen town, and shook its remaining walls. Sanjar shook as the ground beneath him trembled, but a single note rang through the haze of the deathly sound as it died away. Moonflinger had resumed its song.

The vast head shook again as it tried to shake the song out of its ears. Moonflinger parried. The creature shielded itself with its club. Still singing, Moonflinger danced round the creature while Sanjar, his movements perfectly co-ordinated with his sword, performed the steps to follow the involuntary thrusts of his arm. Teasing the creature, they drew a circle round it.

But that was not to say Sanjar was not in control. He had simply let the sword take over. As he parried he watched the creature, honing in on its thoughts to anticipate every move. He let Moonflinger make the strikes, but he had not lost command. And as the creature tired, for it seemed bemused by the speed and accuracy of the thrusts rather than exhausted by effort, Sanjar tightened slightly his grip on Moonflinger as if in readiness to super-impose his will on its action. The creature, treading awkwardly on a fallen stone column, stumbled. It put out its club to steady itself. Sanjar took command of Moonflinger, for the sword was still intent on feinting, and struck the hand which clutched the club with the flat of its broad blade. The blow on the knuckles fetched a grimace of pain on the huge face. It dropped the club, and Sanjar threw down Moonflinger. He stooped and quickly picked up a rock and struck the creature on the back of its head.

The creature looked at Sanjar amazed, and its eyes rolled. It lunged at him as if to pluck him from the ground and dash him against the rocks, but Sanjar, with a deft leap and a sideways kick, caught it with a heavy blow of his foot on the side of its neck. It stood for several seconds with glazed eyes, held upright by the unmoving strength of its mighty legs, then slowly crumpled to its knees and sank to the ground. Sanjar looked down on it, sprawled on its pitted, stony bed. Then he sheathed Moonflinger and strode off in the direction of the church.

The simple building waited silently on a stony hillock looking over the ruins. Over its wooden door was a plain iron cross. The sun cast long afternoon shadows from its walls, which had been painted white and stripped of the murals that once adorned them by order of the Caliph. Under the whitewash, though, shadows of the paintings lingered.

Tadros, who had been waiting all this time, ran over and caught Sanjar's arm.

"Where have you been?" he asked anxiously.

"A small thing held me up," Sanjar said. "Your turn now. I'd rather face a thousand monsters than enter that building."

Tadros had grave doubts that, even if he found a priest inside the deserted-looking church, he would listen to what he had to say. He was not even sure what he should ask. But he shrugged his shoulders, and went inside.

Sanjar sat on a rock. As the time passed he became more and more uneasy, and the scowl on his brow grew deeper. This was all a waste of time, he thought. He did not see where this chase was leading. He felt they were asking themselves the wrong questions, and he doubted the wisdom and sanity of the man who had sent them on this wild mission. He thought it might be for the better if he, and perhaps Tadros, took ship from Iskandriya and sailed to Syria or Turkey. He might even go home. It was a long time since he had seen his family. His mission, his sense of duty, began to waver.

And then in his mind he saw Bahiga as clearly as if she had sprung to life before him. He saw her as he had seen her in her room in the father's house in al-Qahira, he saw her red dress, her pearls, and her black eyes. He saw the sheen on her smooth skin.

"Imagine what might happen if this madman got his hands on the Emerald Tablet!"

He heard the words so clearly that he turned, thinking she had crept up beside him and spoken aloud. The sound even rang round his ears. She had spoken the words aloud, but she was not there.

"If you pursue your venture, Sanjar Mouseback, I shall fight you."

Sanjar fought to banish her words from his ears and her image from his mind, but his will to hold it there was stronger than his strength to push it away.

Then he heard the voice of the beggar at the Bab Mitwalli.

"You will know what to do when your quest is over and you hold the Tablet in your hands."

Sanjar snorted with impatience. The sun was hot, and he was thirsty. The heat and thirst, as well as the encounter with the strange creature and the echoing ruins of the dead city, were playing on his mind. Still Tadros stayed inside the church.

At last he could bear his impatience no longer. Defying his own superstitions, he strode over to the church and peered through the half-open door. Inside it was gloomy. The only light filtered through small windows set under the rafters, but though these were uncovered, permitting a slight, thin breeze, the air was still musty with damp and hundreds of years' worth of stale incense. Slowly, as his eyes became accustomed to the gloom, Sanjar took in the alien scene. The vaulted wooden ceiling resembled the upside-down hull of a boat, as if the ark which had saved the human race and all the creatures of the earth from destruction in the flood now sheltered them within its hold. The aisle was lined with columns looted from one of the temples the pagan Romans had built nearby for their gods and then abandoned. The walls were stuccoed, and here they had defied the Caliph's edict, for they teemed with rich murals that shocked him profoundly with their imagery. Haloed saints, some of them women, mingled on the walls with peasants, soldiers and animals. These representations of figures were, to him, obscenely profane, but curiosity prevented his turning his eyes away. On the wall, a mother dandled a child on her knees. Her piercing eyes held his. Elsewhere there were scenes of torture and death, supplication and prayer. At the end of the aisle was a carved wooden screen set with ivory, very much like the work in the mosques of the region. But the columns and doors were hung with crosses and carvings, and the walls inset with stelae showing small round figures and animals entwined with vines and flowers. To reach the aisle the light which issued through the high windows had to slide over a canopy set over the columns. The floors, like the floors of a mosque, were covered in rush mats, and the only furniture was a stone pulpit.

At the far end of the small church Tadros was deep in conversation with a man robed in black. When Sanjar darkened the doorway they waited for him to enter, but as he hesitated Tadros waved him over.

Sanjar had grave doubts about entering, and still paused. But Tadros gestured again, so he took a deep breath and stepped inside.

No devils stepped out from behind the columns to clutch at him, no earthquakes shook, no thunderbolts clapped. There was merely the gentle clop of his soft boots on the stone floor.

Tadros, unmoved by Sanjar's courage and oblivious of his contempt, called: "Come and meet Brother Paphnotius. Brother, this is my friend Sanjar, who is a great warrior and the bravest man you ever saw. He says he will talk to you," he said to Sanjar, "only he doesn't speak much Arabic."

Brother Paphnotius was a heavy, youngish man, with a thick, black beard and sparkling, intelligent eyes. He wore a black habit and a large silver cross hung round his neck, but the strangest part of his attire was his pointed black bonnet, brightly embroidered in cross-stitching and tied under his chin with a ribbon. He returned Sanjar's look with equal interest, having never seen anyone quite like Sanjar before.

"He says nothing was saved from the library," said Tadros. "It was right here, where the Horseman's Pillar is. He says the Jews rioted because of the injustice of the Roman Emperor, and set fire to the temple, and the library was underneath it and a lot of the books burned. And then two hundred years later the Romans destroyed the rest. He is very interesting, this man. He says the Romans who destroyed the temple were monks, and they burned it at the time of the Emperor Constantine because Christianity was now the religion they had to follow at any cost. They weren't interested in the knowledge that was stored in the library, they only wanted to destroy the temple and burn the pagan books, and they were too primitive and too stupid to know what they were doing. Brother Paphnotius says the only books that were saved were Holy Books written in Greek."

Sanjar mused on this ecumenical information, while Tadros and the monk continued to talk. Eventually Tadros repeated what he said.

"The library here was not the Great Library. It was the library of the great Queen Cleopatra, the place where she stored the books which were given to her by Mark Antony. This was the second library of Iskandriya, and she put her books here because the first one was full. The Great Library was in the university, in the city, quite far from here and nearer to where we are lodging. No one knows what happened to that library. People say the university and the temples and palaces fell into the sea, because at low tide you can see marble floors and steps on the shore."

Brother Paphnotius continued, and Tadros translated: "Great Greek men taught in the university. One of them was a pupil of Aristotle, who was the teacher of Iskander (he calls Iskander "Alexander"), and this man inherited all of Aristotle's books and gave them to the library. When they got old, they were copied and copied. Nobody knows where they are now, perhaps people just stole them or borrowed them and never took them back, because at that time there wasn't much law and order in Iskandriya. Perhaps some of them were taken to Rome or Constantinople. He says that was at the end of the Roman Empire, before the Arabs came, when everybody was quarrelling and there was chaos in Egypt. Brother Paphnotius says he knows all this because he has read history books in Greek. He says that when the library was lost so was all the knowledge and wisdom that had been stored in Iskandriya, but he says a lot of the more enlightened monks and scholars took some of the valuable things away and hid them."

"Where were they hidden?"

"He says most of the things were hidden in monasteries in the desert for safe keeping."

"Does he know what kind of things they saved?"

Tadros put the question. "No, he doesn't know," he said.

"Does he know anything about Iskander – Alexander?"

A lengthy conversation followed, in which there was clear disapproval and a great shaking of heads.

"He says that although Iskander was not a Christian, his body was taken by monks and reburied it in a monastery in the desert for – "

"Safe keeping."

"Exactly."

"He seems very well informed, this brother."

Tadros felt a little uncomfortable. He knew they were lucky to have met this man. Most monks – almost all monks, and most priests – were unedu-

64

cated men who spent their entire lives in seclusion, learnt nothing, and cared less.

Tadros spoke a few words. "I told him: 'My friend says you are very clever'," he told Sanjar.

The monk didn't smile. "I am a poor man, from a poor family," he said. "How else could I have a chance to study, unless I entered the church?"

Sanjar said: "Does he know who can help us further?"

They talked in low voices, and then Tadros said: "He thinks you won't find out anything about Iskander here. He says the only thing that happens in this city is buying and selling. Iskandriya isn't a centre of philosophy like it used to be in the old days. He says the wisest monks are living in the monasteries of the valley of Natroun, and there we might find people who can help us."

"So thank him, then, and offer him payment."

Tadros shook his head. "Oh, certainly not," he said. "You can give a coin to the poor box."

Sanjar dropped a silver piece in the wooden box. Christian poor, Muslim poor, they were much the same.

Tadros was pleased with the information and the favourable impression the brother had made on Sanjar. He wanted to leave the questioning there. He knew they had been lucky.

"I'll tell you what," Sanjar said. "There's something I want to do. You take these coins for the poor box, and try the other churches. I'll see you back at the inn."

He turned in the direction of the sea. He had a tourist's impulse to look at the lighthouse, and he might as well justify his supposed mission to inspect the coastline. The lighthouse, which jutted out into the sea at the northern tip of the town, was a fair walk, but the day was not too hot. However the way took him near the inn, and he thought that since he still had some way further to go before he reached the lighthouse he might just as well ride there on Moonleap, for it would ease him, as well as giving her some exercise that day. So he turned the corner and marched along the street, thinking that before he saddled Moonleap he might down a jug of sherbet in the comfort of his room.

His room was on one of three storeys which opened onto the inner courtyard, and was reached by means of wooden staircases and balconies. The courtyard was empty. The only people about were the servants sweeping the rooms, and the silence was broken by the swishing of their brooms.

Sanjar bounded up the steps to his second floor room and walked silently along the wooden balcony, keeping close to the wall to avoid creaking the boards. He did this because he felt, instinctively, that he should. He drew his dagger before he opened the door.

Instantly something was upon him. The man, however, was small, and Sanjar was prepared. Though the man's dagger was drawn, Sanjar shook him off as though he were a monkey. But his skin tensed in expectation of the touch of steel. None came. The man crashed to the floor and lay there moaning. Meanwhile his accomplice had sprung into place. This was a burlier man altogether, big and bald: swinging a club, he bent his knees and moved his body menacingly from side to side.

But while Sanjar's back was still to the open door, the burly man's was to the window on the far wall, so he was unable to see what was happening behind him. Silent figures appeared at the window, and one was soon engaged in clambering through, as stealthily as he could – and this was no mean feat, as the window was small and some way from the ground. Sanjar stared, fascinated, over the shoulder and the bare bald head of the burly man. The window was so small it was impossible to see much of what was going on outside, but there was a small balcony outside the window and it seemed as though the intruders were climbing on to it from an adjoining room. The first was already noiselessly through, the second had his leg over the sill, and the third was ready to climb in after him. For Sanjar, though, the disconcerting thing about these three was that they were soldiers, and all dressed in the black and gold uniform of the Caliph's guard.

Trying to measure the chance he had of drawing his sword and felling the four of them, not to mention a fourth guard who was standing outside, Sanjar was coming to the conclusion that he had best make the club-wielder aware of their presence, then he could take care of one of them, or they him, thus simplifying his task. But before he had quite reached this decision the first of the guards crept up close behind the big bald man, and, with a quick thrust of his sword, ran him through. The man died with a look of intense surprise. Sanjar seized the moment to draw Moonflinger, but the guards put down their weapons, and the first, without a glance at the crumpled figure he had just dispatched, inclined his head in a slight bow. He regarded Sanjar with a condescending interest. Sanjar winced as the second guard stood over the little man, who was still lying on the floor but had suppressed his moans, and polished him off with his sword before there was time to complicate matters by pleas or argument.

The first soldier, the captain, clapped his hands, and continued to clap them until a slave appeared at the door.

"Get rid of these bodies!" He commanded the frightened youth. The youth dragged the small one out by its feet to the top of the wooden steps, but he needed help with the second. The captain closed the door.

They are going to pin a murder charge on me, thought Sanjar.

"So soon in trouble," began the captain.

Sanjar swallowed. "I wonder who they were?" he said.

"I can probably explain that. You may recall that when you were arrested in al-Qahira you had a quarrel with a Captain Guhar, of the city guards. He would have liked to keep your horse.

"Yes indeed, I do remember."

"It was thought he might try to take revenge. We are here to protect you." He bowed. "Captain Murad Battusta. At your service."

"Then where were you two hours ago when I was out at the great pillar, and I was attacked by a sub-human seven feet tall who wanted to eat me?"

The guards glanced at one another.

"We were watching your room."

"Not very well."

"We concede that, but the villains climbed in through the window."

"Too bad."

"What was the monster, then? Was it also recruited by Captain Guhar?"

"Not to our knowledge. A bit subtle, I think. Everyone knows about the monster, which is why people keep away from the ruins. It just doesn't like soldiers."

"Any particular reason?"

"One cut out his tongue."

"That's quite revolting."

"Probably had a good reason. Anyway, we mostly travel in convoys."

"Very wise."

"If we can be of further service?" suggested the captain.

Sanjar showed them the door.

"I'll keep in touch. And, er, thanks."

"Don't mention it."

It was becoming apparent to Sanjar that Iskandriya was far from the quiet seaside town he had imagined it to be. He needed to spend a little time in reflection, but after looking round the room at the chaos and the spilled blood he decided to carry on with his plan of going to the lighthouse. As he left the room to go down to the stables a slave was already waiting outside his door with a mop and bucket. The inn staff must have been used to such disturbances.

A few minutes later he was riding beside the sea wall. Moonleap stepped lightly, glad to be out of the stall in which she had felt confined after the freedom of the ride to Iskandriya. The stabling was fair, but the horses and mules which shared it were way beneath her status, and their conversation bored her.

It was only a short way to the end of the promontory where the lighthouse stood, and here he dismounted, leaving Moonleap to crop the sweet grass. The lighthouse, or what remained of it, for it had fallen badly into disrepair and much of its upper structure had been shaken to the ground by earthquakes, still towered high. Its massive square walls were of smooth grey stone, windowless and without even a door. Next to it was a second stone building, rather like a warehouse. He looked for a way to enter, and, circling the building, found on the far side a wooden ladder running over his head and parallel to the ground. The ladder emerged from an opening twice his height above his head, while its far end disappeared through a window opposite in the adjoining building, which, if it were removed, would render the lighthouse inaccessible. Thus it was almost impenetrable. There had been a legend that when the lighthouse fell, so would the Egyptian Empire. Earthquakes had taken care of that.

Sanjar entered through the doorway of the adjacent building and found his way through its maze of rooms and steps to the ladder. The building was almost empty, but it looked as though its floors had housed storerooms. A ramp ran round the inside rim of the walls, wide enough to take three or four men – or donkeys – side by side. It stopped at the ladder.

The ladder was more of a wide plank, rotten in places. Once it must have been strong enough to hold a donkey, but now he wondered if it would bear his weight. He stepped under the stone arch of the window and edged his way on. And then he heard voices coming from the open doorway opposite, and a head swathed in a grubby turban peered out.

"Who do you think you are?" said a grumpy voice.

"What is this, man?" snapped Sanjar. "Where are the people in charge of the lighthouse?"

"Why do you want to know?"

"It is not I who wants to know, but the Caliph. Come out and stand on your feet!"

The man leapt through the low doorway as though a devil was behind him, which, in a way, it was. He stood to attention and saluted, but his eyes remained lowered and Sanjar guessed all in the lighthouse was not as it should be. He strode across the plank: if he showed caution he would risk losing face.

He stepped past the man and through the doorway. Inside was an intense heat and the roar of a furnace. Three or four thin, worn donkeys, tethered to a wall, turned to look at him. The three men inside the door had hastily jumped to their feet and stood as a makeshift guard of honour, bowing and saluting as he entered. Their expressions were uncertain but hopeful: never before had their work been interrupted by such a high official. If they succeeded in keeping their lives, and their jobs, until the end of his visit, they were not going to lose a chance of going further and advancing them-selves, and once they saw he was not going to beat them (for he seemed to ignore the steaming cups of black tea, the smell of stale pipe smoke and the imprints of long-seated bodies on the soft rush mats near the door) they became bold and began to petition him. He silenced them with a command to show him the workings of the famous lighthouse.

And so Sanjar saw the great fire which had burned day and night for a thousand years. To reach it he passed through several upper floors, climbing a wide ramp which, like the one in the adjacent building, encircled the inner walls of the wide tower. The heat grew more intense as he climbed, until on the fourth floor he reached the huge brick furnace which roared with the sound of a great wind. Before a hole in its side was an enormous stack of wood, a pile of several cubits. In never ending motion two steaming slaves clad in loin cloths swung the logs one after the other into the fire. Sanjar was amazed. He said nothing, but the lighthouse keepers told him the wood was delivered every seven days and carried all the way up the ramps by donkeys. The slaves worked day and night in pairs, and when they were not working they were chained in a lower room so they would not run away. The Pharaoh Iskander had built the lighthouse, they said, and the fire was never allowed to go out.

From the furnace a huge brick chimney rose to the top of the lighthouse, and through the chimney leapt the flames, giving out a burning glow that could be seen from the northern horizon to the ridge of hills in the desert in the south. The fire showed the world of the enduring might of Iskandriya, and it guided ships into the Harbour of Safe Return on the eastern side of the lighthouse, and the Western Harbour on the other side.

Sanjar went to a window and looked out to sea. The air tasted of salt, and the crying gulls called to him of other, far away places. The waves crashed cruelly on the rocks below, as though trying to wash Iskander's lighthouse into the sea as it had washed the ancient royal palaces and temples, as Brother Paphnotius had said. Sanjar thought of the monk and the many things he knew. Perhaps his knowledge might be useful, and he decided to see him again.

He turned back to the scene inside the lighthouse. While the slaves toiled, the four lighthouse keepers stood in expectation. Sanjar pitied their predicament. Their orders were to keep the lighthouse going, and they did it as they did everything else, with the maximum of comfort and the minimum of effort. They did not disguise their laziness, as they did not hide the hardship of the slaves who fuelled the furnace or the donkeys which toiled up the ramps.

"I shall make my report to the Caliph," he said. "In the meantime, remind me how much you are paid?"

They bowed, sure of a rise in wages.

"Three ducats, sir," they said.

"And the slaves and livestock?" Sanjar's mien displayed his anger.

"There is an allowance," stammered one of the men.

"From now on you are to take over the slaves' work for half the day, and if the fire goes out you're done for. You may lock the slaves in the building at night, but they are not to be chained. That's an order. The next time an official comes, he will ask these fellows here to confirm that you've complied with it. Until then, when you aren't stoking the furnace you must spend your time watching them instead of smoking and drinking so much tea. You are lucky to escape dismissal, but I won't let you off next time."

The frightened lighthouse keepers bowed. Afterwards they would feel extremely sorry for themselves. They faced the prospect of gruelling work, but at this minute they were grateful for escaping with their lives. However, by the time they reached the foot of the stairs resentment had begun to set in, and, sensing it, Sanjar said, "Remember, the slaves will give an account of your behaviour, and you are accountable for their well-being."

He was, he believed, understood.

* * *

It was on the way back along the promontory that he encountered the grizzly monster again, standing in the road ahead of them. When she saw him Moonleap did not slow her pace but kept bravely on, chafing the bit slightly as though to convey to her master, "I've seen it, but I'll keep going until you tell me to stop." Sanjar smoothed her neck. The monster faced them on his tree-trunk legs, his club at his side, his head half bowed in an attitude that Sanjar at first took to be threatening. But as they neared it the creature unexpectedly dropped to its knees and covered its head with its arms, slowly doubling over until it lay in the dust. Sanjar hailed it. The creature slowly lifted its huge and ugly head, which made Moonleap groan, and then it grunted vehemently as though it wanted at all costs to make itself understood. Then it prostrated itself again.

Sanjar was perplexed. Clearly this was an attitude of supplication, but what was the purpose? Moonleap was finding the appearance of the creature, and probably its smell, offensive, for she began to prance. The monster cowered even lower.

"Explain yourself!" shouted Sanjar. But the creature made no movement. It occurred to Sanjar that it might not understand Arabic.

"Well, at least let me pass!"

As there was again no response, Sanjar edged Moonleap gingerly round the grovelling wretch. Moonleap kept her distance, planting her feet distastefully. Without a glance back Sanjar headed for the town, and only some time later, hearing the swish of soft shoes drawn by heavy feet over the stones, did he turn to see the mournful giant, club over his shoulder, trudging along behind.

Sanjar was alarmed to hear the sound of pitiful weeping reverberating through the courtyard of the khan. The wailing grew louder as he climbed the stairs to his room, and flinging open the door he found Tadros prostrate on the bed weeping uncontrollably. He shook the boy. Thoughts flashed through his mind. Had something happened to Bahiga?

"What's the matter?" he demanded. "What's happened?"

At the sound of his voice Tadros raised his head and looked at Sanjar as though he were seeing a ghost. He tried to speak, but failed. Wide-eyed, he continued to heave great sobs and reached out to touch Sanjar's sleeve, and then his hand. He wiped his face with his sleeve, and at last he recovered enough to explain his anguish. He had come back to the room to find a servant washing a pool of blood off the floor, and, in a state of shock, asked what it meant. The servant only replied that he didn't know, but a dozen men had burst into the room and two corpses had been carried out. Sure that Sanjar could not have survived an attack by twelve men, Tadros assumed that one of the corpses belonged to his master. Sanjar pointed out that had the boy kept his wits about him he might have asked someone for the truth, or something a bit nearer the truth, or that he could have gone down to the stables and discovered that after the attack he had ridden away on Moonleap.

He was, nevertheless, touched at the boy's devotion, and wondered at the novelty of someone weeping real tears for him. But there was no time for sentiment.

"Did you have any luck in the other churches?" he asked.

"No one knew anything. One priest said some of the old books had survived, but he didn't know where they had gone. They were hidden somewhere."

"I hope your questions were discreet?"

"I said I was employed by a great historian in al-Qahira."

"Well, I hope you'll be forgiven for such an outrageous lie. Now we must leave at once. I'll settle with the landlord, and while I do that you can get the horse and the mule ready."

"Can't do that."

"Why ever not?" asked Sanjar, alarmed at this insubordination. "We must get to Wadi Natroun as soon as we can."

"The horses can't work today. They have to rest. I've given them only light food, and they can't work again until tomorrow."

Sanjar was indignant. "I don't think," he challenged, "that you have any idea at all about the strength of a horse like Moonleap. I've ridden her day and night over the desert for weeks on end, and she never tires. We're leaving."

"Then you'll have to go without me and my mule."

""All right, you *be* so stubborn. You'll regret it when you try to follow me alone." Sanjar thrust his spare clothes, his razor, pipe and tinderbox into his chamois saddlebag and made for the door.

"See you in Wadi Natroun."

"I hope the monks in Wadi Natroun speak Arabic," grumbled Tadros.

Sanjar dropped his bag. But before he could remonstrate there was a sudden low rap at the door. There stood a small boy with tight curly hair who spoke hurriedly in Coptic.

"He says Brother Paphnotius wants to see us tomorrow morning," Tadros said. "He has something more to tell us."

Sanjar dipped in his pocket and tipped the little boy. "Tell Brother Paphnotius we'll come tonight."

"No, not allowed. He has a service. Monks keep different hours. We'll have to go tomorrow. No choice. We'll come tomorrow," Tadros said to the boy.

With a tight mouth, Sanjar sat himself on the bed.

"Scoot," Tadros said, and the child ran off.

"So you win," said Sanjar. "We have to cool our heels until the morning, then. Now, what we can do here in Iskandriya?"

Tadros thought for a moment. "Eat fish?" he asked hopefully.

He enjoyed being by the sea. He thought that when this adventure was over, he might come back. He surprised himself. Until a few days ago he had not thought much about the future. Now here he was dreaming of holidays by the sea.

"If you like."

"Shall I fix it with the kitchen?"

With half a mind on his reverie, he ran down to see the cook. A few moments later he was back, badly shaken. So shaken he could barely speak.

"Oh master, there's a terrible devil," he gasped. "A huge one, sitting downstairs by the stables. The syces have all run away. They say it's a jinni, and I think – " he confided, a big step for a Copt, believing in a Muslim devil – "I think they may be right."

"Is it seven feet tall, and does it have a shaggy beard, and carry a club?"

"Yes," spluttered Tadros. "Yes, that's the one! Oh heaven help us. It's dreadful to see."

"That's only Rhoorogh."

"RHOOROGH?"

"Yes, Rhoorogh. That's what he says his name is, at any rate. Get him some fish, would you?"

"It eats fish?"

"It has to eat something."

"You think I should go to the kitchen and ask them to feed it?"

"Why not? They feed the horses, don't they?"

With a sigh, Tadros left. But a minute later he was back yet again, with the furious landlord thundering at his heels.

"Get that creature out of here!" the landlord was yelling.

Sanjar opened the door.

"What do you mean by bringing such a monster to my house?" the landlord cried.

"I hardly brought it, it simply followed me," Sanjar replied reasonably.

"Then get rid of it!"

"But I feel quite sorry for it, even though I can't quite understand what it says."

"If that's what you feel, you and your friends had better get going. Out. Scarper."

"Oh come now, landlord, what a silly idea. Haven't you seen how big Rhoorogh is? I'll guarantee that I'll pay you in gold for every morsel he eats. But make the food good, if you please – not that one expects much in a place like this – because we need to keep him quiet. No use upsetting him."

The landlord was shocked into silence, but the abacus had begun to tick over in his mind. Finally he gave a sullen nod and left. As he closed the door, Sanjar roared with laughter.

"Oh! That was worth it! That's what greed will do!"

Tadros stared as if he had gone mad.

"Come on Tadros, just look what people will do for money!" He sat on the bed, helpless with laughter.

"I don't think that's very funny, master. What are we doing, harbouring a devil? And just look what we are doing for money, running all over Egypt looking for a magic emerald, which has such power that the Caliph is prepared to pay a thousand fortunes to possess it. And, worse, what is going to happen to us if we don't find it?"

6 · A Monk's Breakfast

"MOVE YOUR HAND round to the light. I can't see anything. That's better, Yes. Hmm. It's a low building, larger than a house. Domed roof. Urgh! Crosses! Christian crosses. And a – wait, someone is coming. Does this place really exist, here in my domain? Get rid of it!"

The Caliph was in a testy mood. It was one of those days when he liked to be reminded of who he was.

"Sire, Your Highness did agree in your Highness's most supreme generosity and tolerance – "

"Tolerance? When have I ever been guilty of tolerance?"

"Well, sire, not tolerance exactly, no, certainly not tolerance, but well, *intelligence*, that some of these monasteries might remain – "

"Why?"

"Why? Why, so that Your Highness might keep an eye on the occupants, sire. Better in the open and in your sight than hidden in the desert making magic, you said, in your infinite wisdom. Anyway it would look bad, since your mother, God rest her soul, was a Christian – displaying a lack of filial loyalty doesn't go down very well, your Lordship said, and what with your uncle being an Archdeacon... better to let people think they have their own way, Your Highness said, and sooner or later they will go too far. Then you can really show them your power."

"Did I say that?"

"You did indeed."

"Well, quite right. So which monastery is this one?"

"Why, I believe it is not one of the famous ones," the Qadi said, catching the vision in the boy's palm. He recognised the place, and he even remembered the name – St Cyril's. He knew it because it had been the scene of a spot of bother some years before.

"Your Highness decided to leave it undisturbed. Perhaps Your Highness remembers sending emissaries to conduct an investigation because there were rumours that the monks had got a bit uppity with their magic, but the officers you sent unfortunately perished under rather mysterious circumstances."

"Ah yes, I do remember. How curious: does our Turkish warrior expect to find the Emerald Tablet *there?* In a *monastery?* Surely the monks are not in possession of it?"

"Assuredly not, Sire, for their knowledge and power is not so unremarkable as to lead one to suspect that the sacred Tablet has fallen into their hands."

"But why should the Turk, a ghazi, visit a den of monks?"

"Indeed, I know not, Sire," replied the Qadi. He raised his hand, as though trying to catch the sound of distant words echoing from the boy's palm. "Now they seem to be arguing. Why can't I hear what they are saying? Keep still, boy!"

The Caliph tried to make something out of the ink pool which was soaking into the boy's palm and making little rivulets along the creases in his skin. The small boy, freshly scrubbed and dressed in white, unaware that his youth and innocence gave him a measure of immunity from the whim of even this unpredictable man, tried to keep his hand from trembling as the mighty Caliph bent over him.

"Well, man! Why can't I hear anything?"

The Qadi quivered. "Alas, Lord, perhaps God in his wisdom does not give us the gift to hear clearly in these circumstances. One would have to be a fly on the wall... "

"Do it!"

"Do what, Sire?"

"Turn yourself into a fly, if that's what it takes!"

* * *

"He *is* one of God's creatures," insisted Tadros. "He's just misunder-stood."

The monk raised his voice to a roar. "It is the devil himself," he bellowed. "Or one of his own. Do you think our Father would allow it to enter our sacred walls? Take it away! Git! Scram!" He made a threatening move. "And take the Arab with you!"

Tadros stood his ground. "My master brings peace, and travels in the name of the Caliph al-Hakim."

The colour drained from the monk's face.

"Al-Hakim?" What does al-Hakim want with us?" he growled.

"My master cannot disclose such information to an underling like you. He seeks an audience with the Abbot."

The monk hesitated.

"Very well. But the monster will have to remain at the gate."

The monk, grumbling to himself, led the way along the desert track which led to the monastery's towering walls. Coming towards them was

75

another black-cowled monk, and when they met the two brothers conferred in low voices. Sanjar coughed loudly.

"Get along, man," he ordered.

The monk glowered insolently and resumed the trudge to the monastery. The other gazed curiously after the warrior on his fine white steed and the Coptic boy on his mule. Then he turned towards the carefully tended gardens where the monks squeezed sufficient life out of the sand to nurture their fruit and vegetable crops, but as he turned he suddenly perceived a creature so huge, so misshapen that he began to scream – though the wind drove his words away from the walls towards the distant hills, where they echoed with only the rocks for ears. "The devil himself has reached the gate!" he cried into the desert, and rather than return to the monastery, which no longer seemed safe, he ran to the hills. He was missed later at prayer, but it as not until Rhoorogh had left the monastery with his master that it occurred to the brethren that the monster had eaten him.

*   *   *

It had taken almost a whole day of hard riding to reach Wadi Natroun. Their group, which now included Rhoorogh and a pack mule, had set off sharply before dawn, and Sanjar was certain they had eluded Captain Battusta, who, he was now sure, had been set on his tail by the Caliph. On the morning of the previous day they had paid their promised visit to Brother Paphnotius. The monk had seemed somewhat agitated. Drawing them into an inner sanctuary, he had checked every corner to make sure his words were not overheard before he spoke.

"There is something I have heard, something that might help you to find Alexander," he said, as Tadros translated. "I have heard it said that when a new royal palace was built in the city of Alexandria – Iskandriya – many years ago, some tombs were disturbed, including the tombs of kings. And the tomb of Alexander. Rather than allow the body to be desecrated or lost, the elders carried his body in secret to Wadi Natroun."

"Yes," said Sanjar. "You told us he might be in Wadi Natroun."

"I think you should look in the monastery of St Cyril," Brother Paphnotius had said.

Now they stood before the high walls of the monastery of St Cyril's. Set in the walls was an ancient wooden gate, which was opened by an old servant. Through the gate lay the low adobe buildings of the monastery, whitewashed and glaring in the intense late afternoon sunlight. Underneath a cluster of cypress trees, which provided the only shade, a pair of piebald dogs slept. There was no other sign of life. Beyond the small oasis stretched the desert, a bare expanse of sand, rocks and tumbleweed reaching to the far horizon.

A monk approached, dressed, like the others, in a simple black robe and an embroidered black hood. The monk led them past the church, its outer walls festooned with epic murals, and into an office where he motioned them to sit on low stools. It was cool inside. The door ushered beams of light into the windowless room which fell on the bizarre and elaborate decorations – half-burnt candles in ornate silver holders, ivory boxes, embroidered cloths, stone reliefs of cherubs entwined with vines and bearing clusters of grapes, a plaster crucifix, a green bronze statue of a mother wearing a horned crown dandling her child on her knee.

"Some of these things must have been here for hundreds of years," Sanjar said. "If this was where they buried Iskander, they could hardly have chosen anywhere more remote. The question is, was he buried in the sand, or are we looking for a vault?"

"A vault, I think," Tadros replied. "Everyone here was buried in vaults. Until the Arabs came and started just popping bodies into the sand, as you do."

"You know, I've been thinking about it, and it doesn't offend me if you call me an Arab."

"Sorry."

"Ashes to ashes and dust to dust is what we Muslims say. All must return whence they came, and lie with only a shroud for a cover in an unmarked grave, no matter if they are rich or poor, male or female, old or young, and even if they are kings. The idea of leaving a body to rot in a tomb quite offends my sensibilities."

"Don't you believe your soul lives alongside your body? If your body is lost in the sand, how does your spirit find it on the days when it returns?"

Sanjar looked at Tadros in bewilderment.

"What days are those?" he enquired.

"On the anniversaries of the death, when the family meets the spirit at the cemetery and they feast together. We *all* do it, Muslim and Christian. Don't you?"

"Certainly not. That's utterly barbaric. You Egyptians have some very strange ideas. It's really primitive, and as far as I'm concerned when you're dead, you're dead, and you stay in the heavens, no matter what your relatives get up to and where they think you are."

"Do you want to leave the world for ever, then? What about those you leave behind?"

"No. No more trips down to earth for me."

"Well none for me either, I suppose, because I don't have any relatives."

Sanjar paused, then he slapped the boy's thigh. "Oh Tadros," he said, "if that's what you need, I'll remember you on the anniversary of your death."

"And bring cakes to the cemetery?"

"If I can."

"Thank you," Tadros said seriously.

At that moment a monk appeared in the doorway. "Kindly follow me," he said. "The brethren are at prayer, but I have been instructed to show you to a cell where you may rest for the night. The Father will see you tomorrow morning." He bowed, and made a sweeping gesture with his arm. "Please."

He led them to a quadrangle of small domed cells, each with a door opening onto the courtyard. Taking out a ring of massive keys from the folds of his gown, he unlocked the door of a cell on one corner. The room had an earthen floor and was simply furnished with a cane cot, a stool, a water jug and a rush mat. An iron cross hung on the wall, and high above it a small, barred window let in the light.

Sanjar looked quickly round. "It's simple, but we thank you for your hospitality," he said.

The monk bowed, then silently turned and left them.

And locked the door.

*   *   *

The water carrier had tired of grazing near the river. The days were warm, the nights cold, the diet boring, and he was running out of ruses to outwit the peasants who tried to catch him. He had also been badly frightened by a real donkey, which had approached him and then, realising there was something of the supernatural about him, had rushed braying headlong into the river. The donkey swam off, but it agitated the saqui, who decided at all costs to find Bahiga and persuade her to remove the spell she had cast on him so cruelly.

Accordingly he set out one morning to return to the city. On the way he met several farmers and travellers who regarded him with interest, but he trotted straight ahead without a glance to left or right as though he knew exactly where he was going, and he was such an unprepossessing donkey, over-long-eared, thin, and covered in mud as he was, that they let him be.

Negotiating the city streets was more difficult, but he fell in behind a flock of sheep going to market and everyone ignored him, except for the sheep drover, who decided to catch him once he was free of the sheep. But as they neared the Qadi's house the saqui slipped aside and settled in the arched doorway, refusing to budge.

The nurse peered down from a latticed window overhead.

"Why, madam, what a sight!" she laughed. "There's a ragged donkey down below, waiting at the door for all the world as though it wants to petition the Qadi. I wonder who he can belong to?"

Bahiga, robed in red velvet, was reclining quietly on a couch. Her attention, however, was diverted to Wadi Natroun. She did not need to scry to know where Sanjar Mouseback was, or to learn he was imprisoned in a monastery known to be a hotbed of religious and political dissidence. She feared for him. She knew he was untutored in any of the magic arts and had only his strength to aid him. She wondered what weapon that would be against the monks, whom even the Caliph had left alone after he found even the most élite of his soldiers ineffective against their wiles. She had heard through palace gossip, relayed by her nurse, how Mouseback's sword, Moonflinger, had even been magicked away by an adept without his recognising any of the obvious signs. She was beginning to prepare herself for an astral mission.

"Oh, poor thing," went on the nurse. "Now they're beating it, the guards, telling it to move on. Poor little thing."

Bahiga, who could not bear unnecessary suffering, at last looked through the window. "Run down and tell them to stable it," she said.

The nurse, eager to quarrel with the guards, clattered in her wooden slippers down the stone steps.

"And feed it well!" Bahiga called after her.

*   *   *

When the monk locked the door, Sanjar's fury knew no bounds.

"So this is their idea of hospitality!" he cried. "To make us prisoner in a sty of a cell! Barbarians! Don't you have any rules in this place? Where I come from, a guest is a guest, even if he's your worst enemy. The moment we find the Emerald Tablet and get out of this mess, I'm going home."

But at once he thought of Bahiga, and felt a momentary confusion.

"Sir, let's make a lot of noise. Monks hate noise. They might come and let us out. If they just open the door, we can fight our way out and escape."

"Bah! You expect me to howl like a chained dog? There are easier ways out of here, and get out we must so we can find out why they took the trouble to lock us in."

"Shall we wait until its dark?" asked Tadros, not doubting that Sanjar would find a way of escape.

"What can we see in the dark? We'll go – " and Sanjar drew Moonflinger " – now!"

Balancing the stool on the bed, and jumping on top of that, Sanjar could easily reach the window. He drew back the arm which held Moonflinger, and struck the window bars. The magic sword slid through them as if they were sticks. He flicked his arm back and the bars fell neatly out, thudding as they hit the sand. Sanjar hoisted Tadros on his shoulders, and the boy eased himself through the window and dropped to the ground. Within moments Sanjar was beside him.

Dusk was falling and a blanket of chill was settling over the desert. From the church came the low chant of monks at prayer, and in the distance a fox barked. There was no one in sight, and the only sign of life was the family of piebald dogs which lay sleeping outside the kitchen door. Among the low buildings of the monastery stood a single, squat dome, of the type which, all over the country and to all religions, housed a tomb.

They ran across the open space to the dome and crept round the wall until they came to the door, which was of heavy wood studded with silver shields. It squeaked mercilessly as they pushed it open. Inside the light was very dim. They could make out an altar strewn with objects of gold, a carved altarpiece, and gilded pillars and icons.

"Welcome," said a voice from the shadows.

A dusky figure put a spill to his lamp, and was suddenly illuminated in all its finery. Flowing white hair and beard spilled from under a cowl embroidered with gold, and golden silk robes fell to its feet. There was a flash of dark eyes in the light of the lamp. Tadros fell to his knees.

"Is this the Pope?" enquired Sanjar innocently.

"No. I am not his Holiness," the splendid figure replied in excellent Arabic. "Although, it must be said, he does us the honour of staying here from time to time. Of course you must know that we, in the Orthodox Church, have our own Pope. I am not referring to that upstart in Rome. No, I am merely the Abbot of St Cyril's. But I see that you are impatient guests. I said I should see you tomorrow. Do you not accept my word?"

"Word or no, do you lock up his Holiness the Pope when he stays here with you? Do you deny him food, comfort, and companionship after a long journey?"

"O sir, here at St Cyril's we are not, I am sorry to say, running a caravanserai. This is not an inn. We shelter visitors, but that all we do: we shelter them from the cold and dangers of the desert, we offer the comfort they crave for their souls, and we pray for them. You hear the chanting, now, of the brothers at prayer? That is what they are doing now, they are praying for our small friend here, and yes, O honoured soldier, even for you. However when you arrived they were already at prayer, praying no doubt for your safe arrival. They had already taken their evening meal. Normally our guests adopt the life of the monastery while they are with us, and eat when the monks do, and pray when they do. You were shown to your room because we thought you might wish to rest rather than join in with several hours of prayer. I apologise for overlooking your hunger. One of the servants will bring food to your room at once."

Sanjar bowed. "You are aware, Father, that I am come from the Caliph?

That I bear his instructions? And that there is a wish he would have you fulfil?"

"Well, it seems we are to discuss the matter now, after all."

"I hardly think you will find the whim or the reason to refuse."

"So how might our poor brotherhood fulfil the wishes of so magnificent a ruler?"

Sanjar chose to ignore the irony in his words, just as he chose not to see the fine robes of the Abbot and the golden ornaments on the altar as incongruous with a 'poor brotherhood'.

"My master, the Caliph al-Hakim," he said in carefully rehearsed words, "as successor to the long line of rulers of the Egyptian kingdoms, the history of which stretches back to the dawn of time, wishes to commemorate the Pharaohs and Ptolemies, Emperors and Caliphs who ruled before him, the Empire Builders who shaped his land. He wishes to bestow on them posthumous honours befitting their celebrity. He is scouring the land for relics, and for legends. He particularly wants to learn more about the ruler he admires most of all, the Pharaoh Iskander."

The Abbot looked bemused. "Young man," he said finally. "If you are looking for relics of Alexander, who has, so the history books tell us, been dead for more than thirteen hundred years, why are you looking in a monastery here in Wadi Natroun?"

"Iskander was buried in Iskandriya, but his tomb was lost," Sanjar said guilelessly. "We have heard his body could have been moved, and that it might be here."

"Are you aware," the Abbot said slowly, stroking his beard, "that in his own time Alexander was revered as something of a god?"

"There is no God but God."

"Oh quite, quite. Nevertheless, you might have learnt that at one time Egyptians believed in an abundance of gods – creative gods, state gods, local gods, personal gods, animal gods and so on – and that praying to one more was neither here nor there, especially if he also happened to be Pharaoh. In fact it was quite convenient to have a Pharaoh who was also a god. It saved having different loyalties, and if you were in with the king it also meant the Nile flooded on time and your family escaped such curses as being stricken with mystery diseases. Alexander in his day was everything to the people: god, king, leader, hero. Legends abound about such men. I have heard he was brought to Iskandriya to be buried, but I am more inclined to believe he was buried in India, since that was where he died. As for his being buried here in Wadi Natroun, well... " he shook his head. "You may look, of course."

"We hardly know what to look for. We expected a sepulchre, or at least a marked grave," Sanjar said, keeping his eyes on the Abbot and trying to keep them away from the gold ornaments.

"Then you can be assured that, if Alexander were buried here, I would know of it, for we have been the guardians of the this part of the desert since Roman times. We have other relics of course, though I fancy they would not interest the Caliph, for they are the bones of saints, not of kings, and our saints have done little to shape the Egyptian kingdoms as they are manifested here on earth."

"Quite so," Sanjar said. "But even if you do not know the whereabouts of Iskander's tomb you must, as a learned man, know much more about him and about the part of his life he spent in Egypt. Can you tell us anything else we may convey to the Caliph? Are there, perhaps, any other relics?"

"I find it rather curious that al-Hakim should all of a sudden take an interest in history. He is not renowned for taking lessons from the past. However, there is very little more I can say to you. Here we follow the laws of God, and have long forgotten the old ways. Alexander is a myth, a memory. I can tell al-Hakim nothing that he cannot find in his own library. No, there is nothing here of Alexander the Great. Even his great city on the coast is falling into ruin.

"You would do well to return to the Caliph and tell him you have found nothing. There is nothing to find." The Abbot paused to let his words sink in. "Now you should return to your cell, as it is quite dark. The servants will be in the courtyard, probably engaged in idle gossip. I will ask them to bring you some food."

The bright light of the Abbot's lamp had dazzled their eyes, and it took a few moments for Sanjar and Tadros to adjust to the darkness outside. A servant, on seeing them, opened the door to their cell, and shortly afterwards a plate of bread and dates arrived.

"Do you believe the Abbot?" Tadros asked.

"I can't see why he would lie to us. What would the monks want with the bones of Alexander? But then, why did they lock us up? The Caliph has sent us on a chase, all right, without giving us the right directions."

That night Sanjar tossed and turned, trying to piece together the puzzle. Brother Paphnotius had heard that the body of Iskander was at St Cyril's. The Abbot was adamant that it wasn't. Was one lying, or both? Did the Abbot know of the Emerald Tablet? And how did the group of ruffians who seemed to be tracking them tie up with the search for the Tablet?

Towards the end of the night he fell into a deep sleep, but dawn brought a rap on the door. A servant entered, bearing a tray of food which smelled delicious and tickled the taste buds. They stretched sleepily. On the tray was a clay jug, some small, heavy loaves of bread, and a plate of fat-streaked meat which was the source of the sensational smell.

"Bacon!" Tadros, now fully awake, cried with joy.

Sanjar spread his prayer mat on the floor and completed the dawn prayer before turning his attention to the tray.

"What is that?" he asked.

Tadros struggled for the word in Arabic and, to his consternation, found it.

"PORK?" roared Sanjar. "These barbarians are giving me pig meat?"

Tadros was shocked. "Perhaps they forgot you're a Muslim," he suggested.

"Forgot? How could they forget? This is an insult!" Wrinkling his nose at the by now abhorrent smell, he tore into one of the loaves and took a swig from the jug. At once, choking, he spat it on the floor.

"WINE? Is this what your holy men are up to? Breakfasting on wine and pig meat? Or is this simply offered as an insult to me?"

"Not an insult," said Tadros, tucking into the bacon. "Monks are men of God, and people like that don't hand out insults."

"Then you might see what else they can offer," Sanjar said, kicking the boy to his feet.

"The Abbot said last night we had to do what they did and eat what they ate," Tadros said, spluttering bacon fat. Reluctantly he left his breakfast and went out to look for a servant. After a short time he came back wearing a resigned expression.

"I think it might have been an insult," he admitted.

"What are the monks eating?"

At that moment a second servant entered, carrying a brass tray piled with plates.

"Fruit, cheese, eggs, beans, tea. Thank you Tadros," Sanjar said. "Another reason why we should seek another audience with our host."

Tadros had eaten all the bacon. "But do you think," he said, "he would deliberately try to anger us? Isn't he afraid of the Caliph?"

"Perhaps, out here, he doesn't need to be afraid. I wonder what he's having for breakfast. And, for that matter, how he slept last night? He said when we arrived that he would see us this morning: I think it's time to keep our appointment."

The Abbot too had passed a restless night, unable to sleep for the thoughts running through his mind. When morning came he had called for a monk known for his excellent herbal remedies and they had prepared a certain potion.

"He'll be thirsty," remarked the Abbot. "I sent him only wine for breakfast. I would think him too devout a Muslim to succumb to that temptation, even if there were nothing else."

The monk had only just left when Sanjar and Tadros knocked on the door of the Abbot's cell. There was a scurrying movement inside, and the Abbot himself opened the door. The room hardly differed from their own, being similarly furnished and only a fraction larger. The extra space was taken up with piles of ancient yellow scrolls and documents, so old, faded and dusty they looked as though they would fall apart once they were handled.

The Abbot's golden robes were gone. He now wore a rough woollen habit, and seemed a more humble and less sinister figure than he had appeared the night before.

"I am outraged," Sanjar told the Abbot.

"You must excuse them," replied the Abbot smoothly. "Uneducated, untravelled, unsophisticated... personally, I don't eat pork either. I abstain from all meat."

Sanjar was nonplussed by the Abbot's disarming words.

"Let us continue our discussion in the chapel," the Abbot said, sweeping them out of the doorway and across the courtyard. "Such a beautiful morning must be accompanied by a good mood, and the chapel is where I find peace and tranquillity."

In the morning sunlight the domed chapel appeared much more ordinary than when they had first seen it. The gold ornaments were still there, but the gilt paint was peeling off the altar and the pillars, the carved altar-piece was faded and cracked with age and the icons, which had seemed so bright and overpowering, were small and insignificant.

"This is my private chapel, where I study and pray. Those periods of quiet withdrawal are so important. Let me offer you our herbal tea, which we brew from the wild plants we find on the hillside. You will never taste better tea."

He poured the golden beverage and handed it to them in small clay cups. "Forgive me if I don't take tea with you," he said. "I am fasting."

The brew smelled sweet and fragrant. "Flavoured with honey," the Abbot said. It tasted like nectar, and coursed through their veins with a gentle warmth, calming, relaxing, satisfying.

"The ignorance of the monks sorrows me," the Abbot went on. "If they could but learn a little tolerance, they might understand that we are all under one God, all descended from Abraham. More beliefs unite us than draw us apart. You Muslims hold our Lord as one of your prophets, you believe in the equality and humility of man, why, we are virtually brothers, you and I."

Peace had settled on Sanjar. He understood the Abbot perfectly.

"Why can we not strive for love and harmony, instead of living in discord? We are all men of God."

The Abbot refilled their cups.

"Alexander! Now, there was a good man. I wish I could help you in your search for his relics. How I would yearn to uncover the past of such a man! A man, though not blessed with the love and knowledge of God, for he lived before the time of Christ who brought that love to all men, a man – a king – who knew how to rule justly and wisely, who knew and lived with great men, who studied the arts and the sciences, who was loved and revered by all his peoples, and yet was feared by his enemies! Alexander!"

Tadros and Sanjar raised their cups. "Alexander!" they echoed.

They also revered the memory of Iskander, and they loved the Abbot, whose words of truth fell with such wisdom.

"When you go on your way," the Abbot continued, "we shall send with you certain charms to protect you from harm. Ah!" he countered as Sanjar attempted to intervene. "Doubtless you think your strength is sufficient protection! But there are forces in the desert that no human power can allay. We shall ensure that you travel safely, according to our ways. And now the sun is high. It is time for you to leave our community. May God be with you!"

"Allah yisallimak," replied Sanjar. He bowed courteously, and, following Tadros' example, stooped to kiss the ring on the old man's outstretched hand. They then took leave of the Abbot, and returned to their cell to collect their few belongings.

*   *   *

"They've picked up the monster and they seem to be heading off."

The Caliph, exhausted by the elation of committing thirty-five petty thieves to the executioner's sword, had suddenly demanded to see the Qadi's inkblots.

"Where are they heading?"

"It's hard to say, the sun being so high. Now I can see a limestone ridge, so that means they are travelling north again, and they are already not far from the sea."

"Well, keep an eye on them! And call in my masseur, and the dancing girls. I need to relax."

The Qadi's chest pounded, as usual. How long could his heart and his wits hold out?

*   *   *

The Abbot smiled happily. "Excellent," he said to himself. "They swallowed my pretty speeches. We are now quite beyond suspicion."

He lit a torch and placed it in a grease-encrusted stand, and pushed aside a silk carpet and levered open the heavy wooden trapdoor it concealed. Then, holding the torch in one hand, he climbed down the narrow spiral staircase to the tomb below. Slotting the torch in a receptacle on the wall, he knelt beside a stone plinth in the centre of the floor on which lay a large gold casket inlaid with silver. Then he stood, and carefully opened the heavy lid.

With a deep sigh of emotion and adoration he gazed at the bound and gilded mummy. From shoulder to toe the casing was painted in turquoise and lapis lazuli blue with glorious winged beasts and figures of the gods. On the head was the wig and beard of office, and, surmounting it, the double crown of Egypt. And on the face, the death mask of Alexander.

The Abbot choked back his tears. "That maniac al-Hakim," he promised, "that mortal who seeks to cover himself in your glory and to wear your crown! He will never have you!"

7 · Holy Orders

As THEY WERE unaware they had been drugged, and that as a result of this they were now compelled to trust everyone they met and believe everything they were told, Sanjar and Tadros did not realise the danger they were in, nor that they should have paid more attention to Rhoorogh, who alone, though not understanding his master's reactions, had retained a sense of reality. Had they been enough aware and had heeded Rhoorogh's warning snarls, instead of misinterpreting them and telling him to be silent, they might have avoided the fiasco that followed when, before long, they encountered a band of city guards.

Captain Guhar, outlaw and former commander of the Bab al-Futuh guard, infuriated by reports that his men had failed to kill Sanjar in Iskandriya and capture his wondrous horse, had ridden north to intercept the foreign mercenary who had brought disgrace upon him. For no sooner had Sanjar left al-Qahira than Guhar had been dismissed from his post for exceeding his line of duty, and his false arrest of Sanjar had been quoted on top of the list of charges laid against him. Guhar still wanted Moonleap, but revenge was sweeter on his mind. It mattered little to him that Sanjar Mouseback was in the employ of the Caliph, for he, Guhar, had nothing to gain by staying within the boundary of the Caliph's law, and nothing to lose by living outside it. Indeed, his only hope of surviving his disgrace lay in joining the band of outlaws with whom he had connived when there was sinister work to be done, and who at other times had given him gold not to notice where and how it was obtained. A few of his guards more fearful of their necks than loyal to him had joined him outside the law, and through his network of spies and informers he had no difficulty in keeping his sights on Sanjar.

It is not an easy task to stalk one's prey in the open desert. Rocks and ridges make secure hiding places, but come into the open, on the brow of a hill or out on to the sandy plain, and one is visible for miles. Guhar could not keep his cover for long. So he chose the moment when the travellers entered a gorge carved out by one after another of the raging flash floods that scour the desert once every few years or so, and, with fierce cries, he and his small band of horsemen swept down on them from above.

Sanjar and Tadros, their senses dulled by the herbalist's brew, were drawn unwillingly into the skirmish. While Moonflinger deflected the blows aimed at him, Sanjar tried to call the attention of their attackers to the necessity of laying down their arms and making peace. To his dismay, Rhoorogh had smashed two of the guards together and dropped them lifeless on the rocks before he was able to make him obey his command to stop fighting, and even then the creature was painfully slow to follow the call to hold his punches. Sanjar, after warding off the guards in their tattered uniforms without striking a single blow, finally came face to face with Guhar, the man he had once regarded as a horse thief.

"Can't we talk about this?" he shouted as the former officer, on his prancing horse, raised his sword to deliver what he judged would be a fatal blow.

Guhar's arm was transfixed.

"Talk about what?" he asked.

"About why you are attacking us. Have we harmed you? Do you see us as a threat?"

Guhar paused for a moment as he wondered where the trap lay. Then he struck, but Moonflinger's parry knocked the sword out of his hands and into the dried stream bed in the gorge below, and the force felled Guhar from his horse. He lay on the ground, half-stunned.

Sanjar dismounted and sheathed Moonflinger. "I'm sorry," he said good-naturedly. He climbed down, retrieved the dropped sword, and handed it to the captain, who was so perplexed by the gesture he forgot his pain.

"Now, let's talk," Sanjar said.

Tadros picked himself up from under his mule's feet where he had fallen, and the two guards who remained put their hands on his shoulders, then released their grip. Rhoorogh made a move for them, but stopped when Tadros raised his arm amicably. Sanjar stood beside Moonleap and looked candidly at Guhar, who pulled himself to his feet and sheathed the sword, and caught the reins of his bay Arab.

"I'm not interested in a deal," Guhar said. "If it's a deal you're after, I couldn't care less. Your submission doesn't cut any ice with me."

"Sorry about your men, Captain. My friend here goes a bit over the top with excitement sometimes. Now, what can I do for you?"

"You are clearly mad, Sanjar Mouseback," said Guhar. "But whatever your game, we can all play it."

"I have no fight with you, Captain. You made a mistake about my mare, as I recall, but then the Qadi sorted it out and returned her to me. It was an honest mistake, and I forgive you."

Guhar thought the man was either insane, or indulging in trickery. He decided to put his motive to the test.

"That's why I'm here, about the mare. While the Qadi was hearing my appeal at his court, the matter was brought to the attention of the Caliph. The Caliph intervened, and the Qadi has now been forced to reconsider his decision. He has ruled that, since the mare was found lost and riderless, and was claimed by both you and me, she belongs to neither of us, but to the Caliph, who according to the law has automatic right to all horses found straying. This is, of course, to prevent them straying into the wrong hands, because as you know in Egypt only appointed men-at-arms are authorised to ride horses. I have accordingly been sent to bring her to the Caliph."

Sanjar was perplexed. It seemed the Caliph had changed his mind: he was well known to be a capricious man, and now he was claiming Moonleap. He faced the news with a heavy heart. He loved Moonleap, and he relied on her strength, her speed and her good heart. She had always been his. He had been there by the side of her mother, Moonlight, at her birth, he had seen her take her first steps and had watched her golden baby coat change to shimmering white. He had watched her grow beautiful and tall. He had taught her to come to him, and to no one but him, and he had trained her to let him ride her; she had known no other master but him. His eyes filled with tears. Involuntarily he laid his arm on her shoulder, and buried his face in her silky mane. She nickered, sensing his distress.

He looked up. "Then I ask one favour, Captain. That we ride back to al-Qahira together, for I want to see she fares well until the Caliph receives her, and I want to offer her to him with my own hands."

"That will not do, Mouseback, for I am commanded to return urgently with the mare, and for you to continue with your own command."

Sanjar was stunned. "Then, Captain, let us pass this night together here, in the shelter of these rocks, and let me take my leave of my mare tomorrow morning, since I am so loath to let her go."

Guhar sensed a ruse, but he was not ready to call the other's bluff. With the death of two of his four companions, whose bodies lay broken on the floor nearby, their numbers were even at best. He would soon know whether Sanjar were truly insane: he could not kill him if he were. It was a common belief that the insane left their minds with God, and even Guhar would not take the life of one of God's chosen children. He agreed to set up camp, but first he had to eliminate the threat of Rhoorogh.

"This is indeed a good place to camp," he said. "But we have barely enough water for ourselves, let alone for our horses."

"This morning the kind monks filled our waterskin when we left the monastery," Sanjar replied. "We have more than enough."

"But now you have five more horses to water, and three more men. I suggest we water the horses, and you send your friend here back to ask the monks to refill your waterskin. Without that, we have little chance of surviving tomorrow."

Sanjar, in the guileless and suggestible mood that he was, easily agreed. Opening his full waterskin he poured the slightly brackish water from the monastery's well into the wooden bowls they carried to feed Moonleap and the mules and then refilled them for Guhar. When the waterskin was emptied to the very last drop Sanjar handed it to Rhoorogh.

"Perhaps he should take your skin too," he suggested to Guhar.

"No. We shall need it to refill our canteens, for it could be some time before your friend returns. He had best be away."

Rhoorogh made an attempt to argue, but Sanjar and Tadros shouted him down. It did not occur to them, as it occurred to him, that the monks might decline to listen to him and refuse to refill the skin.

That night Sanjar and Tadros slept like babes. Tadros woke first, but dared not rouse his master. For a time he sat by his side, pondering effective action.

Sanjar opened his eyes to the azure sky of early morning.

"They have taken the horse, the mules, the food – everything," Tadros said.

Sanjar cursed, and hit the ground with his fist. He remembered clearly the events of the day before: he had faced one who hated him, and had allowed him to go free. He had lost his reason, he had, again, lost his pride, and he had lost Moonleap.

"We are alive," Tadros said.

"Barely. We have nothing."

"Rhoorogh should be here soon with water."

Sanjar snorted angrily. "The monks won't give Rhoorogh water," he said, "even if he finds his way back to the monastery. They were afraid of him. They'll throw rocks at him and chase him away. Something came over me, I don't know what. I'm ashamed."

"Perhaps we got religion from the monks."

"Religion? No, cowardice has nothing to do with religion. Fighting for God, fighting for good, fighting for family and nation, that's what fighting is about. No, I got a case of cowardice." Sanjar shook his head. "It wasn't that I was afraid to fight, though. I just *couldn't*. I didn't wish the captain any harm. I didn't see him for what he was. What is happening to me, if my wits are deserting me? If I lose the ability to see truth and reason?"

Tadros, too, had failed to see the symptoms of danger, and had taken Guhar on trust, although any sane person might have seen he was lying.

"But you see, now, where we failed, where we did not see the danger," he said. He was frightened now, and sat limply, staring at the hard ground.

"Indeed I do, all too well," Sanjar said, sinking his head into his hands.

"Then this cloud, this feeling, passed. It – what do you call it? When you do something that isn't normal?"

90

"An aberration?"

"Aberration? It was an aberration. You are yourself again. I am myself again too. It's odd, isn't it, that it happened to both of us at the same time?"

Sanjar, though, was recalling the previous morning, drinking tea with the Abbot in his chapel.

Only abbots do not normally entertain guests to tea in a chapel.

And the Abbot did not drink any of the tea.

"The Abbot drugged us," he said quietly.

As the force of his loss and its cause sank in on him, his sharpness of mind returned.

"We must find Rhoorogh, he is our strength," he said. "And then we must recover Moonleap. At least we have one comfort. The thieves forgot to take my sword."

*   *   *

The further Rhoorogh walked, the more he thought about the reception he would get from the monks, and the more he thought about it, the more he feared them. They had treated him none too kindly, and fed him none too well, and he expected to fare even worse if he returned. As he trudged with ever slower and more reluctant steps, he finally he saw a sign that offered an alternative: a sprinkling of goat droppings. These were not too fresh, but they showed people had passed by, and that meant there was life not far away. Going back to the monastery was useless, and he would do better to find water from another source.

The stones at his feet harboured brushwood and small, ground-hugging flowers. Cakes of dried mud showed where rain fell in the wet season, though now there was not a drop to be seen.

"The desert is never as empty as it seems," he said to himself. "Where there is brushwood, there are often goats. And where there are goats, there are people."

Yet the desert was empty, and mercilessly so. Rhoorogh followed the path mapped out by the string of brushwood and the caked sand pools, driven on by thirst and the baking sun, tracking the nomads who had followed this path with their goats, and who would give him water and end his misery.

He did not know how long he searched: night fell, the sun rose, and darkness fell again, or did it fall a third time? The dried stream bed now ran downhill and entered a deep gorge. The yellow sandstone cliffs, the rock so soft that it crumbled at his touch, shielded him from the sun. He stumbled on, and at last, ahead, he saw the people he had been searching. They lay on the sand as though sleeping, waiting for him, but when they awoke and saw him they would offer him water.

He half fell in relief, but a sudden spurt of energy drove him on. When he drew near, though, he was struck with a slow, painful recognition.

They were the bodies of Sanjar and Tadros.

* * *

He was choking. As he tried to catch his breath he realised he was lying face down in the sand and his head shawl was sodden. The water trickled over his face, dribbling the gritty sand through his half-open lips.

"He's coming round," someone said from above the waterfall.

"God be praised."

Strong hands turned him over, and he looked up into several pairs of eyes expressing kindness and concern. They seemed familiar, so he thought he might be dead, and these were friends he had known welcoming him to Paradise.

"We thought you were dead," someone said.

Sanjar drew breath and tried to make his parched tongue work.

"Don't try to talk. Give him a small sip, just a little at a time."

"Who... ?"

"Don't you remember the Ghawarzee?"

Sanjar swallowed the mouthful of water and let his head sink back into the sand.

"My companions... ?" he murmured.

"They are alive."

"You found us."

"Yes, we found you. You are all alive."

"All of us?"

"I'm here," Tadros said. "And Rhoorogh is here, and best of all... Sit up."

Sanjar eased himself on to his elbows, and gazed in wonder.

She munched happily, her nose in a food bowl, blowing the chaff away through her nostrils and swishing her shimmering silver tail.

"Moonleap!" he said.

She looked up at him and whinnied.

"They're very pleased with themselves," Tadros whispered. "They've been looking for you everywhere."

"They should have left me to die, such shame has fallen on me."

"Well, they didn't, so listen to them, they're dying to tell you how they did it."

Later, round the campfire, the Ghawarzee told their story.

Guhar had met up with the tribe on the previous day, a few hours after robbing Sanjar. The Ghawarzee were wary of the captain and his two ruffians. Although they claimed to seek amusement, the three were well armed

92

and were certainly up to thievery. The situation was not new to the tribe. While not blessed with brawn, they said, they had known plenty of chances to practise their guile.

They disarmed the men. They did this figuratively at first, seducing them with enticing words. They promised an evening of debauchery and delight, free from convention and restraint, with wine, and women, and laughter and song, and the dancing of their beautiful transvestites. However these dancers, who, like all beautiful creatures, were drawn to others whose beauty equalled their own, could not take their eyes away from the ethereal Moonleap, who appeared to them a vision of loveliness. They stroked and caressed her, and combed her mane, and whispered sweet nothings in her ears, until the men grew quite jealous and, to lure them away, promised to tell them how they had come by her. They promised an amusing story, and with great merriment related how they had encountered a warrior driven insane by the desert, and how he had not put up a fight but had let them walk away with his horse, surrendering his prize in response to a few words of trickery.

As they listened to the men's description, the Ghawarzee recognised Sanjar.

Much later, as the ruffians lay drunk and sated, the dancers with deft movements stuffed rags into their mouths and bound them hand and foot. Then they struck camp, folding tents and loading camels. As the sun rose they woke their wives and children and, leaving the ruffians but dragging Guhar behind them, saying they would spare his life if he showed them the way, they set off to find Sanjar.

"We owed you our lives," they said simply.

The delight of the Ghawarzee at being able to repay their debt helped soothe Sanjar's wounded pride. He and his companions were alive and restored to health, his mare was returned to him, and so were the mules and all their goods. Yet the irony did not escape him that it was the second time he had encountered the tribe, and on the first occasion too they had crossed paths after he had been tricked by masters in magic.

He sat cross-legged before the crackling fire, surrounded by the banter and laughter of his friends, mulling over these thoughts. Guhar sat bound in the shadows some way from the group, and it was decided they would settle his fate the next day. Before long he felt that someone was watching him. Looking around, he noticed a small figure sitting alone, some way from the fire. The woman was swathed in an indigo gown, and bronzed by her travels in the sun. Behind her the children of the tribe played, and behind them their veiled mothers clustered round their own fire. The lone woman was neither young nor old, plain nor beautiful. Her eyes were on his.

Sanjar asked who she was.

"She is Aisha, a geomancer," they told him. "She travels with us, and throws her bones when she is called upon."

"Why does she stare at me?"

"Perhaps she sees your future."

"Hope it doesn't include any more magicians," someone laughed.

"Alas," Aisha said. "There is much more magic."

"You'd best stay with us, then," the joker laughed. "You'd be safer if you stayed with us."

Sanjar remembered the geomancer in al-Qahira who had told him he would find a horse through a dark-skinned boy, and how Tadros had led him back to Moonleap. "Let her tell my future," he said.

He shifted his position, and the woman knelt before him in the sand. But she did not throw her bones. Instead she bowed her head, and then looked up.

"You plan to go far," she said. "I may not need to remind you that your mission is perilous, and you have many enemies. But you have allies too, very powerful allies. While your enemies will try to use you for ill, your friends will try to use you for good. Beware that your friends do not become your enemies, and your enemies your friends."

Her listeners waited for her to say more, but she had sunk back on her heels as though exhausted, and was looking down at her hands, spread palm down on her lap.

Sanjar's mind suddenly filled with a vision of Bahiga. He caught his breath as her saw her face, smelled her perfume, and heard her say: "You see, I am still with you."

He looked sharply round, sure that everyone else had heard her words.

"Yes, I know it," he said. But one or two of his onlookers looked puzzled, as though he had spoken out of place. Sanjar was confused, but Aisha said: "They could not hear what she said. Only you heard it."

"But such simple words."

"The truth is always simple."

"What does she mean?"

"She means: 'Look, the tribe found you.' "

"Is there anything else?"

Aisha shook her head.

One of the dancers went quickly to her side. "She is very tired, this exhausts her. Come, Aisha, let me help you."

"Can she tell me anything else?" Sanjar longed for more contact with Bahiga.

"Perhaps later, but now she is very tired." Suddenly the dancer shed his veneer of frailty, and, helping the woman to her feet, scooped her in his arms. The sight of the tall dancer dressed in red and yellow silk cradling the blue-robed woman was as sweet as it was odd. He carried her over to the side of the fire where the women sat and laid her down on a rush mat, then stayed beside her for a while, exchanging pleasantries with the others.

Sanjar still held Bahiga in his mind. As the vision of her slowly faded, she rested in his heart. There he held her close, and her spirit comforted him and gave him a great surge of strength. He felt charged with the desire to succeed in his mission, but to show her he was doing it only for her, and to do her bidding.

And he saw then that if he found the Emerald Tablet, she would show him what to do.

* * *

In the narrow street just outside the walls of the Royal enclosure, in the tall palace where the Qadi lived with his recalcitrant daughter, the light in an upper window could usually be seen burning well into the night. At a desk in the small room the Qadi pored over his grimoires. Search as he might, he could not discover the truth he felt must be locked in the secret pages. Even though he looked into the distances of space and time, and sent the jinni on irregular errands, the secret of the Tablet and its knowledge eluded him. He could find no reference to it, either of what it was, or what it meant, or where it was to be found. The Emerald Tablet might never have existed, it might have been one of the thousands of myths evoked by the name of Iskander.

The Qadi fasted, he purified himself, and called on the lesser Princes. But with each fruitless consultation, each failed effort, he exposed himself as a mere incompetent magician, unworthy of his title.

Yet always he felt that Bahiga was closer to the secret than he. At last, forswearing his pride, he sent for her.

After waiting for two days, and knowing he was a laughing stock in his household, he went to her rooms. Bahiga disarmed him by at once apologising for her lapse in filial duty, and offering him sweetmeats baked by her nurse's own hand. The sad and diminished Qadi did not find access to her mind. Deceived by her generosity, he proclaimed his intent, the conclusion to which he was inevitably drawn.

And which, of course, she already knew.

"Let us share our knowledge, Daughter," he pleaded, sitting down boldly on a couch beside her. "For you know, as well as I, that one will only follow the other, should one of us discover where the Tablet lies. So let us work together. After all, it may not exist, and the sooner we know that the better, for we shall need to save our skins before the Caliph learns of it."

"Oh no, Father. You will need to save *your* skin. I am nothing to him, nor he to me."

"There you are wrong, Daughter. For why is it you, though well known to be a sorceress, are let be? Because I'm protecting you, that's why. I come between you and al-Hakim! If I am lost, so are you." He gave her a sideways glance, looking for a sign that she acknowledged this, but her expression did not change..

"I can take care of myself."

"You think so. But what use are your skills against the brawn of the guards? You need my protection, Bahiga. You flout the law! You go about in your sedan chair, you dress as a man... It may seem unjust that women are not allowed out of their homes, but it is *the law*. My position, I need not remind you, is to administer the law. Therefore I should not be seen to disobey it, and nor should my daughter."

Bahiga said nothing. It was true that she did flout the law and that her powers were widely known, and she knew that, were it not for her father, she would have been silenced long ago. Yet the power of the Tablet was so great that it transcended the safety of both her father and herself.

"Father, for the Caliph to gain possession of the Tablet would be a catastrophe. You know that. Why are you aiding him?"

"Of course it would be a catastrophe. But I have no intention of letting him get it. Before it reaches him, the Turk has to find it, and he reports to me. And if he chooses to double cross me he has to contend with my powers. He cannot touch me for strength. I can muster a whole army. And that is only the physical side. My other powers are even more of a danger."

Bahiga pretended to be shocked. "Do you mean to keep the Tablet yourself?" she asked.

"Oh, no, no, no... to put it somewhere safe, away from harm."

"Let it be, then. Leave it where it is now, so safe and hidden that even we cannot find it."

"But if we could only find it, we could prevent it once and for all from falling into al-Hakim's hands."

"I cannot help you," Bahiga said. "Since you will not let the Tablet be, the race to find it is as much between you and me as between ourselves and the Caliph. You serve the Caliph, so be it. I serve the Qutb. The Tablet is his, as we know: before him it belonged to the prophets, and before them to Hermes, and before him to Thoth. It must never fall into profane hands."

"I could withdraw my protection."

"Oh go ahead, threaten me. Have me put to death, if you like. I will not misuse my gifts, I will not betray my heritage. I don't bear you any ill will, Father, and I hope the Caliph will not harm you. But now you have a chance to reject evil, so take it! Take it now! If you will join me, on my terms, we can seal the story of the Tablet!"

The Qadi stood, and without another word he returned, empty-hearted, to his apartments. To punish Bahiga, he sent her nurse away to her village. This was a token rather than a test of wills: he dared not harm the nurse; Bahiga dared not resist the order.

* * *

Captain Murad Battusta had not waited idly by while the Abbot, Captain Guhar and the desert tried to defeat Sanjar. His brief was not to lose sight of Sanjar, and to make sure the warrior kept his mind on his mission. He did not know the precise nature of this mission, only that the goal was a marvellous treasure, and at stake – for he was under the Caliph's command – was his life.

When Sanjar headed south from Iskandriya for Wadi Natroun, the captain allowed him half a day's start. Had he known his subject better he would have realised that was too long.

He came to the monastery by chance, having long before lost Sanjar's trail in the dust. A servant answered his knock at their gates, but denied having had any visitors for weeks: Sanjar and his friends had not been there, they said. The gates closed.

As Captain Battusta turned to remount his horse, his cloak snagged on a thorn bush. He disentangled the fabric carefully so as not to tear it, and as he did so he noticed, caught in the thorns, several long, silver hairs. He touched them: thick and strong, yet soft as silk. And still gleaming white: they had been there for only hours, or less. There was only one tail from which these silver hairs could have come: Sanjar's mare.

Again he hammered on the gate, He spoke a few words to the servant who answered, and shortly a monk appeared and ushered them inside.

* * *

A day later Sanjar and his two followers were back in Iskandriya. They were, however, without Captain Guhar, who on their last night in the desert had slipped his bonds and disappeared. The dancing troupe bade them farewell, and moved along the coast to entertain the Berber tribesmen who lived in the desert there. Many of them had friends among the coastal tribes, and they preferred to spend the summer months there among their own kind rather than wander the hot desert further south,

Sanjar felt the cool sea breeze as he rode west of the town to see Brother Paphnotius. He was alone. Rhoorogh refused to go back to his old haunt, and Tadros had stayed with him in case there was any more trouble at the inn. They had expected to find Captain Battusta there, and he at least might have afforded them some protection, but when there was no sign of him or his officers they assumed he had moved on or returned to al-Qahira.

It would be difficult to communicate with Brother Paphnotius, but Sanjar would try to persuade him to say more about Iskander, and perhaps, if Tadros were not there, the monk would forget his niceties and remember a little Arabic. Sanjar had no intention of intimidating the holy man, but he hoped a generous donation to the poor box might yield results.

Soon they reached the spot where Moonleap had made her first, brave encounter with Rhoorogh. She tensed slightly, as though the memory bothered her, although she was, of course, by now quite used to him and even his smell, overpowering as it was, no longer bothered her. Here they turned away from the shore and followed the well-trodden road towards the group of churches and the ruins of the ancient town. In the distance towered the Horseman's Pillar, and Sanjar laughed to himself as he recalled his battle with poor Rhoorogh, and at the greater fear he felt when he was first brought face to face with Brother Paphnotius.

He left Moonleap to look for grass outside the church: there was none, but it would amuse her to look. In the doorway he removed his shoes as custom demanded, and stepped inside the dimly lit church, making no sound as he trod the cool stone floor.

The church, though, was empty. He called, but no one responded. Not finding the brother there, Sanjar went behind the church where he found two or three small cells.

Brother Paphnotius's cell was sparsely furnished, but it was so small that what little it contained filled every available space. Half of it was taken up by a cane bed covered by a rough woollen blanket. Beside it was a small table piled high with papyrus and vellum scrolls. Brother Paphnotius sat on a low chair. But he was not working on the scrolls. He was slumped over the table, his split and bloodied head, still wearing its cap, crushing the scrolls. The blood soaking into the papers was beginning to turn brown, and the pool of blood on the floor was already dry.

Sanjar was aware of a slight sound, a sudden whiff of cool air from the doorway. He turned.

A small boy was standing there, the boy who had summoned him to the monk's cell a few days before. He was crying, and he was not alone.

Behind him was a bevy of priests, monks, servants and neighbours. And then the desert silence was broken by a sound – the sound of keening women, whose cry hung eerily in the still air.

*   *   *

"The boy found him just before you got there," Tadros explained. "He was bringing him his lunch, and as soon as he found him he ran off to get help."

Sanjar's apprehension at the Christians' coming upon him with the monk's body had been short-lived. Rather, his obvious distress at finding the monk dead – for his instant reaction was that Brother Paphnotius was probably killed because he, Sanjar, had asked too many awkward questions – had so won over the priests that they wanted to learn what he knew, and accordingly they dispatched the boy, partly to distract him from his grief, but mostly because they needed a translator, to get Tadros. Rhoorogh overcame his reluctance and accompanied Tadros, and when they saw him the priests, who had known him by his real name, Giorgios, and had fed him for years, were impressed by the change in him.

While the keening women washed the body in another room, the priests helped them peruse the scrolls in the monk's cell, but they found nothing that might help them learn of the whereabouts of Iskander, or any reference to the Emerald Tablet. The priests said the scrolls were all written fairly recently. They also said that they themselves paid very little attention to matters not related to their church or the contemporary world. Brother Paphnotius, now, had been a bit of a historian. In the old days his interest would have been heretic, but now the bishop humoured such scholarship: history taught about the real Egyptians. If ancient and long-buried beliefs were unearthed in the process of rediscovering their heritage, their bishop, who was unusually enlightened even in these enlightened days, reasoned that it posed no threat to the church. And privately they were both surprised and delighted that, the more they learnt about their forebears, they more they learnt that so little had changed over the centuries. The Copts might have found the one true God through the intervention of Jesus Christ – and of his mother, Mary – but for all the way their means of worship had changed, they might just as well have been worshipping the holy family of Osiris, Isis and the child Horus. Did they not now and then come across little statuettes of Isis dandling the infant Horus on her knee? The only difference was that the services were open to everybody, and not just to the priests and the Pharaoh. And as for the prayers, did they still not make charms with their seven beads, the seven beads of Isis?

Sanjar and Tadros learnt little more. They warned the priests, however, of their suspicion that the murder of Brother Paphnotius might be linked to their questioning about Iskander, and they told them what had befallen them at St Cyril's. At this, however, the priests showed much surprise. True, not much was known about St Cyril's, since it was remote and kept itself to itself: there was no public festival there on the feast of St Cyril, and visitors were discouraged. Yet the Abbot was said to be a holy and scholarly man. Nevertheless, they promised to mention their discussion with Sanjar to no one. As they parted, the priests said they wished they could have more contact with such as he, for they wanted the country to be at peace and united in spirit.

"Then Brother Paphnotius will not have died in vain," they said.

They returned to the inn deep in thought. And it was there, seated beneath the lemon trees in the courtyard, that Sanjar remembered the library which had once stood near the Horseman's Pillar.

"Brother Paphnotius said the monks ransacked this library and burned what was left of the books, but he also said most of them were lost, or borrowed, or stolen. Where did they end up? With people who could read, of course. And then they were lent and used by other people who could read, and so on," he told Tadros.

Tadros spotted a fragment of a leather strap lying on the ground, and picked it up.

"Look at this," he said thoughtfully, turning it in his fingers. "If I turn it in my hands, it becomes hot, if I spill water on it, its gets wet, if I drop it, it gets dirty, if I pull it, it tears. Vellum and papyrus are less strong than this leather. After six hundred years, not much will be left of the library, wherever it went."

"You're a smart boy, Tadros," Sanjar said. "But suppose those books were in the hands of people who did look after them, who did keep them safe? Suppose the people who kept them knew what they had? And suppose they were even taken away and put somewhere safe before the mob of monks came with their torches to burn them? Where would they be now?"

"But monks wouldn't hide them from other monks. They weren't Christian books, they were old pagan books full of Greek and Roman fables and pagan history and dirty poems."

"See! Even you know that, Tadros!" Sanjar had never pretended to be much of a scholar, but he was a pioneer, and now he was on a significant trail. "You see, you know that! Now, how did you learn?"

"Doctor Boutros taught me. He taught me everything I know."

"Why did he teach you?"

"Because he wanted to train me to help treat his patients one day."

"And why did he teach you to read and write? Why did he tell you about old books? Why didn't he just show you how to tie bandages and fix broken legs and mix potions and so on?

Tadros began to see what Sanjar was getting at.

"Well, he taught me because Greek and Roman doctors like Hippocrates and Galen had already written down most of what we know, and if doctors can read they can refer to them."

"Right! Now Doctor Boutros was a Copt, was he not? Yet he would have been quite happy to study old Greek texts to learn how to become a doctor, right? So. These books always had a value! Why, people learnt Greek so they could read biblical books, but that meant they knew Greek, and they could read anything ever written in Greek. And the same with Latin. So! Are you going to tell me every single person who was around when the library was ransacked or robbed or whatever-happened-to-it was either an uneducated soldier or an uneducated peasant or an uneducated monk? No! There were doctors then too, and scholars, and teachers, and priests with a bit of learning. And would they let a mob burn away their pleasures? No! They must have seen what was coming! They must have bundled up hundreds of scrolls and hidden them! And where? Where better than a monastery? The mob of monks isn't going to look under its own floorboards for banned books!"

Tadros was silent for a while. Finally he said, in a resigned way: "I suppose we are going back to St Cyril's?"

8 · Aristotle's Tale

THEY RODE BY NIGHT back to Wadi Natroun, with Rhoorogh, who now knew the way well, navigating by the stars. The desert was still, cool and soundless, and empty except for the odd scurrying fox. As day broke over the desert ridge, casting a soft pink glow over the stretches of sand ahead and the hills on either side, the travellers pitched camp in the shelter of the rocks, well hidden from the open road, and rested until nightfall.

Sanjar found it hard to sleep. His mind was plagued by thoughts of their mission. He wished he could talk to Bahiga, but even if he could she might not wish to enlighten him. She might, though, know a little more about what happened to the precious scrolls that used to be in the Great Library – the first library, the one that might have been spared the burning that befell the one housed in the temple near the Horseman's Pillar when it was destroyed by the Jewish mob. Perhaps Bahiga could tell him exactly what he was looking for in the scrolls, although of course she wouldn't, because she was determined that, whatever it was, he wouldn't find it. The Emerald Tablet must remain hidden, she said, because there would be untold dangers if it fell into the wrong hands. If she were there, she would stop the search.

Yet he wished she were there. He longed to see her, and he could smell her perfume, still fresh in his mind after the vision given him by the strange woman on the night the dancers rescued them from the desert. With Bahiga on his mind, he fell asleep.

He woke suddenly. Voices were drifting over the sand, the sounds sharp and clear in the thin, still air. From where he lay Sanjar could see, through a gap in the rocks behind which they had hidden, the sandy plain which marked the way to Wadi Natroun, and soon two black-robed figures mounted on donkeys came into view, travelling in the direction of the monasteries. Clearly these monks felt free to travel by day: bandits did not bother to rob monks.

Were these the murderers of Brother Paphnotius, now on their way back to St. Cyril's? Trotting on their small donkeys they were making a slow but steady pace. The monks had probably not heard or seen his small group when they silently passed them as they rested during the night.

Nevertheless, when they overtook the monks again, as they would tonight, they must keep up their speed. It was imperative for them to arrive at St Cyril's before word reached the Abbot that they were on their way.

They made camp in the morning within a short distance of the monastery, which was hidden in the hills behind its white stone walls, and there they formed a plan of action. Their object was the scrolls in the Abbot's cell: to reach them they must scale the walls, silence the dogs, reach the cell, and surprise or distract the Abbot. And before they left it was imperative that they refill their waterskin. Their task was not easy: had they known then they had allies within the walls they would have been heartened indeed.

They moved down several hours after nightfall. Rhoorogh was to wait outside the walls with Moonleap and the two mules. Rhoorogh hoisted the near empty waterskin from the back of the pack mule, and quietly poured the remaining contents into a leather bucket so the animals could drink. Then he unhooked from the mule's saddle a coil of strong rope, and lastly he unpacked a small sack of bones, which by now, after two days of travelling, stank unpleasantly. All this was done as silently as they could in order not to disturb the dogs.

Rhoorogh hoisted Sanjar on his shoulders and helped him heave himself to the top of the wall. The dogs heard him, and growled. Sanjar drew one of the sticky bones out of the sack and waved it in the air. After a few moments he heard the excited breath of the dogs below, and a short whine: he threw down the bone, and a second. These would be a treat for the dogs, which would seldom taste meat. As soon as the dogs were occupied with their trophies he turned and helped haul up Tadros from Rhoorogh's shoulders. The waterskin followed. Then Rhoorogh, tying one end to his waist, threw the rope over the wall.

Since they would have no chance once they had broken into the Abbot's cell, their first task was to fill the waterskin. They slid one after the other down the rope and stepped gingerly past the dogs, which looked up from their bones to emit muffled growls lest their prize be stolen. Tadros ran with the waterskin to the well and filled half of it from a bucket already standing there, but when he drew the bucket again the creaking of the rope made so much noise they thought it must awaken the monks. Yet no one stirred.

They filled and plugged the waterskin and carried it back to the wall, where they tied it securely to the rope. They tugged twice on the rope, and Rhoorogh began to pull. The waterskin was heavy: Sanjar and Tadros guided it as best they could, but it balked at tipping over the top of the wall, and Sanjar had to hoist up Tadros who tried to dislodge it, although even with outstretched arms he could barely reach. There was a danger it would split and burst, and their water supply, their lifeblood, would fall into the sand, but at last the skin was over and they heard a dull thud as Rhoorogh caught it. He threw back the rope

Sanjar and Tadros turned their attention to the monastery buildings, and it was then they heard a snicker which, to their horror, was answered by Moonleap behind the wall. They looked, and then crept, towards the sheds which served as stables, and there, in the faint light cast by the moon, they saw horses. They counted four.

In Egypt, only soldiers rode horses.

Nearby was the row of cells occupied by the monks and, at the very end, the cell in which they had been locked when they first arrived at St. Cyril's. Was there not a flicker of light from the high window at the side of the cell, the window through which they had cut their way that first night?

Sanjar lifted Tadros up to the window so he could see what was inside the room. A moment later the boy jumped down and whispered excitedly: "They're the Caliph's guard, four of them, playing checkers."

Sanjar thought quickly.

"Is one of them thickset, with heavy black whiskers?"

"I think so."

"That's Captain Battusta, the one who saved my life in Iskandriya, It seems to me he must have come here in pursuit of us. Well if he's supposed to keep an eye on us, we may as well let him out of this prison."

Sanjar hauled himself to see whether this was indeed Battusta. The window had been hastily mended, the iron bars he had cut with Moonflinger crudely welded together. Below him were, indeed, Captain Battusta and his three guards. But were they prisoners, locked in the cell as he and Tadros had been, or were they mere guests, free to leave and enter the cell at will? There was only one way to find out.

He landed softly in the sand and motioned Tadros to follow him. Keeping in the shadows, they skirted the corner and lifted the huge latch which secured the door. It swung open.

For a second the guards were transfixed with surprise. Then the captain asked, in a matter-of-fact tone: "What kept you?"

Sanjar raised his hands in greeting. Then they slipped inside and quietly closed the door.

"We've been here a week, waiting for you."

Sanjar held a finger to his lips.

"We had to climb over the wall, my friend," he said. "And we hope to escape that way. Perhaps the monks are treating you well: they were less kindly disposed towards us."

Sanjar gave them a brief account of the way the monks had imprisoned and then drugged them. He did not mention his encounter with Captain Guhar or the Ghawarzee, but he told them of the murder of Brother

Paphnotius, and that they had come back to search the Abbot's scrolls. The captain, meanwhile, said the monks at St. Cyril's had finally admitted that Sanjar had visited them, but said he had already left on a secret mission. They refused to say what it was or where he had gone, but had promised that he would return. The guards, knowing it was impossible to follow Sanjar into the desert, had waited, as bidden, at the monastery. But their patience was wearing thin, and so, it seemed, was the monks', for they lived on meagre rations and the guards were constantly asking for more food. The curious thing was that they had spent much of the time there sleeping. The days had sped by. Now they were more lively, and ready to wait no longer but to go in search of Sanjar, for if he were to perish in the desert while supposedly under their watch the Caliph's mercy would be short. Yet here was Sanjar, and perhaps they could now leave.

"They drugged you," Sanjar said. "They wanted to keep you here so you would not follow us, so they kept you plied with sleeping draughts. They want to make sure we have as little help as possible. Now we have to get to the scrolls, and then we have to get out of here." Sanjar made a move to get up.

"Wait," the captain said. "How do you propose to search the Abbot's cell?"

"We'll just have to tie him up and get on with it."

"But the monks get up several times a night to pray. You can hear the bell to wake them – well, we haven't much, because we've been fast asleep. But if you wait until the Abbot gets up to pray you can get into his room then."

"How much time do we have?"

"Oh, they take ages. The praying and chanting goes on and on. At least an hour."

"Well, that may be enough."

"Just wait for the next bell."

The room was cramped, so the three soldiers picked up their bedrolls and lay outside the door on the cool sand, where they were lulled to sleep by the steady gnawing of the dogs on their treasured bones. Tadros had already fallen asleep on one of the two cots: when Sanjar lay down beside him he stirred, and made a move to lie on the floor, but Sanjar stopped him. Captain Battusta lay on the other cot, but the two men made no more attempt to talk. An unspoken barrier had dropped between them. It was best that they, the watcher and the watched, did not become too close as allies. Both owed allegiance to the Caliph, and neither wanted to test that loyalty.

Sanjar had no sooner fallen asleep than the captain was shaking him awake.

"The bell!" he whispered.

Sanjar, in turn, shook Tadros.

"Best get your wits about you, boy," he said. "You have some studying to do."

They had extinguished the light in their room, and now they waited a few minutes, peering from their dark doorway towards the church as the black-shadow monks filed in one by one. Most walked steadily, one or two stumbled as if half asleep, while the last ones hurried for fear of being late. Soon the drone of the monks at prayer drowned the scratching of teeth on bones.

The guards had packed their belongings ready to leave as soon as Sanjar and Tadros had finished their task, and give them cover if necessary. Soon they would saddle their horses: for now they stationed themselves in the shadows while their captain, Sanjar and Tadros ran stealthily for the Abbot's domed, single cell. In the doorway a servant, lying wrapped in a blanket, snored and turned. He was doubtless a heavy sleeper, used to sleeping through the night bells, and he did not wake as they stepped over him or, using a tinderbox, lit the candles in the cell.

There was a huge pile of scrolls, and Tadros did not know where to start. All he knew was that what he was looking for was very old, written in Greek, and probably on papyrus rather than vellum, for this would mean it was more likely to have originated in Egypt. He looked around. Scrolls, papers and roughly-bound codices were piled floor to ceiling, but something told him a fastidious man like the Abbot would not keep any precious documents as haphazardly as these.

And he did not. In one corner was an iron-bound wooden chest, and Moonflinger had cut the iron lock in no time. Inside was no pile of treasure, no gold: merely several dusty old fragments of papyrus. The captain shuffled impatiently. Tadros bent over the box.

The pages were so crumbled and yellowed with age, and the writing on them so faded, that many were illegible. Some of them were, perhaps, more than a thousand years old. On some were paintings of figures of winged goddesses and animal-headed gods, their colours still bright. On others, maps. The writing, in Sanjar's eyes, was squiggles.

"Demotic," Tadros said learnedly. "And Greek."

"Can you read it?"

"I can see the word 'Iskandriya'. This is a map of Iskandriya."

"Is there a tomb?"

Fortunately the Abbot's servant, when at this point he awoke and saw them there, was so drugged with sleep he did not think to raise the alarm before drawing a dagger from under his pillow and creeping up behind the captain. Sanjar and Captain Battusta saw him simultaneously. Both lifted an arm to deflect the thrust, and the servant was turned head over heels. Without a word they trussed and bound him and left him in a corner.

106

"We can't hide our tracks now," muttered the captain.

"That was out of the question," said Sanjar.

Tadros, who had barely glanced up, said: "How much time do we have?"

"Very little."

Tadros was afraid even to touch the pages, it seemed as though they were so ready to decay into dust. He tried to ignore the awe he felt and concentrate on trying to read the Greek scripts, but his knowledge of Greek was so rudimentary and the writing so ancient and so formal – for most of it seemed to be religious text and to have little bearing on history, geography, or the likely whereabouts of Iskander's tomb – that he quickly felt the task would be hopeless. He knew only a few words, and recognised only a few names, the names of Greek-Egyptian gods which he had picked up in the books of Dr Boutros – Amoun, Serapis, Isis, Horus, Hermes.

Hermes.

He read on.

"What can you see? Have you found anything?"

"No."

Hermes seemed to be giving instructions to some dead person. There was a picture of the body, wrapped tightly in white.

He picked up another page. Here was another mummy, this one wearing the double crown of Egypt. The name below it leapt out at him: Alexander.

There was a light at the door. The Abbot stood there, a simple man in his simple grey robe. He offered no resistance. The captain bound his wrists.

"I'm sorry to do this, father," he said. "You gave us excellent hospitality. You just kept us waiting a little too long for our friend."

"I knew he would return."

"Then you should have kept better guard on your treasures."

The Abbot's face was as grey as his robe. He had only one hope: that these heathens would not be able to decipher the precious texts. That hope was short-lived.

"We're wasting time," Sanjar said. "Let's go."

"The papers – " Tadros protested.

"We'll take them."

For the first time the Abbot's composure seemed to break down.

"Don't," he pleaded. "I beg you, don't."

"We have to get them translated. We'll find someone in Iskandriya to translate them."

The Abbot shook his head.

"You won't find anyone in Iskandriya who can read demotic."

"What?"

"Demotic. Egyptian, the way they wrote it when they stopped using hieroglyphs."

"When was that?"

"Hundreds of years ago, when Thebes was the capital of Egypt."

"When was that?"

"Long before the founding of Iskandriya."

Sanjar thought, but thought no further than that the Abbot was trying to outwit him.

"Are these written in Egyptian?"

"Yes."

"So they were written before Alexander's time?"

"Long before."

Tadros stood up.

"Not all of them," he said.

There was a flicker of surprise on the Abbot's face.

Sanjar said, satisfied: "So you thought this little Copt was a simple syce?"

"You can read?" asked the Abbot.

"Yes," Tadros said.

"Coptic?"

"And some Greek."

The Abbot's lower jaw dropped in surprise.

Tadros hoped he would not be examined in Greek. He was bluffing. His knowledge was far too rudimentary for him to read these texts.

It was Captain Battusta who grasped the easy way out of the situation.

"If you want to keep your head on your shoulders and your brotherhood intact, father," he said. "You had better translate these papers."

And that was how they came to learn about Zerzura.

*　*　*

In al-Qahira, Bahiga was preparing for the race to reach the Emerald Tablet. She had assured her father, as she had assured Sanjar, that she would fight any attempt to discover it.

In fact she had no such intention. She knew the Tablet would be found, and that the reason it had to be found was because she could not for ever prevent its discovery.

She merely wished to hinder their movements.

Finding the Tablet had to be difficult so the seekers would be exhausted once they reached their goal. They had to be so exhausted that when they reached it they would not be strong enough to absorb its power. It was imperative that when the Tablet was found it must fall under her control. That was the way it was written, and that was the way it would be.

Only now two of the people who were seeking it were two of the people she loved. How their hearts would have leapt had they known she loved them, just as hers was breaking because it was so.

The other person Bahiga loved was her nurse. She sent money and silks and baskets of preserves to her nurse in her village where she lived in exile, and with them she sent a letter, which the nurse could not read but would take proudly to the village scribe to have it read to her, and all the people in the village would gather to hear that soon Bahiga would call her back to al-Qahira to the house of the Qadi, where she lived in such luxury that she had servants of her own.

The Qadi himself could barely contain his anxiety to leave the capital. The daily audiences with the Caliph were becoming a torture, and the effort of scrying so he could relay Sanjar's whereabouts to his master was draining his strength. Almost every day he hinted that soon he must go north to follow the warrior more closely, to ensure that his mind remained on his task and his loyalty to the Caliph did not waver. The Caliph, however, would not let him go so soon. Why else had he sent Captain Battusta, he reasoned, if not to watch Sanjar? He insisted the Qadi stay in al-Qahira. How else could he, the Caliph, be informed about what was going on, not just in the search for the Tablet, but all over his realm? The Qadi dared not argue, but still he hoped.

Until the day when the Caliph said: "I hear things about your daughter that I would rather not hear."

The Qadi, much as these words terrified him, knew better than to plead for his daughter. If he were to reveal his fear and his pain, the Caliph would have expressed his satisfaction by having Bahiga tortured or put to death in no time.

Now he no longer mentioned leaving the city. He even made excuses not to leave his house, and hurried through the affairs of the courts. As a result many a suspect was condemned without time spent on pleading his case, many another released because the witnesses for the prosecution took too long to give evidence. Bahiga got to hear of this and scolded her father. Who would uphold the law, she said, if it were not him? For a moment he felt like relaxing his watch on her and letting her go to the devil, or rather the Caliph, which was worse – as the Qadi, who had more than a passing acquaintance with the devil, well knew – but once his wrath had cooled he doubled his efforts to protect her, as well as to prevent her getting them both into trouble. He had the house guards burn her sedan chair. "I don't need it," she said, and thus he knew that her powers were even greater than he had feared.

After he burned her chair she was away for days. When she returned, he said: "You are still only a woman."

She laughed.

At last he said, "Make it easier for me."

"I don't fear the Caliph," she said.

What the Qadi feared about his daughter was not the great fear other men felt for theirs. For he, unlike other fathers, would never need to guard his daughter's virtue with her life. He would never have to draw her blood for the unmentionable sin of spilling it if she lay unlawfully with a man.

If Bahiga lost her maidenhood, she would lose her powers.

That was what had happened to her mother.

And that would not be. Both father and daughter knew this, even though it would never be said.

But even the Qadi, although he now knew Bahiga no longer needed her sedan chair, did not guess how strong she had become. Now Sanjar was seldom out of her sight. While the Qadi strained to follow his movements by scrying the inkblot on his small slave's hand, Bahiga followed him with her heart. While her father could make out pictures in the inkblots, she could feel her way to him in her mind. She saw him with her inner eye, and with her inner ear she heard his words. The Qadi feared and envied her because she did not need magic; but she was his daughter, and his fear and envy was tinged with pride.

The Caliph was entertaining a delegation from Baghdad. He kept the Qadi waiting for more than an hour. When he was called in, the Caliph asked: "Where are they now?"

"They are riding in the desert, towards Iskandriya," the Qadi said. "And your guard is with them."

"Too bad," the Caliph said.

Before dawn broke next morning, as the city and its ruler prepared to sleep, four black-robed horsemen of the guard left the palace and rode swiftly north to the Delta.

* * *

A small procession left the monastery at dawn: Sanjar, his followers, Captain Battusta, and his three men. It had taken the Abbot much of the night to reveal what was written in the scrolls, and only when he had finished had he told them about Zerzura.

At first Sanjar was inclined to think Zerzura was a mere plot, an attempt by the Abbot to send them on a wild goose chase. But then the Abbot had shown them an old script, an account by a Roman adventurer (from Constantinople) of how he had travelled many days through the desert and come to a white-walled city with an iron gate. If this were so, the Abbot said, then Iskander, who had travelled in the Western Desert and had visited the oracle of Amoun, where he had learnt of his destiny and had tried to unravel other secrets of the desert, if this were so, the Abbot said, then Iskander himself could have found the city – or even built it – and since the city was supposed to contain great treasure, perhaps it had been hidden there by Iskander, and was what the Caliph was seeking.

Sanjar had started at this. He had not mentioned the Emerald Tablet. "Treasure?" he asked, feigning innocence.

The Abbot gave a wan smile. "I do not imagine," he said, "that this curious interest in Alexander is merely an attempt by the Caliph to set the history books straight. He is either looking for his tomb, or for the Emerald Tablet, which some know as the philosopher's stone."

Sanjar had divined that Captain Battusta knew nothing of the Emerald Tablet, and it was better so. So he said lightly: "I do not know what that is. I have my quest, and that is all."

"No doubt," the Abbot concurred. "But whatever it is you seek, these scraps of papyrus will tell you very little about any tomb, or any treasure."

Some of the fragments of scrolls, he said, had indeed come from the Library of Iskandriya. The Abbot handled them with care and read them with pride. He read aloud from the Greek how Alexander had consulted the oracle at the Oasis of Amoun and been told he would conquer the world, and how at that moment he had changed and become a god. After he became a god, Alexander returned to the coast and went east again to the place where the Canopic branch of the Nile reached the blue waters of the Mediterranean, and there he founded his great city, Iskandriya. And beside the city were vineyards and gardens and orchards and lush grazing, and a huge lake where the people kept pleasure boats and sailed with their comrades, and on festival days they decked the boats with flowers and sailed and sang and beat drums and played music, and feasted on the fruits of the field and wine pressed from the luscious white grapes that grew in the vineyards around them.

But before all this, before the god gave orders for the building of Iskandriya and then left it, never to see it, only to enter it again when his body was brought back to it from India, before this, while he was still in the Oasis of Amoun and learning of his destiny, Iskander remembered the tales told him by his tutor, Aristotle, and he remembered how the army of the Persian king Cambyses, who had conquered Egypt two hundred years before him, had sent an army into the desert from Thebes to Carthage through the place where he was now, at the oracle of Amoun, and how the army had vanished in the desert and had never arrived at the oasis, and no trace of them had ever been found.

What was the fate of this Persian army?

Alexander was obsessed by it. Some said it had perished in a sandstorm, some that it had made its way to Cyrenaeca on the coast. But others spoke of a lost oasis, where sheep and cows grazed, tended by slender black women, and where birds sang all day long.

"Starlings," the Abbot said. "That's what the word means: *zerzura.*"

"Did Iskander go to look for the lost army?"

"We don't think he went himself, he was in too much of a hurry to conquer the world. But he still had to conquer some of its secrets. He sent scouts to find Zerzura, but their mission remains a secret and a mystery, and that may be because they were entrusted with finding a place to hide something very special. These scrolls, these fragments, are the remains of some of the books that were saved from the Great Library six or seven hundred years ago. See how fragile they are, how easily they fade and crumble. No, not all of the library was lost. There are other books like these, in other places, other cities, rescued before time – or marauding monks in their iconoclastic fervour – could destroy them. The scholars of the day saved what they could. But the knowledge, the knowledge that was lost. Ah, there's the grievance, there's the pity." The Abbot carefully put away the scrolls.

As his uninvited guests left the monastery, the Abbot had a twinge of conscience. Such fine young men. That Zerzura existed the Abbot had no doubt, but that these young men would perish before they reached it, of that he had no doubt too.

They rode in a band back towards the coast, camping at night, and resting again at midday in the winter sun. On the eve of the third day they reached the southern edge of the limestone ridge which ran along the coast all the way the Cyrenaeca, and here Sanjar reined in Moonleap.

"Now we must part, Captain," he said. "You are my watch, my guard; we cannot ride together, or share one another's secrets, or forge any bonds of friendship. You obey the Caliph, and so do I. But we act apart, and we cannot ride side by side. I wish you well: I hope that if again I need your aid, you will be nearby, and I hope to be there when you need mine. For now, I shall start, and leave you to follow."

And with that he, with Tadros and Rhoorogh, turned his horse to the west and rode until he reached the shores of Lake Maryut, the marshy swamp which used to be the lake where the Alexandrians of old sailed their boats on holidays, and there they watered the horses, and heard the ghosts of young girls singing and beating tambourines as their silent boats drifted through the reeds.

Captain Battusta never followed Sanjar, but neither did he tell the black-robed guards, when they caught up with him, where Sanjar was bound. For when he saw his men die even after they had told the guards what little they knew he realised he could not betray Sanjar, but could only try to give him a chance to escape the Caliph and perhaps to learn that the ruler had betrayed them before he met a similar fate. So he said nothing, and gave up his life more slowly, and when they had finished their task the officers of the Caliph's guard rode on to seek the warrior and fulfil their master's command.

"So my trusted guards lie dead?" the Caliph asked the Qadi. "Your fine Turk is a murderer, then. Let us deal with him when he has found the Tablet."

9 · In A Persian Garden

WEST OF ISKANDRIYA a well-trodden trail slunk parallel to the rugged and barren coast. North of this trail, between it and the sea, a limestone ridge held back the ghost waters of the dying lake which had once watered abundant fields and gardens to fill the tables of the Greek and Roman colonists. If one climbed the ridge one could see the blue waters of the sea, but the shore was hidden behind dunes and cliffs.

There were few settlements on the trail, and to make the going easier Sanjar purchased a camel to carry fodder and waterskins which they could fill at the villages which had grown around the Roman wells strung along the way, and where they could also buy food for themselves and their animals.

Day after day they travelled, by night bivouacking beneath the stars, wrapping their blankets tightly round them to keep out the chill night. Sometimes they passed the fallen ruins of ancient cities, the stones and pillars of their grand temples as debased and forgotten as their gods. Occasionally they met a caravan of camels bearing wool and woven cloth from Cyrenaeca, or a band of pilgrims making their way – depending on their faith – to Mecca or Jerusalem.

The progress they made was set by Rhoorogh, who trailed behind Sanjar and Tadros on foot leading the camel. It was her reluctance to follow him that slowed him down. Later he exchanged the camel with Tadros for the spare mule, and after that the camel walked more steadily and their pace improved. She was still skittish when Rhoorogh approached her, so he kept his distance, which suited her very well. The truth was she found him offensive.

At first their journey was enlivened by the life which flourished in the remaining shallow waters of the lake. Hippos wallowed, and occasionally roared. There were crocodiles, and wading herons, and vast flocks of white flamingoes, thousands strong. On the shores the Bedouin herded camels and cattle, and cared for the priceless orphans belonging to the fine citizens of Iskandriya and al-Qahira, who sent them their Arabian foals to be nursed on camel's milk to give them strength and save the effort to their precious mares. But as they moved westward the lake dried out, and finally the patches of marshland became scarcer and were replaced by clumps of dense scrub. Hovering on the horizon, through the gaps between the limestone peaks, shimmered imaginary lakes, conjoured by the elements to lie on stretches of sand which were, in truth, as dry as bone. Of bones there were plenty, those of camels gnawed clean by foxes. At midday the sun warmed them through; at night the temperature dropped, and a salty breeze blew in from the sea.

At length they met an old man, ragged and stooped, with a haunted look in his eyes.

"Old man, why are you standing alone?" Sanjar asked.

The old man could barely bring himself to speak.

"I am waiting here to die," he said at last. "I have lost everything, I have lost my brothers, my children, and my wife, and I am waiting here to die.

"Why here, such a long way from anywhere?"

"I am waiting for them. You see," he said confidentially, "they don't seem partial to my old bones."

"Who? The foxes?"

The old man's mouth grimaced into what might have been a smile. "The foxes, aye, I am waiting for the foxes. They are long in coming."

Sanjar handed down his water bottle and the old man gulped from it, the water running down his beard as he made the effort to drink.

"Heatstroke," Sanjar suggested to Tadros as they rode on. Rhoorogh, reluctant to leave the old man behind, tried to lift him on to the back of the mule, but he kicked and screamed so much at this that Rhoorogh feared the struggle might kill him, and abandoned him. The old man sat sobbing, but lifted his ravaged face to call after them: "Don't ride away from the road!"

"I wonder what he meant?" called Sanjar, turning Moonleap off at a tangent towards the hills.

"No! Sanjar!"

Reluctant as he was to counter the old man's advice, Tadros kicked Hermes into a gallop.

"Come back!" he shouted as he tried in vain to catch up with Moonleap.

Sanjar waited for him on top of a ridge.

"It's very trying," Tadros complained, "travelling with a hero."

Sanjar held up his hand for silence. Indeed, the slightest sound would have echoed for miles, to the very edge of the sand plateau that stretched before them. The desert, although empty and silent, was teeming with colour. From the distant blue hills to the mustard, saffron and rose pink sands, from the purple rocks threaded with gold and silver to the nutmeg and indigo shadows.

Yet it was not totally empty. Just below them, sheltered by the ridge on which they stood, was a small hovel built of brushwood, and from a hole in its roof wove a curl of smoke.

"This must be the old man's home," Tadros murmured.

Sanjar gave Moonleap a free rein to manoeuvre her way down the rocky escarpment, while Tadros followed on the more sure-footed mule. Their approach did not go unheard: when they reached the hovel, the family within had emerged and arranged themselves in a thin and ragged semicircle to meet their guests.

However it was not their emaciation, or their filthy, sand-soaked rags that made the blood run cold and tugged the heartstrings of fear, or brought the horses to a standstill as they whinnied silently in terror. It was the evil that flew from their eyes as they stood in their half-circle, and stared.

There were seven of them, five men and two women, and all were so thin their bones all but broke through their skin. From their sparse, tangled hair to their clothes they were the colour of sand, all but their eyes, which stared black and soulless from their bony sockets.

"Who are you?" demanded Sanjar.

The group was silent.

"Can you not speak? Are you mad? Is this why we met the old man on the road over there, did he leave because his family had gone mad?"

At this, the older of the two women began to howl.

This, though, was not a howl of grief, nor was it a howl of rage. It was, in part, the howl of an old woman whose man has gone. More, it was the howl of an old woman whose man has escaped. More than that, it was the howl of a demon which has wind of its prey.

At the sound, Moonleap trembled beneath him and the mule backed in terror. Only Sanjar remained unmoved. Turning to Tadros, whose face was as white as cheese, he asked, "What are these people?"

"Ghouls," breathed Tadros.

"Ghouls?"

"Yes."

"Nonsense!" And with that, Sanjar drew Moonflinger. "Ghouls indeed," he muttered, "don't they know they have to obey the servants of the Caliph, like anyone else?" He waved his sword aloft, but whether it struck fear into their hearts or whether his action provoked their rage he could not tell, for the howls they now began to emit were so terrible in themselves that one would rather shut one's mind to them than try to decipher their meaning.

* * *

A chill wind was running through the streets of al-Qahira. The merchants and messengers passing through the city drew their cloaks about them, and the guards on duty on the city walls stamped their feet against the cold.

A fire warmed Bahiga's apartment, burnishing the copper tables and candlesticks in the room with the latticed windows. Bahiga, in a red velvet dress, stood before the fireplace and watched the flames.

She had too little time. She had not thought she would need to leave al-Qahira so soon, and she had to make preparations before she was ready. But Sanjar needed help now. It was one thing to pit a fearless man against the desert, but the desert was as much a battlefield as anywhere else, and it was quite another to expect him to know how to deal with the perils he might encounter. She had known he would undergo trials in his search for the Tablet, and she hoped that thus he would learn, and through his learning understand the nature of his mission, but she did not want him to die. If only she had given him more warning of the dangers he might meet.

The flames danced before her. The flames, these flames, were under her control: if she added another log she could treble their size, with a drop of water she could extinguish them. But fire had other forms, and of all these forms the most dangerous were the jinn. There were so many types of jinn. There were those who had no power of their own but existed only to serve a master – as her father's helper served him – and there were those with a little power of their own, who could assume the form of animals or monsters and spread mischief and fear, but the worst and most dreaded were the solitary jinn, the jinn of the mountain and desert whose power was fed by the fear they evoked. These were the worst, these – and the ghouls.

The ghouls were almost within striking distance of Sanjar. He would be looking for swords, but their weapons were their claws and their teeth. A scratch or a bite paralysed a victim – and then the ghouls would feast on his blood, and the victim in turn would become a ghoul.

Bahiga, her eyes on the flames, focused her powers and summoned all her strength.

She sent it to Rhoorogh.

* * *

On the other side of the city, the Caliph waited for a messenger from the new guard he had sent to monitor Sanjar's mission. He was impatient for news. The Qadi had been holding a session of his court of justice in a town in the Delta, and had not shown him any inkblot pictures for three days. There was another reason for him to talk urgently to the Qadi, and this concerned his daughter.

It was now late in the afternoon, and the messenger, when he arrived, would bring tidings not much more than a day old. The Caliph watched the palace gates, and felt his heart skip a beat when the rider galloped in. Moments later the man had prostrated himself before him.

The Caliph professed an air of indifference, but decided not to be harsh. "You have ridden hard," he began.

"Sir," the messenger said, trying to regain his breath.

"So get up and give me the news."

The news was that Battusta was dead, the new guard was in place, and Sanjar and his troops had left the hippopotamus-ridden swamps of Lake Maryut and were in the Western Desert proper, west-bound along the coast. Behind him, the new guards were keeping their distance.

The Caliph was gratified by this advice. He took pride in the way he ran his affairs of state. He was the ruler of al-Qahira, and al-Qahira was the mother of the world, and it was imperative that he had a finger on every pulse of his empire. He knew what went on in the palace kitchens, in the merchants' quarter of the town, and in the inns, mosques and government offices of the furthest regions of the Caliphate. Since he was in the habit of walking about the palace, and riding alone and in a plain man's clothes about the city at night, he kept a close eye and ear on the doings of the city from palace household to the slums of Fustat, and he knew to the next word what his subjects said about him, and how closely they obeyed him. His network of spies reported on the further corners of the Caliphate and beyond, from the upper reaches of the Nile valley to the borders with Cyrenaeca, Persia and Arabia and the northern shores of the Mediterranean. Al-Hakim was more secure than he thought in the safety of his person and the security of his borders, but this security depended on his vigilance, and his vigilance never waned.

On his night-time donkey-back forays he could check that taxes were paid and his laws adhered to, that all the females in the city stayed at home, that no dogs were brought within its limits, no church bells rung or shellfish consumed, or cucumbers or pork. He could see that the people were working, not sleeping, at night – sleeping could be left for the hot and unproductive hours of the day. And, in his more benign moments, he checked that the markets were stocked with food, and the little boys were learning to recite the holy verses they learnt in the religious schools he had founded for their benefit. But perhaps his care was not so benign, since hungry subjects were more likely to rebel, and boys schooled in schismatic teachings more prone to leading revolutions. Even the most powerful ruler in the world had to be in touch with the pulse of his capital.

His nocturnal wanderings no longer alarmed his guards. The Caliph always returned unharmed. They believed him protected by holy – or super-natural – powers, and indeed who could say this was not so?

*   *   *

The ghouls howled, but still they did not move as Sanjar, astride Moonleap – who was prancing now with the pain of the sound and the knowledge that her master was about to attack – called to them to obey the Caliph of whom, of course, they had never heard. There was another reason why they paid no heed to his words, for if ever Sanjar was to meet his match in fearlessness, it was in the minds of demons.

Still he hesitated to strike. In war, one faced an enemy arrayed, as was oneself, for battle. These people, despite their demeanour, were poor and unarmed. Ghouls they might perhaps be, as Tadros said – and Sanjar was learning to respect the boy's opinions about the supernatural – but again, perhaps they were not. Perhaps they were indeed just simple souls, driven mad by degeneration or isolation.

All the while the creatures distorted their faces and howled. It took no more than a minute or two for Sanjar to make up his mind, but to Tadros those minutes passed like hours.

And at last Tadros pulled himself together.

"You can't kill them, they're dead!" he screamed, fighting to control the mule. "They're jinn, not humans!"

Sanjar charged.

"NO!"

But Sanjar and Moonleap leapt among the creatures, scattering them and flipping them aside. And that was the little that Moonflinger could do. Tadros watched in horror as the magic sword flailed from side to side but as it cut their flesh only melted for an instant into flame before becoming whole again, while all the time the wailing ghouls raised their scrawny arms to drag Sanjar from the saddle, their eyes bright with hunger and power.

While Moonflinger could not destroy the ghouls, the holy words written on its hilt could keep the demons at bay, but only so long as Sanjar remained unscathed. As fast as Sanjar struck, the ghouls resumed their hideous forms and tried to claw him down and paralyse him with their scratches and bites. The brunt of their attack was staved off by the light chain mail he wore, but his arms, clad only in his white shirt sleeves, for his cloak had fallen back as he rode, were fair prey to their strikes. At the same time the flames that leapt up when Moonflinger made contact with their bodies gave out an intense heat he could hardly bear, and the smell of Moonleap's singed mane and his burning woollen cloak mingled with the whiffs of filth and decay from the ghouls and their hovel was intolerable. At last one of the ghouls clawed at Moonleap's flank, and a thin red stream of blood trickled down her gleaming white coat. As Sanjar felt her strength ebbing, he faltered, and at that point a thin bony hand caught his, and crushed his fingers between its teeth.

At that point, too, Hermes the mule made the first reasoned decision of the day. He wheeled round and bolted for the road, mounting the ridge without a falter as Tadros clung for his life to his back. Tadros, whose relief at escape and guilt at leaving was overshadowed by his fear and discomfort as they ran, was not able to recover his wits until, some way before the road, they encountered Rhoorogh pulling the disgusted camel and the spare mule trotting obediently behind.

By the time they had all hurried back to the ridge there was no sign of the ghouls, but Sanjar and Moonleap were lying prostrate on the ground below. Seeing them, Rhoorogh did not wait to climb down to express his rage. Filled with a strength he assumed was born of fury, he drew himself to his full height, struck his arms on his chest, and roared.

The ghouls emerged from the hollow and began to move into a half circle, but when they looked up and saw Rhoorogh they seemed to freeze. Never before had they encountered such a creature, but it seemed to them, without a doubt, that it was a jinni like them – and one to be reckoned with. They stood their ground, however, until, with a roar that shook the hills, Rhoorogh came crashing down the slope.

The ghouls howled, turned, and fled.

Rhoorogh knew the ghouls would soon think better of their flight and return to protect their meal. He hauled Moonleap to her feet, then seized Sanjar and put him over his shoulders.

Dragging the half-conscious horse, he climbed the ridge and threw Sanjar over the back of the spare mule. Then he slapped Moonleap on the rump, and let out a series of urgent grunts which the horse interpreted as "Run, run like the wind!"

He took one last look over the ridge, and saw that the ghouls were creeping back to the hovel. Their howling when they saw their prey was gone echoed behind him as he ran after the cloud of dust thrown up by the bolting animals.

*   *   *

Bahiga gave a sigh of relief, and put another log on the fire. It would take some hours for the paralysis to wear off completely, but Sanjar would recover. Now she would make her preparations, and when everything was ready she would leave.

*   *   *

They did not stop until they reached the road, where they found the old man still weeping. Yet even here they could not afford to rest. Rhoorogh moved Sanjar carefully to the back of the camel, then he set the old man on the spare mule. Moonleap, who was still very weak, stumbled along by herself. Thus the procession continued on its way.

As they went the old man told his sad story. He had lived all his life in the desert, and ever since he was a boy he had wanted no other life. His four brothers, however, thought there was more to the world than wind and sand, and had gone away many years before. Meanwhile he had taken a wife and lived with her in the hut below the ridge. In time they had a son and a daughter, who had both stayed at home, unmarried. The family had eked out a living from the desert, herding a few goats, collecting herbs and birds' eggs and sometimes fishing on the shore. One day he was overjoyed to see his four brothers returning. As soon as he saw them in the distance he knew who they were, even though they had been gone for many years, and he told his wife to prepare a feast. But when they drew closer he could see that all was not well with them: they had changed. They had not only changed in appearance, but they could not speak. They could only utter the most terrible howls.

His blood had run chill, but though he called on his wife and children to run for their lives, it was too late. The four brothers took them. He had not stayed to watch.

There was a subdued air around their campfire that night. While the old man was wrapped in his grief and Tadros still shocked by the horror of the encounter with the ghouls, Sanjar had come to himself only to realise that he had, once again, been outwitted by demons and saved by someone else. There was no shame in one's life being saved, but it was happening again and yet again... and Sanjar was fast losing his self-respect.

Tadros interrupted his thoughts.

"You were very brave," he said. "I never heard of anyone trying to attack ghouls before."

Sanjar spoke weakly, his strength still drained by the ghouls' poison.

"That's very little consolation," he said.

He wanted to face a real battle, where he could prove himself. He wanted to show this small band of his that he was worthy of their loyalty. He was constantly being thrown up against enemies he could not fight in battles he could not win.

"It is in your heart," Tadros said wisely, "that most battles are won."

"And lost."

Tadros moved a log into the centre of the fire. "Winning is not everything," he said.

"What is there but to win?" Sanjar whispered, watching the flames.

"There is everything," Tadros said. "To win is to bask in the praise of others, to know how to lose is to know yourself. This is why we are with you, not just because you can fight for us, but also because we can show you that you can't win alone, and that you aren't alone. Rhoorogh and I, we are not a fine army, with great weapons and horses, but we can fight with you and for you in our way."

Sanjar poked a stick in the fire, raising a few sparks. He had been so blinded by his own conquests and bravado that he had lost his humility. He had thought of himself all along as the leader, whereas in truth he was a partner, one of a band. Strength was not only in knowing what he could do, it was in knowing what he was.

"You are handsome, and brave, and strong, and good," said Tadros. "but you must know your heart, and you must also the hearts of others, because if you don't, you cannot know how to win, or to lose, or to love."

Sanjar looked at him curiously.

"Have you been in love, Tadros?"

Tadros gave a shy smile. "There was a girl in Fustat," he said. "She lived next door, she was a maidservant. She was so pretty and sweet. I should like to marry her one day, so she won't have to spend all her life serving other people."

"Instead she can serve you."

Tadros smiled sadly. "I may not find her again," he said.

"But you may." He thought of Bahiga, of her brilliance and beauty. Would Bahiga have scorned him for being felled by the ghouls? He realised suddenly that there was so much more he needed to know about her. Their encounters had been so brief, and so unusual, and he knew so little about women, least of all women with special gifts. He wondered whether, like Tadros' little maidservant, she would remain a dream. But perhaps, when this was over, Tadros would find his maidservant, and perhaps he and Bahiga... but again, the thought that she might spurn him was too painful to bear, and he pulled his mind back to the campfire. Whatever Tadros said, whatever Bahiga thought, Sanjar was no longer the man he thought he was, no longer the warrior, no longer the conqueror of all. He recognised feelings he had thought buried, or forgotten; the uncertainty of youth, the questioning of values, the luxury of doubt.

"You are not just a fighting machine," Tadros said.

The flames leapt and danced. In her apartment at al-Qahira, Bahiga watched the flames in her hearth, and through them she studied Sanjar's face. She smiled at Tadros' words. What a wise old soul, she thought, and a tear rolled down her cheek and hissed as it hit the cinders. Sanjar jumped, and Tadros laughed.

"It's only a fire," he said, "not a jinni!"

Sanjar gave him a playful cuff.

"You're a jinni," he said.

But that night, only the old man slept. The others complained in the morning that his snores had kept them awake, but in truth they were listening for other things.

*   *   *

They struck camp at dawn. As they did so, Rhoorogh pointed out that they were low on water and should soon hope to reach the next well in the Roman chain. It was not until they had gone some way that the old man remarked he had heard of such wells, but that some of them had long fallen in, there not being the traffic there was in the old days. Since the wells were two or three days' march apart at best they greeted this news with dismay, although the old man, of course, might be wrong.

The old man was not wrong. Nothing was left of the next well but a stagnant pool, and round it a long abandoned, stone-built town. They wandered among the ruins, picking up small clay pots and fragments of blue-green glass. Sanjar asked the old man, who spoke in an odd dialect, like a Libyan, where they might find water, but he said that if they wanted to find water here they would have to sink a well, and it would be best to move on to the next place and hope they found people on the way.

So Sanjar called Tadros away from his exploring, and they resumed their journey.

Now they rationed their remaining water in earnest. They allowed the horse and mules to drink from their bucket, and filled their own water bottles so the water would not be left to evaporate in the skin. Their main hope now was that they would see signs of habitation before the day was out.

This was the driest area of the desert they had passed. There was scarcely a bird, or a plant, or a wild animal track to be seen, and they would have wondered if they were on the right road had it not been for the occasional droppings and bones of pack animals strewn along the way. They seemed to be the only travellers, however, and it was now some days since they had met a caravan. As far as the eye could see, and that was far, there was no living soul.

That night they saved their water, and slept in thirst. Next morning Sanjar saw the old man had drunk all that remained in his own bottle, and gave him some from his. They moved on.

On the following day Sanjar gave the old man all the water he had left, and by mid-afternoon his head was spinning. Soon they paused for a rest near a rocky outcrop, and the first thing they saw when they climbed round the rock to reach its shade was a drywall house built on to the rock face.

Tadros reasoned that if this were a dwelling, or were once a dwelling, there must be water nearby, and he went off to look for it, starting with the hut. The old man laid his weary bones gratefully in the sand, while Rhoorogh, who gestured that the hut must have been abandoned because the water supply had dried up, found a stick to whittle. Soon Tadros bolted out of the house as though a devil were on his heels.

"A dead man! There's a dead man in there!" he gasped.

Rhoorogh dropped his stick, while Sanjar stood up and followed Tadros towards the shack. The old man called: "Watch it! They could be here!"

Sanjar made his way over the rocks to the door. The rocks were cool, almost damp, as though there might indeed be water nearby, and a vine tumbled over the doorway. He peered inside. The house was windowless and quite dark, but after a moment, as his eyes grew accustomed to the darkness, he could make out two rooms. He entered slowly, determined this time to be more cautious.

"Over there!" said Tadros from the doorway.

He turned his eyes briefly to Tadros and noted where he was pointing, but again he was blinded when he turned his eyes back to the dark. He waited a moment or two, and then he saw it, the body of a man. He crept closer. "Well," he told Tadros, with some relief, "he didn't die of thirst. He has a full water bottle here, and his throat has been cut."

Tadros shuddered.

"I wonder why the ghouls haven't found him," Sanjar said. "Or the foxes."

Afterwards he was sorry he had not thought more about why no scavengers had claimed the corpse, but for now he unhitched the water bottle. "We should bury him," he said.

He uncorked the bottle and sniffed it. "It smells good," he said. "At least it can't be poisoned."

"Let me test it."

"No, I'm thirstier than you. I'll test it."

"Only take a sip!"

"Just a sip."

The water tasted slightly stale. Sanjar drank tentatively, rolling the water round his tongue to test for a strange taste or sensation. All at once his throat closed up as though he were being strangled. He began to choke, and flail his arms about, struggling desperately to take a breath. And then he realised that he was being strangled. He could feel wraith-like hands around his neck, cold as ice. He tried to alert Tadros, but Tadros was staring in alarm, for he could see nothing, only Sanjar and his flailing arms. At first he thought the water had poisoned him, but then he realised he was actually fighting and seemed to be trying to unhook someone's arms from his throat. Tadros leapt to help him, and then he too could feel a physical being, or rather a dense coldness, even though there was nothing to see. Suddenly Sanjar managed to wrench the hands away from his throat, and took a deep gasp of breath. But the cold thing again captured him in a tight clench. The more it tightened its grip, the greater the evil that seemed to pervade the room, so that now the coldness was unbearable. Sanjar was weakening. He sank to his knees, his body heaving convulsively as though in a final, fatal clasp.

* * *

When Sanjar opened his eyes, he found himself in a Persian garden. The light was brilliant. Overhead, an azure sky was sprinkled with small white clouds, while the white paving stones of the garden gleamed and shimmered in the strong sunlight. The scent of roses filled the air, and rose bushes were everywhere – pink, red, white, yellow – arranged in pots on the paving. Fountains played, and small birds bathed in the spray. The garden was ringed by green meadows, with snow-capped mountains in the distance.

He looked around. The only figure he could see was that of an old man in a white turban, clothed in a brown woollen robe, who was sitting with an open book on a stone bench. Sanjar clambered to his feet and approached him. As he drew near, the old man looked up and smiled in acknowledgment. He had fine, noble features and a small grey beard. He seemed familiar to Sanjar, who asked him where this place was.

"I am the poet Firdausi, and this is my garden," the man replied.

"If you are Firdausi, then I am a dead man."

"That need not be so," the poet replied kindly. "I see that news of my death has travelled fast, if indeed I am dead. I am not so sure. As for you, well, you may be but a visitor to the spirit world. As a visitor you may, having come here, decide to stay, but that will depend on how strong are the chains that bind you to earth. You may, on the other hand, be destined to remain. We shall soon see." He paused, as if recollecting something. "The last time I saw you, young man, you were at the court of that dreadful man Mahmud, in Ghazna. We have both come some way since those days. After sending me into exile because he disliked my poetry, he allowed me to return home so I could spend an impoverished old age such as befits a poet. But I'm rambling, and you have many questions."

Sanjar tried to collect his thoughts, but hesitated to ask what was uppermost in his mind.

"I suppose you don't know much about the place where I have just come from," he began. "It's very far from anywhere, and not often visited, and indeed perhaps that's why I'm here, because if we hadn't been so far from a place where people live we wouldn't have run out of water, and then I wouldn't have been tempted – well, anyway, I wouldn't be here." Sanjar was very tired, and sat down on the ground at the old man's feet.

"Please, do continue," Firdausi said.

"I must return if I can, because I have a very important quest to fulfil. If I fail in that quest I will fail all those who have trusted me, and all those who have come to my aid at great danger to themselves."

"A quest, for whom?"

"For the Fatimid Caliph in al-Qahira."

"Ah! A Shiite. But you are a Samanid, and therefore a Sunni. Why have you switched your obedience from Mahmud, who is also a Sunni, to al-Hakim, who isn't? Was it because you realised what an imbecile Mahmud is? But I am indiscreet. Perhaps you are still loyal to Mahmud."

"I am well aware of your quarrel with the Sultan, and that it was largely to do with your differences over religion. It was difficult for you, as a Shiite, to have your work well received at court. You are rumoured to have written a satire, which is to remain unpublished until after your death."

The poet chuckled. "Would you like to hear it? I can say it now, if I *am* dead."

And he began:

> "Free of every trace of sense and feeling,
> When you are dead, what will become of you?
> If you should tear me limb from limb, and cast
> My dust and ashes to the angry wind
> Firdausi would still live, since on your name,
> Mahmud, I did not rest my hopes of fame
> In the bright page of my heroic song,
> But on the God of Heaven.
> O, had your father graced a kingly throne,
> Your mother been for royal virtues known,
> A different fate the poet then had shared,
> Honours and wealth had been his just reward;
> But how remote are you from a glorious line!
> No high, ennobling ancestry is yours;
> From a base stock your bold career began:
> A blacksmith was your sire, in Isfahan."

The poet paused. "I shan't bore you with the rest," he said.

"With thoughts like those, it's no wonder you were exiled. But I had no quarrel with Mahmud. Although his line usurped the lands of my fathers, I admired him. I was exalted when he conquered King Anandpal in the Punjab. I was only a boy, but I cheered when I heard of the battle, and of how when a force of thirty thousand men charged the Sultan's army on both flanks the Sultan was about to call a retreat but King Anandpal's elephant panicked and took flight, and his men, believing their commander was turning tail, fled the battlefield. Thus Mahmud advanced triumphant into the heart of India, and thus I longed to follow him. As indeed I did.

"But now the campaign in India is over, and I wanted to see the world. The Sultan let me go, with a small pension and a letter which allows me free passage and a few privileges. While I was in al-Qahira the Caliph summoned me, and I have undertaken his command partly through a desire for adventure, partly through the need to supplement my pension, and partly because circumstances made it difficult for me to refuse."

"What is the nature of this quest?"

Sanjar thought. "I must find a very precious object, and give it to the Caliph."

"This object is of value, I suppose, to him?"

"Yes, of great value. He says it will make him the most powerful man in the world."

"You believe him?"

"I suppose I do."

"Then why, exactly, are you seeking it? Do you want to give it to him, and allow him to become the most powerful man in the world? Or do you propose to keep it, and thus assume that power yourself?"

"My mission is to return it to the Caliph."

"I can see you are a loyal and dutiful soldier, through and through. Why, do you think, if this object has such unusual qualities, did the Caliph as much as tell you what they were? Would you not wonder that this might tempt you to betray him, and keep it for yourself?"

"I suppose he trusted me."

"Perhaps he does. But that does not mean he will take any risks. I doubt that, once you have obtained the object, he will let you survive."

"That does not change the nature of my duty."

"Ah. Now you are putting duty above all else. That is admirable, in some cases. But not to question one's duty can be a coward's way out. It can be a way of avoiding responsibility, even of denying God."

"I am a soldier."

"Are you a soldier first, or a man? A man or a soldier? Is your first duty to a Caliph, or to God? Have you not thought that the most powerful being, on earth and above it, is God?"

"The object for which I am seeking will grant all earthly powers. It will not conflict with God."

"What are its powers?"

"As above, so below."

"As above, so below. And you say this does not conflict with God? To me, this embodies God. As above – the power that is above – so below – that power will be bestowed on whomever conjures it on earth. That person plans to replicate God."

"Then, to prevent this, I must abandon my quest and my duty?"

"You must choose whether to follow your ruler on earth, or in heaven."

"And if the Caliph appoints another such as I, who succeeds in finding the object of his desire?"

"You must follow your conscience, and you must prevent it if you can."

"How do I know the words you speak are true?"

"Young man, listen." And the poet began to recite from his book, savouring the beautiful words as they rolled over his tongue.

> *"Thee I invoke, the lord of life and light!*
> *Beyond imagination pure and bright!*
> *To thee, sufficing praise no tongue can give,*
> *We are thy creatures, and in thee we live!*
> *Thou art the summit, depth, the all in all,*
> *Creator, guardian of this earthly ball;*
> *Whatever is, thou art – protector, king,*
> *From thee all goodness, truth and mercy spring.*
> *O pardon the misdeeds of him who now*
> *Bends in thy presence with a suppliant brow.*
> *Teach him to tread the path thy Prophet trod;*
> *To wash his heart from sin, to know his God;*
> *And gently lead him to that home of rest,*
> *Where filled with holiest rapture dwell the blest."*

As the poet's words faded away, Sanjar became aware of another sound, the sound of a voice calling his name. The sound rang as clear as a bell, and he turned to see who had spoken.

"I think it is time for you to leave," Firdausi said. "Are you ready?"

Again the voice called.

"Whose voice is that?"

"She is not here," said the poet. "You must return, if you wish to see her. She is calling you."

"Sanjar!"

He looked around the garden, at the birds playing in the fountain and the multitude of roses, and he breathed in their delicate scent.

The voice came again.

"Sanjar! Sanjar Mouseback!"

*   *   *

"Sanjar!"

He was again on his knees, but now he was on the sand, under the open desert sky. Bahiga was leaning over him, calling his name.

Sanjar's first thought was that he was in another part of Paradise. He stared at the vision before him.

"You passed out for a moment," Bahiga said.

"No, I went..."

"Perhaps, but it was only for a moment."

"I was in a garden."

"Now you are here, and you are staying here. Let me help you to your feet."

"I can do it."

But he could not, and weakly accepted as she helped him up.

"How did I get here?"

"Tadros and I carried you out."

"But what are you doing here? And where is it, whatever it was?"

"It's in the hut. We shall bury the corpse, and then it will be still."

"Where is Tadros?"

"I'm here, Sanjar. And Lady Bahiga has found a spring pouring out of the rock behind the hut. We have water."

"How did you get here?" he asked Bahiga.

"Never mind that."

*   *   *

They helped Sanjar to a rock and Bahiga sat beside him while Tadros and Rhoorogh dug a grave for the dead man. The old man, embarrassed by Bahiga's presence, fussed around the graveside, muttering that this was no place for a woman. As they carried the corpse out and buried it, Bahiga uttered incantations for the dead. "He will not rise again," she said.

"Now," she said when it was done, "the Emerald Tablet."

Sanjar regarded her with astonishment.

"There is no time to lose," Bahiga said.

10 · The Roman Trail

"THE GREEKS TRAVELLED this coast by sea, but the Romans weren't so much at home on the water. They couldn't handle it and got washed away by the currents. If you set sail in Iskandriya, you see, and you missed the harbour at Taposiris, the current carried you all the way to al-Baratum, and if you missed that you ended up in Spain. The Greeks loved this, of course, because it meant a few more days in a ship, but the Romans couldn't abide it, so they built a road. And because it took longer overland, and they only had carts to transport their provisions (there were not so many camels in those days) they set up stations along the way and dug wells. It was still green then, or greener than it is now, so they could grow enough food at these places to sustain a marching army. So organised. Not like us, living for the moment.

"There hasn't been much traffic through here since the Arabs came through at the time of the Conquest. They didn't leave much for the Romans, armies or otherwise. Looted and burned the lot, and filled in most of the wells. The Romans liked roads so they could move their armies about and keep order, but the Arabs liked to keep places inaccessible so no one could get up to mischief in the first place. People don't travel along the coast now, except in caravans, because they run out of supplies. Where did you think you were going to find water? Did you ever think of sailing? It would have been quicker."

Sanjar shook his head.

"You heroes," Bahiga went on. "All brawn and no brain."

She was silent for a while, and regarded the wide desert and the glimmer of silver sea beyond the cliffs.

"There is no shame," she said, "in not knowing how to fight the super-natural. I should be helpless before a sword, while you know how to fight a battle. Glory in your talents, but don't be discouraged by challenges you cannot meet. You face terrible obstacles: this is because you have powerful enemies. I will not be there to protect you against them all, Sanjar Mouseback, even if I wish to. Some you must fight yourself."

"You still shame me."

"No, Sanjar, I repeat: there is no shame. When you learn to be less of a hero and more of a mortal man, you will know there is no shame."

"More of a man? Some battles I do need to fight on my own. How do you know I would not have left the garden, had you not called me back? Or that I might have vanquished the ghouls had Rhoorogh not arrived? No matter what, you are always there, as though I'm a kitten which can't be left alone lest it get into mischief. Your words are very fine, my lady, but they strike fear into the heart of a man, fear of being indebted for one's life to a woman."

"Let's not quarrel."

"No, lest you think me short on gratitude."

"You do not understand the magic here, any more than you speak the language. Tadros helps you with one, let me assist with the other."

"Not when it comes to men's things, to the things only a soldier can do."

"Oh, we'll have more of that than I shall care to take part in. I trust losing one's temper will not happen often."

"If I have given you offence, I apologise. But I do not apologise for asking you to keep out of my so-called perilous situations, and leaving me to handle them myself."

She shrugged. "If that's what you want. Can we stop arguing now?"

"Very well, if you like."

She murmured his name again. "Mouseback. How did you come by that name?"

"You embarrass me," he said.

"How so?"

"It was a whim of my mother's, to save me from the evil eye. She was afraid for my strength, and when I was three years old she named me Mouseback so I should not lose it. She thought it would confuse the spirits."

"She did well."

"It became a joke."

"I am not laughing."

"The spirits seem to have caught up with me now, O lady. I have seen them at their worst."

"No Sanjar, Sanjar Mouseback, you have not seen them at their worst. The closer you get to the Emerald Tablet, the more dangerous they will be. And sometimes you will be forced to meet them alone. Only at the final confrontation will you prove what you have become."

"If I have failed you, I would as soon throw myself in the sea now and let the tide take me to al-Baratum."

"Sanjar, you haven't failed. But until now, you have only needed to be a hero to win battles. Now you are pitched against greater things. And now you must show what you are."

For a moment his heart stood still. She was here, beside him. He could see her, smell her fragrance.

At last he said: "I shall do this only that I might win your hand."
She shook her head.
"We must not speak of these things."

*　*　*

Night had fallen, and Bahiga had gone. Sanjar fell into a deep sleep to escape his sudden loneliness, while Tadros and the old man slept the effortless sleep of the young and the old, and Rhoorogh kept watch beside the embers of their campfire. Some hours later Rhoorogh woke Tadros, and settled himself down for his turn to sleep. They stirred when dawn broke over the desert ridge, brewed coffee, filled their bottles and water skin from the spring, and resumed their journey to the west.

This water lasted two days, but by that time they had reached the next of the Roman stations. Here they found the crumbled ruins of a small town, its stones blackened by the conflagration of centuries before. In the midst of these ruins was a pool of stagnant green water and, nearby, a brick-walled well which had been repaired for the use of passing travellers. There was even a wooden bucket hanging from a rope.

The water was slightly brackish, but more drinkable that it might have been in view of their nearness to the sea. They drank, rested, filled their bottles and moved on, not wishing to linger in such a place so full of hidden memories and broken dreams.

Thus a pattern was set as they travelled the coast. Every three days or so they encountered the remains of another station, and at each of these they found water. Meanwhile their provisions were dwindling, and though each night they kindled a fire and baked bread in the ashes, they had besides only dates and small cakes of hard cheese purchased from a Greek merchant in Iskandriya.

At last the ridge which had obscured the sea almost all the way from Iskandriya came to an abrupt end, and soon afterwards they reached the date-palmed fringes of the oasis of al-Baratum where they were almost blinded by the whiteness of the sand and the bright turquoise of the sea. Weary and hungry, they trudged into the town, Sanjar riding Moonleap, Tadros and the old man astride the mules, and Rhoorogh with the camel with its almost empty saddlebags bringing up the rear.

*　*　*

A grey light filtered into the bare grey cell where nothing could be heard but the rhythmic scratching of a quill pen and the occasional scrolling of a page. A knock came at the door, and a monk entered. He whispered a few words before ushering in a tall, dark figure in a black cloak. The newcomer knelt and kissed the Abbot's hand.

The Abbot rose to his feet. "Your response has been swift, and we are grateful that you came," he said.

"I crossed with my page from Antioch to Cyprus, and thence to Iskandriya," the other said. "It took but a few days."

"I compliment you on your knowledge of Arabic."

"Alas, I am still not comfortable with Arabic."

"Then we shall speak French," the Abbot said, slipping easily into the other's language. "Please feel at home here. I trust you encountered no difficulties when you arrived at Alexandria?"

"Your messenger accompanied me, and your agent, the monk, met my ship. They took care of the formalities."

"Very good."

"It is my first time here, but I have heard of your political troubles."

"And you know that is why we sent for you."

"I do"

"We can talk when you have rested."

"First tell me, Father, why you chose me, and called me so far."

"Well," the Abbot said, reseating himself on his stool and gesturing his guest to a bench next to the desk. "Well, where shall I start. I had better start with the Caliph."

"I know about the destruction of the Holy Sepulchre."

"Yes, but that was ten years ago. His behaviour to us Christians has of late become a little less, well, abandoned. Ever since he declared himself the Messiah he has shown more tolerance to those of his subjects not of the Muslim faith. A few years ago Christians were forced to wear heavy wooden crosses round their necks, and Jews stars, Stars of David. That's all stopped now. But now that he thinks he's the Messiah it's the turn of the Muslims to feel betrayed, not by his tolerance to others but by his desecration of their – of his – faith. They know he isn't the Messiah, but what can they do? Do take some refreshment, please."

A monk had entered carrying a tray of sherbet. The visitor took the proffered glass, but the Abbot waved the tray aside.

The visitor remarked on the fine glassware.

"Glass is one of our legacies from the past," the Abbot smiled. "An Egyptian invention, and manufactured near Alexandria ever since."

"I have heard many tales of the splendours of the past buried beneath the sand."

"There has been too much iconoclasm." the Abbot said seriously. "Too much destruction, by too many ignorant people, much of it incited by ignorant monks. They have destroyed the past without stopping to learn its secrets. So much has been lost. So much knowledge, so much beauty.

"And so much magic," he whispered.

"What?" asked the visitor, surprised.

"I digress," the Abbot said.

"But I did not catch your last words."

"I was merely commenting on the loss caused by these fanatical and ill-educated iconoclasts, and all in the name of religion. The monks, the early monks, you see, did not appreciate the wisdom of their pagan forebears."

"But father, you cannot suggest that the condition of mankind before Christendom was preferable to ours?"

"Oh no, indeed not, do not misunderstand me. I merely wish to point out that knowledge, once lost, cannot be rediscovered in its original form. And to know if it is worth discarding, one must first understand it. This the iconoclasts did not do. They destroyed it, got rid of it, no questions asked. There was much beauty in the old world, and much wisdom. But some of it was preserved, and hidden like your treasures buried in the sand. Some, like Alexander, in his wisdom, saw what would happen to the old world, and concealed their secrets from those who would destroy or, even worse, misuse them. And that is why I have sent for you."

"For me?"

"This madman, our Caliph, has commissioned an agent, a fighting man, a veteran of many wars, and sent him on a venture. We think he has sent him to search for one of these treasures, and when he has found it to bring it to him at al-Qahira. The object he could be seeking is so magical, so precious, that if al-Hakim possesses it he will have the power to do anything he wishes, perhaps even to control the world. We can forget our own religion, my friend. We can forget the sanctity of the Holy Cross. There will be no place for Christians, or Muslims, or Jews. If al-Hakim is to be stopped, then the object he wants must not be found. We don't know where it is – it has been lost for thirteen hundred years. But this agent is clever, and he could find it. And I am calling, on you, as a Christian and a knight, to prevent its discovery."

"How may I do that?"

"You must be our champion, and kill the Caliph's man."

*   *   *

Far back along the coast near Iskandriya, Guhar, the horse thief and former captain of the guard, stalked the Ghawarzee. The dance troupe had diverted his attention from Sanjar, whose magic horse had brought him nothing but ill luck – and he saw no reason to throw good after bad.

For some days he lurked near the gypsy camp, keeping his distance, yet he did not know that it was hard to hide from the Ghawarzee, and they were well aware of his presence. One day, as he hid in a clump of reeds near the camp, a lovely young girl in a gossamer veil passed by, singing to herself in a clear tone. The next day she passed him again. He began to look out for her, and one day he heard her name called by other girls at play. "Selima!" they called, "Selima, come and play with us!" But the girl kept on singing, and walked on.

One day she returned with a basket of figs on her head. She carried her burden with an effortless grace, swinging her hips and striding straight ahead on her long legs. As luck would have it, as she drew alongside him she slipped on a patch of mud and her basket jolted, spilling figs about her shoulders to roll on the ground. She set down her basket so she could pick up the dropped figs, and at that point Guhar leapt from his hiding place.

"Lady, O lady, allow me," he said. "Please do not put your fair hands in the dirt."

"Kind sir, you honour me greatly. Do not put yourself to any inconvenience on my behalf."

"For so exquisite a being, what might have proved only a slight inconvenience becomes a great honour."

"Sir, I am but a gypsy girl, quite unfit to accept a favour from a grand ghazi such as yourself."

Guhar was smitten. Her black eyes regarded him from above the veil and seemed to smoulder, black and round as they were, like a buffalo's.

"Allow me," he said, and shouldered the basket.

He asked her name – though he already knew it – and she told him. "Selima," he said. "That is the most beautiful name I ever heard."

When they drew near to the camp, however, he remembered that he could not be seen with her, and put the basket down.

"I would not wish to compromise you," he said. "But promise me you will allow me to speak with you again."

To his surprise she said she would. As he gazed after her, he felt a changed man. Now he must find a way of approaching the gypsies, and he began to devise a plan. He could hardly hope to win their alliance, so he settled on disguise.

*   *   *

Al-Baratum was a little town of wide streets broken by palm and fig groves. The houses were spacious and graceful, their façades supported by marble pillars, their sandy gardens filled with scented trees. The low, whitewashed shops bustled with activity. The streets were swept clean, with walls and even paving stones of scrubbed white limestone. The townspeople, most of whom appeared to be Greek, regarded Sanjar and his friends with cautious stares.

The first thing on the minds of the travellers was food. Here the staple seemed to be fish: all sizes and kinds of fish were spread on trestles beside the road, or spilled in barrels from the shops, or were arranged over charcoal grills on the sea front.

The town was pleasant to them in several ways. Since it was so far from al-Qahira, the Caliph's edict preventing daylight trade was not effective here. Nor was the one binding women to their homes. Women here strolled freely in the streets, and talked and laughed with the men as in any other country, while plump dogs roamed from stall to stall looking for fish heads. Rid of the anxiety that paced the streets of the capital, al-Baratum was a pleasant town, and the elegance of its villas and the beauty of its coast added to their exhilaration.

As they walked among the fish stalls they attracted a large crowd of onlookers who questioned them about their origins and travels, or were merely content to look, or now and again to press a brave finger against Sanjar's silver-studded cloak. They were overawed by the beauty of Moonleap, and all swore they had never seen such a horse, which was doubtless true since no other horse existed such as she. All expressed their wonder at their having travelled by land with a single camel: all, or all those who had ever left al-Baratum, thought only to go by sea.

Although Sanjar did not mention his allegiance to the Caliph al-Hakim, the people of al-Baratum asked many questions about him, and about life in al-Qahira. They seemed grateful that they lived so far from the capital: the Caliph, they said, seldom bothered them, apart from sending his tax collectors and an occasional troop of soldiers to the border a few leagues further along the coast. The soldiers who rode back to al-Qahira lingered as long as they could before they left al-Baratum, as though savouring the freedom the distance from their barracks gave them. Men were never sent twice to a post on the border.

The old man, relishing the attention, related the story of the ghouls, shedding copious tears as he described the death of his family, and even more as he told how Sanjar had rescued him from the same fate. With this tale to his credit, which to these people who so feared the desert counted more than any tales he could tell of heroism in war, Sanjar found himself borne along by the crowd until he and his companions were ushered into a large house in the middle of the town. There scented water was poured over their hands, and they were given goblets of ale and told to continue their tales. At length dishes of fish and bread were brought in, and they feasted and talked. Yet they did not speak of their service to the Caliph, or Iskander or Zerzura, or the Emerald Tablet or the Qadi's daughter, but only of wars and battles, and distant lands, and trials in the desert.

"This too was a famous town," one of the merchants said. "Cleopatra stayed here, the great Cleopatra herself, when the town went under its old name of Paraetonium. She bathed here, in the sea, and she anchored her fleet in the harbour, and here she and Antony spent their last hours alone before he sailed to Cyrene, and she to Iskandriya, where they later killed themselves, of course. This was not always such a peaceful place, so full of pleasure as it is now. It has had its moments."

They stayed there until nightfall, when it was time to look for a place to sleep. There was an abundance of inns in the town, and they chose one near the beach, set in a garden of roses and hibiscus still in bloom despite the lateness of the year. The stabling was good – more than good enough for the old man and Rhoorogh to spread their bedrolls – while Sanjar was given a lime-washed room with a deep horsehair bed and linen sheets, and a couch for Tadros. Careless of their situation and with a mind only for creature comforts, they slept until the morning sun seeped through the cracks in the shutters. Only when they woke did they remember the past weeks and days.

Their reflection was broken by a commotion outside in the courtyard.

The disturbance seemed to be caused by the old man, who was hopping from one unsteady leg to the other and shouting wildly. Now that he was no longer camouflaged by the desert, he was conspicuous in his long grey beard and sandy-coloured rags.

"We'll have to clean him up," Tadros commented.

"We'll have to leave him here," Sanjar replied. "He's too much trouble to take along."

And then they saw why he was shouting. A mounted figure in black robes rounded the trees into view. It was a man of the Caliph's guard, and he seemed to be trying to address the old man.

"No, go away!" the old man was screeching. "I've paid my taxes! Leave me in peace! Get away, you brute of a soldier! Can't you see I'm an old man, not worth hounding? What do you want with me?"

The innkeeper had run into the yard, and with him a servant or two, and they were busily trying to shoo the old man back to the stable, clearly nervous of upsetting the Caliph's man. But the old man still struggled and shouted, even as the mounted soldier turned his black horse, kicked his heels, and rode away.

"Is he after us?" asked Tadros.

"Without a doubt."

"Should we leave?"

"We cannot stay. But that is because we have to find the Emerald Tablet, not because we fear the Caliph's men. I wonder, though, where is Captain Battusta, and I feel I should have asked Bahiga that question. Who is this man, who rides out here when there has been no sign of the Captain?"

"No sign of Captain Battusta, nor of Captain Guhar."

They had last seen Guhar, the horse thief, before he slipped his bonds when a prisoner of the Ghawarzee, soon after the trickery of the monks at Wadi Natroun. Since then there had been neither sight nor word of him, but they did not doubt he was not far behind, waiting to claim his revenge and Moonleap.

"Pray check my horse," Sanjar said. "And order breakfast and packed food. This may be a pleasant way to pass the time, but we have a task to do."

Tadros went down to the stable where Rhoorogh, who was becoming more civilised by the day, had brought a meal conjured from the kitchen of freshly baked bread and eggs to soothe the old man, who was still weeping with indignation. Sanjar looked out over the garden to the white beach and the turquoise sea and reflected on the Caliph's quest.

Only a day before they had been trudging dry and footsore through the desert, with scorpions in their path and ghouls and jinn lurking behind every rock. Now they were in a peaceful town, where rich, seafaring merchants dropped anchor to barter rich pickings from Venice and Marseilles and Catalan in return for water. The sea was treacherous, but these were Greeks, more at home on the water than on land, who kept a home in every port. A wife too, without a doubt. There were perils in a life at sea, but Bahiga was right: it was better than crossing the desert. And was not such a life, a life based on winds and crops and fashions, preferable to a life based on commands and warfare? Was it not better to owe one's taxes to a king, than to owe one's life?

Sanjar pictured the Caliph sending a citizen of this town to find Iskander's Tablet, and laughed. Yet he would have wished a thousand times to be a citizen of the town.

What had Bahiga said: there is no time to lose?

His doubts over the wisdom of his mission were growing. At first he had barely questioned his duty: when challenged by Bahiga, he had cited his command. When she wished him to surrender his quest, he had denied her. Still she was protecting him. Was her protection born of love? He knew it was not: such a woman would have the strength to sacrifice her love, and even her lover, if she thought it right to do so. Then why had she seemed to cease her struggle to change his mind about finding the Emerald Tablet, and why did she now appear to be abetting him?

Perhaps she knew him better than he knew himself. Perhaps she knew he would never give the Tablet to the Caliph. The Caliph certainly did not trust him to turn it over, for why else did he employ so many spies to track him down? Sanjar felt himself a knight played on the chessboard by the principal characters of the game: al-Hakim, the King, and Bahiga, the Queen. Yet perhaps he was not even a knight, perhaps he was merely a pawn.

Yet whatever the outcome of his search for the city of Zerzura, where the Emerald Tablet might lie, he would not drag behind him the other pawns in this game. Tadros and Rhoorogh would stay here in al-Baratum, where they could pay their way if he left them some pieces of silver. He himself would travel on with Moonleap. What he would accomplish, he could only do alone. He could not meet Bahiga's challenge if he had dependents or followers. He would leave that night, while they slept, but he must be sure they would not pursue him.

Tadros returned shortly after the noon prayer to find Sanjar in the garden, seated on a bench and deep in contemplation.

"I have found a scholar of the town," Tadros said. "He is a teacher, an old Greek man who once studied with the Greek monks in Iskandriya. He has heard the legend of Zerzura, where a city, with a locked gate, is hidden in the desert. He believes Iskander built it when he was looking for the army of Cambyses which had been lost in a sandstorm. He told me also of an oasis south of here, where men marry men because the women are of such outstanding beauty that they dare not lie with them, and where the cloth and baskets they weave surpass any others. He says we must pass through there to reach Zerzura, and he says we should leave the horses there, because they will not survive more than a day further south. I think we can trust him to say nothing to anyone."

Sanjar mulled silently over the boy's words. It would be better, then, to take the camel, and leave Moonleap in the care of Tadros.

"Master, you aren't saying anything, but I know what you're thinking. You want to ride on alone now, and leave me here with Rhoorogh. But you can't do that. You need us now. Rhoorogh is strong, and you have seen how he can fight demons. Leave me in the oasis if you must, but I will travel with you as far as I can. It is not safe for me to remain here, nor Moonleap. The Caliph is after you. So is Guhar. I will hold my tongue and die rather than speak, if they catch me, but do not leave Moonleap until we reach the oasis. There we can paint her, and hide her in the reeds with the men who marry men."

"This is not your quarrel, Tadros."

"Yes, it is mine, it's my country's. The Caliph is dangerous, and you need my help. You don't speak Coptic. Your colloquial Arabic isn't brilliant. You still don't know the ways here, you're a foreigner and people know it. And you're working for the Caliph, which makes you everyone's enemy."

"Not everyone. Only Christians, Copts like you. And the Jews."

"No Sanjar, everyone. Everyone hates al-Hakim. The Muslims more than anyone. You're a Muslim, and you're working for him, and no one will trust you or spare you."

"But al-Hakim is a Muslim. Why do they hate him?"

139

"Because of the Qur'an thing, of course."

"What Qur'an thing?"

"Surely you know about the Qur'an thing?"

"No, I don't know what you're talking about."

Tadros sat down on the grass at Sanjar's feet.

"Well, he started by banning the pilgrimage to Mecca, and then he banned Ramadan."

Sanjar looked ashen-faced at Tadros. "He did *what?*"

"He stopped the fast. People weren't allowed to fast."

"But if we don't fast, we are not Muslims!"

"That's right. He wanted everyone to worship him."

For some moments Sanjar was speechless. Than he said: "That's what Bahiga said. First he was the Messiah, and then he was the Pharaoh. But what did you say about the Qur'an?"

"He tried to substitute his own name for the name of Allah."

In his own language, Sanjar cursed the Caliph.

"After a while someone wisely told him that the Messiah wasn't called to earth to replace God," Tadros said. "They say it was the Qadi."

"Al hamda'llulah."

"But you wait till Ramadan."

Sanjar was deeply shocked. He knew so little about this country. Perhaps he had been speaking too little to the people, or perhaps the people were ashamed to be governed by such a blasphemer, and did not talk of the things which caused their shame. Now it appeared the Caliph was nothing more than an apostate. His loyalty to al-Hakim, his doubts about the Tablet and his plan to leave his companions flew away with the breeze. He sent Tadros back into town to fill their packs with provisions and fodder. He knew, too, that he could not even abandon the old man, for he would be sought out and tortured or executed – if he did not give away their secrets, for they had been unwise enough to speak freely before him.

That night they dined on the finest delicacies the inn had to offer, and at dawn of the next day they rode out of al-Baratum. As they left the town was stirring in preparation for the day: stall holders were setting up in the market, and there was some activity around the port as labourers loaded a departing ship with supplies. Sanjar thought of Cleopatra, and of her sad farewell to Antony. How many lovers had parted on this shore, and how many dreams had died?

* * *

Bahiga had one more task to fulfil before she could leave al-Qahira. She requested an audience with her father, and some hours later he summoned her to his apartment, where he sat before a window on a chair inlaid with mother-of-pearl.

It was important that he listened to her, so she appeared the dutiful daughter, bowing before him, and enquiring after his health and well being. She seated herself on a footstool beside him, and waited for him to speak.

The Qadi began to sweat and fidget, and mopped his brow with a yellow silk handkerchief. Life was not so easy nowadays. He was much taken up with the Caliph's foreign politics, and although this meant he was spared the exhausting daily scrutiny of the inkblots he was given the equally exhausting task of smoothing diplomatic paths much ruffled and furrowed by his master, who saw little point in giving way to what he saw as the petty demands of heathens and foreigners. The Qadi saw all too well the expediency of diplomacy, but sometimes he wished his master would fall into the one of the traps he was so busy laying for himself, and from which he, the Qadi, spent so much time trying to save him. A tolerant man at heart, the Qadi had tried his best to dissuade al-Hakim from his more headstrong acts, such as the destruction of the Holy Sepulchre at Jerusalem, which had caused such outrage in Europe and Constantinople ten years before. He had also tried to curb his aggressions abroad, which were mostly of a provocative nature but were dangerous enough. The Qadi was tired. He had all but forgotten Sanjar.

"Father, we have spoken of these things before," Bahiga said at last. "If the Caliph possessed the Emerald Tablet it would be disastrous. Can we not combine to stop him?"

"Daughter, I have told you that I have no intention of letting him have it. The Turk reports to me. And as long as he does not attempt to keep it – and I shall foil any such attempt – I shall make sure the Tablet is beyond the reach of... Daughter, you know we cannot speak of this. The walls have ears."

"Leave it to me, Father. I beg you to leave it to me. The Caliph has no sway over me, he cannot force me to surrender it, or anything, and I owe him nothing. Please, Father, leave it where it is safe, with me."

The Qadi hesitated. "Bahiga," he said, "I know you are strong, and I know you want and will do anything in your power to stop it falling into al-Hakim's hands. But you are still only a woman. You must leave this with me."

"Father, you sadden me, because you know that only one of us can win."

"But we are agreed! We neither of us wants al-Hakim to have the Tablet! Where is the quarrel? Where is the conflict? What is the problem?"

Bahiga smoothed her robe. "Father, I know you are planning to leave al-Qahira, and I know you are not planning to travel the slow and ordinary way. If we are both falling over each other out there in the Western Desert, not trusting each other, both of us trying to control Sanjar and get our hands on the Tablet, we shall probably lose it. Besides, we aren't the only ones looking for it. The Caliph's soldiers are out there, and Sanjar has made some enemies who want to find him – and it – too. Let me handle Sanjar, while you stay here and keep your eye on the Caliph. It's much too dangerous for you to travel this way, and dangerous for you to stay within reach of the Caliph. You must prepare to leave al-Qahira once and for all but, and this is important, Father, so listen carefully, you must take every part of you with you, because there'll be no coming back. So you can't leave al-Qahira on this jaunt of yours running after the Tablet. When you travel you must go the ordinary way, like everybody else. Do you hear, Father? You must escape! You must prevent his getting the Tablet, and you must be free to escape. He will show no mercy. No one can expect any mercy."

"What about you?"

"Don't worry about me, Father. I can return to my body. It's easier for me."

"Your powers," the Qadi whispered, "are so much greater than mine. Mine are just a shadow of yours."

"It really doesn't matter how great is your power or mine, as long as we do not use it for evil. You are too careless, Father, careless above all of your own safety."

The Qadi looked despairingly at his daughter.

"If only it were a simple matter of finding the Emerald Tablet. But I fear there is more to more to our troubles than this. Bahiga, there is something you must know, although what I have to say will anger you. I find myself torn between what I should feel as a father and a man and what I should feel as a father and a magician."

A chill gripped Bahiga's heart. "What is it you are trying to say?"

"I hardly know how to tell you, but I can see I shall have to. The Caliph, as you know, has been busy at his affairs in other parts of his empire. He has not exactly forgotten the Tablet, but he also has his mind on other things. He hasn't been too prudent in his actions, as you doubtless know, especially in regard to our Christian and Jewish friends, and there is, I have to say it, much discontent in the Caliphate, and just as much outside. Well from time to time, as it happens, it is necessary to smooth the way a little, and since this is not a favourite pastime of my master's, such tasks often fall to me. In this case, though, and I swear it, this had nothing to do with me at all, and if it had such a suggestion would never have been made." The Qadi shrugged helplessly.

"What suggestion, Father?"

"Some foolish young man came to the court, an emissary from Europe, very distinguished and handsome, I believe, and the Caliph, with every good intention, I am sure, and wishing to please the man, entered into some degree of intimacy with him, or companionship, quite unusual for al-Hakim, though you know how informal he can be. Anyway this European, who is, I am told, quite well bred and indeed something of a royal prince, told al-Hakim he had heard that there dwelt at court a beautiful and accomplished woman, and that he desired her hand. That woman was, of course, none other than you, my daughter."

Bahiga paled. "But Father..." she began.

"My dear child, of course when the Caliph told me this I made all sorts of excuses, since I, as I have said, might if I were another father acquiesce with gratitude to such a union, but as the father that I am, with other... gifts... and knowing yours, I know you would not agree to the match for reasons not many people, and certainly not the Caliph, would understand. I protested, at last, that in accordance with your religion you could not marry a non-Muslim, but even that failed, for it seems the young man is from Cordoba, and has converted to Islam. To put it bluntly, Daughter, to save our skins you should consent to this match and be away with you and off to Europe, taking your father with you. But I know what marriage would mean. And I am sensible enough to know that, however much I pleaded – if indeed I wished it, and to be honest, I am not altogether sure that I do – I could never force you into a union against your will, since I'm well aware you would sooner turn a suitor into a dog than marry him. There. I've said my piece. What are we to do, Bahiga?"

Bahiga was filled with horror, but she grasped her father's predicament, and struggled to regain her composure. "First, Father, I must say I'm surprised and grateful that you are so understanding and sympathetic to my position. You obviously know marriage cannot be a state to which I can aspire, and though most fathers, in their ignorance, wish to see their daughters well married, you still seek to protect me from such a threat. I know that, in our society, you face disgrace if I remain unmarried, and you must be very tempted to persuade me to conform to what is expected of me. Perhaps it would comfort you if you knew that very often I wish I were like other women, free to marry and bear children, and to hope for a husband I could love. But it can't be, Father. I can't bear to repeat my mother's life, and you know, even though it must be very painful for you to be reminded of it, that she would wish it no other way. I have other duties, and I must do what I am called to do. This European prince sounds very fine, and life in exile might be a prudent step for us both, but it is not my destiny."

The Qadi had expected such a reply, but even so he had entertained a slight glimmer of hope that Bahiga would accept the Caliph's suggestion. Now life would be difficult indeed. Bahiga might well wish she were like other women. So did he.

"I suppose," he snapped, "that if you were to marry at all, you would ask me to arrange a marriage with that young Turk."

"Sanjar?" Bahiga asked. "He's certainly charming and handsome, but I'm not sure about his character. He seems to think himself the Caliph's man, and it remains to be seen what he does with the Tablet."

"You can't fool me, Bahiga. I've seen the way you've run to his aid each time he's threatened by some misfortune, as if he isn't capable of taking care of himself. He's certainly a one to court trouble, and perhaps it were best if he failed to survive. The Caliph might then forget this foolishness. If all is as you say and you do not trust this Sanjar (which I doubt) then perhaps you are casting these obstacles in his way yourself, for he seems to have met more than his fair share on his travels."

"You know that other forces were activated at the very moment he began his mission, and I should not wish him to be destroyed by an evil and inferior power," Bahiga said. She had been touched by her father's loyalty, and decided there would be no harm in taking him into her confidence, or partly so. "There are so many forces at work," she said, "that I believe they are protecting the Tablet. Perhaps the time has come when it should be found. Found and destroyed, before it falls into the wrong hands and we are all lost forever. If Sanjar is the man to find it, we must help him. But we must also protect him from the consequences."

"And after that you will know his character?"

"Only then."

"Pray you are right."

"Sanjar is not the only one whose trust must be put to the test."

"Do you mean me?" The Qadi pointed a finder to his fat chest and stared wide-eyed at his daughter. "Take care, or I'll be settling a marriage for you – and I can force you into it if I desire. Now, what are we to do? How are we to deflect this prince's advances?"

"Can't you say I'm betrothed to another?"

"But you are not, and everyone knows that. We could say you have taken a vow of virginity, but that would arouse suspicion, and in any case the Caliph wouldn't accept it – it sounds too Christian. Perhaps we can give you a disease."

"No!"

"A weak heart, perhaps, like mine."

"Father, for once, be honest! Just say I will not, or you will not! No one can force me to marry!"

"It is al-Hakim's express request."

"He can't!"

"Command."

"Then let us go into exile anyway. Once the Tablet is found and destroyed, we can escape. The Caliphate is not so vast that it has no borders... a boat from Iskandriya, and we are safely in Constantinople, or in Spain! You can make your way to the coast saying you are going to hold a session of the assizes, and I can travel secretly. The servants won't betray us!"

"We have other means."

"We can't go that way! If you leave your body behind, you can never be whole! If they destroy what you leave behind, they will destroy you! You have to leave the normal way, Father, in a sedan or on a horse, like other people do! And for that reason, so you are not vulnerable to the Caliph's whims, I beg you not to leave al-Qahira in an out-of-body state."

"I take my body. I am an adept, you know!" the Qadi said indignantly.

"I know you are an adept, and I know you take your body and everyone where you are going thinks you are there. But you are not really there, and you know it! But you cannot take every part of you, and since you leave something behind you can never be complete! You have to return!"

"I might not need anything else."

"But it doesn't last! Sooner or later you have to eat, you have to go back, or you will die."

"It might be better."

"Father, when you travel this way, what do you take with you?"

"I take my mind and my body."

"And what do you leave behind?"

"I leave a replica of myself, lying on my bed, as if dead."

"Father, that is not a replica, that is you! And, don't you see, if someone who knew no better found you, would they not bury you? And what of me, lying as I shall be in my own room? Will they not say, 'Oh, here they lie, father and daughter, dead of some plague, let's get rid of the bodies.'? One of us must stay! At the very least, the Caliph could destroy us!"

"He will not make a move until he is certain he is not going to get the Tablet. We have plenty of time. He depends on us, on me, I mean, and your Turk. We can make our escape then, if you still think we must."

"I hope you are right."

Bahiga took her father's hand.

"I know we are not always in harmony," she said. "I am sometimes impatient, and you think I do not love you. But I do, and I don't want any harm to come to you."

"Humph," was all the Qadi said.

"Well, you vex me, you would vex anybody. Running off to Europe under the protection of a suitor, indeed! We can run off under our own protection."

But Bahiga well knew she was a burden to her father. If the Caliph really favoured the match and the Qadi did not promote it, he might find himself in disfavour.

And so a plan began to form in her mind. She wished no harm to the European, whom she never knew existed until this day, but she might be forced to cause him some inconvenience, if only for the sake of her father. She might be wise to agree to the marriage. The nuptials need not actually take place, and she certainly need not lose her maidenhead....

"Father, this wedding should go ahead," she said.

"No, not on my account. I forbid it."

"Let us only insist it take place abroad, and we can escape the country, then easily find a reason why the marriage should not take place. After that we shall be free."

"It is too dangerous."

"No, it will be easy."

"You'd turn him into a mouse, I suppose, on your wedding night."

"It won't have to go as far as that. I will, I promise you, make sure this marriage does not take place at all. Only let us pretend it will, and go along with the Caliph's wishes."

"It's a good plan."

"Only one thing, Father, that I ask you, if I will do it."

"And what is that?" But he already knew.

"Stay here in al-Qahira. Let me follow Sanjar and chase the Tablet. Do not come as well"

The Qadi bowed his head.

"I fear the Caliph's wrath over this matter more than over the other," he said. "I cannot agree."

"If you come, it will place us both in danger."

"I may have no choice. It depends on al-Hakim's decree."

"How this man angers me! That our lives depend on such an imbecile!"

"Hush, the walls have ears."

Bahiga had one more request of her father, who in his present mood seemed eager to please her in one way, if not in another.

"Allow my nurse to return."

"She shall come back."

"Thank you "

"And, Bahiga, let us not close the chapter on this marriage. I shall tell the Caliph you accept, but plead a little time. We shall get the Emerald Tablet business over first, and if I can, I shall stay here and leave you to use your skills in the Western Desert."

Bahiga smiled.

"It makes me so happy that we can be, at least mostly, in agreement. I hope it stays that way."

"Yes, yes," the Qadi said impatiently. "But with al-Hakim in charge, who can tell?"

* * *

That night the Caliph called for the Qadi. He had received a delegation sent by the Byzantine Emperor Basil from Constantinople and was in a bad mood. He was making no attempt to entertain his guests. The Caliph considered court banquets a waste of money, but since they were dull affairs everyone was glad that they seldom took place. Instead he was about to set off on a ride through al-Fustat to cool his indignation by harassing the people of the town, while leaving the welfare of his guests in the hands of his sister, Sitt al-Mulk.

As the audience drew to a close the Qadi chose a moment to breach the subject foremost on his mind. "Sire," he began in a tone as far removed as possible from the obsequious, which al-Hakim on most days, abhorred, yet not lacking in the respectful, "Sire, if I might command just a moment of your attention, I have some news you may find gratifying. I have given some thought to the young prince's request for my daughter's hand, and I shall be happy to oblige him if you so wish it."

"Hmm!" the Caliph said, believing these words a mere charade, for the Qadi's daughter would have to marry if he, al-Hakim, commanded it. "Well, if you are willing, and she herself holds no objection – for I believe she has a will of her own, and it would be better for us not to disregard it – then the marriage had better go ahead. I'm sure it will be a relief to you to get her married off, since you can't hide from me that she has caused you some grief with her headstrong ways. Were she anyone else's daughter... So, that's settled. We can tell the lucky young man to expect his bride, and there's an end to it."

"Sire, I request the grace of a few weeks. My daughter is my only child, and the only woman in my household, for you see I did not remarry after the death of her mother, nor did I even take a concubine, since I have been so wrapped up in my duties that I have found no time for such pleasures. So, if you have no objection, I beg that Bahiga may stay a little longer with me, since this will allow time to prepare for the wedding and embroider her gowns and so on, and will give us some last weeks together before she leaves me for a foreign land."

"This is quite touching," the Caliph said. "I am not sure that such an independent woman deserves so much of her father's affection, but if that is your view then I'll agree to it. What are a few days or weeks here or there, so long as the betrothal is made and honour and expectations satisfied?"

The Qadi bowed. "Indeed, you are most gracious," he said. But his heart was pounding. It was not still when he arrived home, and Bahiga sent for the physician.

"I should prescribe a period of calm," the physician said after his examination. "But I know that state affairs give you no time for rest. Instead I shall order you to take motherwort and valerian to calm your nerves, and suggest you avoid anxiety where you can. A man in your state of health cannot take too many precautions."

Bahiga was beside herself, fearing she had contributed to her father's illness, and she sat with him until the following day when her nurse arrived. The nurse's joy at returning to her mistress was tempered by the instructions Bahiga gave her.

"Unless my father is called to the palace, do not let him out of your sight," she said. "He must eat only what the doctor prescribes, and what you cook. None of this magic food. I don't want him conversing with that wretched jinni. And if he says he wishes to leave al-Qahira, do your utmost to dissuade him. Make a nuisance of yourself if you have to. He won't send you away, I assure you."

The nurse wrung her hands. "Madam, you have always shown me the greatest sweetness and kindness, but I cannot say that for the judge. He's such a difficult man. And how can I contend with the supernatural in this house? If you go away, I cannot swear to be able to stand up to him."

"Do your best. I rely on you. Make him some of your honey cakes, and he'll be happy."

"If only it were as easy as honey cakes. Here he is now, ranting and raving about the cost of some dressmaker or other. Always something new to make a fuss about. What dressmaker? You have clothes fine enough, and indeed I have always done the finest embroidery on your dresses."

"Oh nurse, I have so much to tell you."

"Dressmaker, indeed. I wish the silly man would hold his tongue. Anyone would think there was going to be a wedding."

She paused, and looked long and hard at Bahiga.

"Young lady, what is it you have to tell me?"

Had she not been so disturbed the nurse's expression might have made Bahiga laugh, but this was nothing to take lightly. "Yes, I am to be married," she said quietly, casting her eyes to her hands which were nervously toying with the cord on her gown. "I am to go to Europe, and you are to come with me."

The nurse caught her breath.

"Madam, I know so little, but in my ignorance I understood you to say you would remain for ever unwed, lest you lose your special gifts, you said."

"Well, I am to marry, and that will be that."

"Why, pray?"

"It is the Caliph's wish."

"This is not the girl I left so recently. Why are you so changed?" And then she said, "Is it the Turk? I saw that you looked on him with favour."

"No."

The nurse sighed. "That's a pity. He was a fine soldier, so full of courage."

"Yes, I hope he's a good man. A lot depends on his being a good man."

The nurse watched her mistress carefully, saddened by her obvious disquiet, and said, half whispering: "Who is it, then?"

"I hardly know anything of him. But I have heard only good." She fought back a wave of tears.

The nurse reached out to take her arm. "You are despondent," she said soothingly. "But all is not lost. If you don't wish to go ahead with this marriage, we shall find a way out of it."

"You are kindness itself, nurse, and I'm so glad you are back. I know I can count on your loyalty. But just for now, shall we say there is to be a wedding, and there are dresses to be made? It's weeks away, and a whole continent lies between my bridegroom and me. Who knows what will happen?"

11 · Two Weddings

SANJAR AND HIS COMPANY rode several days south from al-Baratum to reach the Oasis of Amoun, where, as Tadros said, women went unveiled, and men married men. The vast oasis was fringed with date and doum palms set in patches of scrub where young girls grazed their flocks of black goats. The travellers aroused much curiosity, as the people lived in so remote and isolated a place that they saw few outsiders apart from caravan drivers. These made the nine-day journey from al-Qahira to bring wheat, flax and spices, and carried back the prize for which they took so much trouble, the black, sweet dates for which the oasis was famed.

Late in the afternoon, after travelling some leagues in from the desert, they came to a village of mud brick huts thatched with straw. They rented two of these, as well as stabling, and then Sanjar and Tadros took a stroll round the village, leaving Rhoorogh and the old man to attend to the animals and unpack their bedrolls.

*   *   *

Bahiga, on the one hand, was assembling silks and satins for her journey to Europe, on the other white linen to wear when she purified herself before she left to keep a watch on Sanjar. Since she wished to fast the next day she had decided to order an early supper, and had called several times for her nurse. Finally she heard her clattering up the stone stairs.

"Where have you been?" she scolded. "I have searched for you every-where."

"Pardon, madam, I was down in the kitchens. That donkey was so pleased to see me, it acts like it's human."

"Donkey?"

"The one that turned up lost, looking so forlorn. It's still down in the stables."

"I'd forgotten about it."

"Well, I just called in, and there it was, all over me. I should have sworn it had something to say."

Bahiga laughed. "Poor thing, it missed you!"

"So it seems. Down there in its stall, with nothing to do."

"We'd better find a job for it."

"I wish it would bring the water up," grumbled the nurse. "This new water carrier is never on time. The old one was a devil, but he was punctual. Funny, they say he just vanished one day."

"Well, I'm about to vanish as well, and I have a million things to do. As if this mission of the Turk's weren't enough, I have to prepare for the journey to Europe and list the things we shall take, and see that the Qadi takes his medication, and be fitted for clothes."

"Such fine velvet that came this morning! What a beautiful gown it will make! Shall you be wed in red velvet, madam?"

Bahiga shrugged. "Maybe."

"You don't seem too happy to discuss this wedding, so we won't. But I take it we are leaving."

"Yes, you can take it that it will be so."

"But what will your poor father do once you are gone? He'll have no one, poor man. He's a mischief maker, that's for sure, but it will be sad for him to be lonely."

"I don't think we shall leave him behind."

"But surely he can't leave the country!"

"Won't he come with me, to see me married? I should not wish to go through such a binding commitment without my father there to give my hand away. I'm sure the Caliph will spare him for so personal an affair."

The nurse took a deep breath, "Aye," she said doubtfully.

"Nurse, I know it means you must leave your family and your country. You are free to withdraw from any obligation to me, and stay with them."

The nurse shook her head firmly. "My place is with you. If God wills I should ever return, then I shall. It is only a short way over the sea, is it not?"

"Yes, only a short way. Perhaps even too close. But let us not be afraid, we must face the future with courage, all of us."

"I don't like to hear you say that, madam. Why, you never expressed any fear or concern about anything, and now you are telling us to face the future with courage! What can happen to us, unless some ill should befall your father, and we find ourselves without his protection and out on the street? But if you wed this foreign prince, our troubles will be over. Unless... oh, madam, you have thrown me into a confusion."

"It's best you just do as I say, and don't ask too many questions."

"Indeed, I see the wisdom of that. But still I pray no harm comes to your father, or we shall end up at the Caliph's mercy, and we all know how he disapproves of you."

Bahiga was too busy with her thoughts to listen. It was time to withdraw to herself and meditate, for she must soon leave, and this time for some days. She did not wish to take the risks she had run when she had last hurried to Sanjar's aid. To help him when he encountered the afarit of the slain man on the road to al-Baratum she had been forced to act quickly, but at much cost to her peace of mind and her well-being. Such an effort was exhausting, but also dangerous, because although she could travel without using sorcery – unlike her father, who relied on his magical skills and was not as gifted as she – if she failed to take proper care before she left she might not find her body there to return to. This time she must do things properly, for there was too much at stake for carelessness.

There was also her father to consider. Would he do as she asked him, and stay in al-Qahira? Or would the Caliph press him to leave? It would be better if no one but the Qadi and the nurse knew of her departure, for then it could not reach the ears of the Caliph. Such news would cause consternation now that the wedding was arranged, especially if the Caliph suspected her interference in the matter of the Emerald Tablet.

∗   ∗   ∗

The red sun sank quickly behind the dunes, and the chill night settled over the fig groves. Late-coming buffaloes with tired, hungry children on their backs threaded their way home for milking after a day spent grazing on the canal banks. As the grubby children shouted to each other they did not see the figure in the shadows of the fig trees, waiting desperately, as he did each evening, for the yellow-robed gypsy girl who was the object of his passion. The last buffaloes passed, and now there was no sound except for the breeze rustling through the wide fig leaves. He was startled by an eerie cry, but it was only a nightjar calling from the water.

At last she came, running lightly along the path. She fell into his arms, and when she had regained her breath she said: "Yes, they say you can ask about marrying me. But I fear that when they see you are a soldier, and belong to a station so much higher than mine, they will ask why you want a gypsy as your wife, so I think you should disguise yourself as a poorer man, a farmer, perhaps, and that would make them more inclined to accept your offer. Oh, and you must provide a dowry, but don't worry about that because money will do and since you are rich I know you have some."

Guhar, although now an outlaw, still thought of himself as a soldier, and certainly not as a farmer. But he saw the wisdom of a disguise, and was prepared to demean himself to win her. Besides he knew, though it seemed she did not (for she could not have seen him that night, when he had suffered such an indignity at the hands of her tribe) that he could not meet her relatives except in disguise. So what she was suggesting presented him with a perfect opportunity to obtain what he wanted, and without her

152

learning of his deceit. For he was sure that if she knew how the Ghawarzee had made a fool of him she would spurn him, and he could take no chances with her love now that he had drawn her so far. So he told her he agreed with her request.

"Do this, and we can be together for ever more," she begged, and giving him a final kiss she ran off into the night.

*   *   *

Sanjar and Tadros wandered through the village, where animals were being stalled for the night and men had gathered in front of their huts to smoke. They were greeted with words of welcome as they passed, but beyond that the inhabitants to a man treated them with studied indifference; while almost beside themselves with curiosity, they were too polite to put any questions to the strangers whose appearance and apparel were so very different from their own.

"Are they friendly, or not?" Sanjar said. "I think they are, because our host who lent us the huts was reasonably affable, yet perhaps they are not, since he had his eye on a coin or two, but perhaps they are, for they don't stare at us or follow us, yet perhaps they are not, because their very secretiveness means they could be up to some devilish business. And again, perhaps they are, for they greet us politely, yet perhaps not, for they do not invite us to join them. What do you think, Tadros?"

"Sometimes desert people like this used to come into the city, but I never had any reason to be afraid of any of them, and I don't think they deserve the reputation they've got. Perhaps the most they might do is help themselves to something, but I don't think they'll try anything like that while we're staying in their village, and I don't think they're up to anything sinister. What do we have they could steal, anyway?" Tadros cast an eye over the saddlebags.

"Nothing. Not yet. Unless anyone tried to get Moonleap again. But they'd have to get past Rhoorogh"

"Do you think were going to find the Emerald Tablet?"

"I just don't know. And perhaps Bahiga was right, and we shouldn't even be looking for it. I wish I knew what she meant, though, the last time we saw her, when she said there was no time to lose. Before she always said she did not want me or anyone else to find it, and now she says there is no time to lose. Could she have changed her mind, or could she..." He wondered whether he should say what was on his mind. "Could this be a trap? Or is it merely a test, to see what I will do with it? Does that mean she has so much faith in me that she will do this? Or am I just a fool? It has already crossed my mind that I'm only a pawn in this game. Perhaps it is time for us to withdraw."

Before Tadros could consider this, something unexpected occurred. They turned a corner and there, standing with two others, probably village men, was a tall, black-cowled monk. Had the monk uttered a greeting and stood his ground they would have passed him by without undue suspicion. But as soon as he saw them he started, drew his hood over his face, and darted away down a side street. Sanjar sped after him with Tadros on his heels, but the village was a maze of lanes and gardens and, as they turned corner after corner, the shadows played with the fleeing figure. All at once, it vanished. Sanjar ran in the only direction the monk could have taken, but there was no sign of him. He returned to Tadros.

"I'm sure I saw him go in there," Tadros said, pointing to a long hut that stood some way from the rest. "There doesn't seem to be anywhere else he could be."

Sanjar strode to the hut and knocked loudly on the door. At first no one answered, although he heard the sound of voices. Then the door was flung open.

He was surprised to see several pretty girls crowding in the doorway. They were laughing and gay, and were dressed in brightly coloured gowns of silk and chiffon threaded with silver, with jewels glittering in their black tresses and gold bangles on their arms. There was no sign of the monk. Laughing, the girls reached out and caught Sanjar by the hands, and drew him inside, and then called Tadros to enter.

The hut was warm and bright, lit by a huge lamp set in burnished copper. Smoke curled from a log fire burning in the hearth in the centre of the floor. It was furnished in a richness unexpected in such a village, with couches covered with rugs of fine wool and velvet, and silver jugs and ornaments and mirrors with frames encrusted in coloured glass and pearls. The girls chattered and smiled, and fingered their robes, and made laughing comments as they ran their soft hands over Sanjar's moustache and Tadros' smooth chin. They poured wine, and offered them sweetmeats from a silver bowl, and all the time muttering promises of love and tenderness.

Tadros was young and had seen little of the world. He had certainly never encountered anything like this. Were these the unveiled women of the Oasis of Amoun? His head spun. Here were fruits until now forbidden and denied being offered him as if free for him to take. The strict scruples of his upbringing flew to the wind, and he laughed in delight. "Wow!" he said.

But Sanjar was taken aback to see something so unexpected and so worldly in so remote a place, and tried to ask the girls who they were. They replied by giving him their names, which rolled off their tongues like pearls. He tried to say that what he really wanted to know was where were they from, and why were they there, but they took no notice and shut his mouth his kisses. Yet something seemed amiss, and he shook them off, but the more he tried to disentangle himself the more they clung, trapping him in their honey-coloured arms. So he gave in to their caresses, and sipped their wine, and allowed them to push him onto a couch, and then one of the girls began to sing. He had never heard such a sound. He had heard of mermaids singing, but if they did then they could never sing as sweet as this. Unused to the wine, drugged with the mingled scent of musk and jasmine which perfumed the girls' hair, and entranced by the sweet song, he relaxed. What was there to fear from them, after all?

It was useless to try to talk to the girls, for they only giggled and repeated names and words of love and seemed unable to say anything of sense or consequence. Yet in spite of his stupor he was determined they should not have their way, and equally determined not to allow them to seduce Tadros. To accept their attentions would be easy but that did not mean it was wise or right. He tried to frame a way of warning Tadros, but each time he spoke the girls kissed their delicate hands and put them to his lips. But he did not return their caresses, and refused more wine for fear he lost his head and did something he would later regret.

As his mind reeled in conflict, he was puzzled by the flight of the monk. Why had he run away? And had he really come here, to this hut? It was impossible, and Tadros must have been mistaken. He asked if only the girls were there, or if there were anyone else, but they just laughed. He asked if they understood his language, and to test them he said: "What pretty bangles you are wearing," and in answer they laughed even harder, and pulled off their armbands and offered them to him, so he knew they did understand, but were too silly or too cunning to make a coherent reply. So he said: "Are you sisters? Where is you father? Where are your brothers?" But they just nodded, and smiled, and muttered sweet-sounding, meaningless words.

Then the singing began again. The girl with the voice as sweet as anything he had ever heard sat beside the hearth and lifted her voice, and everything stood still, so nothing existed apart from her song. She sang without words, but she sang to the listener of whatever he dreamed it to be. To Tadros, she sang of the green fields along the banks of the Nile, the whispering sugar cane, and the girls who strolled beside the river carrying on their heads baskets of grapes and pomegranates. To Sanjar she sang of the rugged mountains of his homeland, and snow, and herds of wild horses sweeping over the Asian steppes. Her voice lulled them into a stupor, so they were meant to forget everything except that of which she sang.

Sanjar kept his eye on Tadros. The boy was usually the one to be alert to deceit or trickery, but he had abandoned himself to pleasures and delights of which, until now, he had only dreamed. Tadros was laying back on his couch lost in a sensual ecstasy, with a slender siren on either side and another at his feet, and staring entranced at the singing girl.

155

Sanjar shut his mind to the song and thought of Bahiga. It was not difficult for him to conjure her: her beauty was so noble, her character so good,
her words so wise that these silly, giggling girls were not even worthy of
hiding in her shadow. The worst he could imagine was that she should chose
this moment to spring once more to his aid. He did not need or desire her
help, and he hoped she was not aware of his situation.

It might have comforted him to know that she was not. At that very
moment, after having dined with her nurse, and having bathed and
anointed herself with essence of jasmine, and dressed in a white linen robe,
and after lighting white candles and purifying her room with incense, she
was deep in a trance of her own.

*   *   *

Sanjar could have put as stop to this play at any time, but he rather wished
to know what purpose it was serving, and why they had been led to this hut
filled with harlots, if, indeed, they had been led there and had not fallen on
it by chance. Tadros seemed to have lost his wits, but it was important that
Sanjar kept his. So he watched, and waited.

At last the song ceased, and the girls turned their attention to Sanjar. It
was hard to resist their caresses. When one tried to undo the buckle on his
cloak, he restrained her, but as he did so the girl who had moments before
been singing so sweetly tried to untie the belt that buckled Moonflinger.

So hastily had they entered, and so wary had he been, that he had not
disarmed himself. The girls had not remarked on this, and only now were
turning their attention to removing his sword. The girl, her face crumpling
into a frown, struggled with the belt. Sanjar moved to stop her, and as he
did so his cloak fell back, exposing Moonflinger's silver hilt. The girl's eye
fell on the hilt and the holy inscriptions engraved on it, and at once she fell
back. And then she hissed, wild as fire.

And so, before Sanjar's astonished eyes, the girl with the golden voice,
with her honey-coloured skin and raven hair, her saffron gown and her
silver bangles, began to disintegrate. Her flesh turned grey and mottled, her
limbs withered, and her long tresses fell to the ground as if torn out by
unseen hands. She seemed to have lost the use of her legs, which doubled up
under her so she fell to the floor and writhed, and her tongue darted in and
out of her mouth. And last of all her yellow silk dress crinkled and dried,
and sloughed off her body.

She lay, hissing, and then she raised the upper part of her body, her
tongue still darting, and prepared to strike.

Sanjar drew Moonflinger and faced the cobra, and then he sliced through
her body below the neck. The last thing she heard was the singing of

Moonflinger as the blade struck home. As the holy sword struck it emitted a pure blue light, the colour of angels.

There was a dreadful pause, and then the room darkened. In place of the copper lamp was a simple iron torch. The rich tapestries were nothing more than straggling vines, the carpets under their feet turned to sand and the couches to hard rock. At their feet maggots writhed in a tin bowl which had once held sweetmeats, while half a dozen serpents slithered over the severed body of the cobra to shelter in the rocky dark holes in the shadows.

Tadros was staring wide-eyed in horror and bewilderment. Never had an illusion been so cruelly shattered.

"Poor Tadros," Sanjar was saying. "Nothing comes easily, but you know that already, my friend."

"That's what it was," Tadros said, when at last he could speak. "Nothing but an illusion." He shivered, and stared at the shadows where the serpents had vanished.

"Well partner, you make the most classic picture of gloom I have ever seen," Sanjar said. "Have you seen the bright side?"

"Is there one?"

"There is, and it's this. We figured this one out ourselves. No rescues, no explanations."

Tadros managed a sheepish smile. "We did?"

"We're doing all right," Sanjar said.

Yet he was secretly disturbed. Tadros was probably right. The monk had not only entered the place and drawn them there, he had perhaps even invented it. Were not many monks highly versed in the skills of magic, especially the monks of Wadi Natroun?

The moon had risen. The boughs of the wayside trees traced a pattern overhead, and a falcon roosting on the tallest branch turned its head to watch as they walked by. They tried to trace their way back to their huts through the maze of streets, looking at the same time for the men they had seen talking to the monk, but it was late into the night and most of the people had withdrawn indoors. It was not easy to find their way, and they had walked well beyond the end of the village before they realised they were going the wrong way. Then they saw another falcon, and a third – or was it the same bird, following them on silent wings?

At last a familiar figure lurched in their direction. It was Rhoorogh, come to search for them.

"Never mind, Tadros, there are still the unveiled women," Sanjar consoled him that night before they fell asleep.

"And the men who marry men," chuckled Tadros.

* * *

They learnt the secret of the marriages between men the following day, but they never saw the unveiled women. Perhaps, they said afterwards, these were merely a manifestation of cobras appearing in an illusion.

They awoke that morning to the sound of merriment. Nearby someone was strumming a lute, and the people of the village were smiling and laughing and gaily dressed, and were strewing flowers and singing. The children of their host came to call them to join the merrymaking, and when they asked what festival this was, they were told there was to be a wedding. Tadros bit his lip to refrain from asking who the lucky couple were, and waited eagerly to see. He did not have to wait long before a procession wended its way towards them, led by a camel garlanded with flowers and carrying on its back a handsome boy wearing an embroidered gown. Behind came a throng of other boys and a handful of adults waving garlands and ululating and beating tambourines.

At length the camel, plodding at a slow pace, turned down a winding street and came to a halt before a hut decked with coloured drapes and tassels. The bridegroom was lifted down, and everyone waited, and then the hut door opened and out came several people, and then they stood aside to wait for the bride to come out of the hut.

And she came. Only it was another boy.

And then the two boys held hands, and the people danced round them, and then the boys sat together on a bench, and a great feast was served to which everyone in the village, including Sanjar and Tadros, and Rhoorogh and the old man, were invited. The feasting went on the whole day and into the night, and then one of the boys withdrew into the hut, and the other mounted the camel and rode to his side of the village.

And then Sanjar turned to a man seated beside him, and said: "And the boy married the other boy?"

"Yes," the man replied.

Sanjar nodded.

"And, er... that's it?" he asked.

"Well, they will live in their own houses."

"Of course."

"Not together."

"No, of course not."

Sanjar waited, but the man offered no further comment.

"So, this is a usual thing?" Sanjar enquired.

"Oh yes."

"Hmm."

"You find it strange?"

"Well, er... yes."

158

"Young men, you know, they can get up to mischief, have ideas... We prefer to make sure they are well behaved until, well, until the time comes for them to take a wife. So these two will not stay married. Only until they find a wife."

"Oh, that makes sense."

"Yes, a great deal of sense."

"So," said Sanjar, "when the time comes for them to take a wife, these boys will marry a girl from the village?"

"That's right. But they won't fool around with the girls beforehand, because they are already married and the boy each is married to will keep the other in check."

"I see," said Sanjar.

*   *   *

"It's a kind of control," Sanjar explained to Tadros. "I marry you, and then you won't go and fool around with the girls, and then the girls will be safe. Perfect sense."

"These people are very strange," Tadros replied, too astonished even to laugh.

Sanjar was not listening, for a crowd had gathered, and a performance had begun. The villages were grouped around a man who had placed several baskets and a sack before them on the ground. The man was none other than one of the two he had seen with the monk the night before. And Sanjar knew at once what was in the baskets.

The snake catcher untied the sack and tipped it up, and out tumbled a tangle of snakes of all sizes and kinds. The crowd shrieked and jumped back. The snakes, thin and fat, striped and mottled, writhed on the floor, and the snake catcher kept them in place with his foot. Then he opened the baskets one by one, revealing the cobras and vipers coiled inside, and picked up some of the serpents with a stick and placed them on his shoulders. The crowd gasped.

Tadros was so entranced by the snakes that at first he hardly noticed the snake catcher. When he did, he said: "That's the man – "

"Hush, Tadros."

Tadros hushed, and turned his attention back to the performance.

"He doesn't get bitten!" he said.

"He's taken out the poison."

"He's charmed them, they're so quiet."

"They're half dead. He hasn't fed them since he caught them."

"How do you know so much?"

"Snake catchers are the same everywhere."

The man was telling the crowd he belonged to a Sufi sect whose founders came from Basra, to where the souls of all serpents flew on death. He said he had been initiated by drinking snake venom, and was thus immune to their poison. He caught snakes by smell, he said. But he never killed them.

"He just puts a scorpion in the sack. The scorpion kills them," Sanjar said quietly to Tadros.

The snake catcher let people from the crowd hold the snakes. He said they would not be harmed, because he had charmed the serpents into a semi-sleep. Those who were brave enough poked the snakes, which were too weak to resist. The spectacle went on. The charmer pitted the snakes against each other, and told tales of how he had outwitted and caught them, and of the lives he had saved and the monstrous serpents he had seen, serpents as big as that killed by St George, he said (for St George was a Roman soldier and had fought the serpent in that country, though some said it was a crocodile), and he told of snakes in Arabia and India. And then he put his snakes back in the baskets and sack, and the crowd drifted away.

Sanjar approached him as he was bending over the sack, tying it with string. Sanjar said: "Did I not see you last night, and you were with a Christian monk, were you not?"

The man denied it. "No, oh no, not I," he said. "I don't speak Coptic. I would not know how to talk with a Christian."

"Strange, I though he might have spoken Arabic.

"No," said the man. "Sorry."

Sanjar showed him a silver coin. The snake catcher did most of his business with village people, and did not see many silver coins. He looked hard at it.

"Oh *that* monk," he said.

Sanjar waited patiently.

"Well," the snake catcher said. "He wanted to know where he could find some snakes. Don't know why."

"And?"

"I told him where there was a cobra's nest, under the rocks at the end of the village. I took him there to show him, yesterday afternoon. There they were, all the young cobras. I wanted to catch them, but he paid me to leave them where they were. Yes, now I think of it, I did catch sight of him again yesterday evening, and we might have exchanged a word or two."

Sanjar gave him the coin. "Do you know where he might be now?"

"No."

"I might reward you."

The man swallowed. "I could not tell you."

Sanjar waited for the man to pick up his snakes, and then he followed. When he reached a fork in the road at the far end of the village the snake catcher paused to put down his burden and rest for a moment, and then he opened the sack and the baskets, and tipped out the snakes, which were far too weak to wriggle out by themselves. Then he picked up the empty baskets, flung them over his shoulder, and set off along a road bordered by sugar cane, his right hand holding the long pole that acted as weapon, basket carrier and walking stick.

The moon was full, so Sanjar was forced to keep well back in the shadows as he followed, but by the light of the moon he took good care to note the way so that later he could retrace his steps. After half a league they arrived at a lonely farm which he thought the snake catcher would pass by, but here the man stopped and went up to the door. He knocked, the door was opened, and he stepped inside.

Sanjar crept to a window. A dog barked, but he stared at it and the dog retreated and quietened down. The window was unglazed, so he could not put his face to it but had to move through the shadows until he had positioned the scene inside within the frame of the window.

He was looking into a simple farmhouse room with bare walls and little in the way of furnishings, and at three men sitting in a circle on the floor. One was the second of the men he had seen talking to the monk the night before, the second was the monk himself, but the third he could not identify because he had his back to the window. .He saw the snake catcher enter the room and address the group, and then the door opened again, and a woman entered bearing a jug. She served them, and left the room. Sanjar wondered how he could get close enough to hear what they were saying.

And then the man who had his back to him stood, and turned, and came to the window, and called: "Will you not join us, Sanjar Mouseback?"

And thus Sanjar was greatly surprised, for he recognised the Abbot from the Wadi Natroun.

"We know you are there, Sanjar Mouseback," the Abbot called. "Do not fear our magic. We shall not take advantage of you."

There was little for it but to step forward. Drawing her scarf over her face, the woman opened the door for him and showed him to where the others sat. As he stood in the doorway he unbuckled Moonflinger and placed the holy sword on the floor.

The Abbot smiled in appreciation.

"Pray be seated," he said.

Sanjar sat on a wooden bench and crossed his legs, and waved aside the jug of sherbet the woman offered him. But the Abbot held up his mug, and the woman filled it, and he said: "You see, it is safe," and so Sanjar accepted it.

The monk spoke.

"Our friend the snake catcher mentioned that you had accosted him, so we were certain you had also followed him."

Sanjar inclined his head.

"I feel you are a skilled man, Brother, so skilled that you can turn a charmer's snakes into snake charmers," he said.

There was a ripple of laughter.

'And you, soldier, have a will of iron, and a gift with words."

"I know what is right."

"Would we all did," the monk said.

The Abbot spoke. "Do not be hard on our guest, Brother. He is a soldier. He does his duty. That, to him, is right. That we disagree with him does not make him a bad man. Be tolerant." He turned to Sanjar. "If that was indeed a test, you passed. Be honoured."

"This is a play of words, Father," Sanjar said. "I do not know the reason behind your quarrel with me, and I have no idea why you wish to thwart me. That you do so could put you in jeopardy, for I serve the Caliph, who is your lord as well as mine."

"Do not speak of a quarrel! That is a harsh word indeed! More than one opposes you, but of them all we alone wish you no personal harm. We admire your sense of courage, and your sense of duty. We are not so sure about your sense."

"Or sense of purpose," added the monk.

"Perhaps," the Abbot said.

"Father, tell me why you oppose me?"

"You meddle in things best left alone."

"That is for the Caliph to decide."

"Then you tell me, why do you want to find Zerzura?"

"I am an adventurer, and what adventurer would not wish to find such a place? Once, through you, I learnt of it, I thought of nothing but to find it."

"I find your words false. You seek Zerzura because you wish to find something that may lie there. It is not the city itself you seek, only the prize."

"You judge me harshly, Father. But if you are right, all you have to do is follow me. You are skilled enough in magic to do the rest."

Sanjar stood up to leave, but the Abbot raised his hand.

"Not so much haste," he said. "You are a soldier, courageous and strong. Will you meet our champion, that he who wins the tournament may lead the search for Zerzura?"

His words took Sanjar by surprise. Who was this champion? But the gauntlet had been thrown, and could not be left to lie.

"I will meet your champion," he said. "Tell me where, and when."

"Here, at dawn."

Sanjar bowed, and buckled on his sword, and left. It was a long walk home, and dawn was only a few hours away.

The Ghawarzee, meanwhile, had put on a show of dancing to honour Captain Guhar. Guhar felt ill at ease in his disguise: he had stolen the clothes from a washing line so they were clean, but they were not of the quality he would have chosen to present himself as a candidate for a bridegroom. He had trimmed his moustache, and rubbed dirt in his face, and practised the gait of one more used to hopping on a donkey than riding astride a horse, and yet his beloved said it suited him well. She did not, of course, know how essential was his disguise, and only wanted him to appear as someone more ordinary than an officer of the horse so as not to arouse the suspicions of her tribe. But although he was unhappy to be dressed as a farmer, he believed his simple gown and plain turban was successful in hiding his identity.

He approached the camp soon after nightfall, and Selima, when she saw him arrive, stayed in her tent and watched him enquire about her, and when he came to her father the two men sat together beside the fire and smoked and talked. And at length she was sent for, and she told her father, in the gypsy way, that she would take Guhar as her husband, and so the other girls uttered ululations, and her father, to Guhar's great surprise, asked why the ceremony should not be performed at once, and asked what Guhar had brought as dowry. So Guhar produced some of the gold coins which had been his illegal earnings in the days when he was in the City Guard, which amounted to a small fortune for a farmer, and when Selima's father asked whether he might perhaps not prefer to offer cows, or camels, or something more befitting a man of his position, Guhar replied that he had considered the coins more serviceable to the gypsies, for what would they do with cows, while the strain of their line of camels was far superior to any he could offer. Selima's father thought this a reasonable suggestion, and said it showed how considerate the bridegroom was, and so a sheep was killed and a feast prepared, and the marriage was celebrated there and then by all the tribe.

And when Guhar asked when he might return to claim his bride, and perform the ceremony known to his countrymen as "the entrance", he was told that this was not the custom at all among gypsy people and that he might claim his bride that very night.

Guhar was beside himself. Here was he, whom they had so recently held prisoner, and who had escaped their custody, now escaping their recognition and being given a daughter of the tribe – of whom he was much enamoured – as his wife. He could hardly believe his fortune. Of course he had no farm to take her to, but what did that matter once they were man and wife? In any case she knew his circumstances – or some of them, for he had not quite told her yet that he was no longer in the City Guard – and she would easily become accustomed to a life with his outlaw friends. Being a

163

gypsy, she would fit in very well, and would raise their brown babies in their rocky fortress in the desert as well as any other bandit's wife.

The feasting and dancing went on until late, though Guhar was impatient for the party to end and the rest of his life to begin. He whispered to Selima that his horse was tethered nearby, and they could ride off together into the desert as soon as the feast was over, but she said she would not travel without her clothes and other finery, and that surely the horse could not carry all this, and perhaps they should hire a cart to carry her and her belongings to al-Qahira while he rode by her side or went on ahead to prepare for her arrival. Now the thought occurred to him that for a gypsy she was making demands way above her station, but then he remembered that the city life he had promised her was not what she would have, and that rather than living in the capital she would still be making her home in a desert tent, at best, and that indeed he did not even have a tent to house her in, and all this would have to be explained to her. And he was angry with her for making things so complicated.

To make matters worse, Selima's father was asking questions about his farm. How large was it, and what crops did he grow, and how many animals did he have, and how many labourers, for surely one so rich did not do all the work alone. Guhar, of course, knew nothing about farming, and although Selima's father probably knew little more, in this case a little might well be a great deal. So he invented reports of beans, and lemons, and milk and buffaloes, and then Selima's father mentioned that the coastal port of Dumyat produced the finest butter and soft cheese in all the world, so fine that it was shipped from there to Europe, and Guhar almost let slip that it was the first he had heard of this, but remembered just in time to say that he himself sent his milk to Dumyat, and that it was his buffaloes that produced the cream for which the port was so famous.

The slender boys-dressed-as-girls again rose to dance, and Selima's father picked up his oud, and drew his fingers across the strings, and others played the tambura and tambourine and flute, and the dancers with their pretty faces and dark-rimmed eyes cast sultry glances at the bridegroom through the flickering firelight. Through all this Selima sat with shining eyes and a happy smile playing round her lips, and he was sorry he could not take her to the city and hoped her disappointment would not dampen her love for him, and he held her hand and vowed silently that he would make up for his false promises and give her riches beyond her wildest dreams, even if – as he certainly would – he had to rob to obtain the gold and jewels he would shower on her.

At last the dancing ceased, and the musicians laid down their instruments, and the people of the tribe went sleepily to their tents, and Selima's father, poking the embers of the fire, suggested that the happy couple withdrew without further ceremony, in the gypsy way, to the tent that had been prepared for them. So Guhar pulled his pretty bride to her feet, and she shook the sand off her dress and let him lead her by the hand to the tent, from where, some minutes later, came the most appalling of the curses he had learnt in the dungeons of the City Guard.

The Ghawarzee had deceived him. Selima was a man.

*   *   *

The tribe had planned the deceit with the utmost care. They had made sure that Selim, who was the prettiest of the dancers, just sixteen years old, and with his voice not yet broken, was often to be seen near the fruit groves and other hiding places from where Guhar kept his watch on the gypsies. They had planned the dowry they would demand, and the feast – the cost of it more than offset by the gold – and even the disguise Guhar would use, a precaution which would make it possible for him to think he was approaching them unrecognised, while at the same time would prevent him from carrying his sword. But they had overlooked one thing. They had not thought that Guhar, perhaps afraid of discovery, would hide a knife in his farmer's gown. And when, some moments after hearing the curses, but hearing no more, they ventured to the tent decorated for the wedding with embroidered drapes, they saw that Guhar had fled, and that he had left the body of Selim lying broken and crumpled on the nuptial couch. Now the curses were theirs, and the camp awoke not to the cries of jubilation for the consummation of a marriage but to the lamentations of a family in mourning for its dead.

12 · The Black Knight

SANJAR ROSE AN HOUR before dawn and opened the door of the hut to find Tadros saddling Moonleap, who was steadily munching her morning feed out of a wooden bucket. She pricked her ears when she heard his step and nickered as she turned to greet him, blowing chaff over the courtyard, and he stroked her smooth flank and told Tadros not to follow him when he left, but to send Rhoorogh to wait at the crossroads at the end of the village and tell him that if he saw another knight ride by he should then, and only then, take the left hand fork through the sugar cane.

As Moonleap walked through the village a single cock crowed. Some days before when they had turned off the road at al-Baratum to ride on sand Sanjar had removed the horse's shoes, and now she made only a muted, hollow sound as her bare hooves hit the packed, dry mud of the track.

It was shortly before dawn, the darkest hour, and Sanjar had some difficulty in keeping to the path, but he took care to stay in the centre of the track. When he came to the farmhouse, which he noticed only because a sliver of light was escaping through a window shutter, Sanjar drew in the reins, and Moonleap stood, prancing a little, her ears upright, her breath forming clouds of steam. He stayed there long enough to make sure he had been noticed, and then turned into an open, sandy field beside some outhouses. At length a door of the house opened and the monk who had played the trickery with the snakes appeared. Sanjar wondered if he could be planning some other ruse, but the monk greeted him cordially, and remarked on the beauty of Moonleap, and then he said their champion was ready, and all was well, and he talked about this and that, and the quality of the date harvest, and if the rains would come. To all this Sanjar nodded politely, and the monk mentioned that perhaps Sanjar had other, sinister enemies after all, for he had heard that a troop of guards had been seen asking questions about Sanjar and his friends. So Sanjar replied that, yes, a detachment of the guard was on his heels, but was there to protect rather than threaten him. And the monk said that was just as well, because the Caliph's guard had a reputation for ruthlessness, and he mentioned that news travelled quickly through the Caliphate, and he always knew the latest events in al-Qahira, such as the news he had received only the night before

166

that a foreign prince, a Christian, had demanded recompense for the Caliph's treatment of his non-Muslim subjects and allies, and for such heinous acts perpetrated in the name of religion such as the sack of the Holy Sepulchre at Jerusalem, by asking the hand of the daughter of the man who carried out the commands of the Caliph, his vizier the Qadi, and that his request had been granted and that she was to be married within the month.

"She is said to be very beautiful, as well as accomplished. A prize for any man," he said.

Before Sanjar could recover from the monk's words and compose himself, the abbot's champion rode out of the shadows. The two faced each other across the sandy space, the one on his white Arab, the other on a black charger, a horse so thickset that it must have travelled across the sea from Europe, since there was no such creature in Africa. The champion wore a light chain mail hauberk and a black surcoat bearing a red cross. On his head was an iron helmet, and he held in his hand a lance and a long shield and by his side hung a mace and a broad sword. The breath of the black horse clouded the thin morning air, and it stamped its foot.

Sanjar called: "Tell me your name, so that I might know who calls this challenge."

"I am known as William of Barenne, or the Black Knight, if you prefer," the knight called back.

"And subject to whom?"

"Subject to the Holy Roman Emperor."

"Why do you come so far, to fight in a land so many leagues from home?"

"For the same reason as you, to fight for the true God, you under your banner of the crescent, and I under mine of the cross."

Sanjar's head spun. It was clear that it was not this knight that asked Bahiga's hand, for the abbot would not have put such a motive for victory in his way. If however the monk had told him this news of Bahiga to put him off his stride then he had taken an unintentional risk, for if Bahiga's promised husband was also a Christian, then this would fuel his fury against the knight. It crossed his mind to dispatch this knight, and then make haste to find the other, but then he recollected himself, and summoned his mind away from Bahiga and back to the dusty field beside the farm.

Seeing that Sanjar carried no lance, the knight threw his aside and lifted a heavy mace from his saddle. Sanjar responded by taking up his own. Their horses stood poised, and pawed the ground, and then Sanjar and the Black Knight, wielding their weapons, kneed them forward and they hurled towards each other, and the thunder of their hooves was followed by the clang of iron as the maces met. The heavy blow sent both men reeling and almost pulled their arms from their sockets, and they withdrew to the edge of the field. With the second charge they met with such force that both were unseated, and fell and rolled in the dust.

Sanjar was the first on his feet, and drew Moonflinger. William of Barenne staggered up and drew his broad sword: both held their swords in two hands. Sanjar was smaller and lighter than the other, but although that might give him some advantage, the knight had strength on his side. They circled each other looking for a chance to strike, then with a cry William raised his sword and let it fall, and there was a clash of steel and a flash of blue light as his weapon met Moonflinger. Sanjar pushed him back, and when he had regained his balance moved lightly into the attack. Then William recovered and fought back, and as they moved back and forth through the sandy dust Moonflinger began to sing and the flashes of blue flew faster from the blade, but while the light illuminated Sanjar's target, it dazzled the Black Knight's eyes. Holding his sword in one hand, he raised the other to shield his eyes from the glare. Sanjar, who now had the greater thrust, harassed him with his sword, and despite his greater size the knight showed signs of weakening.

Sanjar moved to one side and made a great thrust with the intention of disarming him. But the Black Knight, with a surge of strength, stood straight and tall, and uttering a mighty cry he thrust his sword with his huge might. Sanjar tried to parry the thrust, but he was not able to confront the blow head on and thus could not deflect it, and the tip of William's sword pierced his right shoulder. Sanjar was aware that the blade had found its mark, but when after some moments the pain was ready to flood in he refused to accept it and felt nothing, even though the red blood poured from the wound and soaked his tunic. Yet he knew this wound could cost him the fight, because his right arm was now disabled.

He had instinctively prolonged the fight in order to win by weakening the knight. Now he must finish it quickly, before his opponent rallied and gained the advantage. All at once the face of Bahiga flashed into his mind, Bahiga, who was to marry a foreign prince, if what the monk said were true. With this in mind he lifted Moonflinger with his left arm, and let it fall on the knight's sword, and knocked it spinning over the sand, and at the same time William of Barenne slipped and fell.

The sun's first rays were falling around them as Sanjar stood over the fallen knight and pointed the sword at his throat. All passion drained from Sanjar's face as he looked coldly down at his victim, this warrior from an alien land. Yet he knew, at heart, that just as he was a soldier in a foreign land, so was he, Sanjar. Just as the Black Knight gave his service to the abbot for one cause, so he, Sanjar, gave his to the Caliph for another. As one fought for his God, so did the other.

William of Barenne lay his head back in the sand. His face, burned by the sunny climate to which he was not born, struggled to find the words in an foreign tongue to say: "Make it quick, knight, before I think of my homeland."

"No, sir," Sanjar replied. "I shall not make it quick, or any other way. This quarrel is not between us. What does it serve if I take your life? True, we may meet again one day on the battlefield in Cordoba or Sicily, but when that day comes, may God be our arbitrator. Before then, we have much evil to fight, and many wars to win. So I shall not harm you, soldier. Go in peace, and pray God you will see your homeland again." And so he sheathed Moonflinger, and then he noticed his wound.

For a few seconds he swayed, and then he felt a gentle push from behind, and Moonleap nickered and nosed his good arm. With his last strength, for he knew it must not fail him now, he put his foot in the stirrup and swung himself on to her back. Then he looked down again at the knight, who had been hurt by the fall and was trying to raise himself, and with an effort, for his pain was great, said:

"Sir, you are a true and brave soldier, but you are taking up a cause very far from the one you were bred to fight. Go back to your homeland, before they give you any more errands to do and entrap you in their magic. These are not men of God." And with that he turned Moonleap with his heels. Sensing his urgency, she broke at once into a run.

By the time he reached Rhoorogh, who was waiting at the crossroads as he had been instructed, Sanjar had lost consciousness through loss of blood. Alarmed at his condition, Rhoorogh ran along beside him holding him on the saddle so he would not fall until they reached the hut, where Tadros waited anxiously. Rhoorogh lifted Sanjar down and laid him on his bed, fearing he was near death from loss of blood. But Tadros told him he had seen Dr Boutros attend injuries far worse than this, which seemed to be a shoulder wound, and that if Sanjar did not fall ill with a fever he would be sure to win through. So he set about stopping the bleeding, as the doctor had taught him to do, and called for the landlord to give him clean linen for bindings. Meanwhile the landlord's wife hurried to make up a bed in their own house which she said they would find more comfortable than their hut, and then she helped Tadros dress the wound, all the time remarking on the boy's devotion and skill. After a short while Sanjar began to come round, but the landlady had sent a servant out to a wise magician in the village who was renowned for her remedies, and before long the servant returned with a steaming potion in which the wise woman had put herbs and essences to aid sleep and healing. Tadros, who did not waste time in pausing to ponder on the sincerity of this gift, gently poured the warm liquid drop by drop down Sanjar's throat. Sanjar swallowed slowly until it was gone, and then he sank back on the soft down pillows and slept for three days.

The fever did come, and through that time Tadros hardly left the room, but sometimes Rhoorogh or the old man or the landlord's wife shooed him from the bedside and made him lie down in a corner and sleep while they took their turn to watch. But he would soon be up again, until they threatened to give him some of the wise woman's sleeping potion. The magician sent a medicine which she said would cure the fever, but as Sanjar was so fast asleep it was hard to administer it, and when they tried to trickle it into his mouth they almost choked him. So they sent back to the magician, and this time she sent a wild melon and told them to cut it and place each half under his two heels, and when they did this the heat left his brow and the fever began to abate, and on the fourth day he stirred.

While Sanjar slept there was talk in the village of monks, and of a Frankish knight seen riding a huge black horse. These events were so unusual that the residents were not surprised when a detachment of the Caliph's guard rode into the village, but when the guards questioned them they told them nothing, because Sanjar was their ward and their guest, and they all wished no harm to come to him.

And so, on the fourth day when Sanjar opened his eyes, he found himself in another room in another house, with several serious faces around his bedside, and were it not for a smiling Tadros he would have thought he was elsewhere. For he remembered everything that had happened. The Black Knight, and the wound, and Bahiga's betrothal.

Once Bahiga had come into his mind he could think of nothing else. The pain of knowing she was to marry another when he loved her made the pain in his shoulder seem as trivial as a mosquito bite. The people in the room offered goodwill and salutations, but he stared at them vacantly, and wished them away so he could be alone with his grief. They interpreted his expression as one of shock, and his lack of speech as tiredness, and tiptoed away, and once he was alone his agony was so great that he wished them back, but then he realised it was not they he was missing, but Bahiga, and that no one could fill the void in his heart but she. And he wondered how he had survived the combat with the Black Knight knowing what he already knew, or how he had the will to fight and the desire to live, because now he had neither, only an aching longing and the most terrible thought he had ever had: that without his love he did not wish to exist.

Sanjar asked Tadros what day it was, and Tadros told him and thought Sanjar might be angry that they had lost so much time, but he only needed to know so he could count how many days it was since he learnt the news about Bahiga. And the tidings the monk had given him went over and over in his mind, and Tadros saw that it was not his wound that was troubling him, and then finally Tadros said:

"You will have to stop the wedding."

Sanjar was so taken aback by the boy's words that he could not reply, so Tadros said: "You kept calling for Bahiga over and over again when you were in the fever, and I almost wondered why she had not come to your aid, as she has so often, and then I remembered how you got so angry when someone helped you out of a difficult situation, and what you said when you vanquished the magic snakes, that you had won through yourself, and I thought that perhaps she was leaving you to conquer your fever yourself, so you would truly win. But then when the guards were here, whom the Caliph sent to watch you, I put on a turban like an Arab boy so they would not know me and went out to listen to them talking among themselves. And I was so surprised because they were not talking about you or the Emerald Tablet but about Bahiga and the Qadi, and how she was to be married out of politics, and they said other things as well but I shan't repeat them."

"What did you hear?"

"No, I can't say."

"You must tell me now you have said so much!"

Tadros saw he had little choice, and said: "They said it was good she was leaving al-Qahira, because she was a witch and put spells on al-Hakim and that was why he was so crazy. And they laughed. So I left."

Sanjar managed a wry smile. "So in the palace kitchens they blame the Caliph's madness on Bahiga."

"Don't upset yourself."

"If they just knew!"

Tadros bit his lip anxiously. "You did know about the marriage?" he asked.

"Yes, someone told me."

"I thought you knew. You must stop it."

"It's too late."

"No. She won't leave here to get married until you have found the Tablet. You know she will refuse to do anything else. And you can't let her marry against her will, just to please her father and the Caliph."

"It might not be against her will."

"You know it must be! You know how she looks at you!"

"Tadros, cease! How she looks at me is in your imagination, and none of your business." But when he saw the boy's dejection he added, "I love her, she doesn't love me, and I never had any cause to believe she did. What has passed between us, what has bound us together, has been a business matter, the matter of finding the Tablet. There has been nothing else, and it is foolish to think otherwise. In any case, she thinks I'm a foolish soldier, more brawn than brain, she has said so herself. And lacking in education and knowledge. So why would she turn her attention for even a moment to one such as I."

"I think you are too weak to be worrying about love," Tadros said. "You must get strong and let your wound heal, and then you can go and fight for her and show her how strong you are and win her back. You can't do anything now except feel miserable, and if you are miserable you won't get well, so be sensible and think of your health."

"Perhaps I don't want to get well."

"Oh, there you go, feeling sorry for yourself. Well that isn't the way to win her back. Unless you get well and help her she'll have to go through with this wedding, and it'll all be your fault because you won't be strong enough to save her, and you'll both be unhappy for the rest of your lives." And Tadros, in an uncharacteristic temper, went out and slammed the door.

Sanjar slept. When he woke it was after dark, and he could hear Tadros breathing in sleep on the bench beside him. A vision of Bahiga flooded into his mind. Tadros was right, as always, and he must save her. Even if she would not marry him, she would not live with an unhappy match.

Slowly and in great pain he eased himself onto his left side, and sat up. He tried to feel the wound, but the pain was too great. Gently he moved the joints in his arm, and found that not broken, although the rounded tip of the broad sword seemed to have cut through the muscle and broken his shoulder. He rose unsteadily to his feet and took a turn around the room. So far, so good. A lamp was burning but its wick was low, yet it cast enough light for him to see Moonflinger lying on a chest, together with his clothes. Using his injured arm, he pulled the sword from its scabbard. It felt as light as air in his hand, as though, now he was wounded, it would bear its own weight. Slowly he swung his arm, and though he could not swing it far he was satisfied. He sheathed Moonflinger and replaced the scabbard, and went outside to breathe the fresh air before climbing into bed. He lay awake for hours then, wondering how he could save her, and if she loved him.

Sanjar stayed a few days in the village. Each day he practised his skills, and each day his shoulder grew stronger. The magician gave Tadros a balm which she said he should apply to the wound before the sun came up. Meanwhile Rhoorogh played with the village children, who had grown used to his looks and thought he was a giant come down from the mountains. He could carry a dozen on his back at once, and they played at this for hours, shrieking and squealing with delight until the fathers pushed the boys away to fetch vegetables for supper and the mothers called the girls to help with the milking. Even the old man had his cronies, and now that he had exchanged his rags for two linen gowns, one to wear and one for the wash, was able to present himself as respectable.

Since the old man fitted so well in so well with the villagers and in his new clothes was indistinguishable from any of them, Sanjar made up his mind that when they moved on they would leave him behind. The old man suspected this, and complained to his friends, all other old men, that he was to be discarded, hoping to win their sympathy. The old villagers, however, thought him fortunate to stay where he was, and told him so. But he was not convinced, and grumbled that because he was old he was no longer of any use.

"It's not that we don't want to be encumbered with you, it's for your own safety," Tadros explained to the old man. Seeing his disappointment, he added: "Besides, it would help us greatly if you stayed here, because you could serve to put anyone off our trail."

"You mean I'd be a kind of spy?" asked the old man.

"Exactly. Just make sure no one knows where we have gone, so they cannot follow us, and you will be of great service.

The old man thought for a moment.

"But I don't know where you are going," he said. "How can I not tell anyone where you have gone, if I don't know? To keep this secret, I will have to know where you have gone, in order to tell people where you have not gone."

"I think it better you do not know where we have gone, and then you will not be able to say."

The old man still wanted to find out, and asked Rhoorogh, but Rhoorogh did not really know, and even if he had he could not have told him. So he tried to get the information from Sanjar, not from malice, but from curiosity, and to make himself more important by knowledge of the secret. Sanjar, however, was too busy practising with the use of his arm to listen to him, and brushed his questions aside. So the old man took to listening intently to every word that passed between Sanjar and Tadros. It was some time before they noticed this, and during that time the old man heard the word *Zerzura*.

One morning the Caliph's guards rode back to the village. They had spent some days in the desert searching for Sanjar, and had returned to replenish their supplies. They had learnt that horses were ill equipped for desert life, and asked for camels so they might ride longer without water. The villagers had no choice but to comply with this request, and the four guards mounted camels and rode away.

When they had gone, the old man told his friends: "They asked me question after question when we stayed in al-Baratum, and even though they beat me I gave nothing away. But here they don't know me, because now I'm disguised as one of you. So I am to stay here as a spy, and watch for when the guards come back so I can make sure they do not follow them."

The other old men agreed he had a very important role to play, until one of them asked: "How can you make sure of that?"

"Well, I know where my friends are going, and all I have to do is make sure the guards go somewhere else."

"So where are they going?" the other asked.

And so it was that when the day came when Sanjar was well enough to continue with his journey, and he rode away from the Oasis of Amoun with Tadros and Rhoorogh, the whole village knew they were on their way to find Zerzura. The parting itself was not without grief. Sanjar had made a decision more difficult than abandoning the old man: he had left Moonleap in the village, and with her Hermes the mule, but the landlord had promised to keep the horse well hidden and suggested that if they left before dawn not even the old man would know she was still there. In the Caliphate it was forbidden for any but a soldier to ride a horse, and while it might not be that such a flouting of the law would be discovered or punished so far from the capital, yet it would not do to arouse suspicion. Moreover Moonleap was easily recognisable, and by now quite famous, and Sanjar did not want to lose her again.

So they left before dawn, Sanjar and Tadros each seated on a camel and Rhoorogh leading two, one of them the bad tempered female which had walked with them from Iskandriya. They had not long left the oasis before they came across a lone young shepherd squatting on his haunches in the sand, while his few black goats and a hobbled camel foraged for morsels of food in the scrub.

"Why are you riding south?" the youth said.

"And why not, pray?" Sanjar asked.

"There is nothing south but a sea of sand."

"And then?"

"Then there are mountains, and somewhere in them a beautiful oasis with trees and gardens, but it's hard to find."

"Have you been there?"

"Yes. I went for many days looking for a camel, and at last, after going this way and that, I found a green place, where there were running streams, and dates, and gazelle, and many birds."

"Was anyone living there?"

"I saw no one. But I found the carcass of a cow, and I saw what looked like a city, but there were no people about and I was afraid to go near. I was very afraid of the place."

Sanjar began to feel a very great excitement. "Would you know where to find it again?" he asked.

"No. I do not want to go. For days and days there is just a sea of sand."

"But you could find it again?"

"Yes, I think so, by the stars."

"And could you tell us where it is?"

"No, I could not describe the way well enough. I could only tell you to keep on going south."

"Then you must come with us. If what you say is true, you will be richly rewarded. If you do not agree to come, we will understand you speak falsely and disregard your information."

The youth thought. "What if I speak the truth, yet we fail to find the place?"

"Now do you know it or not? If you know it, let's be on our way, and if you don't, we shall waste no more time and ride on without you the way we were going."

"I know it," said the youth. And without another word he unhobbled the camel, and it knelt down and he climbed on its back, and the camel stood up with a painful grunt, and they were on their way.

The shepherd was a taciturn youth, and soon Sanjar and Tadros abandoned attempts to engage him in conversation and they rode on silently. Their pace was slow, for by all the accounts they had heard of the lost oasis they had a seven-day march ahead, and the camels were heavily laden. Sanjar asked the youth if there was any water to be found before they came to the place he described, and he said that yes, there was a spring with water that was slightly brackish, but would do. So they went on for two days, and then Sanjar noticed that they had left the trail which, though little used, was clearly marked, and were now running along a dry watercourse which veered west. The youth said the trail they had left ran south east from the Oasis of Amoun to several city-oases many days' journey away, back towards where there was a great river, and Sanjar knew the youth was talking about the huge green oases closer to the border with the country to the south from where the river came, and he wondered in his heart how the shepherd knew such things. But as if in answer to his thoughts the youth said that caravans came from there and that sometimes, perhaps once every few years, a band of black men came that way to the Oasis of Amoun driving herds of camels hundreds strong, and some of them carrying skins and ivory, and that these man told them of lands far to the south where there were monstrous creatures with necks as tall as trees and where people, even women, wore no clothes. The oasis they were looking for, he said, lay not in this direction, but south west of the Oasis of Amoun.

"Then why have you turned due west?" asked Sanjar. "For I think the lost oasis lies south, and not south west."

"I have to go the way I went when I found it," he replied reasonably. "How else shall I know the way? I came across it by accident, not necessarily by the most direct route."

Almost immediately he turned into another wadi which opened into a wide, flat plain. The distance was deceptive, and so were the contours, and both Tadros and Sanjar said they hoped the shepherd could find the way back. On the far side of the plain they entered another wadi which seemed indistinguishable from the rest.

That night the youth made flat loaves of bread on the open fire. Sanjar watched him and Tadros as they talked, and tried to make the youth out. Who was he, and why had he been waiting there on the side of the road? There was a dull ache in his shoulder, and he wondered if the ache was caused by his injury or by unease. They had travelled a day in what Sanjar thought was the wrong direction, winding in and out through a wadi which the shepherd said he knew. What if he were bluffing, or lost?

There was no sound in the wadi apart from the low voices and the crackle of the fire, nothing moved but wafts of pungent smoke. The fire warmed them, but the air at their backs was chill. One by one they rolled themselves in their blankets and slept.

When they awoke the sun was high, and the rugged red peaks which bordered the wadi were bathed in fresh gold. But they had no time to contemplate the beauty of the scene. The shepherd and his camel were gone.

At once they knew they had been tricked. To guess how they had fallen for such a deceit after all that had gone before was fruitless, for the deed was done. They were now at least a day away from their planned route, and moreover they were quite lost among the wadis and had no way of knowing their way back.

The sun might help them to navigate by day, but they had little knowledge of how to navigate by the stars and it would be fatal to trust to their judgment by night. So they decided to work by their eyes, and try to remember what they could. It seemed hopeless. Each wadi looked much like the next, while a patch of sand looked like this from one angle, like that from another. It was clear they must now travel at a slant to the east, and they studied the crags to see whether a path might lead in that direction, but there was no knowing what might lie in the hollows between the peaks, whether rock falls or flood debris or merely a dead end.

They began to retrace their steps of the day before, but this soon ended in confusion. Sanjar thought they had come one way, while Tadros thought it was another, and Rhoorogh had a third opinion still. The desert, at times so peaceful, so beautiful with its graceful peaks and soft colours, now seemed inhospitable and harsh, a vast graveyard waiting for bones.

They agreed to head towards a black hill which Sanjar thought they had passed the day before. As they neared it they startled a solitary ibex which, alarmed, scampered off in the very direction they planned to follow. This gave them great hope, for they reasoned that the ibex, if it knew its way, would not attempt a path when there was no way through. So they made after it, passing through a gorge so narrow they had to pass in single file, and when they reached the end of it what should be there but the ibex, grazing on a lone tamarisk tree. At the sight of them the ibex moved on again, but this time, strangely, it did not run, but walked ahead, never quite out of their sight unless it turned a corner, and when they themselves rounded the turn there it was again, waiting.

At each fork in the path the ibex paused and seemed to sniff the air, as though to find the find a channel through which the breeze flowed. Many a time Sanjar would have taken this or that path rather than the one the ibex chose, but wherever the ibex went there was always a way through, and always to the east. Following the creature did not seem to any of them to be foolish; on the contrary it was entirely natural.

Then, abruptly, the ibex left the wadi floor and began to climb, pursuing a narrow flood course through the bare rock. This was easy enough for the ibex to negotiate, but quite hard for the camels, so Tadros scurried up to the summit of the crag to see whether the rest of them could pass. When he reached the top he saw below him an open, sun-drenched plain. The ibex stood some way below him, flexing its short tail. The downward path was smooth, ending in a sandy slope, and the greatest difficulty in the crossing was on the lower stretch of the climb where they now stood.

Tadros climbed down again and helped lead the camels to the top. From there Sanjar looked down with relief on the plain and the rocky hills beyond, for a wadi seemed to run directly through them, and the ibex was heading straight towards it.

They did not see the ibex again, but now and again they noticed a fresh cloven hoof print, or a freshly snapped twig on a dry shrub. Now riding, now walking, they followed the bed of the wadi until nightfall, when they camped underneath an overhanging rock. They had now been on the road for four days, but were no more than two days' journey from the Oasis of Amoun, and the lost oasis was at least five days away.

On the next day they came upon an unmistakable trail, which they reasoned from the position of the sun was the one they had been following until the shepherd – who, they guessed, would soon be back with his scraggly goats – led them astray. If it led to the oases far to the south and eventually, if what the youth said was true, into deepest Africa, this trail received little traffic, but that traffic was regular. Several hundred camels left traces even after several years, while wind-blown sand soon covered marks on trails that were used hardly at all. They studied their own map, which they had drawn from the fragments of papyrus they had taken from the abbot's cell in Wadi Natroun. According to that they would reach a twin red peak, and at that point they should leave the main track, which went on south eastwards, and travel due south for three days.

To celebrate finding the track again they stopped to rest and brew tea, and play a game of squares, using pebbles worn smooth by the sand for counters. Thus they stayed for an hour or two while the kneeling camels chewed cud, and then they agreed they had wasted enough time and packed away their pots and threw away their checkers, and made ready to move on.

As soon as they mounted their camels they saw nearby something they could not have seen when they sat on the ground. Just behind them, from where they would have come had they travelled along the track and not over the rocks from the west, lay what appeared to be a heap of rags. They trotted the camels over and there, face down in the sand, lay the body of a young man.

They did not need a closer look to see who this was, for his clothes identified him as the shepherd boy who had so cruelly misled them. Yet how he had died, and why he had been on the path this far south when they would have expected him to hurry back to the Oasis of Amoun? They urged their camels to kneel and joined Rhoorogh, who was already bending over the body.

"What do you make of this?" Sanjar asked. "There seems to be no wound, and the body is not yet cold or stiff. If he had fallen off his camel he might have an injury, but his bones feel whole and he is not bruised or scratched." The youth's eyes stared horribly. "It looks as though he died of fright," he said, "But what is he doing here?"

Since the sand was too shallow to build a proper grave they buried the body under a pile of rocks, puzzling in silence over the mystery of the youth's death. He could have died of thirst, for his water bottle had been attached to his saddle and his camel was nowhere in sight. But that was not likely in one winter day, and in any case how had he come to lose his camel? Had it wandered off in the night, and was it to pursue it he had come this way? Or was he watching to see if they found their way back to the trail, or perhaps he himself had been on his way to Zerzura?

They soon found an answer to one of these questions, though with it the puzzle grew. A little way ahead the track ran into another of the sand plains that received the floodwaters which occasionally gushed down the wadis, sweeping rocks and other debris in their path. Centuries of floods, though these were often decades apart, had baked the surface into a crust so it was easy to follow the trail over the broken plates of hardened sand. Then they saw, lying a little way ahead, the few scattered objects that were to make their flesh creep and bring on the fear which is like no other, the fear of the desert with its hundreds of leagues of nothingness.

They recognised the objects lying in the sand. They had come off the youth's camel: its saddle and bridle, the boy's pack and water bottle, even the red woollen tassels the camel wore for good luck. Everything was there, except the camel.

Tadros shuddered, "Was it eaten by lions?" he said.

"Not like this," Sanjar said. "Lions do not slip the bridles off their victims."

Their own camels were pacing uneasily, and Rhoorogh was looking fearfully from side to side.

"Do you know what it could be, Rhoorogh?"

Rhoorogh shook his head, but made a gesture indicating they should hurry on their way. They left the things lying there, not wishing a repetition of what had come about when Sanjar picked up the water bottle and found himself in a Persian garden. Remembering that incident Rhoorogh paused to kick sand over the bottle lest some hapless passer-by might think someone had dropped it, and pick it up. There remained the mystery. Where was the camel? And what had killed the shepherd, if not thirst?

They hurried to cross the threatening emptiness of the plain, telling themselves that over the horizon they would find the twin red peaks and the path to Zerzura. All at once Rhoorogh uttered a loud grunt, and they looked down to see him kicking something with his foot. It was yet another camel saddle, half buried by sand, and had clearly lain there for some time. They exchanged puzzled looks, and hurried on.

A slight gust of wind whipped the ground, but only Rhoorogh and the camels felt it, and shuddered. After a few moments they all saw what they thought was a dust devil, a small sandy whirlwind, but as they watched and the startled camels stood still, refusing to move, the swirling dust began to assume an entity. Though it constantly reviewed its shape and size the yellow sand was now nevertheless a *thing*, and it blocked their path, and clearly would not let them pass. Then with horror they understood that it was a mariid, the meanest of the jinn, and the curse of the desert and all who travelled there. The camels snorted in terror, but Rhoorogh held up his club.

"The only way to deal with this," Sanjar said slowly and deliberately, "is to address it with extreme politeness. So put down your club, Rhoorogh, for it will get us nowhere."

Rhoorogh did as he was asked, and speaking to the mariid Sanjar went on: "We beg you, let us pass."

The mariid's head, or the part that might be termed the head, darted six feet forward, and hissed. Then it zoomed back.

For some minutes they regarded the mariid, and it regarded them, and then they began to move gingerly to the right, the camels placing their feet with distaste and trepidation. At this the mariid swiftly elongated itself to form a wall from one side of the plain to the other. They all jumped back, their hearts in their mouths. The mariid resumed its former, lumpish shape, and Sanjar, from atop his camel, bowed.

"Master, perhaps we understand that you desire a tribute?"

The mariid rippled.

"We have gold."

The shape suddenly thrashed as though in fury, and Sanjar said hastily: "Quite clearly, sir, you have no need of gold. Pardon the foolishness of my suggestion."

"It wants a camel," Tadros said bluntly.

Sanjar took a deep breath. "Take anything, master. Take one of us. But please, please don't take one of our camels."

At this Rhoorogh turned to give Sanjar a painful look, but Sanjar said quietly: "No, he's not going to take you, and I wouldn't let him. You have to choose which of the camels to sacrifice, and quickly remove its load and add it to the other's. Do this quickly, and we may be able to pass."

Rhoorogh made a protesting grunt which made Tadros quake all the more, for he realised that of the three of them only he was afraid.

Sanjar said: "No, Rhoorogh, we can't fight it. It appears to exact a toll, and the going rate seems to be a camel. We have no choice."

So Rhoorogh, with only a moment's hesitation, unloaded one of the camels he was leading, one they had acquired in the Oasis of Amoun, and placed its load on the back of the female who had shared with them so many of the trials they had encountered on the way from Iskandriya. Then he gave the unburdened camel a push. It took two paces forward, and then stopped in panic. But like a magnet the mariid drew it on, and it stepped forward, its eyes glazed. At last prey and predator met, and the rest, men and beast alike, watched horrified as the camel, its face distorted and uttering a bellow of terror and agony, was consumed alive into the body of the jinni, and as it was devoured it became translucent, composed, like the jinni itself, of swirling dust and sand, and when the camel had entirely gone the dust devil spun around and around and gathered speed, and swirled away across the plain, gathering up loose twigs of scrub in a miniature whirlwind.

13 · The Colour of Pearls

BAHIGA PASSED SEVEN DAYS in fasting and meditation, and would have been ready to meet Sanjar not far from Zerzura had he not been delayed by his encounter with the Black Knight. As it was it was only when she emerged from her solitude that she learnt of the danger he had faced, and then she saw and was glad that he had vanquished his foe and had recovered so well from his wound without her knowledge or intervention. She stayed a few more days at al-Qahira to prepare for the flight to Europe, meanwhile keeping a watch on Sanjar, but all she did to help him was to send the ibex to guide him back to the trail. When he faced the mariid she was not far away: garbed like a Bedu woman, she stayed with the donkey just out of sight behind some rocks. It was all she could do to stop the donkey from braying, and finally she was forced to muzzle him with her scarf.

It had been quite an effort to transport the donkey, but travelling in this way presented one great advantage: like her, it needed neither food nor water, and was therefore no encumbrance. It also presented the perfect accessory to her disguise as a Bedu. For a maiden alone might raise eyebrows but a girl with a donkey was a perfectly natural sight, even so far from anywhere. It was also a companion and something to talk to, and helped keep her warm at night. Bahiga was always puzzled that, while not feeling the need for sleep or food or water while on one of these experiences, she could still feel a draught or suffer sunburn. She remembered a friend of her mother's whose twin son's soul had entered the body of a cat, as the souls of twins often did while they slept, and the child had not woken for three days. When his distraught parents were at their wits' end someone had opened a cupboard door and out had popped the cat, and the child awoke and all was well, but another time the cat's paw was caught in a door jamb and after that one of the twins always walked with a limp. That was why, her mother had told her, no one ever deliberately harmed a cat, in case it harboured a twin's soul. Still it puzzled her. She was like that cat: she could feel pain, and heat and cold, but not hunger or thirst.

Bahiga pitied the camel. To stop their souls climbing into cats, the mothers of twins fed their babies on camels' milk. She wanted to save this

181

one, even though it was a male and could not produce milk for twins, but it had to go because nothing would be achieved unless everyone fought his own battle. And so the camel, bellowing piteously, was sacrificed to the mariid. And the search for the Emerald Tablet went on.

The donkey, running parallel behind the rocks, managed easily to keep pace with the camels. The donkey seemed agitated, no doubt at finding itself in strange surroundings, and had Bahiga known just how alarmed it was she might have talked to it more. For Hanafi the water carrier had never heard of Iskander or the Oasis of Amoun, let alone Zerzura, and had not the slightest notion of where they were now, or why they had come, or even how they had got there. But he had heard of demons in the desert, and he did know a mariid when he saw one, and he had been scared out of his wits.

Bahiga ran beside the donkey, and sometimes she sat on his back, but usually she flew, or rather glided, her feet just skimming the ground. She enjoyed this effortless movement, the weightlessness and the wind in her hair (she always carried a comb) and often wondered what people would say if she let them see her fly past like a bird. But she did not: there were enough problems in the world without everyone wondering why they too could not fly. She held the donkey back as Sanjar and the others entered the narrow wadi on the far side of the flood plain on which they had paid their tribute to the mariid. There was no room there in the wadi for them all, and she did not want them to see her. Moreover, she had to watch who was following.

Bahiga knew the guards sent by the Caliph were not far behind, and had divined that their mission was to intercept the Tablet. They were then to escort Sanjar back to al-Hakim or, if he rebelled, to bring the Tablet back themselves. She had asked the Qadi why he thought al-Hakim trusted the guards with the Tablet more than he trusted Sanjar, and her father had replied that the guards did not know what the Emerald Tablet was, just that they should make sure Sanjar did not keep it, and that besides all four of the guards had families in al-Qahira who would be held to ransom for their conduct. Bahiga suggested that the power of the Tablet was so great that whoever held it would have no enemies, and could easily release a hostage or two, but the Qadi had replied that al-Hakim knew this, and that was why the guards knew nothing of the Tablet's properties or value, and had been instructed most severely to keep it wrapped, and not touch it or look at it directly, and to guard it with their lives and put to death anyone who tried to take it.

However the guards were not the only ones at Sanjar's back, for now the monks were involved. She wondered why the monks were so protective of Iskander, who had no connection with their religion, unless through their scholarship they had also learnt of the power of the Emerald Tablet and had an inkling of where it could be found. The Abbot seemed to be an ardent admirer of Iskander, and wanted either to keep the Tablet from discovery or have it for himself. Bahiga suspected the latter, since that seemed to be the plan of most who knew the secret. The Abbot, moreover, was no dimwit when it came to magic. And some of the monks: she was sure at least one could change himself and others to other shapes. But magicians, all of them, no more than magicians and illusionists.

There remained the other magician, her father the Qadi. Now, though, she had exacted a promise from him in return for her promise to be betrothed. Her task would be easier if he held to his word and kept out of the way. That he would to stay in al-Qahira seemed quite likely, for affairs of state were distracting him from Sanjar's quest.

*   *   *

The Qadi was finding it even more difficult than usual to fathom his master's thoughts. All the power on earth and in the heavens was but a few days out of his reach, yet al-Hakim was bothering himself about the Christians again, and when it wasn't the Christians it was his peach crop. "Isn't that daughter of yours going to marry a Christian?" he barked at the Qadi one day. "Well I'd stop it if I were you. Before you know where you are you'll have your in-laws round your neck, and then you'll come bothering me about some Christian thing or other, and then I'll have to put the lot of you to death. But you're the Judge. How do you sentence yourself to death, Have you ever thought of that, hmm? So you'd better call this wedding off, and tell your future son-in-law to go to go and crucify himself, or whatever it is they do. And don't come telling me about his problems."

But soon afterwards, just as the Qadi had begun to rearrange his life by making mental plans for another way to spirit himself and Bahiga out of the country, the Caliph said the young prince in question had sent a messenger to say he was waiting impatiently for his bride, and begging she be sent without delay. Moreover, the message had reminded the Caliph that the bridegroom was Muslim, though Spanish. "So where is she?" al-Hakim demanded. "Hasn't she gone yet? Still saying your fond farewells?" And then, pleased with the renewed overture from Europe, he made a generous endowment to the Greek monastery in Sinai built on the spot where Moses had seen the burning bush. "If that Prophet found the Ten Commandments at St Catherine's, then we must show him some respect," he said. "We must respect all Prophets, because all they were concerned about was the Messiah, and I am that Messiah."

The city, confused, lived in dread, and as if in response to the fears of his subjects the Caliph issued an edict to say that all found trading before dusk would now be put to death. The Qadi's court was packed with merchants accusing their competitors of illegal trading. Then the Caliph asked again: "Is your daughter ready to travel yet? It's time she was on her way."

The Qadi, of course, knew that although Bahiga's body was sleeping peacefully in her room in his palace, the rest of her was in the Western Desert. He became increasingly anxious, both for himself and for her. Perhaps al-Hakim knew too much about her, and wanted her out of the way in case she upset his plans. For a while her body was safe here, under the eye of her nurse who could put inquirers off by pleading that her mistress was unwell, but the part of her that was roaming the desert was in danger. She might be seen by the Caliph's guard, or by those meddling monks, and in any case what was she going to do with the Emerald Tablet? She was so full of ideals, and so impractical. To destroy the object that could give the owner omnipotence, that was an ideal indeed, but one that seemed to any reasonable man to be pure folly.

"So will you travel to the Western Desert to keep an eye on this Turk?" al-Hakim asked him.

"Yes," the Qadi said.

The Caliph trusted the Qadi. When one was the last in a long line of god-kings one had to know whom to trust. One trusted those who never thought to question one's divinity. Once he had his hands on the Emerald Tablet his god-head would never again be questioned, and everyone on earth, from the last peasant in the land to the Emperor in Constantinople, would bow to him not just as the Caliph, but to a god, the promised Messiah. Then he might even reward the Qadi, if he felt like it.

"Tell your daughter the wedding is off, and that's my final word on it," he said. "I won't have that snivelling so-called prince making demands on me. I don't have to do anything to please anyone. Soon they'll all be squabbling for the honour of pleasing me."

At a stroke a problem that had been niggling at the Qadi's conscience was solved. The cancellation of Bahiga's wedding discharged him from the promise he had made her, that he would not transport himself to the Western Desert to take part in the hunt for the Tablet. The marriage was off, and since Bahiga was no longer obliged to keep to her agreement, there was no longer any need for him to keep his. He told himself that this left him free to go as and where he pleased, whereas in reality he had decided to go before the Caliph's final cancellation of the wedding released him from his pledge. As for the necessity to flee the country to escape al-Hakim's wrath once he was cheated of the Tablet, what would it matter when the Tablet was in his, the Qadi's, hands?

*   *   *

Sanjar travelled warily, alert to changes in the atmosphere, or in the movement of the air or sand, watching for footprints and other signs of presence or passage. He guessed the Caliph's guard were two or at most three days behind, and in this he was right: they followed in the shadows, easily observing the fresh prints of four camels and a man. They were not skilled enough in tracking to notice just when the marks of four camels became those of three, but then they were fortunate not to meet the mariid, which had already eaten two camels and had retired to rest. The guards hoped to move in on Sanjar as he neared his goal, but they did not know what that quarry was, or where: their instructions, for the time being, were to follow.

Meanwhile Sanjar and his companions had reached the edge of the great sea of sand. In the distance they saw great dunes marching on the mountains, and just as high. Here the wind-blown sand had worn down the rocks and left a thick, soft carpet on the desert floor. It was a harsh and empty landscape, and there was little sign of life. Now and again they came across a rock streaked with white droppings marking the den of a hyrax, or sometimes they startled a partridge or a rabbit. Once they saw, basking on a stone, a cornflower-blue lizard which froze as they passed. A solitary falcon regarded them from a crag above. "We see a lot of falcons," Tadros remarked.

"Perhaps its the same one," Sanjar replied.

Bahiga, too, had seen the falcon. Inevitably it had also seen her. It would keep its distance, however. These monks were only magicians. She thought of her father, and wondered about his health and whether he was taking his medication, and she hoped that when they went abroad together they would find peace and a new understanding. He was not a bad man, but weak, and carrying out his duties under a crazed lunatic taxed his strength and his mind.

And so it was with shock and sadness that, after hearing voices two days' ride behind her and mounting the donkey to fly back to search for them, what she found was her father, resplendent in a purple robe and scarlet turban, sitting at a campfire with the four black-coated Caliph's guards, and saying: "And you say the Turk was wounded?"

"In a fight with a Norman adventurer, my lord. The knight vanished back to the coast, but the Turk must have recovered, for the next we knew he was leaving the Oasis of Amoun bound for the south. He killed a young fellow on the way, for we found the body under a pile of stones, and he must have stolen his camel for we found its trappings abandoned."

"Hmm, the more crimes he has committed, the better. Now, where does all this lead us? Where is he heading, and what does he hope to find in this God-forsaken corner of the world?"

"This trail leads to the oasis of Farafra, and the large oases further south. We think this is a wild goose chase, for there could be nothing there."

"Not so fast," the Qadi said. He was not going to tell these men of little education that the Romans – and those who had gone before them – had built cities in the southern oases, and what better place to hide something so precious than somewhere so remote?

Bahiga gave a nod of satisfaction. So her father did not know about Zerzura, or if he did he had not thought to associate it with this quest. It might therefore be possible for Sanjar to evade the guards, and they could continue to Farafra until her father discovered his mistake. That would give Sanjar more time.

The Qadi eased his position and regarded his surroundings with some distaste. Spending a night here would be cold and uncomfortable, and he already had a headache. Besides, these men were rough and not the kind of companions he would choose, and he was glad he would not need to accept their food. He doubted very much if he could rely on them to secure the Tablet, and decided that as soon as he could he would send them in the wrong direction and go it alone.

Since her father was no longer talking and she still wanted to know his plans, Bahiga entered his mind. She had found out how to do this as a child, but seldom did since his thoughts angered her so. This time she was already angry that he had broken his promise, and so, in revenge, she left the headache alone. She wished to know how hard he had resisted if, indeed, the Caliph had pressed him to come, or if coming here had been his own idea. But the Qadi's mind was filled with his headache and the wish that he was seated on a soft cushion, and the smoke in his eyes. So she decided to change his train of thought, and sent him a vision of her mother admonishing him for his weakness, but the Qadi assumed this was his conscience and made the excuse that he was only following his master's orders, which neither he nor Bahiga believed, and nor would his wife had she actually been a party to the thought. Then Bahiga sent him doubts that the Tablet would be found, and he shivered and his heart beat faster. She sent him a picture of himself holding the Tablet in his hands, and he sighed.

And then he bellowed: "Show yourself!"

The rocks around him shook, and the guards jumped up in alarm, and somewhere a donkey brayed. But the Qadi managed to pull himself together and told the guards he had thought, in his imagination, that he had heard a movement, but it was only the wind. However the guards all swore they had heard a donkey, but by the time they said that Bahiga was two days' ride away.

* * *

Bahiga sat wrapped in a blanket leaning against the donkey, and stuck her feet in the sand in the hope it would warm them. It didn't. She dared not light a fire for fear it would give her away, and she dared not sleep since lions and leopards roamed the hills. Through her discomfort, she tried to compose her thoughts. Her first was that her father's betrayal released her from her avowed betrothal. She would still have to leave the country, or go into hiding, but either of those was more easily managed that slipping out of an unwanted wedding. As for her father, whatever happened she had to prevent his getting hold of the Tablet. After that he could accompany her or not, as he wished. Her thoughts then turned to Sanjar, and his strengths – and weaknesses.

A few hundred feet away Sanjar also lay awake. He was thinking of Bahiga, and of how she sometimes seemed so close, as though she were looking into his heart. But the thought was preposterous, and due only to his imagination. She was betrothed to another, and cared not a whit for him. As far as she was concerned he, Sanjar, was only there to find the Tablet.

*   *   *

Dawn broke over the desert. The mountain peaks were tipped with gold, and the sky was the colour of pearls. Sanjar climbed over the rocks and caught Bahiga unawares, combing her hair. She looked up and saw him, and smiled.

"It's funny," Sanjar said. "Nothing surprises me any more." He wanted to tell her of the grief in his heart, but he did not know how to put it into words. He was both overjoyed and dismayed to see her. He said: "Where did you get the donkey?"

"It turned up one day, lost, and we kept it. I brought it with me to add to my disguise. How do I look as a Bedu?"

"Very fine."

He turned away, because he did not want her to see his face clouded with pain.

"Is that all you have to say?"

He said nothing.

Bahiga shrugged.

"Are we close to Zerzura?" he asked.

"It's not far."

"Will you help me find it?"

"No."

"Good."

She looked at him carefully. Something was clearly wrong. "What's the matter?" she asked.

187

"Nothing. Lack of sleep, probably. You should know."

"But I don't know." She didn't know. As she looked at him she realised his mind and feelings were closed to her. She tried to twist her thoughts around whatever obstacle was blocking them, but she could not reach him. She could imagine his thoughts, but she could not read them. Perhaps he was in pain from his recent wound, or he might be thinking of how he was to find Zerzura. For the first time since her childhood she could not perceive what another person was thinking, and she did not understand why.

"Are you well?" she faltered. "I... I hear you were wounded."

"Thank you, I am recovered."

"I'm glad," she said. "I'm very glad." Unaccountably, she brushed away a tear, but Sanjar thought she brushed away a speck of sand.

He said: "Would you like some breakfast?"

"No, no thank you. I have eaten," she said, giving the formal reply.

"Well, we are here, if you need something."

"Thank you."

She watched him walk back to the camels. He seemed to have changed, but perhaps it was that at last he knew where he was. She thought of the prince she would not marry, and wondered if he were as comely as Sanjar.

Bahiga debated with herself whether to tell Sanjar he should make haste, but since he was in such a bad mood she decided instead to go back and see what her father was doing. She found that he and the soldiers had made an early start and had gained ground, travelling, like military men, at a steady pace. The Qadi rode with one of them. To explain his sudden appearance without transport or retainers he had told the soldiers his entourage had been swallowed in a sandstorm. Since there had been no sign of a wind this had surprised them, but he was there sure enough, and as without a doubt they recognised him as the Qadi they had to accept his word. The Qadi found that riding a camel was very uncomfortable, and the swaying movement made him seasick. To add to his discomfort Bahiga now appeared in his mind. She wanted to talk to him, she said. What did she expect him to do, he thought irritably, climb off the camel and meet her behind a rock? No, she said. She wanted to know what were the chances of the guards reaching Farafra. Did they have enough provisions? They had told the Qadi that they had enough food to get to Farafra and back, but they would need to water the camels. But where was Sanjar heading? Was he on his way to Farafra, or further south? Or did he plan to give them the slip and turn off? Bahiga would not say. She wanted to know if he planned to stay with the guards, or follow Sanjar by himself. The Qadi thought very firmly about lunch. Bahiga suggested he give the soldiers the slip so they might meet. Will it be rice and beans, or bread and beans? thought the Qadi. And then he remembered it didn't matter, because he couldn't eat it anyway.

When Sanjar's group stopped at midday to make tea Bahiga was waiting for them, and had even started a fire. Sanjar wanted to know how she had done that without a tinderbox, and she replied that sometimes when there was very little time one had to take liberties with small things. She allowed them to brew and drink their tea in the leisurely, Arab style all three of them had adopted before she told them the guards the Caliph had sent to watch them were less than two days behind, and that her father was with them to make sure that once they had found the Tablet they returned it to al-Hakim.

"They think you are going south towards Farafra, so when you turn off this road you'll have a chance to give them the slip," she said. "But they are closing in on you, and you must not take too long."

"What about our tracks?" Tadros asked.

"You'll have to walk over the rocks. The difficulty is that this will hide the tracks you have made, but it won't show ones you haven't, so at some point they might realise you are not ahead of them. Still, it will give you a little extra time." She stood up and looked at Sanjar kindly, sensing he was still sad. "I must go now," she said. "Look out for the twin peaks," and with that she took hold of the donkey's halter and led it back along the wadi. Before they were out of sight she stopped and looked over her shoulder, but only Tadros turned to wave.

The trail wound on along the bed of the wadi between rocks that changed in texture and hue, broken by floods, tormented by winds and ravaged by ancient seas. From the top of a lone, dead tamarisk tree a falcon fixed them with its beady eye, then took to the wing and soared over their heads to perch on a rock ahead. Sanjar considered the generations of falcons who had watched the trail, and all at once he thought of the army the Persian King Cambyses had sent along this road from the south to launch an attack on Carthage, but which had perished before it reached the Oasis of Amoun. The papyrus they had taken from the monastery said the oasis was then famous for its oracle of Amoun, which Iskander had consulted and thereby learnt he was a god. So Iskander could easily have ridden this road. Had he found the remains of the army lost two hundred years before? Sanjar knew that after one and a half thousand years he would be lucky to find a trace of them, but there might still be swords or other remnants buried in the sand, like hidden pearls. He would have loved to have held and tested such a sword. What of the men who wielded them, who died so suddenly and so far from home? Perhaps they vanished not, as the papyrus said, in a sandstorm, but as a huge sacrifice to the mariid or to an army of mariidin.

They travelled without stopping until nightfall, but still did not reach the twin peaks. That night when they unloaded their bedrolls Sanjar did not eat, but lay to one side with his thoughts. The moon rose, but sleep evaded him, for when he was not thinking of the likelihood that the Emerald Tablet would be found in Zerzura, his thoughts were full of Bahiga and of how indifferent she was to him, thinking only of the search.

*   *   *

Bahiga stalked her father until the soldiers stopped to rest, then she told him to walk over to a sandstone ledge where, if he looked down, he would see her. He did so, being anxious to rid her from his conscience, and there she was, applying kohl to her eyes from a silver bottle. She put the bottle in her pocket and held out her hand to help him climb down, pulling him into a gully where they would be hidden from the guards.

"Why did you come here, Father?" she began. "You gave me your word, and I know the Caliph did not insist you came here but rather you came of your own accord. Why do you want the Tablet? For the Caliph, for me, or for yourself?"

"You spy on me, you follow me around, you get into my head, you intercept my plans – ."

"Your thoughts, Father! I intercept your thoughts, not your plans! It seems I have no influence on your plans, since you do just what you want to do!"

"You will never stand in my way!"

"Calm yourself!" she said. "And don't shout, the soldiers will hear us. This excitement is bad for you. You should have stayed at home. Look at you, here alone with four strangers who could kill you and no one would be any the wiser, except that you would never get back, and you know what I mean."

"No, it's you who should have stayed at home! You and your high-minded, totally silly ideas! What do you know about affairs of state? You should stick to what you know about, not meddle in things that don't concern you!"

"There's no point in arguing with you, you bigot!"

"Harlot!"

For a moment they stared at each other, shocked more at what they had said than at what they had heard. Then Bahiga turned furiously on her heels. Seeing her go, the Qadi wrung his hands.

"No! Wait! We can talk!"

She swung back and put her finger to her lips. "Shhh! "

"Let's talk."

"What is there to talk about?"

"Just, just talk... "

"We have nothing to say to each other. We shall just have to see who gets to the Tablet first." And with that she turned away.

190

There was a shout. A soldier called to the Qadi, who scrambled up the rock. The soldier said he had heard voices, but the Qadi said he had gone behind the rock to say his prayers.

While the Qadi was gone the four soldiers had been plotting what to do with him. Since he had appeared alone, he could disappear just as easily. He had now been with them for a day, and they had watched to see if he had allies hidden in the hills, but had seen no sign that anyone was following. They decided therefore, that night, to kill and bury him (while first taking his purse), for it would later be assumed he had perished with the rest of his party. But at that point they thought they heard voices, and decided to postpone the deed until they were sure it was safe.

*   *   *

That night in the moon-flooded plain Bahiga stayed close to the camels. It was comforting to know that Sanjar was close by and Rhoorogh was on watch. Still she was too cold to sleep, and slowly she crept close to the fire. Rhoorogh covered her with a blanket, and she slept until the sun was up.

When she awoke they were breaking camp. Sanjar, who was tying his bedroll onto his camel saddle, looked down at her with a wry smile.

"I thought we had to rise early and get a head start," he said.

"You don't have to wait for me."

"And leave you all alone?" He laughed dryly. "I suppose you can look after yourself."

"Don't be so unfriendly."

The sun was not yet warm, and she rubbed her hands together.

"You'd better keep the blanket," he said. "Unless it worries you. It's Rhoorogh's."

Bahiga raised her eyebrows a tad imperiously, and got to her feet. She looked down at the blanket. Sanjar climbed aboard his camel. Bahiga looked from the blanket to him, and back again. She had never in her life made her own bed. Sanjar kicked his camel to its feet. Bahiga regarded him with surprise. Rhoorogh came over and picked up the blanket, and tied it on one of the other camels. She thanked him.

That day she rode beside Rhoorogh. They travelled in silence, and she sensed that Sanjar did not want her there. She decided none the less to enjoy herself. The scenery was magical and resounding with space, as though no one had been there before them. The only sound was the occasional snap of a trodden twig and the thud of the little donkey's hooves as it bravely trotted to keep up with the camels. Bahiga was growing very attached to the donkey, and was beginning to feel there was something almost human in the way it responded to what it was asked to do.

191

At last they saw ahead the unmistakable outline of the twin peaks, glowing red in the afternoon sun. It took a full three hours to reach them. As they drew near Sanjar pulled out the map, which indicated that the turning lay between the peaks. From a distance there seemed to be no clear way through, but when they reached the point where the peaks were directly on their right they saw a narrow slit in the rock, just wide enough to take a laden camel. The ground here was covered with pebbles, which would not easily show their tracks and would thus impede their pursuers. Tadros rode ahead through the gap, and soon returned to say the path ran clearly through as far as he could see. One by one they passed through. Bahiga insisted on going last, and before she followed them through the narrow gorge she turned to face the road they had left, just in time to see a falcon lift on the wing and fly off to the north. She looked around. Luckily stones covered the ground for some way. She looked along the way they had not gone, and closed her eyes. When she opened them, camel droppings littered the road for several leagues, and a circle of freshly scorched stones round a ring of ashes marked a camping place.

"That fooled them," she told the donkey.

The donkey brayed. Bahiga was getting used to its responses, and thought that perhaps the magical means by which it had arrived here had endowed it with a special power to comprehend what was afoot. She determined to look in her father's grimoires to see what information she could find on charmed animals. Some magicians used animal familiars rather than jinn, but she did not want to be mixed up in anything as devilish as that. If the donkey had become a familiar it would have to go.

The narrow path wound for some way through the sandstone rock before opening into a wadi paved with crusted sand and dusted with lilies, and here they paused to brew tea. Sanjar's bad mood weighed on everyone and they exchanged few words, even though they seemed at last to be on the road to Zerzura. Bahiga was sad, as well as confused. Try as she might she could not penetrate Sanjar's thoughts. Thinking she might be trying too hard she stopped trying, but still she could not see into his heart. Unwillingly, for she did not wish to spy, she looked at Tadros, and saw he too was dwelling on Sanjar's pain. She had seldom thought exclusively of one thing: now she could not rid her mind of Sanjar. She walked off by herself and sat down on a rock, sifting sand through her fingers.

"Is this anyone's rock, or just yours?" said a voice behind her.

"This is my rock," she said. "You can have that rock over there."

"I'd rather share this rock."

She looked up. Sanjar was bright against the bright blue sky. He held out a handful of lilies. She smiled, and took them, and he sat down and said, "What are you doing here?"

"I don't know," she said. She didn't know. Was it because she wanted to make sure he found the Tablet, or to help him, or to thwart her father, or just because she had nothing else to do?

"I really don't know."

"Don't you trust me?"

There was a pause before she replied, then she said: "It's not only a question of trusting you. If you find the Tablet it will be very hard for you to control it, or yourself."

"Do you think you are stronger than I am?"

"It won't be a question of strength. It will be a question of speaking the Tablet's language."

Sanjar gave a slight, puzzled nod.

"I think you are a good man," Bahiga said. "You seem to me to be a good man. But things are clouding my thoughts, and I'm not so sure of what I know any more." She was afraid that the closer they came to the Emerald Tablet, the more she might lose control. "I don't know what to expect, but we mustn't lose sight of what is at stake."

Her limpid black eyes met his, and Sanjar was struck by how vulnerable she looked. Gone was the strong, independent young woman who had swept him off his feet when she took him back in time, and in her place was a young girl out of her depth. Until now he had thought only of his own sadness and had not considered that she might be as troubled as he. She was different from other women, yet she was forced by the convention of society to behave as they did, to live by the same restraints, to enter into whatever marriage her father arranged for her. It must be harder for her to bear these restrictions than for other women, women brought up to expect and accept them. He stood and reached out and took her hand to pull her to her feet, and her hand felt soft and slight in his. She slipped her hand away, and caressed the lilies. It was time to move on.

Now the donkey, with Bahiga on his back, trotted beside Sanjar. They rode along in silence until Tadros suddenly said: "'Consider the lilies, how they grow'."

"What was that?"

"The lilies. 'They do not work, they do not spin, but –'."

"What?"

"It's something our Lord said. 'They do not work, they do not spin, but I tell you that Suleyman in all his glory was not dressed so finely as one of these.'"

Bahiga said that was very beautiful, but Sanjar asked what it meant. "It means," Bahiga said, "that our spiritual life is more important than working to acquire wealth or riches. It means these lilies are beautiful just for being lilies."

"So we should stop pursuing worldly objects, such as searching for the Tablet?"

"Perhaps we should think what to do when we find it."

"Then perhaps you can tell me, Bahiga, why at first you begged me to leave the country and not look for it, while now you seem to be helping me to find it? What made you change your mind?"

"Yes, I have changed my mind," Bahiga said. "I had better be candid with you, since my actions affect you so much. When you were first assigned this mission, when we first met, you wanted to find the Tablet for the Caliph, and I wanted it to rest where it lay. I was afraid that al-Hakim would succeed in obtaining it, and that you and my father would help him. I was afraid its great power would be uncontrollable in the wrong hands, and I was not even sure what that power would do if it fell into the right hands, so to speak. Would it corrupt even the strongest and purest heart? I did not know, and I still do not. But now I know that too many people want to acquire it, and are looking for it, and are going to continue to look for it until it is found. And one day they will find it. This is inevitable. So now I want to find it, I want us to find it, because you are the only one I can trust, and when we find it we must make sure that no one ever finds it again. Even though we are at risk from the Caliph, or whatever forces are against us, this is what we must ensure."

"And shall we have the strength to do this?"

"I hope we shall."

"All that matters to me is that we are working together," Sanjar said. "I don't care for the Caliph's reward, or fear his wrath, so long as we are of one mind."

"Sanjar – ," Bahiga was about to tell him about her father, and their plan to leave the country. But this plan involved spiriting her father away from the Caliph, and promising to marry a foreign prince. Now it seemed her father's recent action had put into question the first obligation, and eliminated the second. Whatever happened to her promise to wed, both she and her father knew she would evade the nuptials. But the future was too uncertain, and everything depended on their finding the Tablet. So, having nothing definite to say to Sanjar, she decided to say nothing. If only what Sanjar was to do did not matter to her so. If only she could see into his thoughts, and if only she were not so disquieted when she was in his presence – and if only there were something she would rather do than ride beside him though the desert. So, instead of telling him what was in her heart, she said: "Yes, I'm glad of that too."

They rode for the rest of that day, and for two more days. The path, although unmarked, seemed to fall open before them. Always they went south, and each time they came to a point where they might have turned this way or that, a landmark was there on the map, or they chose one wadi over another only to see later from the lie of the hills that there would have been no passage had they taken the one they had abandoned. Shortly before dusk on that third day they beheld a plain in which grew a grove of date palms, the first vegetation they had seen for days. Beyond it was another grove, and another, until the landscape was so thickly wooded with palms and trees that one could not see through them. Not a breath of wind stirred, but soaring overhead was a pair of kites. Had they arrived at Zerzura?

The scroll fragments they had found at Wadi Natroun gave little indication of what they would find in Zerzura. The Abbot had told them of a fabled oasis seven days south of the Oasis of Amoun, where an impenetrable white wall surrounded a city paved with marble, or perhaps with gold. Sanjar had asked himself many times why the Abbot had divulged this information, since it now seemed apparent to them all that he was as keen as the next man to find the Emerald Tablet. Could the Abbot not have come himself to steal the treasure, or sent his flying monks? The more Sanjar dwelt on it, the more it seemed that the Abbot was using him. Had the Abbot not said, when telling him what he knew of Zerzura, that any who tried to enter its walls only perished in the attempt? Perhaps, like al-Hakim, he was relying on Sanjar's prowess and ingenuity: he would allow Sanjar to take the prize, then claim it for himself. By all accounts he would be contending with al-Hakim, the Qadi and Bahiga for possession of the Tablet. What were the Abbot's chances against such foes? That was known only to him. But as Bahiga said, they must ever be vigilant.

They began to walk towards the palm grove. A small herd of gazelle looked shyly at them, but did not move away. Sanjar made to unhook his bow, but Bahiga held up her hand. "No!" she said. "These animals have never seen a human being. Look! They have no fear. You cannot shoot them, that would not be sport, and would betray their trust."

"But we could eat roast meat!"

"Think of the lilies," Bahiga said.

"What have lilies got to do with a roast supper?"

"Don't bring bad luck on us," said Tadros.

Sanjar had divined by now that Bahiga did not need to eat, and that Tadros followed blindly everything she had to say, but nevertheless he did not want to offend and did as they told him. The gazelles watched them with their liquid black eyes. "What tales they might tell," Bahiga said.

Soon they all heard the sound of running water, and ran to where a stream gushed out of the ground under the roots of a clump of palms and ran over a rocky bed to water the trees. They splashed in the water and bathed their arms and faces, forgetting their quest in the pleasure of the moment until Tadros said, "Can you see a falcon anywhere?"

"Not yet. But they will come," Bahiga said. "They will all come."

The rich ripe dates hung over their heads, unpicked and sun dried. "Those must be the sweetest dates you ever saw," Tadros said. "I'm going to pick hundreds when we stop. We shall have enough to last us all the way back to al-Qahira."

Unaccountably, Bahiga shuddered and felt chilled, and gathered her black Bedouin shawl around her shoulders. She never looked into the future: it was forbidden. Her father did that, aided by his wretched jinni. She did not and would not. Sometimes, though, the future settled on her unbidden, like the chill of winter or the warmth of a summer day. When that happened she never allowed the sensation to reveal its secrets, and when, as sometimes happened, she saw clearly what lay ahead, she always pushed the vision aside. The future was not for her or anyone to see.

So when they turned a corner and saw her father waiting for them, no one was more surprised than she.

14 · Zerzura

T HE QADI WAITED beside an outcrop of rock, the purple satin of his gown catching the last rays of the day's sun. He carried no protection from the heat or cold, nothing but his short staff. Bahiga's heart sank when she saw him, and as they drew near she dismounted and ran over to him, anxious that not even the donkey would overhear them.

"What are you doing here?" she demanded.

"I deduced that you would try to find Zerzura. I gave the soldiers the slip, and came here to wait for you."

"Have you lost your senses? What will the guards do when they find you are gone? Do you think they will carry on to Farafra without you? Of course not! They'll come back to find you, and make trouble. You should have stayed with them. Better still, you should never have left al-Qahira in the first place."

"Enough of your insolence! I have more right than you do to be here. Look at you, travelling through the desert with three men and no chaperone! If your intended husband gets to hear of this, there'll be more trouble than you ever dreamed of!"

"Good! Then there'll be no wedding!"

The Qadi's heart fluttered. Bahiga did not know that the Caliph had already called off the marriage, and he would not tell her until it suited him. In any case, once they found the Emerald Tablet the marriage would be of no consequence. What mattered now was that Sanjar should enter the city and obtain the Tablet. After that would follow a battle of wills between him and his daughter to possess it, but he was confident he was wily enough to win.

"Let's stop squabbling and get the Tablet," he suggested.

"Father, I beg you one last time. Forget the Tablet. Go back now to al-Qahira and tell al-Hakim the mission is going well, tell him what you will, but make plans to leave the country. I shall join you soon. Perhaps we shall find it, perhaps not, but as soon as I get back to al-Qahira we can escape the Caliph, get away from all this and start life afresh."

As he listened the Qadi sensed that not all was well with his daughter. Her words were impassioned, but though he had heard them before this time

197

they did not ring true. Was she lying? It was impossible. In all her life he had never known her to lie: she had been outspoken, insolent, unwomanly and ill guarded in her sentiments, but she always told the truth, even when it was the bitter truth. She was not lying, but still there was a weakness in her voice, a weakness he had not discerned in her before. He was struck by a terrible thought, so terrible he dared not dwell on it: but could it be true? Had she lost her powers? He looked from her to Sanjar. Had she lost her powers?

The horror of this possibility struck him dumb. Bahiga meanwhile did not think to enter his mind: she had grown so used over the past days to being excluded from Sanjar's thoughts that she forgot to test whether she still had the ability to enter her father's head, where she could not just read his thoughts, but think them.

The Qadi, however, realised that what was different, what made her seem so weak, was that she was thinking her own thoughts but she was not thinking his. He probed in the recesses of his mind. She was not there.

He spoke aloud: "Bahiga, where are you?"

She did not know what he meant, and turned on her heels. She did not see the walls of the city, their limestone bricks still gleaming white though they had been built centuries before. Sanjar, though, had seen them through the trees, and was impatient to approach. First, however, he must greet the Qadi. He made his camel kneel. Getting on and off the camel was the most uncomfortable part of riding it. The rest was easy. Several times he had suggested that Bahiga rode with him rather than on the donkey, but she always declined with an unaccustomed shyness. The remaining pack camel was too heavily laden to be comfortable, though it might have borne her slight weight. Sometimes she walked alongside, but she refused to take the place of Sanjar or Tadros on the camel, saying she did not want the smell on her clothes. He was glad now that she had not been riding with him when they came upon her father.

Sanjar strode over to the patch of sand where the Qadi was holding court, and knelt before him.

"This is unexpected, sir," he said. He did not question the Qadi's appearing without retainers or tents, or even without a camel to ride, for Bahiga had told him a little about her father's capabilities – particularly of how he used the jinni – and he guessed he was there by sorcery. Neither did Sanjar reveal his disquiet at seeing him, even though he believed the Caliph's right hand man was not there to aid him, but rather to use him – or betray him. It remained that the Qadi was Bahiga's father, and Bahiga, even if she was betrothed to another, was the woman he loved and whose hand he still hoped to win.

"Under other circumstances, I would have you beheaded for daring to ride alone with my daughter," the Qadi said.

"Sir, you have my word of honour that I would not harm or dishonour her, and that my journeying with her has been solely for the purpose of affording her protection."

The Qadi looked over Sanjar's shoulder at Bahiga. She had now seen the walls of the city, and had begun to float towards them. Her feet were almost an arm's length above the ground. She had not lost her powers. He took out his silk handkerchief and mopped his brow.

"My daughter," he began. "My daughter is not even herself. I would say she was bewitched, but that comment would be redundant." He paused, and was aware that Sanjar was waiting for him to continue, but he had already given away too much. He cleared his throat, and went on: "Your task is to enter the city. We do not know if what we seek is there; perhaps it is, perhaps it isn't. Now, how do you propose to enter it? I have heard that whoever tries to climb the wall is a dead man."

"I think I know of a way, sir."

"Yes? And what might that be?"

"All in good time. Let us first approach the city."

The Qadi pursed his lips, and measured the distance to the city walls. He did not wish to be seen flying, yet walking through the drifts of sand that had blown up around the palm groves would not be an easy feat. And so it was that Sanjar, sensing his dilemma, walked humbly beside his camel on which the Qadi sat, or rather bounced, and in this way they came to the walls of Zerzura. Bahiga was nowhere to be seen, and for a moment Sanjar feared she had flown over the wall: but she had not, and a moment later she appeared.

"The city must be huge," she said. "The walls go on for ever." So she had not been tempted to peek over the top. He had warned her of the danger, although she probably already knew the instructions he carried written on the papyrus. She was laughing with the excitement of finding the city the desert hid so carefully, but her father was again alarmed at the way she was behaving. Bahiga was usually so collected, so in control. Now here she was, flushed with excitement and giggling like a little girl. She was betraying herself as something he often accused her of being, nothing but a foolish woman. Perhaps gaining control of the Tablet would not be so hard after all.

"So what do you know about getting in?" the Qadi asked.

Sanjar knew the words on the papyri by heart, but he only said: "We must find a place to camp before night falls."

"It isn't dark yet!" the Qadi cried. "Let's get on with it!"

"I fear, sir, that we cannot allow ourselves to be so impatient. If we wish to secure the treasure within these walls we must make use of full daylight. It would be folly to attempt a search now."

"The falcons are coming," Bahiga suddenly said, shielding her eyes against the evening light as though they were near enough to see.

"Are they here?"

"They are many leagues away, but they will be here tomorrow before sunrise."

"What falcons?" asked the Qadi. "What is she talking about."

"We shall have to risk it," said Sanjar. "Tadros, make slings and practise your shots. Rhoorogh too, though we shall need his strength for other things."

"What falcons?"

"And pick some dates, Tadros, We might as well enjoy them."

"Just beware, father. The falcons are enchanted."

"That's not the only thing that's enchanted around here."

The donkey brayed, and brayed again. He screamed, but nobody listened.

"Shut up," Tadros said. "I can't hear myself think."

But later, when a fire was lit, the dates picked, the camels fed and the tea brewed, as Rhoorogh whittled the tips of several straight sticks into spear points, Tadros used the firelight to fashion a sling from a strip of leather cut from his pouch, and said: "Do we have a plan for tomorrow?"

"I shall enter the city alone," Sanjar said. "No one can climb the walls: Tadros and Rhoorogh must try to prevent anyone from following the way I came. You must also protect our camels, for without them we cannot return to the Oasis of Amoun."

"I'll take care of that," Bahiga said.

"I had better come inside with you," the Qadi said.

"Not so fast, father."

Sanjar shook his head. "I shall go alone."

"I order you to allow me to accompany you."

"I take my orders directly from the Caliph."

The Qadi's face began to assume the colour of his robe. "I am the Caliph's representative here. You follow my orders," he barked.

'No." Bahiga said calmly. "Sanjar must go in alone. It has to be that way."

"We don't even know if the Tablet is there," Sanjar said. "We have to be prepared for disappointment, and to take our search elsewhere."

Bahiga, who had been watching the flames, looked up and said: "This is the time and the place, and soon we shall all be here. Father, because you are with us, sharing our fire, we take you as one of us."

The Qadi said nothing. There was still time. And then there she was, in his mind again. You're out of time, father. Don't destroy yourself, because you'll destroy all of us. You always wanted to do well. Now's your chance to prove what you can do.

Stop interfering.

Power corrupts.

I already have power.

And?

Power can be used for good.

Power makes people evil.

And who's evil?

"I don't know, father, I don't know anymore," Bahiga said aloud.

"We should sleep," Sanjar said. He hesitated, and added. "I don't want to intervene between a father and daughter, but I want to echo what Bahiga has said. We must be together. Our duty is to keep the Emerald Tablet from falling into the wrong hands. It is not my desire to dishonour the man who has charged me with this task, but it is my duty, and the duty of all of us, to prevent disaster from befalling us, and all mankind."

No one spoke. The silence was broken by a sudden report. It was Tadros practising his slingshot.

*   *   *

Bahiga slept very little. Before first light she crept up to the camels, who were gently ruminating their supper, and whispered a few words. Her father was snoring from within the folds of the blanket they had given him, but Sanjar was awake, and whispered her name. She bent over him.

"Sanjar," she replied quietly. "It is time to rise."

"Bahiga, I want to say something. Whatever happens today, I want you to know that I will have tried."

She felt for his hand. "Sanjar, over the past few days we have shared an intimacy I have never felt with anyone before. It has been very sweet, and true, and I've discovered that I can feel something special for someone even though I don't know what he thinks about it -- "

"You know what I feel about you."

"That's... that's not exactly what I mean. But what I mean to say is that now I know you well, or I believe I do, and I know in my heart that you will do as well as you can do."

He caressed her fingers. "Thank you," he said.

Dawn began to break. As the long fingers of light curled round the crannies of the desert, Tadros woke and cried: "The camels! They've gone!"

Bahiga, sitting with Rhoorogh beside the reawakened fire, held her fingers to her lips.

"They are here," she whispered.

"Where?" His face was distorted with anxiety.

"On the ground, look."

"There's nothing!"

"Look."

"Only lumps of rock."

"Well, I couldn't turn them into mice, the falcons might catch them, or they'd run away. And I couldn't change them into plants, or they might get trodden on. So there they are."

"Lumps of rock?"

"Lumps of rock. At least they won't go anywhere."

"How will you change them back?"

"Just –," she flicked her fingers, "like that."

"You'd better make sure nothing happens to you."

"Yes, you're right. You terrible boy, you're always right."

Sanjar spread out his prayer mat and performed the dawn prayer. Rhoorogh was brewing strong coffee, and Bahiga, while she sipped it, regarded the sunlight glinting on the silicone grains in the wind-blown sand, and marvelled at how deeply it had drifted. Perhaps there would come a time when the winds would throw a blanket over Zerzura, and the dunes would march in from the west, and the white city would be buried under a cover of gold.

Yet even that would not be enough to safeguard the Emerald Tablet.

Sanjar, noticing that the Qadi was still asleep, took out the papyrus scrolls and read them for one last time. The script was Greek, but the illustration showed clearly what he had to do. The gate was guarded by a bird, which held in its beak the key to the gate. What could it mean? Centuries had passed since the map was drawn. What if the key were lost?

The Qadi opened one eye, and shut it again, and resumed his snoring.

"I shall come with you to the gate," Bahiga said. "Tadros, is your sling ready? And Rhoorogh, are you prepared?"

As she spoke three dots suddenly appeared in the sky to the north. "Come," Bahiga said.

The Qadi stirred.

"I'll catch you up," Sanjar said.

"Come now."

"Go, I am not far behind."

When she had turned her back and begun to go round the wall he shook the Qadi, who still pretended to be asleep and delayed opening his eyes.

"Please sir, wake up. I have a request, and I must ask it now."

"A request, at this time of the morning?"

"Sir, there is little time, but I must ask you the most important thing I ever asked. I beg you to grant me your daughter's hand. Grant me this, before I go into the city."

The Qadi appeared suddenly to come to his senses, and sat up. What could he say? It was impossible for Bahiga to marry anybody; she would lose her powers. "She is already betrothed," he spluttered.

"Sir, she is betrothed, as I have heard, to a foreigner, a Christian. Is that the best you can do for your daughter?"

The Qadi thought quickly. This young man was in love with Bahiga, and Bahiga, if her odd behaviour were any indication, was in love with him. She was strong minded enough to do what she wanted, even if she later regretted it. He thought fleetingly of her mother.

"She is betrothed of her own will," he said.

"Look me in the eye, sir, and tell me that."

The Qadi met Sanjar's desperate gaze.

"By my life, I was against this match, but Bahiga wished for the marriage and begged me to agree to it. I swear this is true," he said.

Sanjar stood up slowly. All his will and strength drained away. He heard her call: "Sanjar, come, hurry!"

She was using him. Her only need for him was that he would find the Tablet.

Once again his eyes fell on the Qadi's, and the older man read his pain. It was the torment he would have felt had his wife refused to become his. But she had not refused, and the pain had merely changed its nature.

"I am very sorry," the Qadi said.

Sanjar bowed his head, and turned to follow Bahiga. His mind, however, was not on entering the city: he was wondering how he could so have misunderstood her.

As soon as he had gone, the Qadi removed the maps from Sanjar's pack. He read them with some effort, for he had difficulty with Greek, and then rolled and replaced them. All at once he was startled by a strong current of air as a falcon swooped and circled him menacingly, its talons outstretched. He raised his hands to save his turban and received a cruel scratch. He danced about, waving his arms to defend himself, when all at once there came a sharp hiss through the air, and the hawk crashed to the ground. He went towards it, but stopped as the falcon began to fade until it vanished in a puff of steam. "Well," he said. A huge dark shape now lay in the sand. "A dead monk," the Qadi said to himself. "Well I never."

Averting his eyes, Tadros reloaded his sling. He did not know the punishment for killing a monk, and he didn't want to think of it. Two more falcons circled, but they kept well out of range.

Sanjar followed Bahiga's footsteps in the dry sand as she circled the walls in a clockwise direction in search of the gate. He caught up with her before she reached it, and without knowing what he was doing he caught her by the wrist.

"Bahiga!"

The wild look in his eyes startled her. Seeing her look of surprise, he dropped her hand.

"I'm sorry, madam, I forgot myself," he said.

"Sanjar, what is the matter?" His strong grip had hurt her, and she rubbed her wrist. "What is it?"

"Nothing. Let's get on with the task." Silently he led the way. He glanced up to see two falcons circling nearby, but not crossing the wall. He cursed himself for assuming the gate would be as near the trail as it appeared on the map.

"It was a drawing, not a map," Bahiga said suddenly. "It wasn't supposed to be accurate."

"How did you know what I was thinking?"

"I just guessed." It was indeed a guess. But it was a start.

"I wish you had waited to bring the camels closer before you turned them to stone," Sanjar said. "Didn't you know where the gate was?"

Bahiga ignored the sarcasm in his tone. He was in a bad mood again. "It's supposed to be you who finds the way in," she reminded him.

"So sorry, I forgot what I was here for."

"This isn't the time for you to waste energy in fuelling a bad temper."

The gate faced west. It was a double gate, a span again taller than he, fashioned of wrought iron and a little rusted, but unbroken. Bahiga gasped when she saw it. It looked as though it had been in place for no more than a short time, yet they knew it had not been opened for more than a thousand years. Around the gate grew a straggle of damask roses, long abandoned to the wild, yet though they climbed and clung to the walls they had not invaded the gate, as though to leave it free to be opened when the time came. Now was that time.

Then they saw set into the ironwork several birds, their throats uplifted in song. Forged in iron, they sang forever, perched on vines from which tumbled heavy clusters of grapes. In the centre of each of the two gates was a round face, an image of the guardian goddess Hathor with a crescent moon upturned on her head like the horns of a cow. There were specks of gold on her eyes and lips as though she had once been gilded, but the gold had long ago been washed away by rain.

Sanjar began to look for the key. He soon noticed that each of the birds stood on a leafy branch, and that from behind each beak curled a strand of vine. He felt each one of these until he found one that was clipped in place and came free in his hand. It was a small, twisted length of metal, and surely not enough to allow one to enter a city. But now he had the key, he must find the keyhole. He ran his hands up and down the centre rim of the two gates, but could not find anything that resembled a lock.

"The lock for such a tiny key must by now have rusted over," he said.

"Look at Hathor's eyes," Bahiga replied.

The pupils of the goddess's eyes were deep and black, and when he looked closer he saw that they were tiny holes. He inserted the point of the tiny key into one of the pupils, and at once felt a small click. The gate still did not give. He repeated the movement with the other eyes, and as the fourth clicked the gates parted as smoothly as butter cut by a knife.

Sanjar stepped inside. He turned, and for a moment stood looking at Bahiga, but to her disappointment he did not return her smile. Then he took a few more steps into the city. The gates, which opened inwards, swung back and closed. He put the key in his pouch.

Whatever scene once lay behind the gate was now blanketed by sand. He swept the yellow dust away with his foot, and saw gleaming white. He stooped to clear more. Beneath were marble paving stones, as sharp and smooth as the day they were laid. He stood up. Ahead a colonnade of marble pillars led to a tall building, a temple perhaps, much like the ones that lined the streets of the old, and largely uninhabited, parts of Iskandriya. Yet this and all the buildings that surrounded it was perfect in its symmetry and its very completeness. It had not been stripped it of its marble facing, nor had its stones been torn down to make new buildings. This was a city splendid and unplundered, its magnificent villas and courtyards, its tall columns and graceful statuary undefiled.

Where would a treasure be hidden? As he looked from corner to corner he saw a movement, and looked up. To his dismay he saw the two falcons perched on a parapet of the temple. They must have flown over the open gateway as he passed through, and were thus inside the city with him. Why hadn't Bahiga entered too? Only she could have mastered their sorcery. At once he felt ashamed. This was no place for her. In any case, was she the person he needed by his side? He took a grip on Moonflinger. This was his battle, she always said.

He looked carefully around. If everyone who tried to climb the walls of Zerzura perished, then why? Was the city guarded by a magic spell that defeated anyone who flouted the rules? Or was it something more mundane, yet just as sinister? A hidden weapon, perhaps, or a poison?

On the inside of the wall was a smooth drop, with no foothold, and anyone who found himself on top of the wall had no choice but to jump or fall down. The ground at the foot of the wall was, as everywhere, covered by a layer of sand. Gingerly he scraped away the dust, and found underneath a row of ordinary-looking slabs. When he pressed one, however, it gave way and he almost toppled over. It swung back and he tried it again, this time holding it open with his foot so that he could peer into the gloomy hole underneath. What he saw made his stomach turn. Below was a long trough of water, but the water surface was several feet under the level of the stone slab. Anyone who fell through the hinged paving stones would be unable to find a purchase, and would drown. The trough must run all round the wall. He shuddered, then he looked up at the falcons. They could have flown over quite safely. "Stupid!" he shouted, uncertain whether he meant himself or them. Then he thought of Bahiga, and ran back to the gate. He studied the paving stones there, and discovered that these too swivelled when trodden upon, but saw that when the gates were open the slabs were secured by their weight. It was therefore possible to walk through the gate, but not to jump over it. So Sanjar called to Bahiga, who was standing among the trees, to tell her that if she wished to enter the city she should fly, but not land close to the wall. Then he wondered why he had told her this, and turning his back on her he walked along the colonnade and entered the temple.

The Qadi, hiding some way round the wall, heard Sanjar's words and smiled.

Once inside the temple Sanjar paused to take stock of himself. He did not have long, and yet he was concerning himself with the falcons, and booby traps, and whether Bahiga could fly safely over the wall. He could feel his blood running high, and he knew he had been jumping from one thought to the next with abandon. He needed to think, to put himself in the minds of Iskander's men, to think where they would have hidden the Emerald Tablet.

The accounts said Iskander had found the Tablet in the wrappings of a mummy at Giza, probably the mummy of a great pharaoh – perhaps even Cheops himself, builder of the Great Pyramid. Surely Iskander would have wanted to place so sacred an object in a sacred place? Most probably it was here, within the walls of this very temple.

He looked about the temple, which was roofed with huge slabs of stone. Its unpainted marble walls were carved with magnificent figures of giant gods and goddesses with animal heads and pharaohs wearing the double crown, and with friezes showing barges, processions, cattle, flowers, and scenes of battle and of the pharaoh receiving his court. Around the hall were antechambers, and Sanjar walked through all these but nowhere did he see a place where such an object might he hidden. He went back to the main temple, and there his eye fell on a zodiac inlaid into the centre of the solid marble floor. The signs of the zodiac were overlaid with gold and set in a base of porphyry. Was this indeed the city paved with gold? He stood on the circle and looked at it from every angle.

Since the first sign of the zodiac was Aries, his own sign, he began with that. The ram, rampant and resplendent in gold, held its horns as though to attack. He moved onto the next sign, Taurus, a solid bull with thrashing tail and strong, muscular legs. That also had horns. He looked back at the ram. A line, narrow as a hair's breadth, ran across the base of each horn. He studied it, then bent and pressed the two horns. The builders of this city must have been very keen on hinges, for the two horns sprang up perpendicular to the forehead. He pulled them, pushed them, tried to press them together, and finally inserted his index fingers into the sockets. They slipped in as though into a glove. He pulled, and the porphyry paving stone in which the ram was set swung upwards. It was a trapdoor. He lit a taper from his tinderbox to hold to the opening and saw that below was a short drop. Still holding the wax taper he jumped through, and found himself in a small dark chamber leading to a sloping corridor. This was plugged after a few yards by a huge granite slab. Sanjar's heart sank, for it seemed unmovable. He pushed it at the top, at the base, and at the sides, but it would not give. He paused and leaned his arm on the wall, at which the granite plug swung violently open, propelling him backwards. He jumped off the floor and through the opening in case the slab slammed shut, but it remained open behind him.

He was in an enormous domed chamber. The walls were painted in vivid colours with scenes of the ancient world, similar to those in the temple above but more alive, not just because of the brilliant colours but because they showed people doing joyous things: hunting and fishing, dancing and reaping corn. Overhead golden stars shimmered in a midnight blue sky. At the centre of the floor, in a circle paved in lapis lazuli, turquoise and cornelian, was a large stand of polished gold, and on it sat a small casket carved out of solid turquoise.

Sanjar stood for a few moments in awe. Never had he seen anything so magnificent. Slowly he stepped forward to the golden stand and reached out his hand to touch the casket.

There was a sudden scuffle in the doorway and he turned, amazed, to see the Qadi and behind him Bahiga, who with both hands was trying to pull her father back. Sanjar decided that if there was to be a fight, he might as well first look at the Tablet. If this was it. He reached for the lock.

"Don't touch it!" Bahiga shouted.

He paused. He remembered a dim and distant room in a city on the other side of the world, aeons ago, when he had reached out for a honey cake, and the same voice had called: "Don't touch it!"

He dropped his hand, but then he thought: No, I will see it. Again he reached for the casket, and again she called, but this time she said: "Please, Sanjar, don't touch it!"

Perhaps it was because of the sound of his name spoken by the woman he loved that he withdrew his hand.

The Qadi was struggling with Bahiga. "Unhand me!" he cried, and to Sanjar: "I claim this casket for the Caliph! Leave it be!"

Sanjar swung round. "The Caliph sent me to find the Tablet, and take it I will! Step back, or I shall be forced to prevent you. And that I'd rather not do in front of your daughter!"

All at once the Qadi slipped free of Bahiga and, ignoring Sanjar's threat, took a few steps forward.

"Stop it, I implore you!" Bahiga cried. "We must be at one in this! Father, don't approach the casket!"

"Silence," the Qadi cried. "You have no hold on me!"

"Father, you promised!"

"I may have done, but that promise no longer holds! You can't wait to be married, I know, but if it's your wedding you're thinking of, your precious prince can find a bride closer to home!"

Bahiga saw Sanjar's face mask with shock, and gasped.

"Yes, he knows all about your plans to find a husband in Europe! Thought you were being pressured into a marriage you didn't want, indeed!"

"Bahiga," Sanjar implored, forgetting the casket. "Is it true, that you are betrothed, and you agreed to the marriage?"

"I did agree, but – ,"

"You have used me! You didn't care for me, you just wanted me to find the Tablet!"

Bahiga put her hands to her ears. What was happening? They were in this enchanted place, while before them was the most precious and beautiful object any of them had ever seen, and within it, or so they supposed, was the object of their quest. Why were they now quarrelling like a pack of hyenas about an unimportant and hypothetical event, and one that would never have been?

While Sanjar stared at her aggrieved, the Qadi dashed forward and caught up the turquoise casket.

As he did so, the granite door slammed shut and the gust of wind this provoked blew out the taper.

"FATHER!" screamed Bahiga.

"What happened?"

"I *told* you not to touch it!"

Sanjar fumbled with his tinderbox, and after a few moments had lit a wick.

"We should not leave this alight," he said. "There will be little air in here after so many centuries, so save your breath on arguing." He went over to the door and pushed, and examined the wall all round. Then he took the casket from the hands of the Qadi – who gave only a glimmer of resistance – and placed it back on the golden stand. The door did not open.

"We are trapped," he said.

The Qadi bellowed with rage. He was half way through his vocal stream before Bahiga recognised his words. "OSMOLEUS!" he was calling. "OSHPUROTH! Fulfil your promise!"

"Father, no!"

"We are here together, she and I! Return to your sworn oath!"

A sudden chill breeze penetrated the chamber, and the flame flickered.

Slowly a blue and white light appeared, and at length two figures began to take shape.

"Masters," said Osmoleus, and he and Oshpuroth – whose backs, fortunately, for they were not a pretty sight, were turned to Sanjar – bowed to the Qadi.

"The casket!" the Qadi commanded. "Take it for me!"

"No!" cried Sanjar.

The princes turned their heads to look at him, Osmoleus over his right shoulder, and Oshpuroth over his left.

"Wait, wait!" Bahiga said, taking a step forward. "This is a little premature! I am your master too, and I also want the tablet!"

The princes turned to each other while Sanjar, whose hand had again flown instinctively to Moonflinger, looked from one to the other in bewilderment.

"But," went on Bahiga, "the casket is of little use to us unless you can find a way to release us from these walls."

There was a short silence, then one of the princes said: "Where are your symbols?"

The Qadi looked lost.

"Here!" cried Bahiga. She dropped to her knees and, fumbling in her pocket, withdrew her flask of kohl and dipped the short stick on the stopper repeatedly in the black powder, dabbing it quickly on the floor. Before long she had drawn a square, and divided this into three dozen smaller squares of equal size. Then with her kohl stick she drew characters in the squares in a strange script, a mix of Arabic and other signs. When it was finished each line read the same as its opposite read backwards. When she had completed the square she pocketed the empty kohl bottle and stood up, looking expectantly at the princes.

The princes waved their arms, and a mighty wind rushed by. It ballooned their black gowns and swept round the chamber, pushing the Qadi off balance and tossing Bahiga's hair about her shoulders and brushing away the kohl markings on the floor in a cloud of black dust. The flame went out. The granite door shook and with a thunderous sound crashed to the ground, where it shattered.

The noise slowly died away. The princes stood, awaiting the next command.

"Now pass me the casket," the Qadi said.

"NO!" Bahiga said. She stood commandingly before the princes, and said: "Lords, we thank you for your service, so graciously given and so gratefully accepted. Now go."

The princes looked at the Qadi, awaiting also his dismissal. But Bahiga said: "Go, just go! Please?"

The princes vanished, and a rush of warm air flooded through the open door. Bahiga turned to her father, who faced her dumfounded.

"You can't do that!" he spluttered.

"I just did."

"What about all the rigmarole?"

"What about it?"

"There's supposed to be a ritual to dismissing the princes!"

"Well I just did away with it. And now I'm going to do away with the rest of this nonsense. Sanjar, pick up the casket."

Sanjar stepped towards it, but the Qadi recollected himself and held up his hand. He moved it no further, but just stood, as though frozen, with his hand in the air.

"Casket," Bahiga prompted.

Sanjar picked up the box. Although small, it was far from light. He followed Bahiga to the doorway, but before she left the painted chamber she turned and said: "Sanjar, a word of warning, and please take it seriously. Don't open the casket."

Sanjar nodded. Perhaps she was right. There had, after all, been a consequence when her father had ignored her warning and touched the box. Had the princes not arrived they might have been there forever.

Unless Bahiga herself had been able to open the door...

He passed the casket to her while he hauled himself up through the trapdoor, and then leaned down and took it from her, and was about to pull her up when she lifted her feet from the floor and floated upwards, her feet landing with a soft spring like a cat's on the floor above. They looked around. It was remarkably still, perhaps like any other morning in the last thousand years. In the temple and in the city nothing stirred, yet they made their way outside cautiously, not knowing what they might meet. Sanjar had forgotten his recent outburst, and even went so far as to hold Bahiga's hand. But when they were half way across the temple she suddenly stopped and said: "Oh! Poor father! How is he going to climb out of the hole!"

"Same way you did."

"But he'll never manage it, he's too short and fat. I have to go back and help him. You carry on. If you meet a falcon, use your sword. I'll catch you up."

"He's a sorcerer. Surely he can get out?"

"No, he can't. He'll stay like that until... I have to go." Bahiga felt something was wrong. She knew intuitively that her father could not release himself or escape from the underground chamber. "I must go," she said.

"I'll come with you."

"No, you go, you must get away," and she pulled her hand away.

On a sudden impulse he kept hold of her hand, and took her in his arms,

210

and kissed her. But the kiss was swift. It was not the kiss he would have given her had all been well, and instantly he regretted it. He pulled himself back, and said: "Bahiga, make haste, I beg you."

Sanjar left the temple and hurried down the colonnaded pathway, pulling to a halt some way before the gate. He turned, but there was no sign of Bahiga. He faced the gates and, holding the casket tightly in the crook of his arm, took a run, clearing the ground and reaching with his free arm to clutch the iron rails, not knowing if they would hold under his weight. He caught the rails and hung, and the gates swung but did give. It was not easy to keep his balance, and he heaved himself with difficulty over the top to drop to the other side. He stood shakily on the ground, breathless from the effort, and glanced back at the temple. He was filled with so many different emotions, yet shining through them all was the confidence he had in Bahiga now that he had seen the way she had overpowered both her father and the evil princes. Bahiga was stronger than he had ever imagined.

He had kissed her! His head reeled. A kiss bitter and sweet, free and forbidden, a kiss born of desperation and triumph, betrayal and love. She had not denied that kiss. And yet she had not returned it. He had stolen it, and he was ashamed. His heart twisted, and then it jumped to the pretty casket in his hands.

What was it he held? Was it the Emerald Tablet? Why had she told him not to look in the box: was it because she knew it was there? Of course she knew! She had known all along. And that was why she wanted him, as she said: to find the Tablet. Only to find the Tablet.

Why him? Could she not have done all this alone?

All this time he was running back to the camp where he had left Tadros and Rhoorogh and the camel-rocks. He ran keeping to the outer rim of the wall, and it was only when he was in sight of the palm grove where they had spent the night that he remembered he had forgotten to replace the key.

He stopped in his tracks. The tiny key was still in his pouch. He must go back, he must secure the city from the random entry of curious and sight-seers and fortune hunters. He had to return.

He turned at once. It was hard to run in the sand. His legs ached, and sand had spilled into his soft boots. At last he reached the gate. He paused for a moment to draw breath, and then looked for the bird with the empty beak. As he did so he caught sight through the gate of the two falcons who, rather than following him, seemed to be watching the temple doors. They fixed him with their beady stare, and then turned their necks full circle to see what lay within. It was as though the doings of Bahiga and the Qadi were of more concern to them than where he was running to with the casket. Did he, or did he not carry the prize? Had Bahiga dismissed him, sent him ahead in order to carry on some theatre with her father? Were they planning to cheat him and let him believe he had the Tablet when he did not? Were they, right now, seeking and securing it for themselves? Where were they? Perhaps he should open the box and see for himself whether or not it was there.

Instead of replacing the key he opened the four locks of the gate and began to walk along the colonnade. And then he saw the Persian dagger. It hung on the wall at the entrance to the temple, and he was astonished that he had not seen it before. He went across to it, and saw another hanging there, and another, while on the opposite wall hung several long, rectangular leather shields. He recognised them, the broad, lion-headed daggers and the embossed shields of the Persian army that Cambyses had sent to conquer Carthage. So Iskander had found the lost army – or he had, at least, found traces of it. Holding the casket under one arm, he lifted one of the daggers from the wall and felt its weight, and examined the carvings on the hilt. Then carefully he replaced it.

Sanjar closed the gates of Zerzura, and replaced the key, and hurried back once again to where he had left his companions. He did not look in the casket. He did not know if he was betrayed, but he knew he had to get his friends away from the desert and back at least as far as the Oasis of Amoun.

*   *   *

Bahiga ran back to find her father, but paused before she climbed through the trapdoor in the zodiac. She was also shaken by the kiss, yet – though men sometimes died for less – she was not insulted. Was this kiss meant to demonstrate that she was still a woman? Her heart was melting with emotion. Sanjar, she knew, felt that emotion, and the kiss was but an expression of his love, a love tinged now with grief and anger. She understood that now. She did not have to read his thoughts to see his grief. Yet if he did have cause to grieve, it was not the cause he thought.

But this was today, and their task had a thousand times more consequence than a kiss, even a first kiss, and she must push the kiss and Sanjar's love aside. She focused her thoughts back to the chamber below the trapdoor, and jumped down.

It was very dark, with the little light available issuing through the trapdoor from the dimly-lit temple above.

"Father?" she called. There was no answer. She had only intended that he remain for a few minutes in the catatonic trance she had induced, yet when she peered through the broken doorway into the painted chamber she could still see him as she had left him, his arm poised in threat. "Father!" she called again, and she held up the palms of her hands so a stream of energy flowed towards him. He staggered, and she ran to catch him before he fell. He clutched her arms and let her bear his weight.

"You – you cheated me!" he cried, but his voice was as weak as a sparrow.

"Only because you were cheating me," Bahiga replied.

"Where is the casket?" he croaked.

"You are not well. Do you feel well? Is it your heart? Let us get out of here, and get some air, and you can rest."

"I don't need to rest. I must see the casket."

"The casket is safe, don't distress yourself."

"Why did you send the princes away like that? They could have helped us."

"We don't need their help. The princes are evil, they are not your friends. Now, we are under the trapdoor. When I say jump, you must jump."

Her father was, as she had feared, almost too weak to fly, but Bahiga put her arms about him and floated him up. When they were both safely standing on the zodiac she lowered the trapdoor and snapped the ram's horns back in place. She took a step back and scrutinised the circle. It was almost impossible to see the hairline cracks on the hinge.

Bahiga helped her father over to one of the tall columns that graced the temple, and gently sat him on the floor so he could lean on it, and took his hand, not wanting him to move further until he was able. His breath, which should have been light like his body, was short and laboured. They sat like this until the Qadi's breathing grew easier, and then she asked him to wait for a moment, and went outside to the temple steps.

As she left the shadows of the temple she was met by blinding sunshine. When her eyes grew accustomed to the brightness, she looked about. The city was so empty it even had no ghosts. There was still no birdsong, but when she shaded her eyes and looked up she saw the two hawks looking down on her. She could change them back into human form but they might cause too much trouble, so she left them there. On the other hand she could change them into mice, but that was black magic and she drew a line at changing a being from one life form to another. Except for the camels. But that had been an emergency, and now it was time to release them.

Sanjar was hurrying back to where he had left his companions. The casket felt heavier and heavier in his arms, but he had wrapped it in the hem of his surcoat and resisted all temptation to look at it. He paused when he reached the palm grove, but he was suddenly startled by the two falcons which swept over his head so low they disturbed the surface of the sand with the current of air from their beating wings. They rose and flew on, but Tadros let loose his sling and one plummeted to the ground. The other circled back, and hovered. Tadros took aim, but missed, and just as he drew back the sling for a second shot the hawk rose still higher, and then spun round and flew away to the north.

Tadros was sitting on a rock, sling in hand, and with him, to Sanjar's surprise, was Bahiga. There was no sign of Rhoorogh, or of the Qadi, or the donkey, and presumably the camels were still rocks upon the sand. He started to hurry towards them, but at that moment the ground beneath shook, and four camels spilled out from the wadi at the edge of the plain and hurtled towards them at full gallop, the black-cloaked riders on their backs with swords drawn and held high.

Sanjar carried on running towards Tadros and Bahiga. He reached them and stood protectively before them, Moonflinger in hand and the casket hidden in the folds of his surcoat under one arm, just as the four guards reined in their camels. Hidden in the shadows behind the rocks lay the body of the monk felled by Tadros' sling.

The captain of the guard sheathed his sword.

"You must be Sanjar Mouseback," he said. "We are honoured to meet you."

Sanjar did not release his grip on Moonflinger, but when the other guards also sheathed their weapons he stepped forward, and stood straight, and said: "If you are here on behalf of my master the Caliph, I can tell you that all is well and you may ride ahead to al-Qahira to tell him so."

"Our task is to ride with you or behind you, not ahead of you."

"As you wish."

"You haven't seen the Qadi, have you?"

"Since you followed him here, you can see for yourself whether he is about."

The captain muttered something to the guards, and two of them rode over to the walls of Zerzura. Bahiga made to speak, but Sanjar held up his hand to silence her. Without moving his eyes from the captain, he said softly: "Let it be."

One of the men waited at the foot of the wall. There was no sound as the other dropped over it. He did not even cry out. But the second sensed something was amiss, or perhaps he heard the splash of water, for he too started to climb the wall. There were footholds in plenty on its outer surface; it was only on its inner side that the stones were polished and smooth. The second man did not jump over, but he called the name of the one who had gone before.

The Qadi heard the shout from inside the temple. He recognised the voice, and the name, but he did not care. He thought only of the casket, and deemed it best to stay out of sight until he felt well enough to follow Sanjar.

For what seemed an age Sanjar watched the man as he remained poised on top of the wall. To rid himself of one enemy in this way was luck, to rid himself of two would be fortunate indeed. But the second guard had received his instruction: he was to send the other in, and wait outside. With the captain at his back he seemed to have no urge to disobey.

Bahiga wanted to return to her father, but was loath to leave Sanjar with the casket in one hand and his sword in the other. There had been no time to restore the camels to their shape, and for the time being they were safer as they were. The donkey seemed to have run off, and Rhoorogh was still nowhere to be seen. They waited for the captain to make a move.

"How much for the Bedu girl?" he asked suddenly.

"She's not for sale."

"Oh, but I am!" Bahiga said brightly, and to the horror of Sanjar and Tadros she skipped over the rock and past Sanjar and began to paw at the captain's saddle girth. Even the captain could not mask his astonishment as she reached up her hand to his, but in a moment he had hauled her up, and her feet were scrambling for a foothold on the saddle. She laughed at the astounded faces around her, and then she was gone. One second she was sitting with the captain on his camel, and the next she had vanished into the air.

15 · A Shadow Falls

THE QADI WAITED UNTIL the guard had stopped calling the other's name, then he clambered to his feet and moved slowly to the door. He looked out through the marble colonnade, which was baking in the midday sun. There was no one in sight. He climbed slowly down the steps and began to walk towards the gate, and then he paused. If there were a way into the city, there must be a way to open the gate from the inside without stepping on the swivelling paving stones.

Bahiga, perched on the gate, watched as her father prodded the ground with his staff. Then he rested his chin on his hand, thinking. The temple foreground was studded with fountains and statues. Here was Isis, the horned goddess, and the hawk-headed Horus, and a host of lesser deities. Near the gate was a fountain with a marble pediment and bowl with an iron tap. The Qadi searched it, and then, triumphant, found a small lever hidden in the ironwork. He pulled, but the device had rusted over and would not move. Yet he was certain he had found the safe way out of the city.

Bahiga flew down and perched on the fountain, chirping merrily.

"Grrr," the Qadi said. "I might change myself into a cat."

Bahiga metamorphosed into herself, and sat on the fountain with her feet drawn up.

"Then at least you could jump over the wall," she said.

"Well how do you explain yourself, flying about dressed like a sparrow? I thought you were against changing shapes."

"Only changing other people. If I do it to myself it isn't black magic," she replied primly.

The Qadi was extremely irritated. He was unable to change himself, or anyone, with such ease. He took his staff and waved it, muttering a few words, thinking of the image of a cat. Nothing happened.

"Come on," Bahiga said. "You're tired. Let's go."

"Go?" he said. "You came back for me? Thank you, thank you."

Bahiga put her arms around him and levered him up as she had carried through the trapdoor. They landed unsteadily on the other side of the wall, and the Qadi gave a wry smile. "Well, thank you for helping your old father," he said.

216

"With respect, there's only one place you can go now. You are too weak to travel any more, you can't even fly. How will you move about? Go back to Qahira. Go now. And when you get there, sleep."

"You give out so much advice, but it's only advice that suits you. You don't want me around because you're afraid I'll get the casket, I know you."

"If that's all you think of me, Father, then you're on your own. You work out how you're going to get back. I've got better things to do." And with that she was a sparrow again, and flew back to the place where Sanjar was quarrelling with the captain, where she perched on a tamarisk tree well out of range of Tadros's sling.

*   *   *

Bahiga's disappearance, as she had intended, had thrown the captain into confusion. He shouted that the Qadi had his hand in some sorcery, and called for him. Meanwhile Sanjar, whose anger at Bahiga's wanton behaviour had been oddly mollified when she vanished, found his chance to challenge the captain.

"The Caliph might be interested to hear that you spent your time buying young girls while on a highly important mission," he said. "The Caliph is a highly moral man. He wouldn't like it, would he?"

The captain's eyes narrowed to slits. "You should watch your back, soldier," he said. "The Caliph doesn't trust you. We are here to bring you to al-Qahira, and under arrest if need be. You seem to have no way to reach the city. Your camels have wandered off, have they? You won't get far without them. Looks as though you may have to hand over to us whatever it is the Caliph sent you to find, otherwise it has little chance of reaching him."

"Perhaps our camels have gone where the girl went."

"Ha! You think you can fool me with that rubbish!" But his words unnerved the captain, who was as superstitious as the next man. "Where's the Qadi?" he asked again.

"Where's the girl?"

The captain looked over to the walls of the city. Where were his two men? Only their camels were there, grazing peacefully. The fourth guard and he spurred their camels into action and trotted over to the walls. As soon as they had gone Bahiga jumped down from the tree.

"Wake up," she said to the three small rocks.

The rocks grew into the camels, which sat, still ruminating, their aloof expression disturbed by a flicker of surprise. By the time they were fully back to their old selves Tadros had loaded them with the packs and bedrolls, and he and Sanjar had climbed on their backs.

Sanjar, angered by the way Bahiga had run to the soldier, could barely look at her. "Are you coming?" he asked her curtly.

"No, I have to find Rhoorogh, and make sure my father goes home," she said. "Make speed, and remember, don't open the casket."

She handed Tadros the rope leading the spare camel and gave Sanjar a long, last look of hope and encouragement, and then they were on their way.

*   *   *

As he called the name of his fellow soldier, the man on the wall craned his neck to look over the top. The ground below showed a disturbance where the other had dropped, but it was more than the slight shift of sand caused by a footfall. And was there not a slight movement of the floor, as though it were swinging slightly? He looked along the wall as far as he could see. It wound round the city, with waving palms on one hand and ancient statues on the other, but he thought he saw in the distance a break in the white stone, and reasoned that must be a gate.

He dropped to the outer side and walked clockwise round the wall, following the footprints in the sand. He reached the gate and was about to see how to open it when the Qadi appeared on the steps of the temple, shading his eyes from the sun. The guard sprung back and hid among the palms, still watching the Qadi through the decorative ironwork on the gate. The Qadi came slowly down the colonnade, walking as though with difficulty or in pain. He paused to scrape the ground with his staff, and while he was examining a fountain a sparrow flew down and sat on the rim of the bowl, and then all of a sudden it changed into the beautiful Bedu girl he had earlier seen with the Turk.

The soldier rubbed his eyes. It was a common rumour that the Qadi was a sorcerer, but who was the girl? Had he conjured her from a passing bird, or had he turned the girl into a sparrow? The pair exchanged a few words, and then they embraced and clutched each other and, lifting off from the ground, flew over the wall to land a few paces from his hiding place. He held his breath, afraid to give himself away, and listened. So the Bedu girl was the Qadi's daughter, Bahiga the Jewel, rumoured to be the most beautiful woman in al-Qahira. How envious his friends would be if they knew he had seen her face.

But what was she saying, that the Qadi could no longer fly? And what was this casket he spoke of, was this what the Turk had been sent to find?

When, outside the gate, his daughter changed back into a sparrow and flew away, the Qadi sat down on a fallen palm stump to digest her words. Perhaps she was right, for of what use would the Emerald Tablet be to him if he did not survive? He had better prepare to go back to al-Qahira. But he was weak and overwrought, and he could not find the will to concentrate. Half-remembered charms rumbled through his mind, but even his jinni did not appear. He was no longer the powerful, skilled magician he used to be; he was a lonely, sick old man, defeated and abandoned.

While he was sitting and feeling extremely sorry for himself there was a rumble underfoot, and the captain and his man plunged through the date palms on their camels. When they caught sight of him they reined in their beasts.

"My lord," the captain said. "We feared for your safety, but we are glad to see you alive and well."

The Qadi gave a meek laugh. "My dear captain, you must take no pains on my account. Make after the Turk, since I am safe."

The third soldier decided to make himself known, but to make it appear he had only just arrived on the scene lest the Qadi realised he had witnessed what had gone before. So he stumbled from his hiding place and gasped in a pretence of innocent surprise to see the Qadi and the other guards, and said: "I have searched all over for our friend, but I cannot find him at all."

"Did you try inside? After all, we saw him go over the wall."

"Sir, it seemed unsafe to jump over the wall."

"Unsafe?" roared the captain. "What do you mean, unsafe? You scared of a jump?"

The guard hung back, but the captain said: "Well, go."

"But sir – "

"Go!"

The man hesitated. If he told the captain what he had seen and heard then he would be at the Qadi's mercy, yet if he obeyed the captain and climbed over the wall he too might disappear.

The captain shouted with impatience, and the soldier ran for the gate. He looked for a latch, then he shook the gate.

"Climb it!" came the roar from behind.

It was easier to climb the wall than it was the gate, but when he reached the top he hesitated once again.

"What's the fool doing?" cried the captain, cursing.

The soldier studied the ground. If he leaped far enough from the wall it might be safe. He jumped.

"Well, what can you see?" shouted the captain.

There was no reply.

The Qadi fingered his moustache.

"Where is he? What's in there?" the captain demanded.

"Now how should I know?" the Qadi said. "I couldn't climb over the wall if I tried. I was just sitting here, looking at the gate and wondering how to get in."

The two guards rode over to the gate and peered through. They saw no one, nor did the marble halls of the city inspire them with awe. They called and called, and discussed between themselves whether to enter, but decided against it. Eventually they thought of Sanjar and that he might also have vanished, just like the soldiers and the Bedu girl, so they turned their attention from the city. Their parting words to the Qadi were to wish him godspeed, but they assured themselves he would be dead of thirst and hunger within the day.

*   *   *

That morning the donkey had listened appalled as Bahiga whispered the magic words to the camels, and after watching them shrink to stones he had crept quietly away. He hid for a while, but soon saw that everybody was too busy to notice his absence and wandered off. Later he heard Rhoorogh calling him, but he did not much care for Rhoorogh, who was huge and hairy and rough, so he led him rather a dance, in and out of wadis and round corners until both he and his pursuer lost their bearings. He had not caught sight of Rhoorogh for some time, of which he was glad, but he was lost in this deceptive landscape. He had no idea which part of the world he was in, and he didn't know how to find Bahiga or get home.

He had been wandering for most of the morning and had climbed some way up an incline to improve his view when he saw below the green oasis and the gleaming white walls of Zerzura. He brayed with delight, for it was near these walls, at daybreak, that he had last seen Bahiga. He did not know from which standpoint he was observing the wall, but all he had to do as follow it round, and eventually he would come to her. So he cantered over to it, and walked, anti-clockwise, though the soft, untrodden sand. When he had walked so far that he thought he must have circled the city twice he came upon the Qadi, who was sitting on a fallen palm stump, wailing piteously and every now and again hammering his fist into the bark like a bad-tempered child.

He approached the Qadi with a mixture of curiosity, trepidation and pity, and nudged him with his nose. The Qadi looked up, instantly touched by the donkey's attention.

"Have you come to the aid of an unhappy old wizard, my friend?" he asked sadly.

The donkey emitted a short bray.

"Well I can't seem to get back to al-Qahira by myself. Let's see how far you can carry me." The Qadi pulled himself to his feet and reached out for the donkey's stubby grey mane, but the donkey had no intention of allowing the Qadi on his back. He brayed again, and backed away. If he had to walk to al-Qahira, he would walk alone.

220

"Come on, little donkey. Do an old man a favour."

The donkey brayed again and trotted in a circle. The Qadi ran after him, and the two ran round and round in a cacophony of brays and shouts.

Rhoorogh cupped his huge hand to his ear. That was definitely the donkey he could hear, and he lumbered off in the direction of the sound. Bahiga heard it too. The dust had settled since the guards had galloped off after Sanjar. It was now up to him and Tadros to protect the Emerald Tablet: she must return to her body in al-Qahira before she grew as weak as her father had become, but first she must ensure her father was able to return, and she must find Rhoorogh.

The braying shattered the desert silence, and since it came from the place where she had left her father she did not doubt the donkey's distress had something to do with him. She flew over to see what the fuss was about.

The Qadi was running round and round after the donkey, and despite herself Bahiga laughed. The sound of the laughter reached the donkey in a brief silence between brays, and he pricked his ears and looked up. Seeing her, the sorceress he was convinced had bewitched him and who was his only chance of release, he changed course and headed for her, and she, mistaking his gesture for affection, tickled his ears and kissed him. "Naughty donkey, where have you been?" she scolded. The donkey brayed in consternation.

When the Qadi saw the donkey run over to Bahiga he let out a howl of jealousy and rage. The howl echoed through the hills and swept over the plains, and it howled through the Qadi's body, ripping through his chest and tearing him limb from limb with its pain. A thousand daggers tore into his flesh, and a thousand deeds flashed before his eyes. The ground reached up and hit him, and the sun was black.

Bahiga ran over and tried to roll him onto his back. He was almost weightless, as though he were fading, but because he was so round rolling him over was awkward. Seeing her difficulty, the donkey trotted over and helped roll the Qadi over by nudging him with his nose. At this Bahiga looked up and told the donkey: "Why, you really are human!" Then she looked back at her father. His eyes were shut, his features in repose. Bahiga took a deep breath. She was weak, far too weak to perform such a feat as this, but she summoned all her strength and with great deliberation placed one hand on her father's forehead and the other on his breast. At once energy began to flow through her hands, and after some time she felt the life-force returning.

While Bahiga was restoring life to her father she naturally paid no attention to the donkey, nor to the strange effect her simple comment had on him. The water carrier, hearing her tell him he was human, had promptly ceased to believe he was a donkey. His ears itched, twitched, and shrank. His forelegs shortened and his hooves split into stiffened fingers and toes. His back creaked as he stood up on his hind legs.

Her father had begun to breathe again, and Bahiga sat back exhausted. Soon he opened his eyes. The pain had gone, but it had left its shadow to remind him of the force that had ripped through him. He knew at once what Bahiga had done, and weakly he raised his hand. She took it.

"I'm going to take you back in a moment, Father," she said.

The Qadi nodded.

"When you get there, you must sleep. Don't do anything else."

He shook his head.

It was then that Bahiga sensed there was someone behind her. She turned, still on her knees, and saw a middle-aged man with a startled look in his eyes.

"Don't I know you from somewhere?" she said.

The man bowed, easing with his hand the ache in his back. "I am Hanafi, the water carrier," he said.

"The water carrier? What are you doing here? They told me you'd disappeared!"

"You brought me here, milady."

"I did? Well, what a miracle. I thought you were missing. Well, if I brought you you'll have to some back to al-Qahira with us. I hope we can all make it."

Just then she saw Rhoorogh running towards them, and jumped up to meet him.

"Rhoorogh!" she said. "Where did you go? You ran off to find the donkey? Well, it was here a minute ago," she looked about her, "but it's wandered off again. Now listen, Sanjar and Tadros have gone ahead, but they are not too far in front and you can catch them if you run at night, and since you hardly ever sleep that won't hurt you. I am giving you a water flask. Drink all you want from it, because however much you drink, it will always be full. Don't be afraid of anything, Rhoorogh, and if you are ever in doubt think of me. I shall know, and my thoughts will be with you. Go now. You'll find the flask hanging in that tamarisk tree over there."

Rhoorogh grunted and bowed, and again she urged him to leave. She watched until he had collected the enchanted flask, then she returned to the temple to perform one last task.

She was away for only a few minutes, but when she returned she found her father sitting up and the water carrier fussing over a cushion of palm fronds he had fashioned for him.

"We must go now," Bahiga said. "But where's that wretched donkey? Did it turn up yet?"

The Qadi held his hand to his chest.

"I have to take it back. My nurse will be never forgive me if I don't."

"We should go, Bahiga."

"Well, we'll have to leave it. I suppose it will have plenty to eat here," she said.

And so they took a final look at Zerzura, and then all three held hands, and Bahiga closed her eyes and meditated.

*　　*　　*

Sanjar and Tadros rode under the moon for much of the night. They speculated constantly on how far behind the guards were keeping, and whether they had seen the casket, and what tactics they should adopt should they be attacked. Sanjar talked to keep his mind away from thoughts of Bahiga and whether the Emerald Tablet was really in the casket tied on his saddle, but by the time the moon sank and they stopped to rest the camels that was all he could talk about.

They hid away from the track. "If only Rhoorogh were here," Tadros said. "He's the best watch keeper."

"We can't wait for Rhoorogh."

"We should have left him the spare camel, then at least he could have carried some food."

"He'll survive. He's Rhoorogh."

"But he came with us all this way. We can't leave him in the desert."

"He'll catch us up."

It was cold, but they agreed each to take a turn to try to sleep, and Tadros kept first watch. He listened carefully in case the guards slipped by, and then he decided that since he could almost sleep in the saddle while Sanjar needed the strength to fight he would keep watch all night. He ran medical remedies through his mind to keep himself awake.

Tadros dreamed of being attacked by a leopard, and realised he was in the grip of a pair of strong arms and a knife was at his throat. The night was still black as pitch, but there was no time to think of how they had been discovered. No time either for cowardice. He gave a cry of warning, and believed this was his last breath. Sanjar heard, woke, and had his hand on the hilt of Moonflinger in the same moment. A voice said: "Give us what you have, and the boy will not be harmed."

"What we have is the Caliph's, captain," Tadros said.

Good lad, Sanjar thought. Now he knew it was the captain that held Tadros, and where. He knew too that the captain could and would not spare the boy's life, or his. Without a sound he rolled over and crouched, at the same time drawing his sword. Where were the other men? He did not know there were now only two.

Sanjar waited, every sense on edge, and then he heard the soft sound of flowing sand and felt a movement of air over his head. He sprung aside just as a figure jumped, stumbling off balance when it missed its target. Moonflinger found its mark and ran the man through, at which the captain dropped his grip on Tadros and leapt towards him. Sanjar felt him coming and slashed with his sword, and the captain fell wounded. Still thinking there were other guards to fight Sanjar did not waste the time to spare his life, but cut him through with the blade. It was all over in a minute or two, but Sanjar still waited for the other man.

Neither he nor Tadros spoke. Then, so slowly that it crept on them unawares, dawn broke. As grey shadows formed in the gloom they saw the outlines first of each other, then of the two black figures lying broken at their feet. Still there was no other sound or movement, and as the sky began to pale they saw by its light, standing some way off, not four camels, but only two, while their own still sat, silently chewing.

They looked round, but all was still. "Come out!" Sanjar cried, but his voice echoed unanswered. He and Tadros backed onto open ground, but no one came out of the shadows.

As soon as they were certain no one else was there Tadros wrung his hands.

"Forgive me, master," he said wretchedly. "I tried to stay awake, but I fell asleep."

"What is there to forgive?" Sanjar said, wiping Moonflinger's blade before he sheathed it. "Had you not fallen asleep we'd still be wondering where they were. Now we know."

"We must bury them."

"No we mustn't. We must move on. And besides let them be a sign to Rhoorogh, so he knows we are safe, at least from them."

Tadros was not happy to leave the bodies, but he could not argue with Sanjar and he could not stay behind to bury them. And so they packed their camels and rode on, leaving the guards' supplies, and their camels, for Rhoorogh.

At length Sanjar said: "Were it not for Moonleap waiting for me in the Oasis of Amoun, we could follow the trail to the oases in the south and journey up the Great River back to al-Qahira. No one would look for us that way."

"We'd be robbed before we had gone one league along the river," Tadros said. "There's no law and order down there."

"We're not safe yet. You know who'll be searching for us still?"

"The Abbot."

"Not to mention Captain Guhar!" They laughed at this, then Tadros said:

"Bahiga taught you a charm to say to protect you from the mariid. Do you remember it?"

"I do."

"Then we're home and dry, aren't we?"

"Home and dry? How do we know? How do we even know if we have the Tablet?"

The more Sanjar thought about it, the more the contents of the casket gnawed at his mind. If this were indeed the Tablet then where was Bahiga, and why was she not with them to protect it? Why did she entrust something so precious, perhaps the most precious thing in all the world, in his hands, for him to carry across the desert with no more ceremony than a hunter carries game? And there was more. Why had the Qadi given up the chase? He had appeared to want the Tablet as much as anyone, yet now he had dropped out of the race. It could only be that he and Bahiga were in league, and that they, not he, had the Tablet.

The more he thought about it, the more important it seemed for him to look inside the box. It was not that he wanted the Emerald Tablet — or did he? — it was that he wanted to see whether they were making a fool of him, making him think he was in charge of the Tablet while they had it all along. Bahiga had cheated him with her feelings, now she could so easily cheat him with this. And he had been fool enough to believe her.

The ride was tiring, the sun grew hot, and the desire to look in the box grew irresistible. At length Sanjar could bear it no longer and began to untie the pouch that held it to his saddle. Tadros saw him and a sense of dread came over him, and he said urgently: "Sanjar, she said you mustn't look in the box."

"I won't be fooled over this."

Tadros could not explain his apprehension. Again he told Sanjar to be on his guard, and again Sanjar ignored him. He watched helplessly as Sanjar fumbled with the clasp. Why was there no key, why wasn't it at least difficult to open, why only such a small gold clasp, a simple clip?

Sanjar was now so desperate to open the casket that he almost tore off the clasp. At last it was undone, and he flung open the lid.

In the box lay a wrapping of bleached linen, still as soft and white as snow even after so many centuries. Sanjar felt an extraordinary power surge through his hands, a sensation stronger than any he had ever known before. He removed the wrapping, and felt inside a hard object, about the size of the palm of his hand. Carefully, his heart pounding, he opened the wrappings.

All at once a violent force shook his hands and coursed through his limbs, seeming to surge along his body and out through his head. It left him shaking, but he had no thought except to see what was wrapped in the linen, and he did not pause to consider what he was doing. He unfolded the last wrap, and there it lay in his hands, a piece of polished stone so brilliant it emitted a shimmering green and blue and white and silver light. He gazed on it, and thought that nothing existed in the world that was so beautiful.

As his eyes became used to the glare, and as the diffusion of light settled so that he could clearly see the surface of the stone, he saw there were signs and characters engraved upon the surface in a script he could not read. The signs resembled those carved on the temple walls and obelisks of antiquity, and at once he knew that since the knowledge of their meaning was long lost, the Caliph al-Hakim would never understand the magic written on the Emerald Tablet.

The Tablet was fused to his hand as though it held him, and not he the Tablet.

From behind him Tadros said: "You see, she didn't cheat you."

He swung round to face the boy. "So what is it to you?" he snarled. "Do you want it too?" Then he seemed to collect himself and said: "It's almost noon, let's stop and rest."

The camels knelt and they dismounted. Tadros was disquieted by Sanjar's rashness and unaccustomed temper, and by the force that even from a distance he also felt issuing from the Tablet. He started a small fire to brew a pot of tea, all the time watching Sanjar with one eye, and as he watched the way Sanjar looked at the Emerald Tablet he became afraid. At last he could contain himself no longer, and tears of helplessness and fear rolled into the tea.

"She said you must not look at it!" he sobbed.

Sanjar looked up and glared at him angrily. "How dare you tell me what she said, or wants!"

"Please, put it back!" Tadros sobbed. "It's taking control of you, and I'm so afraid."

"Do you do Bahiga's bidding, or mine? Are you her servant, then? What is she to you, that you regard her command over mine? Do you owe her more than you owe me? Why so close to her, all of a sudden? Do you serve her, attend to all her desires, do you?"

"Watch what you are saying!"

"You snivelling wretch! How dare you address me so!"

"Please," Tadros begged, weeping loudly, "I'm so afraid."

Sanjar laid the Tablet back in its casket and strode over to Tadros. "Afraid?" he roared. Tadros looked up through his tears and cowered, covering his eyes with his arms to protect them from the glare of the sun, or was it from Sanjar's eyes?

"You've betrayed me, you betrayed me with Bahiga, you little wretch!"

Sanjar struck him. The blow hit the side of the boy's head, sending him spinning. His head landed on a rock and cracked.

226

A sensation of horror enveloped Sanjar, and instantly he knew he would hear that crack for the rest of his life. He knelt and tried to breathe life into the boy, but he realised it was no use. He uttered a scream of despair so loud it rolled from hill to hill. Rhoorogh heard it, and was filled with dread.

*   *   *

At mid-morning Rhoorogh had come upon the bodies of the captain and the last of his men. He buried them with some compassion but no ceremony in the sand, piled stones on the graves to hold down their ghosts, and caught their camels. With his precious water bottle slung round his waist he led the camels over the footprints of Sanjar and Tadros, hoping they might relax their pace now they had dispatched their pursuers.

Sanjar's cry shook him to the bone. He raced in its direction with his heart in his mouth, and found the crumpled body of Tadros perhaps an hour after Sanjar had moved on. Rhoorogh was overcome with grief. The boy's camel grazed nearby, and at first he thought Tadros might have fallen from its back and so hit his head on the rock. But later he realised this could not be so, for had he died in this way Sanjar would not have left his poor body lying there, and there would not have been a deep bruise on the upper side of the boy's face.

Rhoorogh washed the body tenderly with water from the bottle Bahiga had given him. He sat beside it until the evening, then he and lifted it onto the back of one of the camels. Night had fallen when he set off with the three camels, tied nose to tail, back to Zerzura

He buried Tadros in the palm grove where they had stayed together that last night. Zerzura would be a good place to live, better than the Horseman's Pillar in Iskandriya. Tending the grave would give him a purpose, and he had an endless supply of water, and dates, and six fine breeding camels to give him milk and hides and meat. And no one to bother him, or fail to understand what he was trying to say.

*   *   *

Sanjar, crazed with grief, rode on. Now he barely paused, eating nothing but a few dates washed down with water. When after five days he reached the Oasis of Amoun his anguish and remorse was unabated. He did not open the casket again, and vowed he would never do so. Its life-force still seeped through the box, but shut in there it was safe, and so was he.

He rode into the village one afternoon when most of the inhabitants were asleep. Moonleap nickered in delight when she saw him and rubbed her nose on his surcoat. He ran his hand over her neck and buried his face in the much loved silver mane, soaking in her warm, familiar smell. When he looked up his face was wet with tears. "I missed you," he said.

And now the two of them again rode alone — or almost, for they took with them Hermes the mule to carry their water. They carried provisions to last only as far as al-Baratum, for from here Sanjar planned to take a boat to Iskandriya.

Over and over again as he rode Sanjar relived what he had done. Whatever the reason he had been entrusted with this powerful object, whether or not it was through Bahiga's goodness, or the Caliph's greed, he had not been worthy. He had betrayed all trust. By doubting Bahiga he had betrayed her. He had betrayed himself, he had betrayed the little maidservant Tadros loved, and above all he had betrayed Tadros. He had also abandoned Rhoorogh, his other faithful companion. Had the Emerald Tablet done all this to him, or was the Tablet a catalyst for him to enact his own desires? He was consumed with remorse, and all the time he heard the crack of Tadros's head as it hit the ground.

The turquoise casket hung in its pouch at his side, but it did not tempt him now. What use were all the riches of the world, if one destroyed those nearest and dearest and, by doing so, oneself? Would al-Hakim learn this lesson, and if so, how?

When he was not thinking of the evil he had done, he wondered that even though he carried the Caliph's coveted prize no one challenged him for its ownership. The turquoise casket itself was worth a king's ransom, yet all the highway thieves and robbers that made these roads so dangerous to travellers seemed to be sleeping. Until he reached the outskirts of al-Baratum.

It was now more than seven days since, so crazed with anguish that he could not bury him, he had left the body of Tadros lying where it fell. He had slept one night in the Oasis of Amoun, and that rest had helped restore his sanity. Now, astride Moonleap, he began to return to himself and to anticipate encounters with the enemies he was sure to meet, from the Abbot to the Caliph and their functionaries.

When the monks attacked it was with a rallying cry that would have chilled the blood of a hardened army, but it was the nature of the attack that most surprised Sanjar. Had the Abbot abandoned magic? One moment Sanjar was riding peacefully towards al-Baratum, glancing from side to side at the cultivated vineyards and citrus orchards with their abundance of fruits and thinking he might sleep that night at an inn, depending on when the next ship sailed for Iskandriya, and the next moment the monks were railing down upon him like a flock of black crows. He drew Moonflinger and dropped the mule's rein but he had no time to use his lance or shield before the monks were upon him, wielding clubs and crude swords and shouting fervent cries. Their eyes shone and there was no denying their strength of body or will, yet even their combined fighting skills were no match for his. He beat them back, his blade humming and flashing as it swirled about, and one by one they fell. When there were still a dozen left, a deep voice called out: "Enough!"

The fighting stopped, and the Abbot appeared in the road, standing with his head bare, his grey hair swept neatly back, and his hands folded in the sleeves of his habit. "That is enough!" he repeated.

Sanjar rode over to him. "Well, old man?" he began as Moonleap snorted and pranced. "Your brothers have had enough, have they? Perhaps they should go back to their prayers, and pray to be forgiven! Are these thieves, or are they men of God?"

"My son, you may well speak of thievery, for you have stolen from its sacred resting place a treasure it was not your place to take. Unless it is returned it will bring chaos and destruction in the world, and for its sake thousands will die. I beg you, return it now before it is too late!"

"You speak in the name of reason and peace, but your deeds prove otherwise, Father! I no longer fear your sorcery, I am protected from it now, so do what you will but do not try to thwart me! Call off your army if you want to, it matters not to me!" and with that he pulled Moonleap round and dashed towards the monks, who scattered as he swung his sword. He turned to gallop back among them, but the road was empty. The remaining monks had fled, and he faced only the Abbot. He reined in Moonleap.

"Father!" he called. "I have the casket, but I advise you not to cross me with magic, for I think you know the power it holds within!"

"You win this time, soldier. But this is not your final test," the Abbot said, and before his eyes he faded, and vanished. The monks waited until Sanjar was out of sight, then crept out from among the orange trees to collect their dead.

16 · The Meeting at Muqattam

THE PHAROS, GUIDE and landmark to homecoming seafarers, domi-
nated the Iskandriyan skyline. The port no longer flourished as it once
had, however, and only a handful of trading ships was docked beside the
local fishing fleet. The weather had been rough and stormy and had caused
havoc in the port, and the crowds bustling on the waterfront paid scant
attention to the road-weary soldier who disembarked leading a bay pack
mule and a highly-bred mare which may have been white under the layer of
yellow dust that powdered her. As the soldier wove his way through the
crowds along the causeway that connected the harbour and the lighthouse
to the town, a man accosted him, whom he took to be a gypsy on account of
his bronzed skin and the wave in his moustache.

"Sanjar Mouseback," the swarthy man said. "Don't you remember me?"

Sanjar stopped and studied the man, then he smiled and embraced him.
"Of course! Hamid of the Ghawarzee! And how are the other members of
your family?"

The man from the Ghawarzee tribe took Sanjar to a roadside stall where
they drank hibiscus tea, and there he related the sad tale of the punishment
they had arranged for Captain Guhar, and of how it had turned to tragedy.
Sanjar offered condolences for the murdered boy and asked if they knew
where Guhar had fled, but he replied that they did not. Since spring was on
its way and the winter winds which blew so cruelly in from the sea would
soon abate the tribe was moving along the coast, and he had come to town
to buy supplies. Since the night of the tragedy, he said, they had heard
nothing of the captain. They thought he had fled inland to the hills, where
other outlaws hid.

"If I meet up with him," Sanjar said, "I will remember Selim."

"Leave it to Allah. One of us will find him."

They parted, and Sanjar bade him take his good wishes and condolences
to the tribe. Sanjar did not stay in Iskandriya, pausing only to buy goods for
the few days it would take to ride to al-Qahira.

He was in a dilemma. If he travelled through the rich agricultural land of
the Delta, the most comfortable and the most direct way, he had more
chance of hiding from any pursuers the Caliph might have sent. If on the

other hand he went through the desert, he might more easily see if he were being followed but the route would carry greater hazards. He dared not run too many risks while he carried the Emerald Tablet.

It was February, and the short winter, which was always felt more keenly on the coast, would soon be over. The Delta already showed signs of spring; birds carried food for their young, kids gambolled among the herds of goats, and wheat grew green on black soil made fertile by the rich silt annually carried down river by the flood. He halted early in the evenings so the horse and the mule could graze, and they blossomed on the lush grass. Sanjar bathed Moonleap in a sweet water canal and brushed the sand out of her mane, and rubbed her down with barley straw.

They were crossing a canal one clear morning when Sanjar saw a horseman at the other end of the bridge. The rider wore black, while his horse was a fine bay Arabian which pawed the ground as it waited to cross. Sanjar rode on to the end of the narrow bridge, and stopped.

"Captain Guhar," he said.

The former captain of the guard feigned surprise.

"Sanjar Mouseback!" he said.

"Here to steal my horse a third time, captain?"

Moonleap danced a little, showing her beautiful arched neck, and chafed the bit. The mule, irritated by an accidental push she gave him, pulled back and laid back his ears.

"Enough of your jokes. I have lost all through you, Sanjar Mouseback. My post, my livelihood, my life."

"I hear you lost a bride, too."

"Do we fight man to man?"

"Man to man? A fair fight? Do you know how to play, Guhar?"

"I fancy your tongue is sharper than your sword. If you want to fight, then fight. I have no time for rhetoric."

"Choose your time and place."

"Here and now."

"And the prize?"

"Your horse."

"And if you lose?"

"Mine."

Sanjar dropped the rein of the mule, which wandered down to graze on the canal bank, and faced Guhar on the path. He edged Moonleap forward, and at once Guhar's horse began to back.

"Whoa!" Guhar cried, but his horse continued to move backwards, and beads of sweat appeared on Guhar's brow.

"Your horse is wisely cautious," Sanjar said, pulling his club from its saddle holster.

231

Guhar tried to kick his horse on, but it flared its nostrils and snorted. It flinched as he used his spurs.

Sanjar raised his club, and began to circle Guhar. At this the bay horse stood still, and trembled. Guhar shouted at the horse to move.

"The horse is wiser than you are, Guhar," Sanjar said. "He knows his only recourse is to flee, yet he knows he cannot outpace Moonleap. Will you fight, or surrender?"

Guhar held high his club, but Sanjar, with the merest knock of his own club, flipped it out of his hand. The bay horse, which was still shivering, jumped.

"Now will you surrender?"

In answer, Guhar drew his sword. Sanjar continued to circle him like cat with a mouse. Now he had replaced his club, and Moonflinger was in his hand. He swung the blade, and watched the sweat as it poured down Guhar's brow.

"They tricked me," Guhar said.

"One trick deserves another."

All of a sudden Moonleap, who rarely put a foot out of step, reared on her hind legs and whinnied. Guhar chose that moment to swing his horse round, and the terrified horse obeyed, but swung too far, throwing Guhar slightly off balance. Sanjar lunged at him, and Guhar tried to defend himself with his sword, but Sanjar edged Moonleap aside.

Sanjar paused in his movements. What should he make of this cat and mouse game? He wanted to kill Guhar, had planned to kill him, but why? Because he had tried to steal Moonleap, or to avenge the Ghawarzee? And why did he have the certain knowledge that he would win this fight? Why was Guhar's horse so afraid, and why was Moonleap acting so strangely? He remembered with a stab of pain the rage that had surged through his bones when he made the fatal attack on Tadros, a rage which could only have come from the Emerald Tablet, which hung in its simple bag from his saddle. He made a decision.

"Put away your sword, Guhar," he said.

Guhar did not trust him, and made no move to obey.

"I said, put it down. Throw it down."

The iron blade clattered on the stones.

"Your quarrel is with the Ghawarzee, not with me," he said. "Know what it is to be a hunted man, for you can rest assured that they will find you. No matter where you go, they will come. It is in their nature."

And he called the mule, which trotted up from the canal and came alongside to let him take the rope, and carried along the track towards the capital.

Sanjar stabled Moonleap and the mule at his lodging house beside the Bab Mitwalli, and slept for a night and a day. When he awoke it was dark and the city's night activity had begun. He went out to buy a length of rope, and called for a saddle maker. Then he returned to his room and quietly unhooked the bronze lantern suspended on a long chain from the high wood-panelled ceiling, leaving the lantern with its oil wick burning on the floor. He made a loop in one end of the rope and threw it up to catch the hook. Gently he tested its weight, and when it did not give he used the rope to climb up the wall. With the point of his dagger he carefully removed one of the square wooden panels. With his free hand he sheathed the dagger and took from a pouch tied round his waist the turquoise casket, which he put through the square hole. Then he replaced the panel, filed away the faint scratches he had made in the wood, and climbed down, removing the rope and replacing the lantern. Afterwards he bathed and put on fresh linen, and waited for the saddle maker. He set the man down to make repairs to Moonleap's saddle, and set out on foot for the palace.

When Sanjar's name was conveyed to the Caliph he was summoned at once. Al-Hakim, dressed in plain robes and seated on a wooden chair, was impatient for news and dismissed all the lackeys in the audience chamber, and only then did he ask Sanjar: "Have you got it?"

"Has the Qadi not told you?"

"The Qadi is sick," the Caliph said. "He can tell me nothing, and I was only waiting for you to return before I put him to death. The foolish man is not right in the head, he believes he can travel great distances by the use of magic, but that's false, for the whole time he pretended to be away he was asleep in his bed. He's up now but he pretends to be ill, so I won't have him around here and I keep him under guard at home so he can't escape. That's what happens when you try to cross me. As for that daughter of his, I told the European who wanted to marry her that he couldn't, because I don't have to please anyone unless I want to. I might bring her here into the palace and use her again as a bargaining point, but this time I'll insist the price is high, since she is very beautiful, though I don't see why anyone would want her because she doesn't keep to the rules. I'm digressing like this because I can't bear to wait to hear your news, yet I like you and if you haven't got the Emerald Tablet I'll have you instantly put to death. Anyway, have you got it?"

"I have it," Sanjar said.

The Caliph uttered a cry of triumph and relief. Then he said: "Are you telling me the truth? No one tells me the truth any more."

"I am telling you the truth."

233

"Give it to me, then."

"The power of the Tablet is very great. I have felt this power while I have carried it, and it has taken great strength not to allow it to overpower me. Therefore I have not brought it to the palace, but I should prefer to hand it to you in secrecy, in a place where you may receive it without its causing you harm or even being intercepted."

The Caliph's eyes widened and he clutched his chair. "Where is it?" he demanded.

"It is hidden in a safe place. And I shall hand it over to you, but I must ask that we meet in the way I shall describe." Sanjar paused.

"Yes?"

"You must agree."

The Caliph struck the arm of his chair impatiently. "Yes, yes, I agree."

"You must come to the place I suggest, and you must come alone. The power of the Tablet is so great that it can be seen by none other than yourself. You alone must receive it. If you bring any others, I shall not be able to appear or to hand it over to you. Agree to this, and the power of the Tablet will be yours."

"Yes!" al-Hakim cried triumphantly. "Yes, it will! And the rewards I promised you, they will be yours!"

*　*　*

It was while he was walking though the streets that had been his haunt when he first came to the capital that he remembered the sedan chair for which he had watched with such anticipation, and the words of a man in the crowd came back to him. "That is the Qadi's daughter, Bahiga the Jewel, the woman they say no man may win, for she knows the secret of her destiny," the man had said.

There was no sedan chair that evening. Sanjar ignored the Caliph's guards at the door and asked the Qadi's doorkeepers if he might be allowed an audience with Bahiga. They must have had orders to admit him because he was shown at once into the Qadi's audience room, and after some moments the nurse appeared and told him to follow her to Bahiga's apartments.

Bahiga was robed in crimson silk, a golden band embroidered with pearls around her brow. She held out both hands to him, but her smile of greeting was tinged with sadness.

"Sanjar, welcome back to al-Qahira," she said. "But I know your journey was marked by grief, and I am sorry you suffered so."

Sanjar fell to his knees.

"Madam," he said, "I failed you. I doubted you word, and I looked in the

234

casket. I held the Emerald Tablet in my hand, and I paid dearly for it. My punishment for disobeying you was the greatest I could suffer. I killed Tadros."

"Nemesis was cruel in her swift reprisal," Bahiga said sadly. "But the struggle within you was too great even for you to bear, Sanjar. The Tablet has powers beyond those of the gods, and you are only a man. I blame myself for leaving you with such a great burden. But the task had to be yours, and you performed it well. You fought to save the Tablet, and you brought it safely back, and you had the strength to withstand opening the box again. No one else could have done that."

"With the Emerald Tablet, there is one last thing to do. But there is another matter, Bahiga, that I must speak of, and that concerns the little maidservant Tadros wanted to marry. She lives, I heard him say, next to Boutros the Physician, who brought him up, and her name is Maryam. If you can find her, will you give her this purse, which is the last I have of the Caliph's gold, and will you take her into your service or find a place for her where she will be cared for?"

Bahiga promised to fulfil his wish, and then Sanjar lifted his eyes to hers. She had never looked so beautiful. Her skin was as clear and delicate as the moon, her eyes like lustrous onyx and her lips as red as rubies. She wore the ancient bracelet set with turquoise and lapis lazuli, as she had the first time they met, and the crimson dress was tight over the bosom and embroidered with seed pearls. Sanjar said: "I cannot leave unless I speak of my love for you. In spite of what you say of my conduct, I failed you and am not worthy to be accepted by you. When my eyes fell on the Emerald Tablet I even told myself that nothing existed in the world that was so beautiful, but now I know that was false, and it is just a stone, while there is nothing so beautiful as you. I truly believed you had chosen another, but I know now that was wrong and the choice was not yours. I also thought you might consent to be my bride, but in my thoughts I once debased you and now I do not consider myself worthy of you. Still I remain here, on my knees, to tell you I wish to serve you, and to beg that you forgive me for my base doubts and false accusations."

Bahiga held out her hand and took his and bade him stand, and led him over to the seat next to the latticed mashrabiya window, and there she said that in her eyes he was not unworthy, but perhaps even too worthy of her, and she told him she loved him and would love him always, but that she could never be his.

* * *

A few hours later Sanjar rode Moonleap up the steep path which led from Fustat to the Muqattam Hills. Behind him was the mule laden with everything he possessed, the most prized of which was a shield which Bahiga had taken from the temple in Zerzura to give him. She said he needed a good shield, and though it had failed to protect its Persian bearer from a sandstorm, it would save him in battle. The shield was so old and fragile that he not see how this could be, but he would never again doubt Bahiga, and he had gladly accepted it.

It was still some hours before dawn and the city below sparkled with lights, but the cragged limestone hills were dark and the path treacherous. When he reached the highest point overlooking the city Sanjar reigned in Moonleap and tied the mule to a rock, and waited.

It was not yet the appointed time, but he did not have to wait long. The Caliph was too eager to delay gaining the prize he still feared might elude him and arrived early, riding a white donkey. He saw Sanjar and said expectantly: "Well? Have you got it."

"Greetings, sir," Sanjar said, looking keenly into the shadows. "Are you certain you have not been followed."

"Yes, yes, quite certain," the Qadi said impatiently. "No one is allowed to follow me unless I say so. I like to be alone, so I can see what's going on. Now tell me quickly, have you got it?"

It was plain to Sanjar that the Caliph, who had only the Qadi's word of the existence of the Emerald Tablet, did not have a true notion of its power or importance. He spoke of it as the giver of all power to he who possessed it, yet he appeared to regard it as a trinket to be bought and sold like a pearl in the bazaar.

Sanjar dismounted, and without a further word he took the turquoise casket from his pouch. "If I give you the casket, what is my reward?" he asked.

"Where is the Tablet? In the box?"

"It is."

"Your reward will be given you tomorrow, at the palace."

Sanjar knew there was to be no reward. The Caliph would destroy whoever knew he possessed such a talisman.

"I need a token."

Impatiently the Caliph drew from his finger a ruby ring.

"This ruby is smaller than my finger nail," Sanjar said. "Would you exchange the most precious object in the world for such a trifle?"

"I am a simple man," the Caliph spluttered. "I do not ride out with bags of gold. You will be given your reward tomorrow, at the palace, at a fitting occasion."

"A fitting occasion? Are you going to barter all the power in the universe for my presence at a fitting occasion? Are you not indeed insane, and if I were to hand this power to such a madman would I not be more insane than he?"

"Hand me the Tablet, it is mine by right!"

Sanjar had chosen the meeting place with care. The hills were hollowed out by quarrying, and movement was hazardous. Beside them the cliff fell a thousand feet to a bed of jagged rocks, and beyond that was the glimmering city. The mantle of the calm, dark hours before dawn was thrown over the hills, and the Caliph on his donkey was a faint shadow under the deep night sky.

As he handled the casket, not once did Sanjar move his eyes from al-Hakim, who stared at the box as if transfixed. Still holding the casket and with slow, deliberate movements, Sanjar opened the linen wrapping that enclosed the Emerald Tablet.

Sanjar could see the Tablet's brilliant light reflected in al-Hakim's eyes. The Caliph jumped down from his donkey and made a rush for the box, but Sanjar spun it out of his reach. Still without removing his eyes from the Caliph, and by a great effort of will keeping them from falling on the casket, he slipped one hand inside it and withdrew the Tablet.

The Caliph lunged, and caught Sanjar's hand. As they struggled the Tablet seemed to imbue them both with strength, as though three and not two were fighting for possession. Then Sanjar pulled free his hand, and as he did so the Caliph lost his balance and fell, and both spun to the ground. Then Sanjar, his hand now free, pushed al-Hakim and tried to stand, but the other snatched at the Tablet again and as Sanjar pulled his hand, still holding the emerald, was dashed on the ground. The stone took the brunt of the blow and tiny fragments splintered off its edge. Sanjar felt a pinprick as one of the splinters scratched his wrist.

He stood, and the Caliph too pulled himself to his feet. Waving the Tablet enticingly, but still averting his eyes from it, Sanjar backed towards the quarry shaft. When he reached the edge he stood poised as the Caliph came ever closer. And then, as the Caliph reached the edge, Sanjar flung the Emerald Tablet into the shaft.

The Caliph teetered on the edge, gazing in horror as the Emerald Tablet fell into the blackness, and then dashed into a million stars. Sanjar did not look but jumped back, and a moment later was sheltering with his terrified mare under the bluff.

Al-Hakim stared down the shaft at his shattered dreams, his illusions of conquest and glory. In those terrible moments his fantasies ended. For a few seconds there was silence, then a sound came from the shaft as of a wind in voice. The sound rose, and with it the tumultuous wind rushed up, and enveloped in the wind was an intense emerald and blue and white and silver light. The Caliph cried out, and flung his arms wide, and the luminous wind caught him and lifted him from the ground.

Sanjar watched as the Caliph ascended, engulfed in emerald light. Slowly the vision drifted upwards, and when he had watched it reach the stars, and the wind had ceased, he mounted his mare and, leading the mule, rode down to Fustat and from there over the desert plateau towards Kolzoum, from where roads led to Damascus and Jerusalem.

Dawn was breaking. Moonleap pranced, knowing she had a long journey ahead. Beside her, the mule walked quietly. Sanjar would go where the road took him; perhaps even as far as home. But with him he carried the parting words Bahiga had spoken the evening before. "Don't be sad, Sanjar Mouseback, because some things about the future I can't help knowing, and I know this much: this is not the end for us. We have more battles to fight together, you and I." And he knew he would be back.

*   *   *

The nurse had been so delighted to see Bahiga come safely home she begged her not to worry about leaving the donkey. "It'll be safe," she said, "if what you say is true, and there's grass and water there." She was also glad the water carrier was back, and it was curious that he was even better than before, always punctual and no longer insolent. Sometimes they would remember the donkey, and the nurse would say: "I wonder how the little donkey is doing out there in Zerzura?" And Bahiga would look up from her embroidery, and look wistfully out through the mashrabiya window, and say: "I wonder?"

Author's Note

The Emerald Tablet is a fantasy rather than a historical novel, but some of the characters and events are based on fact or familiar legend. It is set in Egypt in the early part of the 11ᵗʰ century, nearly 400 years after the Muslim invasion under 'Amr ibn al-'As in 639 AD. At that time Egypt was ruled by a dynasty of Shiite Muslims from western North Africa, the Fatimids, who conquered Egypt in 969 and built the city of al-Qahira (Victory) – now more or less corresponding to the Khan al-Khalili (bazaar) area of Cairo.

Al-Hakim bi-'Amr Allah (985-1021) became Caliph of Fatimid Egypt in 996 at the age of 11, and was brought up by his Christian mother and her brothers. Al-Hakim was mentally unbalanced, and the eccentric decrees he issued during his rule threw the country into confusion. The Caliph himself chose to follow a simple, ascetic lifestyle, and refused to wear fine clothes or stand on ceremony with his subjects. From time to time he persecuted Christians (he put his own uncles to death), Jews, women, and dogs. To prevent women leaving their houses he forbade the manufacture of women's shoes. He also put restrictions on the consumption of certain foods – honey and cucumbers were prohibited. He insisted that all business be conducted at night, and often rode round Cairo on a donkey, alone, to make sure his orders were carried out. In 1011 he destroyed the Holy Sepulchre in Jerusalem, where more than half the population was Christian (repercussions from this helped lead to the First Crusade 80 years later). In 1016, at the instigation of his Persian Grand Vizier al-Darazi, al-Hakim proclaimed himself the Messiah, after which he eased his intolerance of other faiths but incurred the wrath of his fellow Muslims by banning the pilgrimage to Mecca and the fast of Ramadan, and by substituting his own name for that of Allah in the reading of the Qur'an. Under him the Fatimid dynasty, famous for its culture and art, began a long decline, and law and order, which had never fully been restored following the collapse of Roman rule, fell into disarray, especially in the provinces.

The population at that time was divided roughly equally between Christians (Copts) and Muslims. Many of the latter were descended from the invading Arabs while the rest were local converts, many of whom changed their religion on marriage. Under Islamic law, a non-Muslim man cannot marry a Muslim woman unless he converts to Islam, and any children of the marriage are automatically Muslim. (This partly accounts for the gradual decline in numbers of Copts up to the present day.) The word *Copt* comes from *Aegyptos*, and is the name the Byzantine Egyptians used to refer to themselves. The Arabs did not adopt this name and the converts to Islam dropped it, so Copts are therefore those indigenous Egyptians who remained Christian. It was only recently (in the 19th or 20th Century) that the word became associated with the Coptic Church, which until then was called the Egyptian Church. At the turn of the first millennium, about half the population spoke Coptic and the other half Arabic, but the Arabic language was soon to take over. The Coptic language has now disappeared apart from its liturgical use, although some words are incorporated into colloquial Egyptian Arabic, especially those pertaining to the agricultural calendar and to the 'baby talk' used by mothers with their children.

In 1020 the Fatimids ruled North Africa, Palestine and Syria from their capital in Cairo; the Buyids, under the Abbasids, held Iraq and western Persia; while the Ghaznavids under Mahmud II, whose father Subuktigin had overthrown the Samanids, ruled the rest of Persia and Afghanistan.

Al-Hakim disappeared while riding his donkey in the Muqattam hills near Cairo one night in February 1021. His body was never found. Most people assumed he was murdered, perhaps by accomplices of his sister Sitt al-Mulk.

Tadros, the young Copt who is befriended by Sanjar, echoes the Mesopotamian mythological youth Tammuz – Osiris in Egypt, and the Greek Adonis – who loved Ishtar (Isis) and was killed by a boar or, in the Egyptian myth, by his brother Set in a fit of jealous rage. In Judaism this myth is echoed in the tale of Cain and Abel. That the object of Sanjar's quest ever existed is pure conjecture: according to legend the Emerald Tablet of Hermes Trismegistus (the Graeco-Egyptian god of learning) was found by Alexander the Great on a mummy inside the Great Pyramid of Giza. The Tablet, it was said, was inscribed by Hermes (who was identified with the god Thoth) with all known magic, beginning with the famous words: "What is below is that which is above, and what is above is as that which is below, in order to perform the Miracle of one thing only."*

Explorers have been searching for Zerzura, the lost oasis, for at least a thousand years (the desert expedition in *The English Patient* was loosely based on a search for Zerzura by Count Almasy accompanied by Sir Robert and Lady Clayton-East-Clayton). No one knows exactly where Zerzura was,

* Quoted from *Sacred Science* by R.A.Scwaller de Lubicz, Inner Traditions International, New York, p.170, tr. from the *Commentaries de l'Hortulain,* in Bibliotéque des philosophes alchymiques ou hermétiques (Paris 1756).

but I have placed it somewhat north of its generally supposed location since the logistics of so small a group attempting to cross the Great Sand Sea in those days would have been insurmountable. The legend of Zerzura and the mythical city with walls that could not be climbed without certain death became entwined with the story of the army of Cambyses, King of Persia, which was lost in the Western Desert south of Siwa in the 6th Century BC, presumably in a sandstorm.

The Qutb was – and perhaps still is – the spiritual leader of the Sufis. When it was time for each Qutb to leave the world his powers – or spirit – passed to a successor (as from Elijah to Elisha, both regarded by Sufis as earlier Qutbs), and his body ascended. Some Sufis claim the god Thoth, or Hermes, was the first Qutb. According to Cairene legend one Qutb, the Qutb al-Mitwalli, used to frequent one of the original gates of Cairo, which was called after him the Bab Mitwalli. This gate was replaced in the 1090s by the Bab Zuweila, which stands a little way away from the original but to this day retains its old name locally in memory of the Qutb. When the Bab al-Futuh was rebuilt, also in the 1090s, it also retained its old name although it was officially given another one (the Bab al-Iqbal).

According to folk belief adepts are not able to speak during astral travel, but to liven up the narrative I have granted them the power of speech even when they are out of their bodies. In other respects the local magic and beliefs are similar to those current in parts of Egypt until the present day. The historical and geographical references, including place names, are also, to my knowledge, accurate for the time. I have called Siwa by its old name of the Oasis of Amoun, as for a long time it went under the name of the oracle there (which Alexander consulted in antiquity). Alexandria at that time would have been much as I have described it. The lighthouse was working until it was demolished by an earthquake in 1031. The Horseman's Pillar, now called Pompey's Pillar, where Rhoorogh first appears in the story, was probably topped at that time with the figure of a mounted horseman, thought to be the Emperor Diocletian, and lay well outside the ancient boundary of Alexandria.

Cairo would have been known by the Arabs, who founded it after the conquest, as al-Qahira (Victory), and Alexandria as Iskandriya. Throughout the story Alexander is called by his Arab name, Iskander, when referred to by Arabic speakers, and as Alexander by the Copts. I have called the modern seaside resort of Mersa Matruh by its old Arabic name of al-Baratum (derived from the Roman Paraetonium) and Suez by its former name, Kolzoum.

I am very grateful to Dr George Scanlon and Dr John Rodenbeck for helping me with the history of the period, and to Dr Jason Thompson and Elizabeth Rodenbeck for reading the manuscript. The quotation from Firdausi is adapted from *The Shah Nameh*, translated by James Atkinson,

Frederick Warne and Company, 1886. Firdausi died in poverty after being ousted from court by Mahmud II either in 1020 or 1025 – which of the two is not known for certain.

JENNY JOBBINS
Cairo, June 2002